Jamaica White

Visitors to Jamaica will know the ruins of
Rose Hall, one of the great tourist attractions of
that wonderfully beautiful island. Rose Hall was
the name of Jamaica's largest sugar plantation,
and over a century ago it was run by the
notorious Annie Palmer, a sadistic white woman,
known as 'the Witch of Rose Hall', who, according
to rumour, murdered her husband and was
responsible for the murder of many of her slaves.

This savage and tremendously exciting novel,
based on a Jamaican legend dating back over a
hundred years, tells the story of Rose Hall and
Annie Palmer, who for all her faults had a
notion of grandeur and responsibility for the
future of the colony. It begins in the early 1830s,
when young James Arthur arrives from England
to take the job of book-keeper at the plantation,
only to find himself immersed in the problems
of the slaves in the mills and in the fields. His
relationship with the lovely, fascinating, hard and
brilliant Annie makes up the core of the book. The
revolt of Annie's slaves and the manner of her
end make up the climax.

This very powerful, graphic novel, explicit in
its descriptions of cruelty, passion and the lot
of the slaves, is also filled with the magic
atmosphere of Jamaica. It is full of action, and
has a hypnotic quality that many readers will find
irresistible.

Jamaica White

HAROLD UNDERHILL

W. H. ALLEN
LONDON
1968

*The author wishes to express
his appreciation to
Mrs. Vivienne Harper
of Kingston, Jamaica
for priceless help in
researching this book.*

© Harold Underhill, 1968
Printed in Great Britain by
Northumberland Press Ltd, Gateshead
for the publishers W. H. Allen &
Company, Essex Street, London W.C.2.
Bound by Richard Clay (The Chaucer
Press) Ltd, Bungay, Suffolk.
491 00340 4

For my beloved wife
Agnès

'Where love stops,
power begins,
and violence, and terror.'

C. G. JUNG
Civilization in Transition

1

'THERE'S YOUR Jamaica,' the captain said. 'I know she looks pretty but don't let her fool you. You know what they say about her? They say she's a bad place to live but a good place to die, because you die fast.' The captain slapped Arthur on the back and went aft to his bridge.

The captain was a bluff man who had seen too many people and too much ocean to be diplomatic or even vaguely friendly. When a passenger or two complained about the food or uncomfortable bunks, he reminded them that they were lucky they weren't aboard a slaver. He had captained slavers, he said, for five years, carrying five hundred blacks where fifty people should have been, and those five hundred in chains and eating, like dogs, out of a communal pot, digging out bits of tripe and pig's tails and boiled cabbage with their fingers.

Some of the crew had whispered the true story about the captain but before many days he told it himself over dinner one evening—how he had, to stop a slave mutiny one bright morning just off Barbados, taken ten blacks, all chained together, and had them thrown overboard in fifty fathoms of water as an example to the rest. He told it only because Miss Jenkins, a young lady from Edinburgh who was going out to marry a planter, said she knew little about slavery and hoped to get to know her fiancé's 'employees'.

'There were just a few bubbles on the sea,' he said calmly, '. . . because the chains were good heavy ones. After that we had a quiet trip. You'll pardon me, ma'am, but that's the best way to handle them.' Miss Jenkins excused herself and went straight to her cabin, looking ill. The captain laughed and said it was all right, there were enough niggers left for her and within six months she'd be squirming in bed with one.

After the captain's story one of the crew told Arthur that nobody had given a damn about just ten blacks. The captain had had the best record among all the slavers for bringing his live cargo safely into Jamaica, Barbados, Antigua and Santa Cruz. But one of the mates had told his parents about the drowning back in Leeds that winter. His parents had gone to their minister, and he to higher authorities and there had been a scandal reaching all the way to Parliament, started by 'that interfering Henrietta in his clerical frock. They're such busy-bodies they're always yapping like lap-dogs. There's a few in Jamaica too. There's also a few who don't mind havin' slaves at all, and they're in between them black thighs night and day. You'll see. The more we bring out here the more fun they'll have. You'll like it too, but stay away from them Henriettas. They're sick, most of them are, and they'll have you on your knees in front of them when you should be on your knees on top of one of them black girls, mate.'

The crewman left to swing up the tall mast for his trick in the crow's nest and when he got there loomed free and somehow majestic over the deck, in control of a circle of space limited only by the horizon of the moment. Arthur agreed with him silently, remembering the minister back home who had cautioned him to stay in Manchester and serve 'his parents and his God'. The minister was an ugly man with heavy jowls and a spreading belly who came for tea once a week and dinner once a month, always ate and drank too much and always took Arthur's father aside for 'just a few bob' for the church. A gossip and a leech and a big man in a small neighbourhood, he would, it seemed to Arthur, know nothing of the problems of slavers, of planters, of people such as himself who chose to go out to Jamaica instead of rotting in Manchester or London.

They had been sailing up the Jamaican coast for four days and were coming into Montego Bay. The island had been one continually awesome sight. Convoluted green mountains dug up into

· 8 ·

brooding clouds. Dark sheets of rain swept across the sea, passed over the frigate casually, rushed on towards the land and surged up the valleys to the slopes of the high green hills. Jamaica vanished in the clouds and reappeared, proud and awesome, looming out of the sea. At night, as the ship slipped through the moonlit waters, Arthur had come up on deck to peer out at the brooding island and listen to the fruitless thrust of the surf against the coral shore. The waves sent up an eerie phosphorescent glow as they turned to foam against the shore. Beyond that, there was nothing, except an occasional twinkle from the dark hills produced, the captain said, by a dozen or more candles glimmering in the dining-room of a great house among the sugar fields.

The ship eased into the harbour at Montego Bay shortly after ten in the morning. Small boats, paddled by broad-shouldered blacks, converged on it. They shouted, begged, offered coconut, pineapple, bright cloth, little wooden statues. Arthur was now used to them. They had done this at every island up through the Caribbean. These were the freedmen who had escaped slavery or been let loose by their owners. They were all healthy and happy-looking, free in the sun and on the bright waters. But there was something pathetic about them, coming out at every port to peddle essentially the same things, each one of them trying to out-manoeuvre the others to gain a momentary advantage and perhaps a thruppence from the people on board.

Some were good divers, and Arthur had come to enjoy throwing a penny or two into the water and watching the blacks leap overboard, head first, and come up with the coins. Then, too, they called everyone *Maws-ter* and it made him feel important to stand high on the deck with the sheer wooden wall of the hull between him and the shabby naked crowd. *Maws-ter*. It sounded absurd at first, but as they stopped at port after port he began to savour it.

Maws-ter. He flung a coin, then another, and the naked black men jumped, then begged again. In London, he had made ten shillings a week and called the head clerk *Sir*. Here he would make almost a pound a week and be *mawster*. He began to feel stronger, and unconsciously squared his shoulders under his shirt. He had no conscience to betray him. The woman from Edinburgh had been nasty as they entered the harbour. She had come up on deck and they called her *mistress* and begged for coins. When Arthur threw one she had said 'No—don't do that. Don't make fools of them. Don't make them act like animals after meat.'

He had looked at her in surprise. 'But that's what they do.' he told her. 'That's how they make part of their living. You saw them at Barbados and the other ports. It's the same thing. They *like* this. Look at that man. He's got his coin and he's proud of it—see him getting out of the water?'

The black was naked, his buttocks hard and glistening as he rolled over the gunwhale of his little dugout. The woman looked and then looked away quickly. The black called to her from the boat. *Mis-tress, mis-tress, I beg yu a penny.* . . . She turned again and screamed down to him 'No. *No.* I am not your mistress. Go away. Oh good *God* . . .' She turned away abruptly and went down the gangway towards the passenger's saloon. The black man sat in his pirogue, disappointed, his face still upturned, wondering at her. He squatted in the dugout, his knees apart. The girl from Edinburgh had, surely, seen his sex, uncircumcised and full as a fresh banana, casually exposed to the bright sun. If she was a virgin come out to marry in Jamaica, then the island had been an immediate shock to her. Arthur smiled. Would she tell her bridegroom?

The black man, still looking up, said softly 'Mawster . . . mawster. I beg yu . . .' and Arthur flung him a bright shilling. The man vanished into the water like a lithe fish without disturbing the balance of the slim dugout.

The frigate moved towards the dock. The town was starkly white in the morning sun. The angle at which the light fell brought peaked roofs and the white grillwork of balconies into sharp relief and left the verandas looking dark, cool but impenetrable.

The dock was a melee of people and things. Bales and boxes from all the Empire were scattered like the debris of war—shipments from Hong Kong, Sydney, Brisbane, Alexandria, Ceylon. There were huge crates and boxes from London too. Arthur thought that he had, on his tiny desk near the quays of the Thames, probably written the manifests for some of them months before and thousands of miles away. He had seen enough commerce in London but here it was again, a quarter of a way around the earth. The looms of Manchester and Leeds had put cotton on the backs of the blacks who were manhandling the shipments from London or bringing green bunches of bananas to dockside. English nails had driven planks together to make the homes that scaled up the hillsides of Jamaica. Englishmen like himself had come out of the tangled web of London and built a world a long way from home. When he tried to think of it, the Empire was too vast to consider. He, an Englishman, was only twenty-four but shared in the ownership of half the earth. Only the fools, he thought, stayed in London, pale little men scratching in their ledgers or working the dusty looms in the factories and eventually dying of tuberculosis. The world began out here, fresh and green, warm under the sun, scrubbed by the offshore breeze. *Mawster*, he said to himself. *Mawster*.

The word was echoed from below. The blacks on the dock milled about and shouted it. Mixed in with them were cocoa-coloured people, almost-white quadroons, Chinese, and white men who stood apart from the turbulence. Only the blacks shouted and begged, peddled and haggled loudly among themselves. Now and then a cocoa man would talk with a white, then shout orders at the blacks in a garbled dialect that made no sense to Arthur. Obviously there was an order of authority. The black man, a noisy, prancing but handsome clown was at the bottom. And, black would turn to black and shout, even as the cocoa man had, as though imitating an authority he would never have.

Arthur went belowdecks to be sure he had forgotten nothing on board. It was hardly likely, because his belongings all fitted into one little satchel and one small trunk. In the saloon, he saw the girl from Edinburgh, looking moodily through a porthole. She turned to face him and said, 'I'm sorry. I lost control of myself.'

'Nothing to be sorry for. I suppose the tropics are surprising for all of us.'

He wished he hadn't said it. She glared at him as though he had mocked her. He let the moment pass. In her ruffles and heavy dress and all her petticoats she looked pathetic in the gloomy ship's cabin. She was just a frightened little Edinburgh miss coming out to a new world. If her first experience had been the sight of a naked black man she would get over that in time.

'May I help you off the ship?' he said quietly.

'Someone . . . he . . . John . . . my fiancé is coming for me,' she said.

'They may not allow him on board. You remember at the other ports. They're afraid of fever. . . .'

'Quite so. Perhaps I should go then.' She moved towards the

gangway and then turned and looked him directly in the eye and indicated that he should go first. This time he almost laughed. She did not want him to see her virginal ankles as she went up to the deck. John would have an interesting time with his little bride.

At the gangway the captain was shouting at an assortment of black men trying to arrange to have his cargo removed, calling them thieves and ass nigger fools and, without cajolery, reducing them one by one to his price of a sixpence for a day's work. Arthur and the girl said good-bye to him. His only answer was, 'Remember what I told you.'

They moved down the gangway into a shouting mob of blacks. Arthur took the girl's hand to steady her. As they descended he saw a white man pushing through the crowd. He shouted the girl's name, Mary, over the babble of the blacks and pushed them aside. Arthur moved aside and the man lifted the woman down the last few steps. He set her down and went to kiss her. She pushed him back and reached out to touch his face. It was scarred and atop the scars were small bloody blotches.

'Nothing,' he said, 'nothing. I . . . I had a touch of the fever this winter and it left some little scars. The rest are bites from mosquitoes, is all. They will go away by tonight.' Apart from the scars and the blotches his face looked unhealthy, as though he drank, or ate badly. His eyes were fatigued and lonely. The girl involuntarily touched his face with her fingers, as though trying to cure him right there on the noisy dock. He was obviously not what she had expected to find. Around them, the blacks shouted and pushed.

Finally the girl turned to Arthur. 'Mr. Arthur, I would like you to meet my fiancé, Mr. Williams. Mr. Arthur has been a fellow-passenger, John.' Arthur put out his hand and Williams took it, grudgingly.

'Pleasure to meet you,' Arthur said.

'Have you come out to work?' Williams asked.

'Yes of course.'

'At what may I ask?'

'On a plantation.'

'Whose?' Williams looked surly and impatient.

'It's called Rose Hall.'

'Rose . . . Hall?' Williams enunciated it carefully and with obvious surprise.

'Is it a nice one? Will Mr. Arthur like it there?' the girl said. Williams ignored her.

'What work?' he asked Arthur.

'Book-keeper.'

'You know the work?'

'Very little but they said I would be taught.'

'You'll be taught a lot at Rose Hall. Good-bye.' He turned and led the girl away. As he did a black woman ran up to hold a parasol over her head. The girl tried to take it but the Negress kept it and padded along behind her. The couple got into a carriage and rode off, the Negress standing behind the seat, still holding the parasol. Obviously, Williams had some standing. The girl said he had been an overseer on a large estate, then had bought one of his own. Arthur watched them ride up the rough, bumpy street. He turned to look back at the ship and found the captain puffing a cigar and watching him impassively. The captain looked away from him and out over the Jamaican hills. Arthur's trunk came down the gangway, borne upon the head of a black man. He had one arm up like an iron tentacle clutching the trunk to steady it. The other held Arthur's satchel.

'Where him go, mawster?'

'Let me help you put that down.' Arthur reached for the trunk.

'No, mawster. Where him go please, mawster?'

'Into the city. An office. Johnson and Carruthers, Solicitors.'

'Yassuh.' The black man turned majestically, like a ship tacking in a slow breeze, and preceded him down the dock at an easy flat-footed pace, his head held high and his body moving lithely as if the trunk and satchel were weightless.

At the end of the block he stopped and revolved slowly to see if Arthur was still there, and then sauntered into the streets, the burden on his head unmoving, his own self majestic and un-affected by the swirl of people around him. They passed a Chinese dry-goods store, a ship's chandler's reeking of hemp and turpentine, a millwright's, and a small branch of Barclay's Bank in a neat white building with virtually no windows and heavy iron bars where there were openings. Arthur paused to peer in and saw a pale English clerk bending over a huge ledger, copying off the figures from a pile of invoices and manifests. He was a strange image compared to the bright, noisy street. He was, Arthur thought, England. In London now he would be doing the same thing. As it was, he was free in the sun on a Caribbean street with a strong bearer ahead of him cutting a swathe through the crowd.

'You are?'

'James Arthur.'

'James Arthur, *sir*, if you please. We do keep our dignity, even here.' Carruthers was an old man with a splotchy red face. He peered over a tiny pair of bifocals.

'Yes, sir. Sorry, sir.'

'If we lose our dignity we lose everything, don't we?'

'Yes, sir.' The old man was not even looking at him. He was picking at papers on his desk and merely talking to himself.

'. . . Especially here. We are especially lost here, in Jamaica, if that happens. But you don't know about that. I hope you will learn. Yes, I hope you will learn better than some of your associates have learned.'

'Yes, sir. Thank you, sir. I hope to.' What in God's name was the old man talking about?

'There is no room here for vice and wickedness, nor for undignified people who disgrace the white race and the good name of England.'

'Yes, sir.' He was watching the old man's large, arthritic hands fumbling on the desk, and he saw his own name on a piece of paper.

'Arthur—James Arthur.'

'That's right, sir.'

'You left Manchester and then you left London to come here?'

'That's right, sir.'

'And why have you done so much leaving? Have you come from prison or left stained women behind or stolen from someone?'

'I have *not*—none of those.' He was sharp with the old man.

'Sir.'

'Sir.'

'From Manchester?'

'Yes, sir.'

'What street?'

'Harley—sir—thirty-seven Harley is where my father's shop is.'

The old man stared at him thoughtfully. Then he took a quill pen, dipped in ink, and wrote down the address. 'I happen to know Manchester,' he said softly. 'I was there twenty years ago

. . . and Harley is a nice street. . . . Will you ever go home do you think?'

The old man's attitude had veered. His eyes took on a softness and, Arthur thought, a sadness, perhaps of exile. Conceivably the old man had stolen, or killed, and could never go back to England. There was always talk at home of those who had gone out to the colonies for one reason or another.

'I don't know if I'll ever go home, sir. That remains to be seen.'

'Yes, of course. Yes.' The old man put Arthur's papers away, tucking them, with a thick packet of others, into a large pigeon-hole on his desk. 'A lot remains to be seen. And you will see it, here in Jamaica. See it and think about it. Try to understand it, to make some sense of it. Don't let it sweep you away. Don't slip on the slime around you, and dirty yourself. Good Englishmen came to Jamaica, good men, in the old days. Strong men. And fine women. . . .' The old man paused and his wide, arthritic hands moved as though groping for something.

'I think I understand, sir.' Arthur was more conscious of his own discomfort than of the old man's words. The little office was hot and confining and like all solicitors' offices, boring. There were no pictures on the walls, only a few dusty documents. The old man's desk was crowded with thick briefs and old lawbooks open to yellowing pages. A louvred door, opening on a small veranda, faced the sea. The water was a blinding sheet of metal, the frigate a stark silhouette, the throng on the dock a restless, faceless mass that looked like a parade of mummers walking off into a sunset.

'Understand? You can't understand. No one can understand. Can those niggers understand? They understand what they see and what the black magic man tells them. And what do they see? The white man turned to trash and sometimes the white woman too. A whole Empire dying because we are crumbling away into trash. The niggers are just waiting for us, like the ocean is waiting for that ship. Two hundred years ago we came and laid out the fields and built our houses and in those days men's heads were high. But not anymore. Try and keep your head high, Mr. Arthur, and you will do us all a service.'

'Yes, sir.'

'Fifty pounds, fully found, is that correct?'

'Beg pardon, sir?'

'Your wages.' The old man's voice was dry and hard again.

'Yes, sir.'

'And transport back to England if you survive your contract
—or rather if you complete it. Two years. Correct?'

'Yes, sir.'

'So much for that. And now, since we are all entitled to our
bit of grog, this is a good time for it, don't you think?'

'Yes, sir.' Because of the heat, he didn't feel like drinking, but
this was no time to alienate the old solicitor. Carruthers took a
decanter from the desk, and two small silver mugs. He poured a
quantity of almost-black rum into each. They touched mugs.

'Good luck to you, Mr. Arthur, and remember what I said.'

'Thank you, sir.' The warm rum brought tears to his eyes.
They sat in silence for long moments, the old man staring at the
stuffed pigeonholes on his desk.

'Begging your pardon, sir, but have you been in Jamaica for
many years?' Arthur said carefully.

'Thirty-seven years,' Carruthers said, '. . . since 1795. Before
all this madness about emancipation. Seven years before the
fools in London outlawed the slave trade and the smuggling
began. Back when some decency prevailed. Before anyone thought
we could live like black men and still survive. In those days,
Mr. Arthur, I called Jamaica home, and so did my good wife. Now
I am just an old man keeping the accounts and the papers for a
diseased and dying friend.'

Arthur finished his rum and put the mug on the desk to
indicate he was done. Maybe the old man would let him go. Old
men talked and talked and for them nothing was ever right.
Arthur's father had gone on for hours about duty, responsibility,
the old days, the little shop on Harley Street and then, when Arthur
was ready for Jamaica, about England's shame, slavery.

Thus for his father slavery was a shame, but for Carruthers it
was desirable. Arthur was indifferent to it. If there were slaves
there were slaves, and no cause for him to give tuppence either
way. It was hard enough for a man to get decent work in England or even abroad without worrying about men who were
black, yellow, blue or whatever colour. Whatever happened to
them was their own fault. The world was full of big thoughts
for which the working man had no time. He thought for a
moment of Mary, the girl on the ship. There she was, all worked
up about the poor black men diving for coins, until she saw
his masculinity and then ran away from him, all her big ideas

· 16 ·

gone. All the black had in the world was the tiny dugout he floated in, his naked body to dive for coins, and his handful of manhood to give him some peace and some fun in this world. And she couldn't stand any of that. Now the old man was telling him that Jamaica had gone to seed, thus welcoming him, apparently, to nothing at all after he had travelled five thousand nautical miles to get there.

'. . . your life here will be harder than you think, Mr. Arthur,' the old man went on, '. . . but at least you will see how your Empire was built. I think there are no sugar growers buried in Westminster Abbey, but perhaps there should be. Perhaps there never could be and we'd best hide the whole subject. Well, good luck to you, young man. Go to the Steed and Bridle Inn down the street for the night. Tomorrow Mr. Broderick will come for you to take you to Rose Hall. By the way do you have a bearer?'

'Yes, sir. That chap outside.' He pointed to the porter through the window. The man was sitting on the ground in the shade, his arms on the trunk, his head cradled in them.

'I know him. Strong but a thief. Give him no more than thruppence to the inn.'

'Yes, sir. But he's been waiting for some time. . . .'

'No matter, no matter. He was born to wait. He's asleep and you are awake, and no one pays *you* for sleeping. Certainly I never will. And neither will Mrs. Palmer, as you will soon find out. Good day now.' The old man had become brusque again.

'Good day . . . sir.' Arthur went out into the searing daylight and awakened the bearer, who got up wearily, heaved the trunk to his shoulders and stood there blinking.

'The Steed and Bridle now.'

'Yassuh.'

The inn, on a side street near the harbour, was run by a hawk-faced Scot who said immediately that the Steed and Bridle was respectable, and women were forbidden. Arthur had not even considered the subject and, as he paid his night in advance, told the man so.

'You new ones all say that,' the little man snapped. 'We try to be hospitable to decent men and women. And then a year ago a fancy man from an estate came here one night with three black swine. He has a lovely white wife at home, mind you. But he comes here with three swine and they act like animals all night and we can't throw them out because he is a man of property and owns part of our mortgage. Or rather he *did*. I tell you we scrimped and saved to buy him out and be sure he can never come back.'

'And how did you know what they did in the room?' Arthur asked softly.

'The next room was empty. We heard every filthy bit of it, the wife and myself. Or she heard part of it until I sent her away. Unnatural things that no *decent* human being could believe. Like animals, *animals* I tell you, panting and licking after one another. Like *cattle* in the fields, watching one another.' His eyes bulged and his face stiffened like a death mask. Only his taut little mouth moved. Arthur took up his change slowly, shilling by shilling. He had known only a limited amount of pleasure with Manchester shopgirls and a few indifferent London tarts. The crotchety old innkeeper had inadvertently fired his imagination.

2

Broderick the overseer came early the next day. He pounded on the door just after the church bell had struck six-thirty. Arthur had long since been awake in the terribly bright morning. He had not slept well since the frigate first entered the tropics, where the day begins suddenly, like bright lights going up on a stage. Long before six, the Montego Bay street had resounded to voices, the clattering of donkeys, and their masters going to market, the shrill squeals of pigs, the escalated squawks of chickens and cocks. The Caribbean day was immediate and unstoppable.

Bed had been a horror. After a dull meal at the inn he had gone to a tiny tavern that stank of urine, been largely ignored except by a drunken young white man of about his age but with a sick, gaunt face who had said all plantations were hell and muttered about having his horse taken away and being, somehow, free at last and ready to go home.

On the way back from the tavern a black girl had come out of the shadows, quickly touched his pants and then pulled his hand to the front of her dress and said only 'ting an' ting . . . ting an' ting, mawster, only five shillin'. . . .' He was afraid of sickness and afraid of the night and afraid of the black body he could barely see under the half-moon and stepped swiftly past her. Back at the Steed and Bridle he had fumbled drunkenly with the voluminous mosquito net after first trying to sleep without it. It

· 19 ·

proved useless because of a hole in one side. Then, because of its thickness, it helped make the bed a hot hell in which he had sweated and suffered delirious dreams in which old Carruthers the solicitor droned at him unintelligibly. Then the Edinburgh virgin appeared and she was standing in a bright shaft of sunlight boring through an open porthole in the frigate's saloon. She was bare-breasted and stripped to her flowing white cotton pantaloons and screaming at him and pointing to the scalding white brightness of the porthole until finally he closed it and she vanished in the darkness and he awakened to the bright morning.

Broderick, the overseer, was short and cocky-looking, and had a very short haircut. He obviously thought of himself as handsome. His face was leather-brown from the sun and for all his shortness he looked commanding and healthy. Arthur envied his good looks and felt at a disadvantage. The sun had burned him painfully early in the voyage and he had avoided it, thus keeping his English pallor, and probably *looked* like a book-keeper. The dreary, half-sleepless night and the abortive encounter with the black shadow on the streets made him feel worse. Broderick looked as though he read all this instantly on Arthur's face.

'You're Arthur?' Broderick said as he came in the door.

'Yes. Good morning. I . . . I'm glad to see you.'

'That's interesting. Not many people are glad to see me. Are you ready to leave?'

'Yes of course. I woke up early and . . .'

'Everyone wakes up earlier in Jamaica. Have you eaten?'

'Not yet.'

'Then have your breakfast and I shall be back in an hour. I have a few things to do. But promptly, in an hour. Downstairs, with your luggage.'

'Yes of course.'

Broderick left without closing the door, and Arthur stared out into the gloom of the corridor. He heard Broderick's footsteps disappear down the stairs, then stop.

'Arthur.' His voice was loud and deep in the stairwell. Arthur went out to the balustrade.

'Yes.' He was going to say *sir* or *Mr. Broderick* but avoided both.

'You saw Carruthers as you were supposed to?'

'Yes I did.'

'And he told you about hell and damnation and dignity?'

'Yes he did that.'

'Ha. And your wages are established?'

'Yes.'

'That's all. I'll be back in an hour.'

Arthur felt better after the small remark about old Carruthers. The old man must be a plague to everyone, but with the plantations far apart in the hills he was unimportant. Arthur was eager to get out of Montego Bay and to his job at Rose Hall. Carruthers suggested England, his father and mother, his supervisor at the London import firm. He hadn't come out for that, but to leave it all behind him, even if it meant going straight to hell.

Broderick came back in an hour in a small wagon driven by a tired-looking black. Arthur went to help the man put the trunk and satchel in the wagon but Broderick touched his arm to stop him.

'Never,' Broderick said quietly.

'I'm sorry. I should know by now.'

'*Know* it. One step downward and they have you started. And they look for it now, especially the younger ones.' Broderick spoke matter-of-factly as though discussing the price of sugar. Arthur watched the man, who was stringy and emaciated, but muscular, trying to heave the trunk on to the wagon, his eyes bulging, his neck muscles taut ropes.

'Is he . . . is he a slave?' Arthur asked quietly.

'Yes of course.' Broderick looked him in the eye. 'What in hell did you think he was, my brother?'

'And he's not . . . he's not paid or anything?'

Broderick stared at him, boredom and scorn on his face. 'London is full of fools, isn't it? I wonder how they find you all. I wonder that they don't educate you. Your sugar tits didn't fall from the skies over Warwickshire, you know. They came from Jamaica. No, little boy, he is not paid. He's a slave. He's glad to be alive. He gets four fish, a pound of grain, a half-pound of sugar and a pint of rum every week, and two changes of clothes a year and a place to live and all the medicine he can whine and wheedle for. Do you have any more stupid questions?'

'Look, Mr. Broderick, I . . .' He was infuriated but Broderick's scorn was obviously deep, and he *was* the overseer.

'Yes, you what? Get into the wagon, Arthur, and let's get to Rose Hall.'

Arthur climbed on to the wagon, tense with anger but already feeling it begin to pass. He had learned to accommodate himself to managers and overseers and all the rest after one bad incident in London. He had tried to punch an officious head clerk in his first job and been sacked. The owner had heaped scorn on him and called him a 'Manchester shop boy' and 'common, without civilization' and talked about 'self-control, law, order, politeness and the prestige of one's superiors . . .' before sending him away to walk through the office past the triumphant head clerk, who merely flicked a glance at him and turned over another page in the ledger on his desk as Arthur walked out.

Now, it was Broderick. But he could take it. Jamaica was not London and on the green vastness of the island surely there was a measure of freedom for him.

The black man took the reins and the cart clattered along the street, the little grey donkey that pulled it ignoring the dense masses of people that drifted around donkey, cart and occupants the way fog drifts around a moving ship. Arthur and Broderick sat perched in silence on the hard board seat, lurching slightly with the wagon. The curved back of the black driver hunched over the reins in front of them, his bony spine protruding through his cheap cotton shirt. Beggars came up to them saying, *Mawster penny for me nigger belly, mawster . . . mawster, me mash up bod and me beg a tuppence, mawster. . . .* One boy clung to the side of the wagon for a few seconds until the driver reached out casually and clapped him on the side of the head with the bit of stick he carried for a whip. The boy yowled and then tripped down the street towards the next wagon.

The road curved up gradually out of the tiny town, the donkey labouring evenly and the cart creaking as the two men, the vehicle and the slave rose higher and higher until they looked way over the flat, glassy sea. Arthur turned to see the frigate etched on the vast blue water. One of its sails was being hauled up as it prepared to ease out to sea and move on to Cuba and perhaps America before the passage back to London. For a long second Arthur wished he were aboard but then remembered the ten days he'd spent puking into the mid-Atlantic and another four days becalmed under the pitiless sun off Antigua. He could live without ships for a while.

The town ended and the countryside began quickly, with the exception of a few scattered houses at the edge of Montego Bay.

The road, paved with disconnected stone stabs, was hemmed in by dense banana plants with huge tongue-like leaves, by scraggly green walls of sugarcane that looked like monstrous enlargements of grass stalks. Silence settled over the road, except for the creak of the wagon wheels and the donkey's clopping hooves. The sun, unobserved by clouds, struck their faces and made them squint. The silence and the vastness of the rustling greenery that witnessed their passing conspired to stir a vague fear in Arthur. Sweat trickled down from his armpits, and his bowels stirred involuntarily. He would have liked to get off the wagon and relieve himself, telling Broderick to keep going, and then running after the wagon when he was through. But he had had enough humiliation from Broderick for the day.

In a few minutes Broderick stood up and swung away from the plank that served as a seat, and sat on the flooring in the back, stretching out his legs. 'You might as well do the same,' he said, '. . . it's twenty-four kilometres to Rose Hall.'

'And you came all the way out this morning?'

'I didn't say that.' Broderick squinted at him.

'I'm sorry.'

'Mind your own business on this island and you might get along.' He said it indifferently, without rancour, and closed his eyes against the sun.

Arthur stayed on the plank seat for a few minutes, watching the donkey's interminably slow progress and noticing the thick spatulate hands of the black man, holding the slack reins. The driver looked at the passing ground and only occasionally up at the twin converging parallels of the road. Now and again he nodded and muttered inaudibly to himself as though confirming some sweet familiar truth. Arthur tired of watching him and went to the back of the wagon. He sat clutching his knees, peering back at the vanishing scenery, and dozing off for long minutes. Perhaps an hour passed as he dipped in and out of torpor, the sun growing like a hot burden on his back, the vanishing road and greenery framed in the shape of the wagon's tail end.

He was awakened by a loud oath from Broderick, who leaped over him, grabbed the driver and flung him out of his seat. The wagon had gone off the road, began to tilt crazily, and then stopped. The indifferent donkey munched at the grass and sprayed the earth with a thick stream of urine. Broderick leaped off the wagon and as the driver screamed, kicked him in the ribs and then, rolling him over with his foot, snatched up the little stick he had used on the donkey.

'Son of a whore go to sleep. Nigger bastard drive us off the road . . .' Broderick flayed at the man's head, then he tore off his shirt and whipped at his back as the driver grovelled and screamed. His back, bright in the early morning sunlight, was embroidered with old whip marks running from his shoulders to his belt. Most of them were as high as the ridge made by his spine as he crouched in the road.

'Mawster . . .' It was a scream not just a word, muffled in the warm morning air. Broderick flayed at him and finally threw the stick away. He gave the black one final kick and then grabbed the donkey to pull it back on the road. The donkey held firm, linked momentarily to the earth. When it finished, it brought its head up from the grass and moved back on the paving stones. Arthur clung to the wagon as it righted itself with a jolt.

'And what the hell are you doing, may I ask, attending the theatre in London?' Broderick shouted up at him.

'I'm sorry. How can I help?' He perched himself on the wagon's edge, ready to jump down.

'Forget it. Stay there.' Broderick pulled at the grovelling driver's arm. 'Get up and get on that driver's seat and stay awake. No rations this week and five lashes when we get home.' The driver got to his feet, retrieved his torn shirt and arranged it over his back. The wagon creaked forward. Both men sat in silence. Arthur remembered the thick welts gleaming on the driver's back and was tempted to ask Broderick a question, could not frame it and in fact did not even know what it was. There were the welts and that was all. The ricketty wagon jolted along the stones and dropped in and out of deep ruts. The wheels grated harshly on stones and pebbles in sections where rain had swept down the valleys and bisected the road with small gullies. Arthur thought of getting out to help push the wagon past these points, but Broderick sat still as though ignoring them.

A half hour later Broderick dug into a small satchel and pulled out a pint of rum.

'Drink?'

'Thank you.' Arthur took the bottle and had a small, fiery drink. Broderick took the bottle and drew at it once, waited a minute or two, and then drank again.

'More?' Broderick offered the bottle again.

'Thank you no.'

'It's here.' He indicated the satchel.

'Thank you. I should have thought to get some in town.'

'You'll think about what you'll think about, because you have to think about it. What are you thinking about now, for example?' Broderick was not aggressive. He had a distant impersonal look as though he were just toying with the whole idea of thinking.

'Nothing particular . . . just getting there, perhaps, getting to Rose Hall.'

'You mean getting off this stinking bumpy road and out of this wagon and out of this hell heat.'

'Yes, all right. Yes, all that too.'

'It's hot at Rose Hall too.'

'I suppose it is.' For a moment Arthur remembered Jamaica as he saw it from the frigate—lofty and lovely, green and mysterious. A faraway vision, the mountains cloud-capped, the surf a glowing line at the edge of the dark nights at sea.

'I think you're thinking of something else, such as that nigger . . .' Broderick nodded towards the driver.

'Nothing particular. I . . .'

'Did you ever see scars on a man's back before?'

'Not . . .'

'You mean not at all.'

'No. Not at all.' The wagon jolted and creaked. Broderick stared at him insolently. Broderick was very few years his senior but had some command of life that he, Arthur, lacked. Broderick made him feel like a clerk in his father's haberdashery shop again.

'And no one in England told you that we beat the niggers out here, eh?'

'It wasn't . . .'

'. . . wasn't in your contract. Old man Carruthers never mentioned it either when he gave you the lecture about decency and dignity. Did he?'

'No.'

'All Carruthers wants is sugar, Arthur. Ten tons of cane, a ton of sugar.'

'I see.'

'That nigger's back has been well educated. He was one of my best cutters five years ago. I graduated him to wagon driver now that he has six sons working for me. But I educated him. I gave

· 25 ·

him his first ten lashes the first time he tried to run away. Didn't
I, James. Didn't I?'

'Suh?'

'Didn't I give you your first ten?'

'Yassuh. Yassuh, you did.' The driver nodded.

'And today you'll get five.'

'Yassuh.'

'Mr. Arthur will give them to you to learn just how you like
them. Mr. Arthur is new *buckra*.'

'Yassuh.'

'You see? James is all yours, Mr. Arthur. We can have the
lashes tomorrow because you're tired after your journey. Tonight
I'll give you a cat-o'-nine-tails so you can practise a little if you
like. They have to come down smartly and evenly to do any real
good. It can be your introduction to Rose Hall.'

Broderick dug in his satchel, took the bottle out again, and had
a short pull at it. Arthur wanted to join him but was too furious
to ask. Broderick had humiliated him, using the old driver as a
foil. The driver's scarred back meant nothing. Five more lashes
would add only a little to the embroidery of welts. Broderick only
wanted to push him, Arthur, out on to an unfamiliar stage and
then mock him if he failed. Arthur felt a pang of nerves across
his bowels. *All right, all right*, he would practise with the cat-o'-
nine-tails that night and do whatever had to be done the next day.
He tried to visualize the scene. Broderick of course would be
there, but would there be other white men watching? Would
the other slaves be there to watch him too? What would he look
like, to all of them? He saw himself in the middle of a curious
circle, facing the black man's scarred back and the moment when
he would have to hit it with the flailing nine-tails. He envisioned
the nine-tails scattering, landing ineffectually, or looping around
the man's body and only tearing the taut flesh around his ribs.
He, then, would be humbled and not the old driver. The old man,
tied to a post or whatever they did, would stand there and be
beaten badly and the victory would be his, the humiliation Arthur's.
He felt this, without the words to carry the feeling.

Broderick sat silently, his eyes half closed now and his head
nodding with the wagon's movement. Arthur wondered where he
had been during the night, if he had not come out to Montego Bay
that morning. He had probably been with a woman in town.
Arthur, heading for the plantation and work, wished that he had

gone with the black girl on the street. But she had come too fast out of the shadows and frightened him because she seemed part of the unknown night in a strange place. Broderick, content and at home, had all the advantages that morning.

Arthur watched the road inch by inch and noted the silent passing, in the opposite direction, of barefoot, wide-hipped market women, their heads erect and supporting enormous baskets, going into town. Then he drew up his knees and cradled his head in his arms and dozed in the growing heat of the day. The wagon's joltings seemed to smooth out into movements not unlike the frigate taking the Atlantic waves that had brought him to Jamaica.

3

He awoke in a morass of heat and soreness, not sure whether he had been asleep or merely rolling in and out of consciousness like a sick man. Broderick was awake too and sitting up on the seat looking down on him.

'We're here,' Broderick said.

'Where?' Arthur said without thinking.

Broderick didn't answer. They were passing through huge iron gates and entering a narrow road bordered with high stalks of rustling cane. Up the road more than half a mile, he saw the great house, rectangular and bright against the deep green of the fields, its windows looking over the land like great baleful eye sockets.

'We might as well stretch,' Broderick said and leaped off the wagon. Arthur followed him, still dazed. From the ground, the great house seemed to hang in the morning like a mirage. His exhaustion turned it into a hallucination, made the thick green fields into solid carpets, like trimmed English lawns. The word *hallowed* crossed his mind as he viewed Rose Hall through the green tunnel of sugar, along the gravelly road and up over the fields to the summit where the house crouched.

'Good God.' He said it involuntarily.

'I said that too,' Broderick said quietly.

They strode up the rutted road past the silent stands of sugar until the wall of stalks broke suddenly. There was a big clearing thick with the leafy trash of cut sugar and the cut stubs of the plants. Broderick turned into the clearing, Arthur following, stumbling over the rubble. At the far end a gang of black men, half stooped over, advanced on and through the green wall of sugar, their machetes flashing in the sun. They were chanting softly but then stopped. As Broderick came up the only sound was the chop of knife on stalk and the rustle of the long slim leaves.

'I told you no singing.' Broderick went up to the slave driver, a black with a thick muscular body and a long whip coiled loosely around his neck.

'Yassuh. But dem just start now and dem stop.'

'Because I'm here.' One slave looked quickly back over his shoulder, but Broderick saw him.

'Him,' Broderick said quickly to the driver. 'He was singing too. Three lashes now. Quickly.'

'Yassuh. Jeremiah, suh.' He called the slave out of line. The man made believe he didn't hear at first, then turned, his head bent. His eyes on the ground he walked straight to Broderick and said very quickly, 'Suh, no suh, not Jeremiah. Not him. Ho, suh, please, Mistah Broderick, suh, don' beat nigger Jeremiah dis time suh.'

A few of the other cutters stopped and looked back. 'Get back to work!' Broderick shouted. They faced the cane again. The driver took Jeremiah by the arm and had him lie down in the trash then had him crouch instead because the new trashy leaves were too deep and soft. He took the whip from around his neck, uncoiled it, flicked it experimentally and brought it down once, twice and a third time, making three neat parallel bloody stripes low on the man's back.

Jeremiah half-screeched at the first lash and made only deep grunts at the second and third. As he scrambled to his feet the driver kicked his machete towards him and he returned to the faceless advancing line to hack at the sugar, the blood sparkling on his back and oozing slowly down over his pants. None of the others looked at him or said a word.

Arthur had watched the whip land once and then looked at the solid, impersonal face of the driver, who seemed to be concentrating on hitting the man's body accurately, as though it were a target. It was hard for him to believe that the cutter could or would walk back into the line and keep working. Arthur kept quite still, moving only to wipe away some sweat on his forehead. He was too tired to think very much about the dreamlike scene.

'They finish and then load this field today,' Broderick told the driver, 'and I mean finish it, load it and get it into the mill. Tomorrow morning the second gang can clean it before breakfast.'

'Yassuh. She sure a big field to finish an' load today, suh.'

'I said today. Unless they want no dinner and to keep working all night. I'll send torches over for that. And if they work all night you will too. You'll cut cane. You hear?'

'Yassuh.'

'Today?'

'Yassuh, today.'

As Broderick turned away the driver moved quickly towards the line, cracking his whip in the air and shouting at the backs of his men. Arthur stumbled across the hot field after Broderick, twisting his ankles frequently in the trash and coming down hard on the soles of his cheap boots on the thick stubs of cut cane.

'He's a good driver,' Broderick said, 'but he has to be reminded now and then.'

'Yes, I suppose so,' Arthur said.

'Don't suppose, Arthur, remember.'

'Yes.' Arthur turned his head to look at the line again. It was hacking silently at the sugar, including the beaten man, who stooped no less than the rest. It occurred to Arthur that if he failed, the rest of the work gang would turn on him because there would be one less hand to get the sugar to the mill that evening. Beaten or not, he had to keep going. As Arthur looked back he stumbled over a cane stalk and fell with a groan at Broderick's retreating heels.

'Best watch where *you're* going,' Broderick said, glancing at him. Bruised, Arthur got up and kept following him, the morning sun bright in his eyes.

They turned and moved up the road facing the looming great house.

'He's a good driver,' Broderick said, 'one of the best. And very good with the lash. You noticed?'

'I . . . he made even lines.'

'That's not the point. That's just something he likes. They try never to hit twice in the same place with the whip. Rips too much flesh. Over ten lashes it's hard to avoid that however. The point is he hit low down. When a man is cutting you save the upper back and shoulders. You need that for the cutting. This way he can still work.'

'I see.' Rose Hall took more light from the morning sun. Arthur barely heard Broderick, he was so hypnotized by the building.

'. . . but if you don't need the man right away for cutting, it's all right to hit him higher, and give him more lashes.'

'I see.' Watching the building, he stumbled slightly in a rut in the road, but caught himself quickly. Arthur was not at all accustomed to walking in the countryside.

'. . . and if you hit him higher it will start to hurt him like hell the next day. They seem to remember more that way. Do you get the point?'

'Yes, indeed.' Broderick's voice seemed far away. He could not connect it all with the lovely home on the hill.

'Are they very rich?' he asked.

'Who?'

'They. Up there. The owners.'

'*Her* name is Mrs. Palmer and whether or not she's rich is neither your business nor mine. We just produce sugar for Rose Hall, Arthur.'

'Mrs. Palmer. Is there a Mr. Palmer?'

'There was.'

'He left?'

'He died.'

'Oh? He was old?' Arthur barely heard himself speak. He was thinking that the house was greater than anything owned by the Manchester mill owners, the men from whom his poor father had bought cloth, the men who loomed so large and powerful in the city. He had no idea there was this kind of incredible wealth in Jamaica. The big green slopes and the home suggested a vastness, peace and extraordinary wealth that was beyond him.

'No Mr. Palmer was not old. Nobody gets old in Jamaica except grey lice like Mr. Carruthers who lives off the rest of us.'

Broderick turned off the path again and headed for a building. Smoke poured out of it and there was a clot of activity around it. Slow oxen dragged carts of sugarcane up to it, and the slaves lugged the rigid stalks off the wagons and into the gloom of the building.

'This is the mill. We'll start you here, Arthur. Not today but tomorrow morning.' They moved into the hot gloom of the mill. Inside, it clanked and clattered and the sick-sweet sugar stench made Arthur want to retch. His stomach squirmed. The rum in it turned to bitter fumes. He clenched his jaw against vomiting and blindly followed Broderick's broad back into the shabby place. The mill crew began to materialize like the shadows of shadows Against the bright squares of the doorways the men from outside came in lugging stalks on their heads and shoulders and stopped to feed them into the slow rollers that gnashed and pressed at the cane. The rollers were turned by six more men pushing at a spoked wheel, leaning and walking into it as it turned a gear that turned a gear that revolved the rollers. At the other end of the mill, cane juice the colour of foamy spittle ran into a wood trough.

Broderick paused to watch the juice spill out, an abstracted look on his face as though he were thinking of something else. Four or five of the slaves looked towards him but turned quickly back to their work. The air was dusty and the *crump* of the fresh cane as it was dropped before the grinders mingled with the rattle of the gears and rollers in the thick heat of the wide room. The process was simple enough. There seemed nothing to ask Broderick except where the pressed cane was going. Arthur saw it being pushed through a big hole in the floor.

'It goes below,' Broderick said, 'and they move it over under the boiling pots. Sugar consumes itself. Or maybe I should say it creates itself. We burn the trash to heat the boiling pots where we get the sugar.'

He turned and moved on. Before him, out of the darkness, another white man appeared. He was lean, tired-looking and about a dozen years Arthur's senior. A shaft of sunlight probing down from near the roof made his face look angular, pale and somehow tormented. Broderick spoke with him briefly, pointing out some trash on the floor, and a place where the wood trough was broken and dripped cane juice. The other man nodded, his dark eyes serious, almost frightened.

Broderick turned to Arthur. 'Wilson, this is Arthur, the new man. He starts here tomorrow. See that you talk to him tonight and tell him about the work, hear?'

'Yes of course, yes.' Wilson had not expected Arthur to extend his hand and so grabbed for it quickly at the last second, shaking it nervously with a tight grip.

'Where . . . where are you from . . . England?' Wilson said.

'Yes, Manchester.'

'Manchester, I . . . I know Manchester. At least I have uncles there. Weavers. A . . . a factory that is. They're well off now, I understand. Well off. Manchester is growing, isn't it?'

'Yes, still growing.' Even in the dark hot mill the lie echoed in his head. Manchester was a grim tangle of dirty unpaved streets clustered around the horrible mills. One of Arthur's uncles had died at his machine at the mill one night, some said from inhaling lint and dust from the cotton cloth being made for Wellington's soldiers. The mill owner stuffed his pockets with sterling and his uncle's lungs with cotton lint, or so his father the shopkeeper had always said.

'Yes, Manchester, very nice . . .' Wilson looked wistful, and eager to cling to his vision.

'Let's move along. Fix the flume, Wilson,' Broderick said.

'Yes, yes of course. I'll come by your house, Arthur. Supper together perhaps?'

'Fine.' Arthur followed Broderick towards the steamy boiling house, leaving Wilson alone with the mill crew. On his tongue was a comment about Wilson, but he held it. He sensed Broderick too well by now. He was suddenly grateful for Wilson, someone on his own level. But on the other hand Wilson looked ill and half-destroyed. His existence was a warning, his gaunt face in the dim mill gave lie to the white vision of the great house, the thick, grandiose carpets of sugar undulating over the hills and down to the sea.

Broderick showed him the boiling house with the immense copper vats bubbling with cane juice and the silent men with long paddles scraping scum off the top of the brew. The place was insanely hot and they left quickly. Broderick took him to the little house that would be his, said lunch would be sent to him, and dismissed the driver who had come with the wagon and the baggage. Arthur looked at his little two-room cabin. It had a narrow bed with a thick rustling mattress, two crude chairs and a small deal table, and the other room was a small kitchen with a table to eat on.

He went back and sat on the bed first, his head in his hands, aware of being hot, tired, and having seen too much for one day. He wanted to sleep but was afraid Broderick would come back, so he got up and hung his few clothes on pegs in the cabin walls.

4

BRODERICK'S HOUSE was on a knoll just west of and below the great house. From it he could see most of the fields between Rose Hall and the sea, and out east almost to the boundary of the properties. Altogether, he could see nearly half of Rose Hall's six thousand acres.

He could watch the fields as though they were parts of a chessboard. After three years as overseer he could tell from a distance when a field was ripe for cutting. He knew the best ways to manoeuvre the slaves to keep the cane moving towards the mill and the smoky boiling house. He watched the grinding and the boiling with some care. He kept thievery to a minimum and held the slaves in close check. They played sick as often as they could. but always ran the risk of Broderick catching them and having them flogged.

Broderick knew that Carruthers hated him but in the face of Carruthers, and with his own talents and Annie Palmer's backing, he was secure. Rose Hall was known as a hard place but also a productive one. Out on the long Jamaican coast there were other plantations failing, their fields lying fallow or grown cane rotting in them, their great houses gone to seed, their owners sailing for England and leaving old skinflints like Carruthers to cheat them, cheat the land, cheat even the slaves who had, years before, begun to filter off the plantations and into freedom in the mountains and now even appeared brazenly in Montego Bay, Runaway Bay, May Pen and other towns, free, insolent, unafraid of capture.

But there was a way to beat that. Just six months before, one of Broderick's best slave drivers had run away, been caught and even after two months in The Hole beneath Rose Hall, chained to a wall and with a chain snubbed short around his neck and then linked to his foot irons so that he could not even sit straight let alone lie down, he had run away again. After the second capture, Broderick had sent him to Rodney's, just outside of MoBay.

There, where specialists had more time to make a slave think, they spread-eagled him face down in the dirt once a week and flogged him for a solid hour. They starved him, hung him by his thumbs, beat him with clubs, starved him more and continued the weekly floggings—did anything except touch him with human hands, talk with him, reason with him, demand anything of him or indicate anything except their will to keep him alive, and in torment.

It worked admirably and the black returned whole and fell back into the cutting line, still not meek but perhaps permanently dazed at the true, final and fierce power of the society for which he laboured.

Thus Broderick, as overseer, communicated the little pressures of history in his own time. The runaways began gradually after Parliament decided to end the slave trade, but Broderick had been a schoolboy in Ireland then, learning his Catechism and the rudiments of English in the morning, digging peat with his mother through the afternoons and until the sun's gloomy evening death on the fringes of the endless bogs. He knew not of slavery, or of its end, or the years to come when the illegal slavers ran hulls full of blacks, chained together into their own excrement, out of Dahomey and the Ivory Coast and brought those that survived surreptitiously into the little pink and white town of Montego Bay as it dozed under the Caribbean moon—or half-dozed because well aware that the ship gliding into the harbour, and the muted clink of chains, meant more labour, more sugar, more money for Jamaica, regardless of what ignorant London parliamentarians and wild-eyed hysterics wanted.

Broderick had come out only five years before, barely twenty and with a prison record for having broken a man's jaw with a crowbar when he tried to rob a London shop for a pound of bread. He had travelled from the peat bogs of Limerick as far as a Leeds woollen mill, baulked at the clatter of the creaky English machines in the dim factory, left after a week and gone on to be a cabin boy then a gunner in the British Navy, and finally was punished and cashiered for insubordination.

He had at least been fed and had time to think in prison, Naval and civil, and then, because of his strong-boned Irishman's body, had been tapped by a smart warden who arranged an early release provided Broderick allowed himself to be taken straight to a Plymouth pier by the book-keeper of a Jamaica commission agent. He could have killed the book-keeper with ease and stayed in England but the prison had been near the Thames and for more than a year he had been able, by stretching on his toes, to clutch the rusty slime of the prison bars and peer out at the river, sometimes clothed in sensuous fog, sometimes an incredible silver roadway under the sun, and see the ships coming and going. So, upon release, he went to Liverpool and to sea, with no idea where Jamaica was or what he would do there.

At Rose Hall he had been dumped into the same cottage where he had just put Arthur. He had been a supervisor in the fields, the mill, the boiling house and by dint of great luck became a favourite first of Mr. Palmer, then Mrs. Palmer. The husband drank, and between that and hard times in Jamaica his will had eroded to the point where he needed Broderick to hold Rose Hall together with his fierce Irish temper and the almost calculated viciousness bred into him by the humiliations of his life in Britain.

The slaves came to know Broderick not just as a terrorist. They could have lived with that. There were whole carpets of black backs to be whipped. There were infinite varieties of ways of slackening the work after Broderick had tried to tighten the discipline at Rose Hall. The slaves were a century ahead of him, deviousness was their birthright and salvation. He outwitted them by infiltration. His untutored Irish soul somehow absorbed them and yet was dissimulated among them so that he could anticipate their next try at besting him merely by the way they looked or moved. They knew him best on the plantation for the time he got wind of a revolt. The idea had been to burn a cane field at night and when he went to supervise the fire fighting, kill him in the confusion and throw him into the burning field where he would, in about two thousand degrees of swift fire, be consumed and vanish.

He heard about the planned revolt accidentally, in Montego Bay, where he had been for a week. He returned from there the afternoon before he was supposed to die. As evening fell he sent for one of the slave drivers he had been told was behind the uprising. Broderick took the man inside his house, killed him quickly with a knife and then cut his head off, on the veranda, with a machete. Then he went out into his yard and thrust a thick cane piece in soft dirt and stuck the driver's severed head on top of it.

He told no one, knowing that someone was always watching in Jamaica, that the night was constantly alive. He went to bed early, sure that the field would not burn. If through some miscalculation it had, he planned to walk to it, carrying the head on the cane stalk, the remaining blood dripping down over his own head and shoulders. The Jamaican fear of their own dead would have kept him alive. But there was no fire, and having made his point he took the head down at dawn shortly after roll-call in the fields.

After leaving Arthur, Broderick went up to his house to take off his boots, waggle his toes thoughtfully, throw his damp linen shirt on the floor and have a small rum with some tepid water. It was close to noon and he felt a certain somnolence after the night and the wagon ride. He reflected on the night, with three black women ranging in age from twelve to twenty, in a bed in an empty great house on the edge of MoBay.

The deep satiety that follows prolonged depravity had settled over him, and led him to smile to himself as he looked over the green fields to the sea. The black women were like a private kennel of talking animals.

The twelve-year-old had been particularly interesting—the other two had brought her for her initiation, had coaxed her and even held her for him and then had used her with their big lips and teeth in their own private ways for his amusement and theirs.

By the end of the night, in the candlelit room thick with *Ganja* smoke, she was in a frenzy of excitation and mindless erotic joy, giggling, sleepless, inventive, jealous of her prowess, converted to the worship of Broderick's strange (to her) pink-white male rod. He slipped himself into the taut folds and crevices of her forked, agile self with detached glee. *Thy Kingdom Come*, he thought once, *Thy Will Be Done on Earth*, and laughed. Then he took out his bottle and passed it, briefly, among the women to liven them up even more and in passing spilled some down over the smooth small of the back of the crouching twelve-year-old and watched it trickle down, a stinging lubricant christening the darkness of her new womanhood. He slithered happily in the stinging wetness of the rum, poking at her as she moaned, her head buried deep in the calm lap of one of the older girls, who sat naked and dazed, puffing *Ganja* in a pipe like a bizarre chaperone. He had sent them all out before dawn, with two shillings apiece, and slept for an hour before waking with the dawn and riding on for Arthur.

From his veranda Broderick could see the ocean frigate on which Arthur had arrived, edging up the coast under full sail. Where was it going? Cuba, then America, then London. Its voyages were uninteresting. Some Americans had come down within the past few years, bringing their slaves with them. There had been a revolution, they said. No, they were not Americans, just frightened British escaping with what they owned. Good for them and this revolution against the pompous English, Broderick thought. The Americans must be good people to have brought that off. He had considered going to America but it seemed foolish to give up his hilltop at Rose Hall for an uncertain future. And London? He had forgotten it except for the slimy prison bars behind which he ended up while Napoleon was holding court at Elba, and beyond that remembered the moment he had smashed the wiry baker's jaw with the crowbar and run with the bread, gnawing at it as he ran, wolfing the last of it as they caught him and took him to prison.

Ireland was out there but he had served his apprenticeship in the dreary bogs, beside his stooped mother. Served, survived, would never go back and never knew whether mother or father or friends were dead or alive, and cared less. He smiled again— thinking of the incalculable distance between his tropic night with three niggers, his skill enlarging and ripening a fat squirming twelve-year-old—the distance between that and his chill mornings, teeth chattering, as Father Fianna's altar boy in Couny Limerick, Ireland, dreary place of his birth. He toasted the ship as it passed, then went to splash and wash himself with water from an expensive English ewer that Annie Palmer had given him.

Broderick kept no woman at the moment except for a toothless old cook for his meals whose little child tidied up around the house. For about a year he had had a mulatto mistress and as he washed he missed her momentarily. She had always taken off his boots, kneaded his feet, poured him a drink, stripped him and washed him and, if he pleased, had lunch and supper with him. He had tired of her and there had been complications with Annie Palmer so he told her to move on but did so with some gentleness, not wanting to make enemies. She knew, of course, about his affair with Annie but so did the entire plantation and probably every person down the seventy-five green miles of sugar and coconuts between MoBay and Port Antonio.

The important thing was that the mulatto girl had no particular desire or reason to murder him, either by poison or by hiring a runaway to come out of the bushes on the MoBay road and hack him to death. Both were easy to do in Jamaica. Overseers vanished and their corpses were found in the forests weeks later or their mouldering bodies suddenly emerged out of the cane as it was cut, revealed by the cutlasses of the cutters as though by the trowels of archaeologists. Owners and their wives suddenly doubled over in screaming pain at their dinner tables, scattering crystal, silver and good Madeira over the polished mahogany as the houseboy tiptoed in to clear away the rubble around them, stealing what he could in the process. The militia always came to 'enquire', hung a dozen slaves and whipped a dozen more until their backs were ragged meat and then left the great house to the rain and breezes until some smart attorney sold the plantation to a London merchant who wanted to dally in sugar at a distance.

Broderick had cornered and beaten his fear of death. At twenty-nine he was old for Jamaica. Few men lived to thirty or beyond in mill, field or on horseback, or by too much rum. Broderick without getting caught by fever, lockjaw, improbable accidents had no dreams of longevity, or even of any job beyond that of overseer. He was a good overseer and a hard one, saved about half of his two hundred pounds a year. His private delights did not go much beyond the previous night's orgy with the two women and the child, or an occasional alligator hunt in the swamps to the south.

As he finished washing himself, the little deaf-mute from the great house came up the path. Annie Palmer kept the child as a body servant and message runner. The child stood at a distance from Broderick's house and motioned to him. He nodded, and the child left. *Damn.* She wanted to see him now, probably to ask about his trip to MoBay. She would be jealous, maybe furious, depending on her mood. He never knew what to expect. If she was in a good mood she might have had a little orgy of her own. She was famed for them. But after those she was usually not seen for a day or two.

Broderick put on a clean linen shirt and went up the hill to Rose Hall. He climbed the wide steps and used the brass knocker. A house girl let him in. He waited in the hall just outside the sitting-room. It would have been bad form to walk right in. At least she didn't like it, and he felt better within the confines of ceremony. The house *was* impressive, solemn and sombre and polished against the rustling disorder of the fields and the cattle pen, the steamy heat of the boiling house. The ceilings were high, the whitewashed rooms cool; the burnished mahogany and cut crystal bespoke some calm perfection that had been created out of disorders that the house excluded. Broderick was always ill at ease in Rose Hall, even in Annie's bed. The widespread green factory that was the plantation was his world. Silver and cut crystal, chandeliers, carpets and polished woods made him ill at ease because they were too static.

He knew that Palmer, after creating the estate and Rose Hall, had had the same sort of reaction. He was always coming down the hill to Broderick's house to drink half the night, and enjoyed taking any slave woman he wanted. Drinking more and more, he had grown progressively more unbearable to Annie Palmer. Broderick believed she had killed him one night. No one knew. By tradition he was buried on the plantation and the same day Annie's two house servants vanished, believed to have been strangled by Annie herself and then buried in an old tunnel said to be under the house. It was generally a matter of indifference or at least an unprovable story on an island where no story could be proved but only vanished, diffused like the smoke of the burning cane fields into the atmosphere of legend that lay like a palpable haze over everything in Jamaica.

'Good morning, Broderick.' The house girl had come and ushered him into the sitting-room.

'Good morning, Mrs. Palmer.' The formalities came naturally as they scanned one another's faces. She looked well for a woman of about forty-five. She kept out of the sun so her skin was dead white. Her eyes were clear, deep and dark and she had a medium mouth, neither hard nor soft but straight as a wide slash across her face. This day her black hair lay long over one shoulder, an inky cascade over a simple white dress. All he could see of her were the little black shoes she still imported from Paris and her delicate fine-boned forearms and small but, he knew, strong hands.

'Please sit down.' She waved him to what he thought of as the second chair. The first was a wide, soft green velvet chair her husband used and Broderick had often sat in, sometimes with a naked Annie Palmer in his lap. The second chair was straight, with a leather seat, and uncomfortable. Broderick perched on it.

'And how was Montego Bay, Broderick?'

'Very well thank you. I went to get the new book-keeper.'

'Thoughtful of you.' She let silence fall for long seconds and gazed at him. He looked at her and then over the polished andirons before the immense yawning mouth of the fireplace. He knew enough to wait before talking. In Jamaica there was always time. The arbiter of time was the cane rustling without. Man and time came to grips only when the cane demanded it and was ready to be cut. Broderick heard the soft bong of a clock in the upstairs hall announcing the quarter hour, but which hour he didn't know. He stared at the fireplace conjuring a fire and remembering odds and ends of the first night, in the middle of a roaring rainstorm, when Annie Palmer had called him to the house and made him her lover of sorts.

Annie sat still, looking at him. A flying beetle whirred in the room and bumped into a crystal bowl, making a soft ping. A door creaked in one of the outbuildings and there was the sound of wet slops being thrown on the earth.

'And how is the new book-keeper, Broderick?'

'All right I suppose. About twenty, from Manchester. Pale tired-looking like they all are. He's in my old house.'

'I didn't ask where he was. I assumed we had a roof left to put him under.'

'I saw the importer in MoBay. Our next salt fish should arrive in a fortnight and some mill parts in less than a month. . . .'

'You can spare me all those details. I was sure you'd manage to get some work done if only early in the morning? I'm amazed at how you are able to get up after a night like that. I assume that you will be with us here for a while now?' Her face was very serious but there was a sly wit in her eyes. She knew all about his little night. There was no escape in Jamaica. Word about everything circulated like the garbage endlessly flowing, exposed, around the piers of the Thames. Servants, pedlars, slaves, ministers, parish council members . . . everyone who moved carried some gossip of someone else. And the speed of the stories was out of proportion to the speed of travel. In this case it might have been the wagon driver but it could just as well have passed from one of the women to a friend, thence into the market-place and on to a horseman who knew a book-keeper who knew a hostler at Rose Hall and he, in turn, had told the cook or a maid in exchange for a bit of meat or a bone for soup.

'Yes, Mrs. Palmer. I'll be here for a while now.' He went back to staring at the fireplace.

'The sugar is coming in properly?' Her voice was a little softer than usual. It ripped easily and lightly around her English accent.

'Yes it is. We're cutting from here to the sea now, then we go east or west, depending on where we can burn best.'

'Must we burn? It makes so much soot.'

'We cut faster if we burn, and hold the sugar. If the cutting is too slow we lose the sugar to the sun.' His voice was flat. He had explained it all before. It seemed a ritual she demanded.

'All right. And that book-keeper Wilson, the one in the mill, is he sick?'

'Sick.'

'He looks pale and unhealthy. And I came upon him last night . . .'

'Last night?'

'I was riding last night. I came on him sitting on a stump in a clearing. He was holding his head in his hands. He looked as though he could have been weeping. I don't know. I told him to get back into his house, and he went away. When I want people out at night on the property, I'll tell them.'

'I'll talk to him.'

'Put him in the cattle pen if you can. We can't have an idiot in the mill. He said he's in the mill.'

'Yes.'

'Put the new man in the mill and train him.'

'Yes.'

'One more thing . . .' She sat very still but was kneading her hands together gently. They might, he thought, hurt a little after riding, or after what she usually did when she was out riding. Wilson had been lucky. She had killed one book-keeper, accidentally, the year before.

'. . . you heard about the Edwards?'

'No.'

· 42 ·

'About Mount Pleasant?'

'Nothing.'

'Then what the hell *have* you heard besides the black swine you went to in Montego Bay. *What*, Broderick? Don't think I don't know about your London prison, and don't think I won't send you back there.' She was on her feet, fierce, shrill. She threw a lovely switch of soft black hair back over her shoulder. Her unframed face, pristine as a cameo, was alive with hatred, with some fear that created it. Broderick sat still. It was the first time she had mentioned the prison, even though fury was a common thing with her. The threat was real. She had done worse. She knew no limits except the confines of the great house.

'And what happened at Mount Pleasant?'

'It was burned last night.'

'The house too?'

'Everything. He tried to stop them with a gun but there were too many of them. There were so many they crushed him to death. They just walked on him, on his stomach and his face and everywhere.'

'Did the militia come?'

'. . . and they went straight for her. They would have let her leave if she hadn't screamed at them, and even started to throw her chinaware. . . .'

'So the militia didn't come?' Annie Palmer was entranced and he wanted to stop her.

'. . . she was always a fool, that woman. Her slaves *liked* her. She sucked around them while he tried to hold the place together. Do you know what they did to her? They took off all her clothes and made her dance with them. Then they poured oil all over the balustrade, and straddled her on it, and slid her up and down for half an hour, laughing at her. You didn't know her. She always insisted on keeping her furniture so well oiled that this was their *joke*. They *humiliated* that fool. They wouldn't even kill her. They wouldn't even rape her. Finally they poured oil all over her and fifty of them rolled her in the dirt all the way down the driveway and into the cattle pen and left her in some wet dung. . . .'

Broderick was accustomed to these stories. Annie Palmer got all the details swiftly from her servants. From them she demanded accuracy. They tried an occasional lurid lie but were always found out and punished. She had an impressive command of rumours and could sort out information so well she was believed by the slaves to be half witch. Yet she rarely left the estate, except for her night riding.

'They have a wit about them, haven't they?' Broderick said. 'Is she still alive?'

'No. They say she tried to . . . to do something . . . to a bull in the pen, and he trampled her. She was probably quite out of her mind. And the mosquitoes had eaten her half alive before dawn.'

'And the militia?'

'As a lieutenant in the militia, Broderick, you know where some of them could have been last night. They are not different from you, are they?'

'Will there be a burial?'

'Ah yes. Gordon is on his way to Mount Pleasant now. I'm wondering if he will scrape and clean her body with his own hands, or hold a little prayer meeting of the household slaves and convince them they should wash her. Mr. Edwards will be easier of course, since he was merely crushed to death. No mess at all for Mr. Minister Gordon. Ha. *She* certainly was baptized, wasn't she?'

Hunger and a growing somnolence began to overtake Broderick. It was probably well past noon. He shifted uncomfortably in the hard leather chair, which creaked in shrewish annoyance. Annie Palmer stood by the fireplace, her arms folded, looking out at the day, a bright rectangle formed by the long window. On a distant hill, sugarcane blossoms lay like the last sifted snow clinging to the English hills in early spring. Broderick made mental note that the field would be ready to cut within a fortnight. Perhaps he would cut east, then, instead of west. He would have to ride out tomorrow and see.

'All right, Broderick. You may go now.'

'Thank you.' He got up slowly and stretched his legs, watching her. She turned her head and dark eyes to him.

'But stay alert.'

'Yes.'

'There are too many troubles in Jamaica now. Too many. But we . . . but Rose Hall will not have them.'

'Yes.'

Before he turned to leave she moved towards the stairs and started to climb them, one delicate hand on the balustrade, the other holding her long white dress, her figure alternately bright against the wall, then silhouetted against the fierce sunlight outside. Broderick imagined that it would be a week or so before he was invited upstairs with her. She wasn't jealous of his Montego Bay women. There was none of that silliness between them. And she didn't resent his independence, because she had her own varied and exotic satisfactions.

5

THE DAY'S heat and the silence of the little house became too much for Arthur. He slept, lulled by the buzzing of the bees outside and the occasional rhythmic bumps of a flying beetle against the louvred doors.

Jamaican women came to look at him as he lay sprawled deep in the corn husk mattress. First they looked through the louvres, then quietly opened the simple door latch.

The first was Samantha, a black who had lived for some time with his predecessor. She cooked exceptionally well. He had liked her and taken her hot Calalu soup when he was very drunk at night and he had sobbed like a child sometimes when she put him to bed. After a few months on the plantation he got the fever but before he could die of it took a horse and a rope and rode out to the edge of the forest and hung himself from a tree.

The other niggers laughed when she cried and cried over him and made his grave alone, digging it with an old iron pot in the soft earth of the forest, under a mahogany tree, burying him herself to be sure no one touched him. Before she buried him she rubbed a tiny, almost-formless doll she had managed to scrape out of a bit of white birch wood over him, then tucked the doll swiftly into a little cotton bag around her neck where it reposed along with a scrap of one of his pencils, a crumpled page from one of his three or four books, the pretty stamp from the one letter he had received from England, and a few of her other magic things—an alligator's tooth, a rusty nail, and what she believed to be a bit of dung from a Roaring Calf, the noisy, fiery spectres that sometimes roamed the night.

Samantha stood silently by Arthur's bed, studying his young face. He was not unlike the other man—the same shock of hair, the same cheekbones, reddish and ruddy. He could have been sent to her. He could have.

Samantha was observed leaving by Mary Lou, who said nothing and flattened herself against the side of Arthur's little house. Mary Lou earned soup bones from the cook for information about the new book-keepers, and any other gossip she could pick up. It was she who had found Broderick's prison discharge paper, taken it to cook, who had passed it up to Mrs. Palmer. Cook traded information to Annie Palmer's personal maid in exchange for a tiny bit of scent or a discarded linen petticoat or even a good metal button or two. The maid knew that the cook was between her and Mary Lou but never told Mrs. Palmer because she, the maid, passed information down to cook, who dealt directly with the slave drivers. By mid-afternoon for example two drivers knew that Wilson would be transferred out of the mill and that the mill work might become harder, or easier, depending on Arthur, who was still an unknown.

Wilson they knew, in the mill. The pilfering of sugar had been good that year because of him. The mill slaves sensed his reasonableness. Instinctively they cherished him. They knew enough not to take too much advantage of him, thus destroy him. By his very reasonableness he defined the limits of their theft and trickery. But they could not save him from sobbing alone in the night and being caught by Annie Palmer. So now they had to cope with his loss. Mary Lou came to look at Arthur to tell the cook, who could tell the drivers. She stared at the sleeping Arthur. He told her nothing. He looked very ordinary. Ordinary hands. Ordinary legs. A good young face, dead asleep. Ordinary shoulders. No rings on his fingers or chains or lockets around his neck. She tiptoed over to his clothes. The usual cottons and linens. With swift hands she felt through them and probed his open trunk. No watch, no chain, nothing to steal. No papers. She found his purse, snapped it open carefully. A few quid and nothing more.

She left the money. It was death to be caught with money at Rose Hall.

She tiptoed back to look at him again. A board creaked and he awakened. She stood perfectly still, knowing how the English reacted. She wondered at their fright. Within a second after his eyes opened he sat up on the bed, terror in his eyes.

'Yes . . . yes what is it? What?' It was almost a plea.

'Well ah just come, mawster, to see if yu awright and need somethin'.' She looked infinitely placid.

'Nothing. Nothing thank you.' He rubbed his face, recovering.

'Yassuh, well then ah'll just go . . .'

'No, wait.'

'Well suh the mis-tress she wan' me soon an . . .'

'What mistress?'

'Well de mis-tress say dat I shouldn't go too far and . . .' She had taken on too much and trapped herself, mentioning the mistress. Only her good tongue would save her now, although she had little fear of him. The new *buckras* tended to be stupid, and even quite helpless in the vast confusion of the plantation.

'Mistress? You work for Mrs. Palmer?' Arthur blinked sleepily, rubbing his face still, and scratching his head.

'Well, suh, I'm Mary Lou and born on Rose Hall, suh, and come to see jes' if you needed somethin' suh.'

He caught the sly whine and the evasive excuses in her tone and decided to forget them.

'Nothing, Mary Lou.' The bright, hot day thrust itself at him again and he resented her for waking him up.

'Yassuh.' She turned to go, casual, shambling.

'Wait a minute.' She was by the door and stepped easily away behind it, so as not to be seen by anyone passing by.

'Yassuh.'

'Broderick. The overseer. You know him? Where is he now?'

'Yassuh. Him live on de hill, suh, on de hill dere.' She pointed vaguely.

'Uh-huh. But where is he now? Is he there now? Is he home?'

'Don't know, suh. Don't know. Him go to de fields. Him go to Muntegah Bay, suh . . . sometimes.' In fact she knew that Broderick was at home eating, had spent some time with Annie Palmer, had been in Montego Bay the night before, had ordered the wagon driver to be beaten the next day, and Arthur to do it.

'If you see him . . .'

'Suh?'

'Never mind.'

'Suh?'

'What time is it, do you know?'

'Suh?'

'Time. *Time*. Do you know the time?'

'Afternoon, suh? Dat time?'

'Clock time. What time by the clock.'

'No, suh. Whistle blow for dem field hand breakfast. Long time, suh.' She was afraid. He looked impatient now. She sensed strength in him. He might decide to hit her. He might press her to prove that she had come with good intentions. He was too low on the ladder to give her over to Annie Palmer, but he knew Broderick, who could put her back in a field gang.

'Is there any food?'

'Suh?'

'Food dammit. Something to eat. Soup. Meat. Tea. A kipper. There's no food here.'

'Yassuh. I get yu somethin'. You got no woman now, suh?' She knew he didn't. Mary Lou didn't particularly want him but whoever she sent to him would owe her a favour. The *buckras* ate well enough. A lot of chicken, and beef or pork when there was enough on the plantation. But you had to watch them. Some were mean. Or rather they got mean after a while. They drank a lot of rum and got meaner and meaner.

A nigger was almost never mean, but the white man seemed to have a kind of curse in him. They always liked Jamaica at first, always liked a Jamaica woman too, and they made love like healthy young bulls just let out of a pen. But then they got to hate. They got to hate so that they hated the sun, hated the rain too, hated the sugar (hated the constant green of it, one of her *buckras* told her once), hated it when you tried to be kind or when you made a good dish of greens with pork or even when you wanted to lie down and do it with them. When they fell into the fever it was different. They cried and talked about strange faraway things then. Or they screamed as though in some terrible fight. They whined. They even prayed. One *buckra* had screamed over and over again, all one night OUR FATHER WHO ART, OUR FATHER WHO ART, OUR FATHER WHICH ART, and the slaves had crept through the bushes to come and listen to him, hoping he could live with the witch in his soul.

'Woman?' Arthur eyed her levelly. The commission agent had talked about this. He would have a harem in Jamaica.

'Yassuh. You got no woman now?'

'No.' He sat still on the bed, conscious of his newness and aloneness and of the way she was bargaining with it. He was hungry and she bargained with that. He had probably been stupid to ask her about food. Broderick would doubtless have a comment.

'Deys many nice Jamaica girl for you.'

'I suppose. Are you going to bring me some food now?'

'Yassuh.' Mary Lou took the opportunity of fleeing out the door. She came back in a few minutes with a thick green soup, a plateful of rice with a gravy over it and some lumps of dark meat in it, and a cup of coffee. She set it down on his table, went out again, and came in with an old bottle and a cracked china cup just as he was sitting down to eat.

'Watah, suh,' she said softly, and stood beside him for a minute, watching him taste the soup.

'Thank you. Are you going now?' His look told her to go.

'Yassuh.' Mary Lou sauntered out into the bright sun. She wore a cheap cotton dress, no shoes, and he noticed that her hair was almost straight and came down to about the middle of her neck. He had seen a lot of women on the road that morning with the little ugly pigtails the blacks made with their fuzz. There would then be another strain in Mary Lou—a little white, or perhaps Chinese. He had heard there were a few Chinese in Jamaica.

She paused in his yard. He watched her stoop and take a red flower and put it in her hair. Then she came back hesitantly, and stood at the door.

'What is it now, Mary Lou?'

'De goat meat wit de rice special, suh. Special to get . . .'

'Oh?'

'Beg yu a sixpence, suh, for get de rice meat.' Her eyes searched the floor then the walls then the ceiling and her pink tongue came out to search her lower lip.

'I have to pay for this?'

'*No*, suh. No. No. Just special from . . . from a woman on de way here.'

'The mistress knows you charge sixpence for the meat on the rice? And does Mr. Broderick know that, Mary Lou?' She looked

frightened now. He saw the game. You played *mawster*. She had
the food and maybe a Jamaica girl for him. But he had the ultimate power, or at least excellent leverage.

'No, suh. Not for de meat. Just Mary Lou beg yu a sixpence.'
Her eyes became dull and she stared at his shirt front. He remembered that he had almost begged in London. He might have
looked like this if he had gone back to the manager and the head
clerk and stared at their chests, humble, offering himself up for
their amusement, scorn and regal decision.

'Wait, Mary Lou.' He went to his satchel and took a shilling
out of his purse. Then he changed it for two sixpence pieces, and
one sixpence for two thruppence pieces. A shilling itself would
probably attract too much attention to her if a dockhand worked
all day for sixpence. Her hand was open and out when he returned. He put the money in it and closed her hand over them
with his own.

'Thank you for the food. . . .'

' 'kyou, suh.' She looked up as far as his chin, and went off
again, running over the front yard out of sight behind a flowery
bush and out on to the road.

Arthur sipped some of the coffee. He had never liked coffee
but this wasn't bad. Dark and smoking hot, with a lot of sugar in
it, the cup seemed to centre his life around itself. He stared at its
darkness for a while and in his mind heard soft echoes of home,
of his fat, patient mother in her kitchen, his worried father,
scurrying to please and keep his customers and telling the family
what a fine job he had done of converting worsteds into waist-
coats for 'gentlemen' that day. The steaming cup reminded him
of Harley Street winters, the shutters closed tight, the charcoal
making a circle of warmth around itself that extended out six
or eight feet into their little parlour.

Their home had been better than most. The factory workers
had suffered after the end of the wars in Europe, many of the
Manchester mills closing. Now and again he had brought a
school-fellow home for bread and jam and some tea in the cold
afternoons, at his mother's insistence, because she knew what
poverty lay out on the streets of the city. She often named the
boys he might bring home. He never knew why until years later
when a friend told him that his mother's bread and jam and an
occasional kipper had been his breakfast and lunch that day and
he went home nights to a dish of pig's foot or some ox-tail soup

with maybe a dumpling now and then. His mother had known, then, about each family and their problems and had been good, a good woman, in her way.

His father, too, had by some miracle survived the bad times after Napoleon's wars or perhaps not by a miracle but just by going to his little shop every day and serving people well. Momentarily oblivious of the bright Jamaica afternoon, Arthur hoped that his lonely father on Harley Street would forgive his leaving. His obscure need to go alone into another world was not unlike his father's solitary way of work and, he hoped, not beyond the old man's comprehension.

He was grateful to Mary Lou for the food and the coffee. He had a home now and the food was a good pause after the long sea trip, the night in Montego Bay, and after Broderick and the dreary wagon ride. The house was crude enough, just boards intersticed with something resembling plaster, but its shutters opened out on a warm, colourful landscape. There were flowers just outside the window and a tiny breeze moved in the house. A small yellow and black bird the size of a sparrow flew through the room. He sat still and it came to the far edge of the table, cocking an eye at him, and then dug at invisible crumbs at the tabletop before angling away towards the window, then the sky. He would have to put some sugar out for it. He watched it vanish, and then dug into the hot rice and meat gravy.

As he ate a small black boy came to the door, carrying a bottle. He stood in the entrance alternately looking at Arthur and at the food on the table.

'Yes.'

The boy moved the bottle in his hands. 'Mary Lou send dis,' he said.

'Come in.' The boy shook his head.

'Come in, lad.' The boy stared at the ground. Arthur got up and went to him, squatting down to look in his face. The boy surrendered the bottle without looking at him.

'Beg you a bite, suh.' The boy looked at the floor, his mouth loose with fear. Were they all craven that way? He thought of himself again, going to borrow a cup of flour from Mrs. Pringle, their Manchester neighbour. But he would never have dared ask her for a bite of food, even though he could smell hot buns from the kitchen or the scent of a new pudding cooling on the dining-room table. Arthur gave the boy a bit of his rice and gravy on a small dish, with a spoon. Ignoring the spoon, the boy pushed the food into his mouth all at once, with one hand. Then he licked the plate, put it at Arthur's feet, and ran away down the path. Arthur stared after him.

After eating he took a short walk. There were two other houses within fifty yards of his. From the path he could see up to Broderick's house, several hundred yards away. When he got out as far as the main avenue into the estate he looked up at Rose Hall again, serene and magnificent. The louvred doors parted outside an upstairs room. A woman stood there for perhaps half a minute, in a white gown.

She looked out to the east, where the sugar cutting work was going on, making a wide scar on the neat carpet of sugar. Then she looked down the avenue and saw Arthur. He was too far away to see her eyes. Just her slender outline and dark hair were visible, and that was probably all she saw of him too. He was going to step away from the avenue but checked himself and stood still. In a few moments she stepped back into the room, closing the doors to a narrow V. Lest she be watching him from in there, he walked away back to his house. He had nowhere else to go on the property where he had business, at least that first day, and it seemed best not to wander aimlessly.

Mrs. Palmer, he reflected, was a bit of a vision, at least from a distance. He had imagined a grey old lady, possibly fat, a crone of sorts, the counterpart of the MoBay solicitor. But what he had seen was handsome and with the delicacy of expensive porcelain. At least she looked that way in the white gown. As he went back to the empty house, past fiery bougainvillea leaves, deep red hibiscus blossoms and a mango tree heavy with the green, unripe fruit, desire pervaded him like a sinister music he had not wanted to hear, or had ignored because of the long sick boat trip and the shock of the newness of Jamaica. Now he felt better, and would gladly mount a woman. If Mary Lou came back he could try her, although he had no real taste for black skin and stiff hair. They also stank, from lack of soap and water. The girl in Barbados had been acrid and had a big unattractive triangle of thick wool at her crotch. One of the sailors had told him they were all that way, with thick hair half-way up their bellies. Her best assest had been movement. Lord, how she moved and wriggled, as though she had been created solely to writhe around or under or over or beside or in front of a man. Never had he known anything so sinuous. She made English whores seem like stiff pigs incapable of pleasure. He had to admit that, even though he didn't much like them black.

With nothing to do he lay down on his bed to daydream for a while in the warm, drowsy afternoon.

6

ANNIE PALMER saw Arthur on the road, watched his passage from the partly closed doors as he walked back to his house. She had thought of calling out to challenge him, but was too tired. She made mental note to ask Broderick what the new book-keeper was doing wandering around the property, staring at her windows.

The little deaf-mute was with her. He was short, almost dwarfed, as though one infirmity had led to another. His head was large, his eyes always bright and alert. He was sturdy and strong for his twelve or thirteen years, and as friendly as an amiable dog. When she had found him he had been given to rages induced by his muteness, and because of terror. He could not hear horses or cattle or people coming upon him. She had in fact almost trampled him while riding on the properties one day, and that way found out about him. The slaves were going to abandon him in the forests in hope that he would somehow survive as he might have in Africa. As far as Annie could determine they thought of him as a throwback, the reincarnation of an ancestor, thus somehow scared and not to be killed, and probably displeased with them, because of his rages.

To control his rage Annie had a collar and chain fashioned for him and broke him gradually, interspersing food and comfort with chained exposure to the cold rain or hot sun in a garden behind the house. Her husband had despised all this but she kept close watch on the boy to be sure her husband never arranged, as he wanted to, the child's murder.

Now, with her husband gone, he was a safe, permanent part of the household. He had watched Arthur with her, standing in the shadows behind her, and then went to squat in his usual place in the corner of the bedroom, where she had a cushion for him.

Annie sat at her dressing table and looked at herself in the mirror. She was tired from her night riding, and her face showed it. But the new moon had graced the plantation and she had gone out to ride, for how many hours she could not remember. She recalled stopping at Broderick's house and learning from his old hag of a cook that he had gone without telling her. Sometimes she allowed him to ride with her. If he was in the right mood they would race down the road. towards Runaway Bay, or Oracabessa in the other direction, and inevitably catch a slave out illegally at night, corner him and either tie him to their horses and drag him down half a mile of paving blocks, screaming and kicking, or make him run between them while they trotted along, whipping him with their crops as they went. Three times deputations from other plantations had come to complain about having the slave, their property, damaged but Annie had told them either it was not she, or the man had attacked her, and they had gone away to gossip helplessly among themselves about mad Mrs. Palmer.

She knew her reputation, but ignored it. Years before, she had chosen to withdraw from it as though it were not hers at all but some incredible fabrication of lunatic gossips, isolated in their great houses, stranded in their seas of sugar and watched, constantly, by shifty battalions of silent slaves, padding through all the rooms like amiable silent ghosts, and so watching each other in town. All privacy vanished and no one could be distinct but had to merge into Jamaica talk and legend. She stood apart from this, becoming her own legend. She withdrew from the drawing-rooms, avoided town, and only on rare occasions allowed Carruthers to visit her to discuss Rose Hall's accounts. She stayed in the great house, silent, with her memories and wtih her playthings, the men and women, black and white, whose lives depended on her.

Annie brushed her hair before the mirror. She thought about that fool, Sarah Edwards, humiliated and dead now. Dead in her own cow pen, trampled by a bull. A few years before, Sarah had rejoiced at the legal end of the slave trade. A sweet, vague woman she had cajoled her husband, a retired army man, into having a party to celebrate the end of the trade. They told no one what the party was for and when they proposed their first toast to '. . . a healthy, moral Jamaica, freed from the stigma of traffic in human flesh, a proud part of Her Majesty's Empire . . .' nine-tenths of their guests stared in silence and then excused themselves gradually, walking away from the candlelit veranda, the glowing chandeliers, the roasts and wines, and out into the darkness to their slave-driven carriages. Several clergymen remained, one a former solicitor who had left the profession to become an Anglican lay brother. Two other planters, both mulattoes, stayed too.

But the Edwards had toasted their own doom and Jamaica's too. It took them years to realize it, but their demented hope of changing the world gradually led them, and Jamaica itself, into a creeping genteel poverty. As Sarah Edwards polished and re-polished her furniture and was sweeter to her blacks, production fell, the plantation grew shabbier, the slaves drifted away else-where, and those remaining finally got hungry to the point where, in an anguish of perplexity and hungry fury they burned the fields and moved on the great house itself. Annie Palmer, brushing her hair was not sorry for any of them.

Annie touched herself lightly with the cologne she still had sent out from Paris occasionally, and then took off the simple white gown she had on. The deaf-mute watched her, his brain stunned as ever, by the shock of her dead-white flesh. He thought her the only white woman in the world, a palpable miracle. His heart beat a little faster. He kneaded his fingers. She gestured to him and lay face down on the bed. He hopped up beside her, on his knees by her side, looking over her like some strange surgeon. Then he began to knead her back, starting at the base of her neck and slowly working downward, making little croaking sounds in his throat. His sturdy little fingers massaged her well. Annie had had one of her best maids teach him how.

When the little mute had passed to the small of her back—which hurt from riding a horse until three the previous night—and then on over her narrow white buttocks and down along her thighs to her knees, she turned sideways towards him. She drew up her knees a little and he lay down beside her, his woolly head butting softly into the warm cove made by her belly and thighs.

He could not have known that Annie had always wanted a child. He just found it comfortable, there against her white softness. His eyes were open and bright. Up between the swells of her breasts he could see her eyes, see them close, knew by the feel of her when she went to sleep. He lay still and wide awake, guarding her and wondering if she would cry out in her sleep this time, as she sometimes did. He was quite calm, unmoved and satiated merely to lie there. She had made a eunuch of him several years before.

7

'I TELL YOU she gave me a turn. I was just out for a walk in the moonlight and stopped to sit in a clearing for a minute when she came crashing out of the brush at a gallop. She wears a man's clothes when she rides, you know. A black suit, and sits a horse like a man. Thought it was Broderick. Then I looked up and saw the face and her long hair. A sight in the moonlight, I tell you.'

'What did she say?'

'She asked what was I doing in the fields at night,' Wilson said. 'Damned lordly she was too. As though a man had no right to leave his house. But then she had the whip curled in her hands. So I said I was merely out for a breath of air.'

Wilson seemed to talk a lot, and was on his third or fourth rum, so Arthur encouraged him.

'She's famous, you know. Rides out like a holy terror, unannounced. Flails a black alive if she catches him out at night. They're all terrified of her, poor people. They really believe she's a sorceress. They say she's been seen in five or six places at once. They say she can hex a man and kill him at will. These Africans are mad, you know. No man in England could believe it. And no plantation owner wants anything to do with Christianity. They're quite the same as the Romans. I think one can be hardly proud of what we've done here. Let's have another drink, eh?' Wilson clapped his hands together to summon his servant, a fat black woman with sleepy eyes.

'Your house is pleasant,' Arthur said, '. . . mine seems very bare.' Wilson had two seats of woven straw, a straw carpet, several small carvings of faces and figures, a few small paintings.

'Too bad. The chap who was in your place seemed to have very little interest in life. He drank even more than I do and finally killed himself. I never did discover what his trouble was. His woman buried him herself. There was talk that she killed him, but they found him in the forest hanging from a tree. Ah yes, the furniture and things. They make these here. They can copy anything, and really have a good bit of talent. The paintings are by a free mulatto I know in Montego Bay. Crude, but he's improving, I'll take you to see him one day if you'd like.'

'Thank you.' Arthur really had no desire to meet a painter. It was a world he knew nothing about. Obviously Wilson had unusual tastes that were beyond him.

'Well what are your feelings the first day, Arthur? Think you'll like Rose Hall?' Wilson's voice was thick after the rums.

'It's work. I . . . I was sick of Manchester and London. Do you—do you like it here?' He disliked the way Wilson queried him so directly. In the mill that morning, the man had looked weaker and more confused than he seemed now.

'Yes it *is* work. True. With care one can save a few pounds here, if one lives, and perhaps plan a future. I may start a little school for the freedmen's children one day.'

The maid came back with the drinks, rum with tepid water. They drank silently for several minutes. Arthur had no idea what to say about Wilson's idea of starting a school. He felt inadequate to Wilson because he had no plans himself. He had come out just to escape from England. He felt stupid because that morning his best thought had been that he was free in the sun on a Caribbean Street, peering at a book-keeper through the bars of Barclay's Bank, and scorning him.

'By the way, did Broderick say anything to you about me?' Wilson said. He looked down into his mug of rum.

'Nothing at all. Only that we should talk about the work at the mill tonight.'

'Yes. I hear he's moving me from the mill.'

'Is that bad for you?'

'Not at all. Good, in fact, back out in the sun. But I had hoped

to make a change or two in the mill. I guess it's too late
now.'

'Anything I could do?'

'Not really. It's best you just do your work. Never pays to
make suggestions to Broderick.' Wilson downed his drink and
clapped his hands again.

'Not an easy man, it seems, Broderick.'

'Not easy? Beast is a better description. Be cautious with him.
He would kill without thinking about it, and kill any of us as
well. *That's* who we work for, Arthur. The other overseers are
much the same, I've heard. He's not unique. One body more or
less means nothing to them. The sugar does. Grow it, cut it,
refine it, sell it. There are plenty of *us* to go around, happy to get
out of England.'

Arthur considered him. A bright man, obviously, if he had
taught school. A man with education, working in a grinding mill
and now moving to the cattle pen. Hating Broderick, but also
fearful of him, for some reason. Arthur failed to understand
Wilson's problems, but knew they were more than his own, or at
least more abstruse.

'So . . . so she rushes at you out of the night, eh?'

'Yes. Days, she stays in her nest up there, like a black widow
spider. Rides out to whip the niggers in the dark of the night, if
she catches them out. Lucky thing she didn't take me for one and
lash me proper.'

'You mean she's alone up there *all* the time?' Arthur recalled
her attractiveness, from a distance at least, that morning.

'Well not *all* the time. Broderick is in and out of there, and in
and out of her, probably. And they say she'll take on a healthy
nigger now and then, no maybe even two or three of them, or
perhaps have a half dozen up for a little show. . . .'

'A little show?'

'Arthur, we English are rather strange people. We think the
French and Spanish are depraved and we assume that the nigger
is an animal at base'—Wilson's voice was thick from the rum—
'but our own capacity for viciousness and filth exceeds theirs by
far because we have the gift of imagination added to some centuries of intelligent thought. This allows us to plan and carry out
remarkable things that would cause some of our ancestors to
blush for us. But we're still always able to justify them before
Parliament and the Throne. Here for example we have created

Jamaica. And Jamaica has created Mrs. Palmer, who is probably an insane, murderous animal. And yet Jamaica, and in turn England, understands her the way, say, in the past the world has understood Nero, Caligula, Judas, Alaric and Visigoth, Cleopatra, Genghis Khan and so on.'

'Yes.' Arthur had not really followed Wilson's monologue. He had stopped back at the immediacy of Mrs. Palmer, alone in the house. He was reminded of a woman back in Manchester about whom everyone talked. As a boy of twelve he had delivered a bolt of silk to her shuttered house on the city's fringes. She had asked him in, given him little cakes to eat and showed him her collection of pottery figurines and a copper gong from Hong Kong. She let him heft what she said was a real Japanese samurai sword once brought home by her husband, a sea captain who had vanished in a typhoon off Australia.

He remembered that she smelled wonderfully fragrant and had delicate hands that touched him lightly on the neck and down along his back as she walked him around the house. That evening he had told his mother about the sword and figurines. She had shouted at his father for more than an hour about what, he didn't know, except it had something to do with the woman 'having visitors'. Whatever Wilson was talking about had stirred at least that memory but nothing else.

'Someone may even think of us as brave some day. Imagine that,' Wilson smirked. He looked into his glass, finished his drink and clapped his hands again. 'Brave. Whipping niggers who can't even read. Brave, sitting and watching the cane grow and the niggers cut it for us. Brave Irishmen like *Broderick*. . . . Were you informed about militia duty?'

The late evening sun was dying, reddening the sky. The room darkened gradually, and the servant paused to light an oil lamp. It cast sharp shadows over Wilson's lean face. A crude wooden statuette near him on the table was elongated in inky shadow against the wall.

'Militia? No one mentioned that to me.'

'Of course not. They only told you about getting rich in Jamaica and wallowing in black flesh. But there's one more thing, old boy, it has to be defended.'

'From what—invasion?' Arthur's history and geography were vague. He had not the remotest idea what the French, Dutch, English, and others had been doing around the Caribbean for so long a time. Drake, Nelson, and others. Fighting to sell goods to the natives, he supposed.

'Invasion yes. From within, my boy. Place is crawling with runaways. We have to go out now and then and kill them in the hills before they outnumber us.'

'You mean we go out like an army?'

'Precisely. Crusaders at the throat of the infidel. But there is no holy city to take. The niggers just melt into the forests. We capture trees, vines, streams and hills and occasionally a few of those woolly heads. This is England's second wool trade, largely unknown to the British public. There really should be a black section on the mighty red Woolsack in the House of Lords.'

'And we bring the niggers back to work?'

'If they can still work. Of course a good body is worth two hundred quid—in other words, four years of your wages—now that the trade's been stopped. We try not to kill them unless they charge us with cutlasses. Now and again we have to kill one in the field, if he goes wild. Oh you'll see, you'll see. There should be an operation in a month or so. It's getting time again. General Broderick will keep you informed. You really had no idea at all what you were getting into here, did you?'

'I suppose not.'

'They like it that way. Don't let them beat you down.'

Arthur wanted to ask Wilson if he knew what *he* had been getting into. The man seemed supercilious now. But for all his impotent sarcasm he had a certain dignity and a vague air of having known better days. He would be a class or two above Arthur, his father in government, perhaps, or a teacher too, or conceivably a wealthy merchant. Not wanting to talk about his father's tiny Manchester shop, he avoided questioning Wilson.

The servant brought dinner, on cracked old English pottery. There was soup, a roast wild pigeon, mashed yams, boiled greens, and Wilson opened a bottle of port.

'At least the food is good here,' he said. 'More than you'd ever dream you would see. Chances are we will never dine at one of their rich great houses, but they live opulently, the devils. But then Jamaica is so rich even we inferior creatures can eat well. Quail, snipe, plovers, pigeons, doves, geese, turkey. Lord, the woods are teeming. The place is like Eden. I don't know how England ever deserved this. And the sea, God, it's a storehouse. The wretched Africans are just beginning to learn a little about it. See this?

It's fresh turtle soup. I doubt they're having it at Buckingham Palace tonight. There are fellows here on the shore who'll take you out in those little dugouts. Throw a line overboard. Hell of a ride when you get a turtle. Drags you about for an hour. If you're lucky you can beach the boat and then drag the brute in. Ever see a live turtle?'

'No.'

'Neither did I before this. Big creatures, flapping their fins down there under the sea. Delicious meat. The boatman keeps the shell. They use them for dishes. Tortoise shell dishes in a nigger's shack. Turtle soup for dinner on a book-keeper's fifty quid a year. Wild pigeon. Oranges. Oranges! . . . ' He clapped his hands, and the servant appeared, hefty, implacable. 'Bring an orange. Bring three or four. Look, look here, Arthur, aren't they lovely? How many of these have you seen in Manchester?'

'At Christmas now and then, is about all. They came all the way from Spain, I think.'

'Right-o. Let's see what else. Pineapple. Mango. Breadfruit— marvellous when you bake it. We must have that some night. Yam, pigeon. . . . It's marvellous. They say even alligator steaks are good. The 'gators are out there in the swamps. They say our dear forebears in the last century used them on the niggers. An example of the Empire's intention to maintain stability and order in the name of the Crown. Niggers terrified of 'gators too. Say their eyes glow in the night, looking for them. Black meat. Never seems to occur to them that 'gators like white meat too. Perhaps one day the niggers will have a 'gator pit of their own, throw white men into it. Maybe *women*. I wonder how Annie Palmer would like to have a 'gator chewing her?'

Wilson opened and poured the port, a gift, he said, from his friend the Reverend Gordon. He was quite drunk. But his mood had shifted. He liked something about Jamaica, if only the food and drink.

'To your good health, friend Arthur, and all the wealth you came for. I beg your pardon for such early dining, but our day begins at dawn and we must be up and about for Sir Broderick and the Lady Anne.'

'Thank you, Wilson. To your good health too.'

'I will likely never have good health, in these surroundings. The only thing that saves me is the prox—prox—proximity of the sea down there, at the base of these hills. You see I came from the downs hard by Dover. I was brought up smelling the sea, loving it. I could never go to sea because I had asthma. And now here on the land, with the same damned asthma. Foiled in either instance. You know Byron? Know what he said about the sea? He said . . . no not *about* the sea. He said it *to* the sea—*to* it. Very important difference. He said:

> *Man marks the earth with his ruin—his control*
> *Stops with the shore; upon the watery plain*
> *The wrecks are all thy deed, nor doth remain*
> *A shadow of man's ravage except his own,*
> *When, for a moment, like a drop of rain,*
> *He sinks into thy depths with bubbling groan . . .*

'We must go down to the sea, Arthur. No runaways down there to come and kill us. No mosquitoes. No yellow fever. No grinding and boiling. Just good turtle to catch and eat. And that bubbling groan . . . into the depths with us.'

'They used to throw the blacks into the sea, all chained together,' Arthur said. 'Tough blokes, those old captains.' He was proud to have some small knowledge to contribute.

'Yes, but neat. Gone without a trace. No gore, no beating. No ugly traces for history to ponder. Much nicer to drown a man than whip him to death. Has less of a touch of the Inquisition about it. Civilized, drowning. Byron was right. We do mark the earth with our ruin. Broderick likes to cut up the fields and cut up men, mixing a little blood with the sugar.'

'Wilson, can a fellow have any fun out here?'

'Of course. Good eating, as I told you. Enough women to cripple you. There's riding, if you get a horse. They're too expensive for us. Otherwise nothing. Get accustomed to it. This is not London. It's the end of the civilized world. I'm personally thinking of sending for books on botany and zoology to do some studying before I drink myself into oblivion.'

'I never drank much, except a pint now and then.'

'Get accustomed to that too. The days are long, and the nights worse, even though we get up at dawn. You'll find that you need companionship in the glass.'

'Don't you keep a woman? I heard that everyone out here did.'

'I try that off and on. Jabbering smelly idiots. Steal from you. Pester you. Want a bolt of cloth, a pound of meat for their worthless families, want you to sneak them an extra salt fish ration. Pad about the house like ghouls after you. Before you know it everyone for miles knows how often you change your underwear or whether or not you snore. You're not yourself any more. You're just a shadow. They could snap their fingers and do away with you. My servant. If she wanted to put a bit of poison in the food tonight, there'd be the two of us, gone. And she'd be gone, too, off with the runaways in the hills before dawn. It's all very tenuous, Arthur. You'll begin to feel the web around you soon enough.'

'Web?'

'Web, net, whatever we want to call it. We're fishermen who have caught only ourselves. The net is deceptive because we think we're outside of it, instead of inside. But a Jamaican hamadryad is probably at this moment peering at us through the shutters. Or a runaway, with a sharp cutlass in his hand. The possibility of instant death is always with us.'

Arthur cut at the delicate meat of the wild pigeon and drank a bit of the port. He could not remember eating so well in his life. London seemed a long dreary line of hard bread and dry cheese, of watery stews and dried out kippers. Whatever Wilson's attitudes, Arthur was at least grateful for this moment of his life, as he had been while eating Mary Lou's rice and gravy that afternoon.

The servant glided in and out from the back of the house, bringing more yams and greens for their plates, more legs and breasts of pigeon, finely roasted over charcoal. The servant was fat and dull-eyed, wore a spotted calico dress that hung about her as though she were unaccustomed to clothes and didn't know what to do with them. Arthur was reminded of the driver he had to beat the next day. He hesitated to ask Wilson about it but there was no one else before he went to Broderick, and he also had to learn about the mill from Wilson.

'Wilson, I have to whip a man tomorrow. Is that—is that a usual thing? And how do you do it?'

'Don't be absurd. No white but Mrs. Palmer whips them. They make the drivers do that so it's all kept in the black family, so to speak.'

'But Broderick said . . .'

'The hell with him. He'll have forgotten it tomorrow.'

'But if he decides to . . . the cat-o'-nine-tails, is it hard to use?'

'I don't know. I either shut my eyes or look a little away when they do that. There is quite enough ugliness in the world without me being a student of it. At the school, they always wanted me to cane those little boys, make them pull down their trousers and beat them on the flesh with a stick. I defied them, defied them all. One day I beat the headmaster, on the face, with his brutish stick to see how *he* liked it. We English are sick, I tell you.'

'What did they do to you at the school?'

'Nothing. A term in jail and the end of my teaching. And so I came out here, but never escaped the madness of Englishmen.'

'What about the headmaster?'

'What about him?'

'You said you beat him on the face.'

'He's all right. They transferred him to a school in the Midlands where nobody would know how he got the scars. He's probably whipping little boys' behinds to his heart's content.'

Arthur sensed the end of the evening, and Wilson's growing drunkenness. He had to take away an answer or two before the evening disappeared and left him alone in the mysterious newness of Rose Hall. 'What's it like in the mill? What do I do there? Broderick told me to ask you.'

'Nothing to it. Be king in the mill and the field. King. Oh, I mean the Queen—Victoria, I forgot for a second.'

'Please, Wilson. I've got to be there tomorrow morning and will be no kind of king at all.'

'A toast, a toast to the Queen.' Wilson jumped to his feet, drank, threw his glass on the floor, and stumbled out to the veranda. The servant came to sweep up the pieces. Arthur followed Wilson outside. The darkness was profound, except for fireflies in mid-air, a minor glow on the horizon that came from cook fires in the slave quarters below, and the stars above, speckling the Jamaica sky.

'So that's all there is to the mill?' Arthur said after a while.

'You threaten me now,' Wilson said, his head sagging towards his chest, '. . . threaten me with Broderick, who sent you to me.'

'Look my friend . . .'

'I see. Broderick has claimed you already. Smart of him. I surrender. In the mill watch them to see that they don't steal cane, don't steal the juice, don't steal the gears or the grinding knives, don't sleep on the job and don't try to sneak in a relative to work and do the stealing for them. They'll keep testing you.

You'll find them imaginative in the extreme, although the ultimate power belongs to you—to us—because we have the whips. Is that enough?'

'But—but exactly what do I do in the mill?'

'I told you. Watch them. And also push them. Keep them doing one thing after another. The moment they have a chance, they stop. A man brings in some cane, drops it on the floor, and stops. He just stands there. He would sit down if he could. Or he talks with one of the mill hands or the women pushing the cane into the grinders.'

'Talking isn't allowed?'

'You have a specific mind haven't you? Talking is up to you. Broderick won't have it, or singing. Neither will Mrs. Palmer, but she's rarely seen by day. If you want to let them talk or sing a bit, that's your responsibility. Personally, I found it soothing. The African chant is a wonderful thing. And if they like you they may bring you a gift or two. The pigeons we had this evening were a gift from one of the mill hands, a young boy that carries trash to the boilers. He likes to chant a bit during the day, and I let him now and again.'

'I'm sorry to bother you with all these questions.'

'I trust that Broderick will not be told all of the answers. What you do over there is your own responsibility. Each of us must work and die separately, in his fashion.'

Arthur remained silent. Strange fellow, Wilson. But with many feelings and ideas. And now he mentioned dying, odd for a youngish man. Arthur stared out into the black night. He had seldom seen such darkness, except during the sea voyage. The night was a fathomless well, the stars unreal. And yet he knew it was only eight o'clock. He realized that there was not even an inn to go to or a street to walk. He was confined to the veranda with Wilson, who disliked vague things, such as the Empire and the plantation, and spoke of death. He would have to see about getting a horse and learning to ride it, if he were to move at all. And then where was there to go? Montego Bay? For a moment he missed London's teeming streets and saw that he might have made an irreversible and terrible error in delivering himself to Jamaica.

Wilson reached out and touched his hand lightly. 'You'd best go now, my boy,' he said softly. 'Tomorrow arrives soon and the dawn is rather cruel to us inebriates.'

Arthur thanked him for dinner and went up the dirt path towards his own house as Wilson stumbled off to bed. He had decided not to go and see Broderick but thought better of it. He looked up at Broderick's house on the hill, reluctant to submit, but knowing there was no choice. He breathed deeply and walked slowly, fighting the effects of the rum.

Going to Broderick's he felt poor and beaten again, not free and proud the way he had on the Montego Bay street with the bearer in front of him. Mosquitoes bit his hands and face. He moved up the path quickly, stumbling over roots and vines, to evade them.

Broderick came to the door shirtless and ordered him in to keep out the night bugs.

'What is it, Arthur?' The overseer looked annoyed. He appeared to have been studying some large property maps spread out on the floor.

'You told me to come about the cat-o'-nine-tails for tomorrow.'

'What cat-o'-nine-tails?'

'I'm to . . . to whip the driver that brought us here this morning. You said . . .'

'Yes. What have you been up to all day?'

'Nothing. I unpacked and someone brought food, and I saw Wilson this evening, as you said.'

'Who brought food? Where?'

'A girl. A black girl. To my house.'

'Name?'

'Mary Lou.'

'Oh. She found you already. Be careful of her. Did you bed her too?'

He stared at Broderick. How far did his ownership of a man's life go? The overseer stared back, assured, implacable.

'No. Not that I wouldn't mind. . . .'

'I don't care about your tastes. Just be careful of her. She'd like nothing better than a white or a mulatto child. Most of them would. And she may be crawling with disease. But that's your business. And she talks. And begs. Be on your guard.'

'Surely. The . . . the cat-o'-nine-tails? Should I take it tonight?'

'What did Wilson say?'

'We talked about the mill work.'

'Was he drunk again tonight?'

'I'm not sure.'

'You are, so he must be.'

'I did have a few rums.'

'You know we start at four in the morning?'

'I hadn't been told.'

'You're told. The bell will ring. Was Wilson alone?'

'Except for his servant.'

'The fat woman?'

'Yes.'

'No boys about?'

'No one else.'

'What did he tell you about the mill?' Broderick's gaze was level and noncommital.

'To . . . watch everything carefully. Keep them moving. Watch for theft. To keep them from singing and chanting, and talking.'

'Good. Nothing else?'

'That was about it.'

'Does he seem . . . all right . . . to you?'

'I don't follow you.'

'Forget it. Just be careful of him. Every man has to make his own way here. And this will be a bad season. We're short-handed. Here's the whip for you . . .' He went to a corner of the room and brought back the flailing tails. They cast a brief splayed-out shadow over the maps on the floor as he crossed the room.

'It takes time to learn to use them well,' Broderick said quietly, like a schoolteacher discussing the alphabet. 'But you should know how. You have to stand back a few feet, and take a good, full swing, with your arm straight out, like so. Then come across and down. If you hesitate, the tails will bunch up on you. Remember, straight, and keep a full easy swing. This one is tarred to keep the tails stiff, but you still have to do it properly. I think there's a nigger in the tunnel tonight. Let's go and see.'

Broderick picked up a lamp and strode out of the house. Arthur followed him up a winding path towards Rose Hall. Then they went down steps and through a heavy wooden door to an underground passage. At the end of it was a cave-like room. A woman lay in the corner, both wrists chained to the wall. She looked up as Broderick raised the lamp high over her.

'Venus. What you doing here? Miz Palmer catch you a-steal her scents again, or you make off with a chicken, eh?'

She was plump and looked absurd, almost comical, lying ın a heap in her calico dress, her chained hands extended towards the rough rock of the wall, almost as though in prayer. A tear gleamed in one eye and trickled across her nose.

'No, suh. No, suh, Mist Broderick. You know me, suh. No such a ting, suh.'

'Miz Palmer lies, Venus? That what you say?'

'No, suh.'

'Well, we've come to visit you for a minute or two.' He took a bunch of keys from his pocket and undid the lock holding her chains. She got to her knees, rubbing her wrists.

'Just stand over there,' Broderick said, '. . . face the wall.'

'No, suh. Miz Palmer don' say about whippin', suh. She don't . . .'

'Now.'

She faced the wall, her arms at her sides. Arthur heard her sob softly. Broderick undid the top of her dress and pulled it down over her body to the floor. Like the driver that morning, her back was scarred, and her protruding buttocks too, and below them her thick thighs, slightly scarred down to the knee line. The lamp on the floor accentuated her soft rotundity, the great width of her hips, the ample flesh of her behind. Desire and a sense of shame touched Arthur all at once. His fingers tightened on the hard leather handle of the whip.

'Now if you'll stand over here, Arthur, right about where I am.' He looked up into Broderick's sharp eyes. '. . . right here, at this angle. We're just going to hit her once. Hold your arm out and down at an angle like this. Right. And now swing and as you do turn your body into it. Wait. First untangle the tails. Swish them a little. Right. Now you're ready.'

Arthur looked for a second at his human target, standing still and unreal, passive, nude, defenceless in the flicking lamplight.

'Now,' Broderick said.

He swung fast, blindly, but remembering to keep his arm straight and turn and duck into the blow with his right shoulder. He expected a sharp crack but there was virtually no sound— less than his father had made hitting him with a belt when he was a boy. There was just a small sob from the woman. Her massive bulk had not moved.

'Excellent. You have that all right. You'll learn to do it harder when you get your distance established. Your arms are a bit longer than mine. Here, wipe her off with this. . . .' He took a wet rag from a wood bucket in the corner and threw it to Arthur. He wiped the woman's welted back with the cool cloth, and turned away.

'Bless you, suh,' she said, still staring at the wall.

'Put your dress on, Venus,' Broderick said. She turned and they watched her pull clumsily at the dress around her ankles, her huge breasts swinging like dark heavy fruit in the lamp glow.

Broderick said, 'They're like great cows when they get older, and there's always a pickaninny pulling at them. Venus . . .'

'Suh?' She stood up, the dress just at the edge of her circular, fleshy belly.

'You got de bigges bubbies in de whole plantation.'

'Yassuh.' She looked serious, frightened, then smiled.

'Let's see them. Show them to *buckra* Arthur here, who beat you. Hold dem up.'

She let go the dress, which fell to the floor again, and held up her mountainous breasts with their wide purple nipples. They spilled out over the edges of her short fingers. She looked at Arthur, expectant, friendly. He looked back pleasantly, but felt himself blush.

'There's some dinner for you, Arthur,' Broderick said, nudging him, '. . . she fed six children with those . . . all right, Venus get dressed.'

When she finished she lay down quietly on the floor while he chained her again.

'I'll speak to Miz Palmer for you. You want to go back to the house soon?'

'Yassuh.'

'You have no pickney in your belly now?'

'No, suh.'

'You lie.'

'No, suh.'

'Then I can take you back to the field to cut cane?'

'No, suh. Please, suh.' She stared at Broderick's boots, her eyes huge.

'Did you see me tonight?'

'No, suh.'

'Did you see *buckra* Arthur tonight?'

'No, suh.'

'And you didn't feel no whip tonight?'

'No, suh.'

'That's good. An' I hope no duppy come to get you tonight.'

He took up the lamp and Arthur followed him through the tunnel and along the path, carrying the cat-o'-nine-tails. Broderick turned off at his own house, saying 'good night' over his shoulder. At home, Arthur dropped the whip on the floor and poured himself some of the rum that Mary Lou had sent over. He drank it but within minutes was out in front of the house, vomiting rum, turtle soup, yams, greens and wild pigeon, leaning dizzily against the house with both hands, his head down, the stars at his back.

8

His PRACTICE on Venus was wasted. That next day Broderick assigned a young field driver to give the old man his three lashes. Arthur merely watched as the old man was called out of line at reveille, just before dawn. The whole thing was barely visible under the light of spluttering torches in the cool open fields, and over in a few seconds. The old man, his grey woolly head bowed just a little, walked off the field alone. Because of his age, and with six sons in the cutting lines, he was specially privileged and had only to tend the creaky wagon. The young cutters paid little attention to what was happening in the pre-dawn gloom.

The next weeks were lost in Rose Hall's battle with its crop. Before dawn there was the torchlit reveille. Lateness for it was rare, and severely punished.

At work by five, they all had breakfast in the fields at ten. Dried cod from Nova Scotia, some rice, a boiled banana, and tepid water to drink from a tin dipper. There were exactly forty minutes for this and then they went back to assault the walls of a million stalks of cane, bending low to cut them close to the ground, the cutters thrusting each stalk behind them like a spear thrower putting his weapon aside, the clean-up men coming to cradle clusters of stalks in their arms and lug them to the oxcarts.

Rose Hall's fields were soundless, by Broderick's edict, except for the *chuk* of cutlasses as they bit into the cane, the occasional grunts of the clean-up squad, the crack of whip over oxen, the squeal of wood and wheel as full carts moved away and empty ones came forward. Only the black slave drivers spoke now and again, urging the men forward, telling them to keep the cane cleaner, to strip away more of the leafy tops, leaving hard, clean cane for the mill.

Arthur was in and out of the fields and the mill, moved about by Broderick. The overseer would indicate how far to cut a field, pointing out the middle of a knoll where he should turn the men east or south down a hillside to meet cutters coming the other way. He knew the terrain well, came and went like a field marshal inspecting units in the lint. He carried maps. He told Arthur to stay out near the driver and give his instructions through him and not hide in the shadow of a wagon. He said they had more respect for a man who exposed himself and who was ready to step in to stop trouble.

The sun—lambent in the morning, backlighting the last of the sugarcane blooms on the hills, picking out the easy majesty of Rose Hall, turning dewdrops to gems on red hibiscus, etching playful palm fronds against the sky—was a hot terror by eleven and an implacable pole-axe by noon, its power reinforced by the ground, then thrown back by the wall of cane, felt more as a weight, a will, than mere light.

Men's shadows vanished at noon and sometimes their sense left them too—now and again a cutter would fling his cutlass into the air with a whoop and run screaming in circles, holding his head, then rolling over and over on the ground, mindless of the sharp stubs of cut stalks, tearing his skin even before the driver got to him to whip him swiftly into blubbering near-silence, throw a dipper of water over his head and tie him by the neck, his hands loosely bound behind him, in the shade of the wagon. Unless he was ready to go back to work the wagon dragged him along with it to the mill, giving him a choice between strangulation and getting to his feet. All but a few got up. Those that did made one long round trip with the slow wagon, slipping and falling along one way but scrambling to their feet again to avoid horizontal hanging, finally coming back to the cutting line in the field. Those who didn't stay on their feet merely strangled, being either to ill to move or ready, finally, to end their own lives. Their bodies were taken down to the slave quarters and thrown before their wailing women. Suicide had been common in the early days when slavery was unbearable for a proud Ashanti or Coromanti. But that had passed within a generation and the new arrivals had been filtered in among the older slaves. The agony of their frustration was diluted in the common mass of docile blacks.

The sun that grew the crop dropped Arthur twice during the first week, twice again the second week, once the third week as he adapted to the climate and the dullness of standing in a field, squinting at the brightness all around him, watching the cutters at their monotonous work.

When he fainted the drivers had one or two cutters carry him gently to the shade of a wagon and they dipped cool water on to his head. Then he would lie there gazing at the white-hot sky for long minutes before getting to his hands and knees, finally up on his feet, and walking back near the work line. He always thanked the driver for his help but got no answer except perhaps . . . *she hot, mawster* . . .

If it rained, as it often did in the afternoon, he rejoiced, watching the bright edges of thunderheads nudge towards the sun, quench it, then turn the sky smoky black. Then the ground colours came to life—the earth reddish brown, the cane a soft green, the knolls to the north and south of where he stood mobile soft colours and ambient form, seemingly heaving like the sea as sun and cloud crossed overhead. Then the rain swept in from the east, a dark wavering veil moving over the land, urging a cool breeze before it that sent a wavy shudder through the cane and dried the sweat on a man's body. The rain came down in huge drops, joyous, flamboyant, turning to an avalanche of sweet water as the big-bellied clouds emptied themselves on the land.

The bodies of the blacks streamed with the cool rain. They paused to acknowledge it by looking up at the sky and rubbing their faces and heads in satisfied circular motions. Arthur always took off the helmet Wilson had loaned him and let the rain spatter on his head, cooling, fresh, not like the pallid drizzles of Manchester or London. The Jamaica rain was as much of a force as the sun. Its power and tempo rushed out of floodgates in the sky that opened and shut in random succession. Now the rain was a soft hush, a steady shower. Then it turned to a roar. The cutters kept to their work, vanishing and reappearing in heavy veils of rainfall, the only sign of them sometimes the regular small flashes of their cutlass blades. Arthur and the driver moved in close to keep watch. But the work never slackened. If anything, it went faster in the rain, the back of the heat broken, the day's monotony eased, the world alive with the choking smell of earth, the gentle scents of faraway flowers borne on the wind. The cane rustled and danced, losing its timeless unconquerable quality, suggesting long grass waving on an English meadow instead of a demanding crop to which all of them, on the plantation, were chained.

There were times when it rained for days. After the first day Broderick would usually stop the work. The cane sucked up too much water, diluting itself and its sugar content. And, after twenty-four hours of downpour, even walking became dangerous. Rivulets spilled down the slopes and became streams. They cut their own veins in the body of the land, tearing out rock, tree and bush as they went. The waters turned the colour of the red soil they stripped away, and surged on towards the sea. They took houses with them, mostly the pitiful slave shacks, sending them toppling and then rushing in furniture, mattresses, and what rags the blacks called clothes. The water snatched up small children, clogging their nostrils and mouths with muck from the high hills and then dragging them down along gullies to the sea.

At those times the water was a wide wet scourge chuted down from the high mist-hidden hills behind Jamaica's coasts, picking its victims at random. After a dozen or more hours, the ceaseless, monotonous rain was an unbelievable, tiring presence. At home, Arthur would nap and awaken, nap and awaken, disconnected from time except to know night or day, hour after hour linked in monotonous continuum by the evenly pounding rain. The first downpour came just a few days after he had started work. Intermittent, it made the first day bearable, and was welcome. Then it came in force, and Broderick, cursing, ceased operations.

The next day, Mary Lou came to see Arthur. Glistening wet, she carried some fish and a few handfuls of rice, some yams and a breadfruit. He made her undress and towelled her with a rough piece of muslin he had drawn from Rose Hall's storehouse.

Her body was still damp and cool as he put his mouth on hers, touched her damp flesh, carried her to the bed and mounted her. She flailed under him with a wildness that seemed to verge on terror brought on by the storm.

For two more days they were confined to the house by walls of rain. They ate a little and drank a lot of dark heavy rum. In the day's soft gloom or the hellish glare of the lamp by night, they copulated easily and, it seemed to Arthur, almost constantly. They seemed to be carrying out a private phallic tribal dance celebrating the rain.

For Arthur, Mary Lou was a revelation. At first, he took his pleasure rapidly, exploding in a single burst of English nerve and flesh. He felt superfluous, lying with more woman than he could cope with. She scratched him in frustration, rubbed herself on him, whimpering softly. She bit him, licked him, tried to bring him alive the way a bitch does a sick pup. She had something to give him. Her crotch was her life. Under her wide triangular clot of dark wool lurked all the sensation and knowledge she carried, or wanted. He took it more slowly the next time, and the next, enjoying the rippling of her muscles, the lissome way that spine, hip, belly and thigh all co-ordinated around, and for, the centre of her, that wet tunnel leading to her mysterious black soul. He took it more and more slowly each time, jabbing less, playing more, sure, detached, relaxed, inventive, his body an instrument charged and changed by repeated shock waves going down to his deepest muscle, farthest nerve, beyond sex, beyond himself. Jamaica had something for him. Jamaica, in the flesh of Mary Lou, took him.

She said little. She had no life to talk about. She was the child of a union between John Palmer and a fourteen-year-old slave girl, thus had white blood in her. All it had done was lengthen her hair a little. She was exempt from fieldwork because of that. She was free to leave Rose Hall too, but stayed because her fish and rice were there. She was not a fancy girl who could attract a wealthy white man. She wanted no part of sharing a hut with a field nigger and sinking back into the bottom of the black world. Yes she liked to be mounted by either black or white and had already given birth to two black children, both destined for the fields, but never saw them, or wanted to. They had been absorbed into the family of whomever she thought had made her pregnant. Another body for work, even that of a child, being useful on the plantations, there were no arguments about paternity.

As the rain pelted down hour after hour, she had no clear knowledge as to whether or not her own shack would be there when she returned to it. The rain, she said, took what it wanted. She would survive it. *Cow no dead him wi' shake tail*, she told him. As far as he could determine it meant that merely to be alive was enough and gave hope for the future. Her only quirk seemed to be an obvious but indefinable terror of Mrs. Palmer. It was not until the second day that Arthur saw why. High up on the inside of her left thigh, on the delicate cocoa skin fractions of an inch from her bushy sex, he saw the puckered welt of the brand that, she admitted, had been done by the mistress herself one day. He fingered it thoughtfully, wondering at the probable pain of cherry-red iron hissing on the skin. In his young half-drunken enthusiasm he kissed the place and ran his tongue over the brand—AP. She laughed, saying she was lucky that Miz Palmer had stopped where she did and had not done what she *said* she would do. Whatever had earned her this attention was never mentioned, nor could he draw it out of her.

When the rain lifted after three days, the sun peered suspiciously at a shambles. Acres of sugar lay flat, tumbled by the wind, swept horizontal by the beating of the rain and the rush of mud and water from the hills. The path from Arthur's house was a rocky gully. The bodies of several slaves were found immured in mud beside their houses. A child whose foot showed above the surface was carefully dug out and its rigid body wiped clean by moaning women. Black flies gathered to pick at its bloated lips and torn face.

Special food was issued because no one had eaten for three days. It was given out in the road near the flimsy shacks. The sun that had seemed such an enemy was welcome again as Rose Hall came to life. The blacks seemed almost eager to get back to work in the sugar after being cooped up at the rain's mercy.

But again the sugar became a defiant green wall and the sun took its revenge. From dawn until past sunset the work went on, seven days a week. Besides his fieldwork, Arthur drew night duty in the mill and the boiling house, and stumbled up to his home on the slope only two or three hours before dawn and the sound of the bell to rise again. He often wondered how the slaves felt, or if they felt, or could feel, anything after a day of such labour. He had no way of really knowing because they seemed to be universally docile, hovering out there on the edge of his own life like a vague cloud formation. Few of them ever spoke to him. Sick call was held at reveille, and if a man had to plead to go to the infirmary, or stay at home that day because he was sick, he had to argue it out with Broderick, who always won.

Marse Broderick. Nathaniel him sick today. Sick bad, suh.

Where?

Arm, suh. Lawd, wot a pain. It come in de night, suh, by de bad air. Please, suh.

Which arm?

Dis, suh. Him lef arm fo cut de cane, suh. Him bad need a day to res', mawster, please, suh.

Cut with the right arm today.

Cyawn't cut wid de right, suh. It lack schoolin', suh.

Today it goes to school. Arthur, see that Nathaniel cuts all day with his right arm . . . and no rum for three weeks—long time no rum, you hear me, Nathaniel?

No, suh. Nathaniel need him rum, mawster.

Then you cut today.

Yassuh.

What arm? Lift it. Nathaniel lifted the left arm, as Broderick half-smiled at him.

Thank you, Nathaniel. Any more for sick call?

Broderick knew them well. Even had Nathaniel chosen to cut his right arm, Broderick would have kept after him, discovered him drinking rum that was not his, ordered thirty lashes and a week in the stocks for him. Arthur came to admire Broderick for keeping the slaves so well in line. In the dark mornings there were only the three white men facing two hundred strong blacks, most of them carrying cutlasses. It was hard to grasp what strange sense of order kept them from revolt. One man could be whipped; two hundred were something else.

'The point is,' Wilson told him one evening, '. . . there would be no point to killing us. If we all go, the plantation goes, and with it their fish and rice, their iron for barrel staves, their salt, calico and everything else. And so it pays them to run away, and then sneak back to steal what they can. And, believe it if you will, and you should, they regard our ability to write as pure magic. Besides the whips, pencil and paper hold them.'

'Ah, so we are safe?'

'Of course not. We may have our heads removed at any time. They're savages. We are worse savages, hence our triumph over them. But they are pure savages. They don't think rationally, so their instincts are correct. They want freedom. That would include cutting off your head and mine and dancing over our bodies. Same sort of thing as the Parisians did. Rush this place as though it were Versailles, the way they did at Mount Pleasant a few weeks ago. But with a difference, a tremendous difference. The French, after they had their orgy, started building again. And the Americans, I suppose, and so on. But if the blacks decide to rise it will be like the coming of black Visigoths and we'll have another darker age, darker, even than the one we have now.'

'There aren't that many to overrun the place, are there?' Arthur asked.

'There aren't eh? There are a third of a million of them and fifteen thousand of us. And they breed like jack-rabbits. More seed is being put into more black women tonight alone than all the molasses produced in Jamaica during the past year. The lowlands, dear fellow, are drowned in seed while Milady Palmer sits barren and alone on her hill, and you and I sit here getting drunk. And back in England they think the sweet picnic on the Jamaica health will go on forever. In any event don't be too sure of those blacks we supervise. We may all lose our heads tomorrow if they decide that freedom is preferable to salt fish. And God help them then, when the niggers finally *own* Jamaica. Which they will one day. I wonder what they'll do then? They couldn't very well have slaves, could they—unless they started their own trade and imported Chinese or South American Indians. . . .'

Wilson rambled on drunkenly. Arthur never recalled more than a part of what he said. But he did watch the field hands more carefully for rebellious signs. None were visible, in his crews. So docile were they that Arthur put a stop to the practice of tying a sunstruck man by his neck to the wagon. He merely had him bound loosely, put in the shade, and had cool water poured over him. But then it happened several times in one week, and when he saw one black chatting with the wagon driver he realized that the hands had quietly taken him one step too far, luring him out of position with their docility, calling forth a sympathy it would be fatal to give. He regretted withdrawing it, but still knew he was not convincingly harsh with them. He had the neck ropes restored but it didn't stop the men from feigning sunstroke. They lay in the shade, got up to follow the wagon on its circuit, but at the field's edge began to sing, chanting

we flesh belong only to whip, and we blood belong to de groun'.

Arthur thought about this for a day or two, saying nothing to Broderick and with the field driver neutral, waiting on his orders. He finally abandoned the wagon altogether, had the man beaten briefly, then pegged to the ground, beaten again in a while if he feigned unconsciousness.

The afternoon that he had three men pegged down, and the driver hitting them one by one, while the cutters chanted for them and Arthur, furious but frightened, shouted at them to stop. Mrs. Palmer appeared in the field, a hat pulled low over her eyes, and asked him why he was trying to kill three costly field hands. She stayed up on her horse, straddling it, wearing trousers. Against the bright sun she was more of a silhouette to him than anything else. Her voice was sharp, but sounded cultured. He stood in an agony of embarrassed rage, the field dreamlike, unbelievable, the three slaves flat on the ground, the driver, whip extended, head down, out of it now, waiting, and in the distance the now silent cutters hard at their work.

'I . . . they . . .' He pointed to the men on the ground.

'They what?'

'Sick or . . . or crazy . . . from the sun, but they won't get up.'

'How can they get up if they're ill?' He sensed amusement in her voice.

'Because they do this. They do this to lie down like this. I'm going to beat the hell out of them . . . *beat* them. . . .' His voice rose to an hysterical squeal.

'Until they die, Mr. Arthur? Goodness we mustn't do that. Have the first one there untied.'

'Yes.' Nervously, he started to fumble with the knots at the man's neck.

'I said *have* him untied. The driver, Arthur,' she said softly.

He stood up, gritting his teeth, and told the driver, who had not moved, to untie the man.

'Stand up,' she said quietly. The driver stood back and the man got to his feet.

'You sick now?' She uncoiled a whip from the side of her saddle. The black shook his head, blank fear in his eyes.

'Good. Run. Let me see you run across the field.'

The man shook his head again. He was tall and lean, with strong muscles in his arms and shoulders, and a flat, muscular belly. He stood there surrounded, passive and contained, his eyes serious but with a peculiar blankness, as though within himself his own existence had somehow been erased.

'I said run now, or I kill you where you stand, hear?'

He ran, slowly and uncertainly at first, jogging, then moving faster as he heard the horse start up behind him, its hooves rustling the cane trash on the ground.

She circled wide of him, to the right, and then bore in towards him at a gallop as he began to zigzag uncertainly, looking over his shoulder, shouting something unintelligible at the chest of the now thundering horse. He ran as he watched her come on and tripped and fell just as she drew abreast of him. The whip caught him in mid-fall, directly across the face.

There was a strangled scream in the hot afternoon and a cutter or two turned around for a brief look, then went on with the work. Arthur noticed that his fists had tightened, although his panic had gone and the field was under control, as it had not been before she came.

Annie Palmer drew off as the black came half-way to his knees, clutching his face, dark blood streaming through his fingers. But her voice came clear over the fields.

'Run again.'

The black wailed, a high-pitched wail, like that of a woman.

'Run again now.' The voice was casual, almost coaxing.

He came up to his feet, crouching low, still clutching his face, and ran fast, his head very low, towards the nearest edge of the field. Again she circled wide, and he picked up speed as he approached the safety of uncut cane, his head back now, arms pumping, blood a smear all over his chest, but safety only a few yards away.

This time she came up at right angles to him, between him and the cane, giving him a chance of veering at the last second and running for it in the other direction. For a moment it looked as though he might vanish in the wall of cane, and Arthur hoped he would. But she spurred the horse hard at the last, passed in front of him, brought the whip past his head and down with a loud crack down the length of his back, the force of it snapping his head back. As he fell forward the horse thundered past and he rebounded off its flank, splayed out like an acrobatic tumbler, landing in a heap.

She reined in sharply beside Arthur and the driver. 'Put him in the stocks now,' she said, 'so they can see him. No food for three days. Stop at the infirmary first, to fix his face. Who is the next one now?'

The driver called to two cutters to carry the first man back to the group. The other two cutters cowered on the ground. *Good*

God is she going to do this with all of them, Arthur wondered. He felt himself trembling. It was his own fault. He had let the field discipline go to hell.

'This one is next.'

'Then have him untied.'

The man stood up, his face piteous, distorted with fear, saying nothing, waiting.

'Are you sick?' she said softly.

'No mis-tress. No. No, ma'am.'

'Den how I hear you sick and don' work for me?'

'No, mis-tress. I work cuttin'. Work in de fiel'. Work for *you*, mis-tress.' He looked at Arthur and then the driver, as though for support, as though this were a trial and he believed in its reality.

'I see. Den *him* sick?' She pointed to the last man on the ground, his neck held by a thong to a peg.

'Don' *know*, ma'am. Don' rightly *know*, mis-tress.'

'Get him up too.' The driver undid the third man, who immediately babbled that the second was a liar, that he didn't cut well, that *he* was a good cutter, that he wanted only to cut cane but had been tied in the field because the sun made him crazy but that now he 'fight de sun, *fight* 'im, and 'im have no power now . . .' He was interrupted by the bloody body of the first man, flung down on his back beside the horse, his mangled face looking at the sky, the upper lip dangling loose in a welter of blood and dirt, the nose smashed just below the bridge, the shards of two broken teeth sticking through the pulpy remains of the lip.

'Then go and cut,' Annie Palmer shouted, lifting the whip in the air as the blacks ran for the cutting line, snatched up their cutlasses and went back to work. Arthur saw the ghost of a smile on the edges of the driver's mouth.

'I guess that should do it, Mr. Arthur,' she said. 'And now if you will come up to Rose Hall this evening after the work is finished, at about sunset, I should like to have a talk with you.'

'Yes, Mrs. Palmer.' He said it to the rear of her horse, so quickly had she wheeled and galloped off towards the road.

9

'HIM DIRTY lak a fiel han,' Mary Lou chided, scrubbing his neck.

'I *am* a bloody field hand, right there all day with them.'

'Den tomorrow you be overseer.'

'I'm afraid not, girl.'

'You na gwine see de mis-tress this evenin'?'

'How the hell did you know?'

She came around to the front of him, rubbing his face and his chest, then stroking cool soapy water down towards his groin. She always washed him on the grass just outside his tiny house, as day became evening and a cool breeze slid down out of the mountains.

'Know ever-tin in Jamaica. Come a-mek yu smell sweet fo de mistress. De mis-tress lak him, him be boss *buckra*. Sleep in de mis-tress big bed, and sen' salt fish to Mary Lou.' She rubbed vigorously around his groin and worked her lathered hands between his legs.

'The mistress may put me to work with a cutlass instead,' he laughed. 'You heard what happened today?'

'Some of dem han bad. Mek fo sick but de mis-tress am smart. Mek a neger run an crack him good, him swallow him taste for run. Jodie in dem stock tonight, lock up, not a-run and have no mouf to cry wid, no mouf to lie wid. Jes his han to work wif, an that best fo neger.'

'You think she should beat them like that?'

'Neger know nothin but de whip. Neger wan sleep, eat him fish and rice an mek ting-ting. Cut sugar jes to fill him mout befo he sleep. Grow him yam for him alone an fo pickney an no work plantation. Neger lazy. Need de mis-tress fo mek him' work de lan.'

She knelt before him, stroking his legs with the soapy water, running her hands up and over and around his crotch in swirling motions. He stood looking over the darkening hills to the great chasms and rills of benign evening clouds far over the sea. He felt tall, handsome and aware of his good body and her strong hands kneaded and relaxed his numb legs. The morning's terror drained out of him. Mrs. Palmer had swept into a field where he had failed. The mess had been created by his own weakness. Or so he mused, watching the brilliant red sun work its will on the clouds, turning them purple, orange, blue or silhouetting them, shooting long beams past them down to ground or up to sky.

It was hard to visualize just how he had failed. He had been lenient with the niggers, then harsh, neither succeeding, she galloping into the field and in one minute in one dramatic act dominating it. He would go back the next day like a rag doll, a stupefied figure in shirt and pants, but not the cutters' master. Only she was their master.

Mary Lou poured cool rinse water over his head. He barely felt it stream down over him. Then she towelled him roughly. He took her in his arms, kissed her and hugged her close, as though she could stop or absorb his lonely fear.

'Dem night mos-quito bite soon,' she said softly, '. . . we go in de house.'

'Yes. Let's go inside. I have to get ready. . . .'

'Love yu good befo yu see de mis-tress.' Mary Lou clung to him, her hips rotating, her hands stroking him.

He was numb to her. He felt her hair. He heard her breathing. He smelled her sweet-acrid flesh, the sweetness from the permeating scent of sugar and molasses that hovered over the plantation. But between the morning's failure and the confrontation to come, he was numb to Mary Lou.

'Shall we have a bit of rum, eh?'

'Don need. Need yu. Love yu good befo you go up.' She held him tighter, her kisses warm on his neck and face. He stood still, waiting for her to let go. It was getting past sunset. Annie Palmer was waiting. He had to dress and go. Mary Lou slid downward, still clinging to him, on her knees in front of him, at him with her mouth. A tingling warmth spread over the centre of him, a drawing down, almost gravitational, his fear of going up the hill almost vanishing, the great house and the woman in it unreal. But he caught himself, and pulled her away gently.

'Not now, Mary Lou. I'm sorry, girl. I have to go up there. It's after sunset now, I'm late.'

He stepped away from her, leaving her on her knees, hoping she would be no trouble. He had his work, his contract, his new life in Jamaica, nothing behind him, all before him. He had the terror of the morning, the vengeance of Annie Palmer on the nigger he had been unable to control. He had to face Annie Palmer herself now.

God. If she gives me trouble I'll walk off the plantation. On the way to his clothes he stopped to pour a little rum. Mary Lou was still on her knees, sitting back on her heels, hands on her lap, staring at him.

Shameless little idiot. But then I suppose it's rough. The white men come and go. Someone new possesses her every year. And the niggers too.

'Hey d'you want a drink?'

'Yes.'

He brought the glass to her, squatted, still naked, beside her. They touched glasses, as he had taught her to do.

'Thanks for the bath.'

Her wide eyes looked at him amiably, without hatred. *Stupid women. Cow eyes looking at you. As though they knew everything. As though they were thinking. She thinks between her legs, is all.*

'Don' be 'fraid of her, Ar-thur. She no gwine hurt you.'

'Afraid of who? That one on the hill? Don't be silly. She just wants to give me a school-teacher talk is all, about how to be tough with her cutters. I'll be tough all right. I'll cut their miserable backs for them. I'll make them yell and scream if that's what they want. We'll go back to the rope and the cart tomorrow and choke the useless black breath out of them if that's what they want.'

'Don' whip dem han'. No good. None of it good. Dem no wan' kill yu. Dem know you go to de mis-tress tonight, an no trouble. No trouble.'

'Lord. It's just me in that field, and not her ladyship. They'll

· 87 ·

listen to me or I'll break them in two, the brutes. If I have to go up for my schoolboy lecture tonight, they will have to pay for it.'

'You fight dem, you die.'

'Not me, I won't. I didn't come here to die, I didn't. No dirty nigger is going to kill me and I'll take no nonsense from any grand lady on the hill either. And you can wager on that.' He knew his own abysmal fear even as he spoke against it.

'Den why you come to Jamaica if you don't die?'

'Nobody goes anywhere to die, Mary Lou. I came here . . . I came here . . . to live. That's it, to live. To live somewhere new and do something different.'

'Nobody live in Jamaica now. Dem die. Pickney die. Fiel han die. *Buckra* die. Maybe mis-tress die. Nobody know. Duppy come in de night.'

'Stop . . . stop that duppy talk. Sounds like those mad ones in England with their haunted castles. Listen, girl, I must go now . . .'

Her small chatter bored him. Her wistful gloom was even worse. Jamaicans seemed strange. Three hundred black men and women out there at dawn, quiet and subdued. The sad chants they sang about their blood and the ground. Mary Lou's talk about the duppies. He knew they had ceremonies that no white man had ever seen, knew they believed in magic and spells. Madness, all of it. They called ghosts out of cotton trees, buried their dead beside their shacks to keep friendly ghosts nearby, believed in one stupid thing or another. Wilson had told him some of it. He couldn't remember all he had said.

The sky was dark now, almost black. Night had come down on it like an eyelid, leaving only the last squinting glimpse of the western light. He fumbled with the lamp and the matches, then was blinded by the glare from the wick. He pulled on pants, shirt and boots, then felt his face. There was stubble. He would have to shave. He went out the door and looked up the hill. Lights were flickering in the great house. *Damnation.* He was late already because of Mary Lou.

He took the lamp to the kitchen, poured water from a pitcher into a tin basin. His razor needed stropping but there was no time. Without using soap, he wet his face with one hand and drew the razor over one side, then the other, wincing as he went. He cut himself when he got to the upstroke on the underside of his face.

He hung over the basin, droplets of his blood colouring the water. He bled easily. It would be difficult to stop it, and he had to go up the hill. He pressed at it with a cloth.

'Stan dat way an don' drop blood on de shirt. I soon come.'

Mary Lou was in the lamplight, but vanished as he looked up. His lateness frightened him now, but he had no recourse but to wait. His blood dripped into the water.

She returned in minutes, crumpling some leaves in her hand. She stuffed them in her mouth, chewed them, spat out the pulp into her palm. She took a bit of it on one finger and held it on the cut beneath his chin.

'What the hell is this?'

'Jamaica medicine.'

'What's it called?'

'Don rightly know. Green leaf.'

'Is it working?'

'Wait.'

She held him a minute or two, one finger under his chin. The drip of his blood into the water had stopped. She wiped his chin cautiously with the towel, and they waited together.

'All right now,' she said.

'Thank you, girl.' He kissed her quickly, her face a blur, her lips trying to cling to his, and went out into the night.

He walked carefully, wanting to avoid stumbling, falling or tearing his clothes. Lights glimmered in the great house above him. *Late, damnation, late.*

He got to the wide steps, and slowed. Up close, they were impressive, rising massively from either side towards the main door. Half-way up, he paused to look out over the fields, undulant and quiet under a half-moon. From here, he could see the ocean, tranquil, dark, the shoreline hidden by tall cane and taller palms. He kept going up the steps, the big mahogany door ahead. Its brass knocker was cool to the touch. He rapped too lightly at first and tried again, the final knock foolishly loud. He probed his chin with one finger. It was all right. Dry. But he was nervous now. He felt a need to urinate. The collar of his rough shirt itched. He was aware of a blister on his heel from his field boots.

The great door swung open. A fat maid stood bulging against the edges of the widening crack of light from within.

'Yassuh.'

'Here to see Mrs. Palmer. Arthur is the name.'

She viewed him in silence, as though he hadn't spoken or didn't exist.

'Arthur. James Arthur. Book-keeper. I work here. I . . .'

'Moment.' She floated away, leaving the door half open. He could see only a table and a lamp, and part of the polished hall floor. He peered in at them and at the maid's vanishing bulk, wondering if she knew about his shame that morning. She probably did so to the nigger maid he was just a weak man unable to control a field of cutters. He wanted to run down the steps on the other side and urinate quickly in the bushes. He took a step sideways but stopped. The maid was returning. No time. He would have a bad evening. It was impolite to ask where to relieve yourself in a good home, or so he had been taught.

'You come.' The maid's face was blank but her eyes told him she knew of his failure, and that knowledge scalded him. Then he remembered her face—Venus, the one he had hit with the cat-o'-nine-tails. Impassive, she led him to the drawing-room.

Annie Palmer sat before a small fire, in a green velvet wing-back chair. She looked up at him, her face slim and surprisingly white, her eyes deep and dark, but also accusing.

'You are late.'

'I'm sorry ma'am, I . . .'

'You left the fields well over an hour ago.'

'Yes . . . yes'm, I cut myself, I . . .' He stared at her, a mixture of fright and curiosity in him. *She is not an old woman.*

'And you have been bleeding for more than an hour?'

'No, ma'am.'

'And what *have* you been doing?'

'I'm sorry, ma'am.' He feared and hated her now, both pervading muscle and bone, paralysing him. His hands seem to hang at his sides, exposed, absurd, too large. His clothes were rough and poor. He one class, she another, this his fate. He remembered his father, buying cloth from the rich, sewing, selling clothing to the rich. *My poor father.*

'I said what have you been doing?'

Wilson said she was insane.

'I'm sorry, ma'am, I was too slow dressing.' She had good big eyes, wide deep. And a full mouth, full lips. Always a good sign, his father had liked to say, warmth in a good full mouth. Never marry a thin-lipped woman, my son. He was afraid to look down at her chest, but saw that she wore black lace. *Very dear*, his father always said about lace, and was afraid to work lace. *One mistake and you lose a lot. I'd rather muslin or wool.*

'Slow dressing indeed. I should imagine so, with Mary Lou soaping you in your yard.'

Ah! Binoculars, spies, whatever. But she had a beautiful accent. High-born. A lady for sure. Peculiar that she would want to keep such close watch on his movements.

He brought his hands together before him, clumsily, then brought them behind, gripping one hand with the other, kneading his knuckles.

'. . . and I suppose you lay down with her when you went inside the house? Did that delay you further?'

'No, ma'am.'

She sat staring at him as though he were an errant child. He avoided her eyes, looking just past them at her dark, shining hair. Then he looked down at his rough unpolished boots and then back towards her, his hands clenched tighter behind his back and sweat pouring from them and him.

My poor unhappy father. They always made you feel so poor. His father had taken him on visits to clients—fittings, adjustments, discussions of materials. His father on his knees before them, pins in his mouth, adjusting trouser or skirt. Himself perched on a chair, hands on his lap. *Do tell the boy to sit down if he pleases. Or he can go to the scullery for a sweet. Handsome son you have, Mr. Arthur. He will carry on for you in years to come.* His father looking proud on his knees *thank you, mum, thank you*, then briskly inserting his alteration pins. And then he, meek son, following the skirt of a white-capped maid through long corridors to the scullery for a dish of trifle and a mug of milk.

'So you didn't lay with her. She must be losing her . . . charm, eh? But never mind that. What happened in the field this morning?'

'I'm sorry, ma'am. I lost myself. I lost control. It won't happen again, ma'am.'

'I hope not. Did you intend to beat those three valuable hands to death?'

'No, ma'am. Just teach them a lesson, I suppose.' *God.* He was ashamed of the morning's hysteria.

'And what kind of a lesson?' Her voice seemed calm and not unkind.

'To keep them from malingering. They do everything to try and stop the work. I suppose, ma'am, they're taking advantage of me, but they shan't again.'

'You're quite sure?'

'Yes, ma'am.' He looked straight into her eyes, and squared his shoulders.

'Ah, then you're more stupid than I thought, aren't you?'

'Ma'am?'

'Niggers, Arthur, do you know anything about niggers?'

'No ma'am.'

'Did you ever see one in England?'

'No ma'am.'

'Do you know anything about Jamaica?'

'Very little, ma'am.' *She's playing with me now. Five thousand miles from England and under contract to this mad woman. Perhaps I should service her. But Broderick is pleasing her already. Maybe I should show her my manhood. Would that please you, ma'am?*

'You may sit down, Arthur, over there.' She waved him towards a straight-backed chair. She rang a tiny bell beside her and Venus padded out on bare feet.

'Venus, see what Mr. Arthur will have to drink, and bring me a sherry.'

'Yassum.' Venus looked at him.

'Rum, please.'

'Wid watuh?'

'Yes, please.' She padded away, soundless on the burnished floor.

'There is no need to say please to servants.'

'Sorry, ma'am.' *How must I behave? If only I were anywhere but here.*

'Are you sorry about everything? One thing after the next?'

'Ma'am?' He stared at her as though he had not heard her, his gaze asking her to repeat or abandon the question.

'Nothing. Tell me, do you like your work here?'

'It's all right, ma'am.'

'Standing out in the fields, or in that hot mill—is that all right?'

'I'm—I came here on contract, ma'am. I don't know what else there is to do.'

'I suppose you don't. And your work is everything to you?'

'I don't understand, ma'am.'

'Heavens—I mean you live for your work, so to speak?'

'I don't know, ma'am. A poor man must work. My father always worked. A man must always work. A poor man at any rate.'

'You work just because you are poor?'

'A man must eat, ma'am.' *Strange, in her rich house. What would she know. Servants, everything.*

'Is that why you came to Jamaica—just to work and thus eat? You came five thousand kilometres over open sea just for that?'

'I suppose so, ma'am. I'm the first of my family to come out.' He was proud of that. At least he had left. But he hadn't left for this. He wanted to get away from this woman. He hoped that Mary Lou would be there when he went back down the hill. At least the lamp was on for her, and she could always scrounge food. She had a strange way of wanting to sit in the dark sometimes, just sit with him there, in the room, or lie with him holding her, in the bed. It bored him, as it did when she talked about the night spirits. Inaction was dull, the spirits unreal. But now he missed her. She was better than this fine lady.

'Tell me, did you kill someone in England?'

'No'm.'

'Did you leave a stupid little girl with two or three children in a Manchester kitchen?'

'No'm.'

'Astonishing. Five thousand kilometres just to work and eat. You amaze me, all of you.'

He took a deep draught of the rum, wondering what she wanted of him except to play cat and mouse. *Idle hands,* his father always said. *Hold your tongue, always hold your tongue, my son. The rich are not like us. They say what they please, and we must listen while we do their work for them. Why they make us do that, I shall never know. I suppose they're lonely people in their fine mansions and all. With idle hands.* His father measured and sewed and counted, day and night. Even when he sat before the fire with his wife, sipping a mug of ale before bed, his mother always knitted or sewed and he always made some small repair or adjustment as they chatted quietly, their hands eternally busy.

Silent, he waited on her. Like the others: she made him feel foolish to have come out at all. But what had he known about

Jamaica? Nothing. He saw a chance to leave England, and did so. And so she had him, perched on a chair in her house, with nothing real outside for him in the Jamaican night and nothing on the morrow except to stand in her fields, see to her cutters. *I am no better than my poor wretched father.* He would have liked to go home in the morning, even as far as Manchester. He had friends there. He had known a girl or two there. He could have a little house and a small grate for the fires. Work in a mill. Marry and raise a son or two. Drink his pints and play skittles on Saturdays.

'Amaze me. All of you. Five thousand miles. For fever to get you, or a scorpion, or a nigger to strangle you in your bed some night. I suppose there's hope for we English. Do you smoke?'

'Smoke, ma'am?'

'Yes, smoke. A pipe. I have several clay pipes here if you should like one.'

'I never tried one, ma'am.'

'A pity. Would you care to try? It seems to be a pleasant thing for a man. And I take a puff now and then. If you'll have a pipe I shall have a bit of it.'

'All right, ma'am.'

'Good. I'll fetch it then.' She crossed the room and went towards the stairs. 'And if you need to go outside for any reason go now. I know how it is when a man's been drinking.' She went up the stairs without looking at him.

He strode through the drawing-room, out of the front door, and went to some bushes at the end of the garden, gratefully spilling his water into their dark mass. *It was time.*

Relieved, he ascended the steps and stood at their centre, looking out at the property. A half-moon was up, barely illuminating the tops of the cane stalks. On a knoll to the left, he could see Broderick's house, and then his own and Wilson's down below it, set back from the road. Far in the distance to the east, at his right, he thought he could make out the next plantation house, with only the utter blackness of dark fields in between. The night was silent now except for barely audible drumming and chanting coming up from the slave quarters. He listened for a few moments to that foreign, rhythmic sound. *Strange that would be in Manchester now. Find it hard to believe, they would. Write the folks, I should, and tell them about this place.*

He went back in the house. Annie Palmer was in the drawing-room waiting.

'Here's the pipe, and the tobacco . . . and you fill it this way. Scoop some up and then press it down but not too hard or it won't burn properly.' She seemed changed, pleasant now, engrossed in what she was doing.

'I never tried a pipe before. Do they make you ill at first?' They stood facing one another at the mantel.

'I shouldn't think so. At least a strong chap such as you. Here, I'll get you a coal.' She bent to the fire, took up a small coal with the tongs, and held it over the pipe. He puffed, the smoke making his eyes water.

'All right?' She smiled a little, and her eyes were softer.

'All right.'

'I shan't lose you immediately, then, of deathly illness?'

'No ma'am. It appears not.'

'I can't afford to, really. You haven't even worked off the cost of your passage. Let me have a puff now.' She took his hand and held it, and with the other hand took the pipe. She held the stem delicately with three fingers, and puffed carefully.

Not really a mad woman perhaps, strange Wilson called her insane. Her mouth was pretty, sucking at the white clay pipe-stem. She had wide-set eyes, a straight little nose, cream-white skin. She had delicate fine-boned hands. He thought her at once lovely and frightening. He felt the fright, comingling with desire, in his groin, down along his legs. *A beauty she is.* Except the one in his childhood, warm and wondrous, the widow of a sea captain gone in a typhoon. And this one, a strange one. On the horse that morning, then furious with him, then allowing him to go relieve himself in the bushes, then nice to him.

Venus came again with full glasses. Annie Palmer gave him back the pipe and took her glass, and he his tankard.

'Good health.'

'Good health, ma'am.'

They drank and he puffed again at the pipe, trying to master it without snapping it in his fingers or choking on the smoke. She went back to her armchair, leaving him standing alone and self-conscious at the mantelpiece.

'So you came . . . so you came for no reason, just to work, Arthur?'

'Yes, ma'am.' The rum was deep inside him and the pipe smoke making him dizzy. He leaned against the mantel but felt too exposed standing before her in the centre of the room. It all seemed too vast, the room, the house.

'It must be strange to be a man and just leave, and come so far, to no one, to nothing, so to speak. And you are not at all afraid, you say?'

'I suppose not.'

'But you were terrified this morning. You were like a foolish schoolboy. Why was that? You must have been afraid then.'

'All right, ma'am, I admit I was afraid. No one ever told me how to handle them.'

'Broderick hasn't told you how to handle the niggers? Is that it?' She sounded sharper now. He remembered that Wilson said she went to bed with Broderick.

'I suppose he did. I'm sorry, I suppose he did, and I didn't remember.'

'He let you hit Venus once and that was the end of your education at Rose Hall. I suppose that's what it amounts to. A poor teacher, Broderick. A will, but no mind at all. Cunning without intelligence. I suppose Jamaica needs him now. It could be all we have between us and our graves.'

'I'm sorry about hitting your maid, ma'am, but Broderick . . .'

'I know him thank you. And it doesn't matter. She got what she deserves. She's like the rest, a thief and a liar. We never did much with the niggers in Jamaica and probably never will. In fact they may be hopeless and a vast waste of our time, except to cut sugar and grind it and get it on the ships to England. They all want to go back to their African jungles but they can't, now, and so we must deal with them here. The best way to do that is to whip them and chain them and keep them working. Broderick just happens to be enough of a beast to do that for me. That's why I still employ him. And you will learn, in time. It doesn't bother you, the business of the niggers, does it?'

'Bother me, ma'am?' He left the pipe on the mantel and went back to his chair.

'You're not sorry for them . . . not concerned one way or the other about slavery . . . none of those priests have preached to you to tell you it's a sin?'

'No, ma'am. They . . . they're just there, seems to me.'

'That's good enough. Just do what you can to keep them in control. Think of them as . . . as children. Strong children, and murderous sometimes, but children. They are satisfied with very little. And we really have nothing to answer for. All great civilizations were built on slavery of one kind or another. Did you know that?' She smiled and looked at him with patient condescension.

'Not really, ma'am. I had very little schooling.'

'The Egyptians, you know, and all those things they built. The Greeks. All that magnificence built by the backs of slaves. The Romans. And so on. Jamaica was nothing at all. This would be a wilderness without us, without the white man.'

'I suppose so, ma'am.'

'But they will try to drag you down. They will try to confuse you. They will try to defeat you, the way they did this morning. But that is what they must *not* do. Do you understand that, and do you understand why?' She leaned towards him, her eyes wide and, he thought, a little sad.

'Yes'm. My work is to keep the work going. I think Broderick said ten tons of cane, a ton of sugar.'

'Oh no, man, I don't mean Carruthers and his wretched economics. I mean what I said. Not drag us down. Not destroy Rose Hall. Not destroy us, and what has been created here. Not let the rabble take command of the earth. Not be *eaten* by them. The world has been built by excellent people, do you understand, people who *excelled*. It has not been built by whining niggers. . . .'

Venus entered the room and crossed it quietly. She closed and latched the shutters against the night, noiseless, graceful in her motions. Arthur observed the twin globes of her meaty rump moving up and down under her worn cotton dress. She finished and left, all in one somehow contained loop of silent motion.

'Not built by whining niggers, Arthur, but by white men who came those thousands of kilometres over the sea to build these plantations. And what do the niggers do—whine for their fish and rice and rum and squirm around in their huts making more and more niggers that we are supposed to feed. Whine and steal and lie down every chance they get and let the earth go to ruin unless we watch them every minute.'

'Yes'm.' Her face had a beauty and intensity about it now— whatever she was talking about. He gathered that she hated the niggers. He recalled Wilson's talking about her riding out at night to whip them. *She's mad. She's mad after all.* He sipped at his rum again and remembered the gentleness of Mary Lou, washing him in the sunset. That was better than listening to this woman.

'Do you understand me, Arthur?'

'I believe so, ma'am.'

'That's all I wanted to tell you, really. Try to be part of our world and not theirs. We built this world. All this'—her hands indicated the house—'and more. A great civilization. England. And in Jamaica we grow the sugar that helps feed the niggers, and we put clothes on their naked backs. Without us they are nothing. They will die for lack of sense and management and even the will to go on. They take everything and give nothing. If they were left alone there would be only ruin in Jamaica, such as there is at Mount Pleasant now. Ruin . . .'

Her voice trailed off. He wondered why she had to tell him, a fifty pounds a year book-keeper, all this. He wanted nothing to do with grand people. Nor could he care much about her Jamaica. The most he could lose was his job. If need be he could always work his way home, or go on to America. *A man can get on without all this high talk. Ruin and all that. So much talk of ruin. Ruin her in Manchester or Leeds, they would, if they got her in a mill fourteen hours a day. Take her blood for small wages, like all the rest. What in heaven would she know about ruin?*

She stared into the fire for long minutes, sipping the golden sherry from her glass.

'You don't . . . you don't know what I'm talking about, do you?' she said sadly.

'Perhaps I do, ma'am. Just . . . keep them from spoiling its work here.'

'That's something like it, I suppose. I don't expect you to understand it all. Perhaps no one ever will again. Or there will be fewer and fewer who do. Can you hear them drumming out there?'

'Of course.'

'They drum and drum until they are exhausted. They drum and sing and dance and lie down together to love in the night. They are fortunate people, you know. They cannot read, they seldom think, they don't know what a column of figures means. And they have no responsibility to the estate, the land, or to one another. Their women crouch in the dirt and bring children into this world, and I am responsible for them until they are old enough to cut for me and earn their keep. I alone. Mistress Palmer of Rose Hall. The pivot and centre of all their lives. They could destroy me in an instant if they wanted to. And they will, when they are ready. Destroy me. Murder me, burn me, dismember me, whatever they do, and they will . . . they will, believing that this will free them. And it will not. They will find . . . they will find their chains again. They will sink into a slavery . . . a slavery of their own creation that will confuse them more than this, much more than this. Because they will not be answerable to me or to any of us, any of the few of us here in Jamaica now, the few of us anywhere. . . .'

He listened. *A strange one*. His bones were tired from the long day in the fields. The fire glow soothing. He blinked, then rubbed his face to stay awake. He examined the heavy pewter tankard containing his rum. Initialed J.P. Her husband. The dead man. He wondered, idly, how she had killed him.

'Try to save yourself, Arthur.'

'Save myself?' Her voice had been oddly friendly.

'Yes. Save yourself. You could be useful to yourself, and even to Jamaica. Has that occurred to you?'

'Yes, ma'am. I suppose so, ma'am.'

'You don't suppose anything, really, do you? Yes, ma'am, no, ma'am, I suppose so, ma'am. Five thousand kilometres . . .' She stood up and paced the room, cutting at the air with a small white hand. 'Five thousand kilometres over open sea from England to live like a dog and you *suppose* so. You have no visions, I presume, of owning a plantation or becoming a MoBay trader? Of going back to your dear folks in Manchester with a trunkful of gold, coming home like a Drake or a Columbus? You came for a game, eh, and you'll settle for your bottle and Mary Lou? And keep your belly full and get your regular sleep like all the niggers?'

She stopped walking and bent over him, hands on her thighs, her hair falling towards him. She smelled of some sweet cologne or perfume, its odour distinct and soothing after the persistent reek of sugar and molasses and Mary Lou's acrid flesh.

He looked into her mocking eyes. Fierce eyes. He gritted his teeth against them, against hitting her or cursing at her. Against himself. *My father my poor father*.

'No answer, eh? No answer from you, Mr. Arthur. The glorious heavens have manufactured and sent another ninny . . . how brave your face, how noble your ambitions, how grand the empire that . . . that . . . what's that they say in the Bible . . . that gave you suck. Were you suckled, really, or *knitted* in a Manchester mill?'

She flung her hair back over her shoulder and twirled in the centre of the room, laughing, her head tilted back. He followed her gaze up to the strong beamed ceiling. What she said seemed immaterial. She might be drunk and was probably half mad as Wilson said. *A crazy woman.* But she was graceful, fragile. *A lady. They go mad alone*, his father had said, *nothing to do with themselves. They live with ghosts and dreams. Never envy them, son.*

'Mrs. Palmer . . .'

'*Knitted.* Ha. Or *loomed*, is that what you call it, *loomed*? It's a better word. Loomed like a bolt of wool and shipped out here. Oh, Lord, wool is one thing Jamaica does not need, Arthur. We need steel, perhaps, but not wool. Steel . . . oh, goodness, where do you all come from? . . .' She went back to her chair, covering her face with one hand.

'Mrs. Palmer . . .'

'That is my name, yes. That was my name. Or is. Or was. No matter. What is it, my loomed friend, my Manchester woolly lamb? What do *you* want from me?'

'May I please leave now, ma'am?'

'Why must you leave now—you mean to go wet my bushes again, woolly lamb?' She looked at him with quiet scorn.

'No. I'm very tired, ma'am.'

'Ah yes, I forgot, your big day flailing about with your whip, messing up my fields. And of course you would want to get home to Mary Lou. She must miss you, poor thing, and you her. She makes only one simple demand of you. Of course you may go.'

'Thank you, ma'am.' He gulped the last of his rum. It was a fine one, not the rotgut he'd had with Wilson, or that Mary Lou brought. He stood up and walked across the heavy Oriental carpet, noticing its beauty for the first time. Around it the wood floors were burnished bright, and reflected the firelight.

'Do something for me when you go, Arthur.'

'Yes'm.'

'Go down to the quarters. You know where they are—to the right over there and down?'

'Yes'm.'

'Ask for Jason. A big fellow. He cuts in one of your crews, I think.'

'Yes'm.'

'Just tell him I'm here waiting.'

'Yes'm. Is that all?'

'That's all. The world is strange isn't it . . .' She looked at the fire, a little smile on her mouth, then looked at him. 'Strange. You have your Mary Lou and I have my Jason. I sometimes wonder, really, why white men become so tired and black men do not. Have you ever wondered that?'

'No, ma'am.'

'Unfortunate. Good night.'

'Good night, ma'am.'

He barely saw the front door ahead of him and was just enough aware of the glittering chandelier in the hall to glance up and want to smash it.

All her fancy talk. The big door swung towards him, wider and heavier than he'd thought it was. It pushed him back until he circled the edge of it and got out into the night. He drew it towards him and closed it quietly. He faced it for long seconds, his fingers spread out on the weathered mahogany.

Then there was one solid metallic shot of sound from behind the door. He fled in a rush, dragging his hand along the rough sandstone wall for balance on the way down the steps, cutting it, stumbling on the steps, falling and hitting the gravel with his shoulder, scrambling to his feet but knowing all along it was the door bolt he'd heard, rammed home by Venus. He looked back to see the last of the servant, hauling the drapes together across the paned and leaded window just above him.

Wretched woman. Wants her nigger. I'll summon him. Half-way down the path he stopped to look back at the house, its lights dimmed downstairs, a solitary glow above in what was probably her room. He tried to conceive of her room, but could not. Nor was she herself credible. A woman of quality, so she seemed. Delicate, fierce. But strong as a man, surely. Indomitable in the field that morning, in control of the horse, the snake-like lash and the racing, terrified nigger. And then demanding to know why he had come out. And all her fancy talk. *Excellent people.* Rose Hall squatted on its hill and she within it, enigmatic, fragile, mad, more his conqueror than his employer. He felt imbecilic, confounded, without rage and void of fear too, nothing having prepared him for her, the island, the plantation, or his errand to get the nigger for her bed. He clutched the wrist above his hand, scraped on the wall and stinging. *Excellent people. Quality.* A woman who ordered a lover as though he were buttons or cloth. And he her messenger now. And Broderick? Another servant. So he and Broderick were not that far apart. She ruled them both. He gripped his wrist hard and went down the hill to the quarters.

The blacks were around the embers warming their cook pots, some eating, some chanting softly. He saw low firelight, dark flesh, muscle, breast, belly, flashes of light palm and foot sole, brightness of their eye whites. He saw nothing, really, except their total presence, audience for his shame, dozens of eyes on him, defeated in the field that morning and now come to do her will. Later he would remember a bright-eyed high-breasted girl, nursing her child. He had never before seen that.

'Jason.' He said it to no one in particular. A horde of faces. Around him a half dozen naked children leaped like puppets, chanting *buckra buckra*, their hands out begging.

'Jason. Send Jason up to . . . up to the great house.' This time he picked a group to say it to. Two bucks leaning in a doorway, three women squatting around a black iron pot. They gazed, eyes neutral, mindless. One of the women, gnawing on a scrap of fatty flesh from the pot, stopped long enough to screech the message down the line of shanties.

'Jay-son, *buckra* wan' yu, mon.'

'Tell him up to the great house. Now.' He turned, not wanting to see the buck. The day had been enough, the scope of his humiliation numbing, his will gone or rather subsumed and tendered impotent by island, plantation, blacks, the woman on the hill, his being evaporated into nothingness. His body trembled as he walked away from the quarters and he momentarily feared the onset of fever. Mary Lou had talked of the fever.

He looked up towards his own house but could not go up there for the moment. He turned down the path again, his legs weak, but wanting to walk. He came out on the drive and went down and down until he reached the gate, its dark scroll-work written against the sky, clear under the half-moon. It was chained and locked but he went to it to hold it and look out on the silent road, all the black coast of Jamaica asleep and silent save for the rustling of a mongoose, a rat in the cane, and in the trees the foolish melodic noise of a kling-kling bird.

'It's locked.'

He turned in fright to face Broderick, sitting in the shadows, on a rock.

'Yes . . .'

'Yes. It's locked every night. I lock it.'

'Yes . . .'

'Were you going somewhere, bucko? If so there are lots of other ways off the property.'

'No. No, sir.'

'Just came to see the gate, eh? I like it too. They say it cost more than three thousand pounds, wrought in Birmingham. It cost more than you.' Broderick's face glowed momentarily. He was puffing on a pipe.

'Didn't she ask you for dinner?' Broderick said.

'No.'

'Ah. She must have. But that's personal, between you and the lady. Of course. How about the pipe? Did she bring you Palmer's pipe to smoke?'

Arthur stared at him. Then he and Broderick did share something.

'Cat got your tongue? Down off the hilltop and full of great secrets?'

'Yes. Yes the pipe. She did that. You just surprised me is all.'

'Brings it out for everyone, it seems. Palmer's pipe. Makes her feel at home again, I'd guess. She butchered him, of course, right in that house. And maybe more. No one's quite sure. Now she goes 'round with that old clay pipe of his like it was Cinderella's slipper. Well. And she sent you for Jason?'

'Good God.'

'Ah. So I thought. You're young yet. You thought it was all for you. She belongs to none of us, only her own self. We're lucky to get in there for a good meal now and then, and drink what's left of the good wine, and get taken to her bed . . . and get out alive. That's the way some of them are. That's the way she is.' Broderick's voice was detached and cold but reassuring in its simple certainty.

'Good Lord.' Arthur leaned on the gate, feeling the solid wrought iron, still warm from the day, against the length of his back.

'Best I tell you while you're here. While you've had it, which you have. I've seen better men than you broken by her. Less than a year ago a man went out that gate because of her. She rode him down that same night and left him for dead. The stray niggers finished him and took his clothes. The dogs got the rest and they brought me his bones and a little meat in the morning. No good to me, any of it. No sense in that happening to you, eh?' Broderick's face glowed again from the light of the pipe, then dimmed and he was visible only as a form in the moonlight.

'Then what do you want of me? What . . . what do I do here? What about this place? Damnation, man . . .' He shouted without realizing it. Broderick sat still for minutes, then got up off the rock, a short, porky little man, his face white-cold. He came close, his eyes level and calm, his voice metallic, hands on his hips.

'I don't care at all what you do so long as you do your work. Hold the crews in line. Tell me what you hear, so we don't all get our throats cut some night. That's all I need from you. And I need it. If I don't get it the dogs are outside the gate waiting for you too. And you can believe that. And they'll get you before they get me. Is that enough?'

'Yes.'

'You better stop dreaming out here and get to bed. Tomorrow starts double duty for three weeks. You get an hour between the fields and the mill, and three hours to sleep between the mill and the fields.'

He strode away up the hill. Arthur spread his fingers, feeling the iron of the locked gate behind him. He sensed fully if wordlessly that he was a fool without alternatives, having bound himself over to the place, the gate's iron lacework constraining him like a web, the plantation sprawled out there waiting to engulf him. *Mawster mawster*—where was the day he followed the bearer down the MoBay street, free in the sun?

We're lucky to get in there for a good meal now and then . . . and be taken to her bed . . . that was the full extent of Broderick's thoughts. He was probably right. There was no proving him wrong. Broderick had in fact made of him an ally, a sort of brother. Yes she could break him. Yes she had tried. The shame of going to fetch her nigger was still with him, but abated because he shared it with Broderick or thought he did, or shared it with others through Broderick, who had perhaps avoided that, who had mastered her, his fierceness the equal of hers, the nonchalant viciousness packed into his stubborn Irish self an antidote for her.

He continued to feel the gate, his fingers exploring the curvature of the scroll-work, finding the places where the scrolls converged, then fanned away again.

Beyond him. She was beyond Broderick. He had, at least, restrained her, certain of his utility to her, to Rose Hall and to

Jamaica, that restraint his triumph, that triumph, shared with him, offered as a compact for their mutual protection. *That's the way some of them are. That's the way she is.*

Beyond him. Beyond him. Self-assured. But afraid. *So we don't all get our throats slashed, he said . . . he's afraid of something. He's afraid but she's not.* He remembered her fragility. Delicate hands, a fine-boned face, the long soft hair. A slim figure in the lace dress. *Excellent people.* She meant something by that. Something held it together. The dark land around him. The high house, magnificent, dominant. The moiling slave quarters. Something held it all besides the whip.

Reminded of tomorrow, he pushed away from the gate and went up to his tiny house, glancing only fleetingly up towards Rose Hall, quenching the thought of the black buck on his way there, replacing him, and with him Broderick.

Mary Lou was waiting in the bed. She gazed at him, fearful he would dismiss her. Silent, he blew out the lamp and undressed in darkness. Within minutes he was at her revelling in her heat, the acrid smell of her, breast belly and thigh. He bore down, pushing her into the bed, thrusting and thrusting at her and when she screamed, as she often did at her climax, he rushed on alone. She rubbed his face with hers, wetting it with her tears, sensing his estrangement, hoping for his deliverance. Which came, but only with Annie Palmer in a clear irrevocable obscene picture in his mind. The picture then scattered, awareness shifted to his hot outpouring, high up against the soft unseen centre of Mary Lou.

Relieved, he let his breath take him, his lungs pumping. He settled on her, mindless, wordless, sweat streaming between them. When he began to hear the mosquitoes, he got up to arrange the net over them and then slept, without a word to her.

10

ARTHUR SAW nothing of Annie for three weeks after his first visit to the house. Rose Hall's harvest edged forward, biting into the fields, the work ceaseless, its horizons limitless and thus exhausting. He stumbled through it, in the fields by day, in the torchlit mill by night, the mill phantasmagoric, the boiling pots at one end the temperature of molten lead, the other end dusty choking heaps of cane flung out of wagons on to the mill floor.

He was in bed at midnight, up before dawn, no clock guiding him, just a clanging angle iron that roused the whole plantation like an army, overrun and wiped out but summoned from their graves to fight again.

Lateness or malingering ceased as Broderick became more strident and ferocious. One feverish black, caught asleep in a cottage full of women too old to work, was hauled out and lashed for an hour before supper one evening, the process consuming the strength of two black drivers, impassive, efficient, working in relays without visible sign of shame or sympathy. The man stopped screaming after the first few minutes. The rest was just leather on flesh, his twitching and his trickling blood the only signs of life. Broderick stopped it once, to feel for the man's heart, then let it go on. The gangs, including the women, watched soundlessly, there being only a tiny groan when a piece of the man's flesh fell away, revealing some rib. Broderick looked at them then, but none dared look back. At the end of an hour Broderick signalled for the supper bell, and walked away. Arthur was tired, too tired to be concerned, and his sense of order accepted whatever Broderick felt had to be done. He walked the long way around to his house to avoid meeting Wilson on the way. Wilson would have had to talk about it.

Otherwise the harvest pushed along, Broderick like a ubiquitous eagle, alighting in field and mill, dominant and alive every morning with an overall sense of the plantation, the fields to be cut, the method and order of delivery to the mill. He stood in the assembly field each dawn, neat, impressive in his way, a complete anachronism, a tiny white facing two hundred burly blacks. He ignored the first tongues of dawn touching the tops of the coconut palms, singling out the last cane blossoms, pushing pink into the last of the clouds, fading the stars, reddening the earth and picking out the flesh, form and ragged clothing of the little army confronting him.

Arthur wondered at his tireless will. In the hot fields, he remembered Broderick and stood straighter, less out of fear than emulation. He began to criticize the cutting. He found willing allies in the drivers, free with their whips, loud in their commands.

Broderick noted his progress and came one day with a tabulation of tons per field, congratulating Arthur in his laconic way and asking him to help at a field burning that evening. Between them they took forty hands, cut firebreaks around the field, stationed the hands with buckets of water at its edges, and when the wind was right put the torch to the green sugar. The fire sputtered at the edges, an insignificant disappointment, then caught and raced through the field in the direction Broderick said it would, flame buttressing flame to form a castle of fire in the night, sucking air into itself, creating a near-vacuum around its edges, its inhalation tangible, an inrush of atmosphere that he could feel on his flesh. Rats and mongoose scurried out, some afire, others luckier, the Negroes scurrying to try and catch some of them for their cooking pots.

'Remember,' Broderick said when it was over, '. . . if you ever have to do this alone, to watch your windage and be damned sure of your firebreaks. If it ever got out of control half of St. James Parish would go up, and take the houses with it.'

'Yes. Will we burn them all, or just this one for some reason?'

'Ah. You don't know. The mill is slow. Haven't you noticed that?'

'I can't tell.'

'Ah. You wouldn't know. The tonnage going through is too low. Carruthers . . . well, never mind him. You burn the cane to clean it so it cuts faster in the morning. Strips the leaves and the rest. It's still there, see?'

In the last of the fire glow, the ground a bright bed of embers, they looked at the forest of dark slim stalks, all of which had survived the swirling waves of flame.

'Beautiful, wasn't it?' he said to Broderick.

'What?'

'Beautiful, the fire. One of the strangest things I've seen. . . .'

'Beautiful indeed! A lot of work. Queer one, you are, if you think that's beautiful. Another hard job is all. Watch it for two hours now, until the moon . . . until the moon is . . .' He regarded the sky, hands on his hips, jaw stern, as though to shout commands at it. 'The moon is about over that palm, standing where you are now. Then collect the gangs and see they get back to quarters. You did a good job tonight.'

'Thank you.'

'So did I, so I'm going up to supper with her ladyship. Shall I bring you her regards?'

Broderick walked away before he could answer.

He waited out the last of the fire, patrolling the firebreaks, being sure the blacks let no sparks get to other fields. He became hungry and hoped that Mary Lou had food ready for him. She was often erratic about that, appearing or abandoning him at will. He envisioned Broderick, dining well on the hill, an insouciant butcher but still an overseer, with his privileges.

When the moon rose far enough—as far as Broderick had said it should—he collected the gangs and herded them to quarters, a lone figure behind them as they jabbered among themselves in their dialect.

On balance the slaves worked well enough. They moved automatically, they and the work one thing. Only interruption of its rhythm disturbed them. A ravine or a rock in a field stopped them and they had to be realigned quickly before chaos set in. In the mill, if too long a lapse between one cane truck and the next let them pause, they looked helpless and lost, then tried to slump to sleep on the floor.

Arthur tried to keep at them, making work for them: a bit of cleaning, a mound of trash to be moved, a small repair. Over the weeks he tried to become their will. They had none apart from the task at hand. Whatever they had been, they were no longer. If they had been free in Africa's jungles, they were no longer. *The brutes had best work*, he thought. Annie Palmer had said something, but he didn't remember it. Holding it together, or something. That was it.

Nights in the mill were an agony of heat and an interminable corridor of a bizarre museum through which he seemed to stumble onward towards a void, there being no rest, no conclusion, no door through which he would at last escape into a glade, a garden, a home, a decent room; escape to anything.

He wavered under it, one night found a black shaking him in the mill, awakening him from eyes-open sleep, pointing to a jammed grinder, blades snapped and a shaft bent by a rock in among the cane. He looked at it in panic but remembered to stop the blindfolded mules who turned the wheel that powered the grinder. He looked, knowing nothing of the machinery, the gang silent, helpless but silently demanding, aware that he faced the choice of letting them go for the night or solving his peculiar white man's problem, the machine.

It was past three in the morning but he went to Broderick, leaving a driver in charge of the mill while he ran, terrified, torn between asking Broderick's help and preserving his own power of decision, hating his impotence but defeated by the machinery. He pounded on Broderick's door in near hysteria. The pressure of the sugar, the mill and the black men were on one side, Broderick and beyond him Annie Palmer on the other.

'Who is it?' Broderick spoke through the door.

'The mill . . . the mill is broken. It's Arthur.'

'Anyone with you?'

'No.'

'Come in.' A bolt was thrown and the door opened.

'Sorry to wake you but the mill, the grinder, stopped and I don't know what to do.'

'How stopped?'

'Blades . . . blades broken, a shaft bent. A rock in there.' He stood there, self-conscious, childlike, Broderick contained, mildly quizzical as though the rock were an absurdity, the visit foolishness.

'A rock?'

'Yes. In the machinery, caught between shafts but it only bent one, and broke some blades. I stopped the machinery. They're waiting. . . .'

'Who?'

'The gang. I left the driver. . . .'

'All right.' Broderick pulled on trousers and a shirt and went out, Arthur following. Beneath the house was a shed. Broderick unlocked it and fumbled in the darkness, cursing. He came out with a rusty, bladed shaft.

'The last one. I hope they don't know it. Wait.' He circled the house and entered it again, emerging a minute later, buckling on a pistol belt.

'Bring it.' He indicated the shaft. Arthur followed him along the path to the mill. Broderick worked silently, unbolting the bent shaft. He replaced it, ordered the machinery started, saw the new one work, indicated with his hand that the gang should start again, watched them fall to.

As they began, he looked carefully at each of their expressionless faces. Then he took Arthur outside. They stood side by side, looking at the night for long minutes. The mill was on high ground and the shining edge of the sea was visible. A cane truck squeaked up from the fields, the driver encouraging its mules *geetchup geetchup*.

'You went to sleep?' Broderick asked.

'Not exactly. I . . .'

'It comes to the same thing. I know how it gets in the mill. I did two years of it. But I warn you, man, let it happen and we're done for. That's our last shaft, and when the next one gets here, I don't know. Carruthers expects me to run this place on nothing, and still turn a profit.'

'I'm sorry, Broderick.'

'I don't care whether you are or aren't. In fact I don't care at all about you or what you feel. Feeling is for women and niggers. If there's anything Her Majesty's navy taught me it's that. They like to whip Irish gunners when they get a chance, and they don't feel it when they do it. So stay awake.'

'Yes.' Broderick's talk was discontinuous but in the mill's torchlight Arthur could see his face, his thin Irish mouth tight, his jaw solid, his eyes haunted. He was much shorter than Arthur but seemed more powerful in his compactness, his steady, directed rage.

'And now you do one thing,' Broderick said. 'Do it quickly. And now. Better you do it than I. You have to work with them. They expect it of me, now we'll let them expect it of you.'

'And what's that?'

'Go in and shoot him where he stands.' Broderick yanked the pistol free of his belt and held it out. 'Scipio, the big one feeding the grinder.'

'Dear God, why?'

'He threw the rock in to break the grinder. The rocks are common now along the coast. They've just discovered that. Take it.' He held out the pistol.

'But—are you sure?'

'Yes. Go and kill him. Now.'

'But suppose it was a mistake, an accident?'

'We lose nothing either way. But a rock like that doesn't just slip in. They know what they're about. We have to tell them the price of it. Now. Take it. Shoot him.'

'I never killed a man Broderick.'

'TAKE . . . IT. He's not a man, he's just another nigger, and he's the nigger who stopped this whole plantation in five seconds, while you were asleep. He could have killed you with the same rock. And that might be his next idea. TAKE IT. Do it there, in front of all of them. You go first. I'll follow you in.'

Arthur took the mahogany butt of the gun and looked in towards Scipio, busy at the grinder, lifting armloads of cane to thrust into the machine. It was impossible to conceive of him as an enemy. But Broderick might be right. The rock itself was too large to have just slipped through. Even so it seemed excessive to kill him, but then Broderick knew his people.

'Get it done, will you?' Broderick was gently impatient, his voice low, verging on the confidential. Arthur confronted Scipio's back, bent to his work. He called him. Scipio ignored him. He called again, louder. Scipio turned and saw him, and the gun, and Broderick behind him. He fell to the floor, grovelling, clinging to Arthur's boots, keening *no, mawster no, mawster*, crouched, his head on Arthur's boots, the only target his bare back, already stitched with scars from whips of bygone years.

'Go ahead,' Broderick said quietly. Arthur looked quickly at the others in the mill. They bent to their work, only one or two flashing him momentary, frightened glances. Scipio was alone, surrendered up by them as though he had never existed.

He stepped back and fired point blank into the back beneath him.

· III ·

Scipio screamed, a high awful scream and rolled away from him, screaming still, clutching himself where the bullet had come through his stomach.

'In the head now. In the head.' Broderick's voice was cold, strident. Arthur pointed the gun again, closing his eyes as he fired but not fast enough to avoid seeing the impact demolish Scipio's right eye. The screaming ended. He looked to Broderick, who held him with his eyes and reached for the gun as though reaching to take his hand. His grip on it was so tight that Broderick had to take his wrist and manipulate the gun away from his fingers.

'Fine.' Broderick called out and had two hands take Scipio away on a cane wagon, with orders to bury him that night.

'Come have a drink,' Broderick said. 'You probably need one now.'

They went in silence to Broderick's house. On the way Arthur heard and saw a cane wagon, creaking off with Scipio's body. He was a murderer, he thought. But not a murderer. No more so than a soldier, and the shooting a simple requirement. He followed quickly after Broderick, the speed of events and, for the moment, Broderick's quick pace, giving him no time to think.

Broderick preceded him through the door, then closed and bolted it behind them. Broderick handed him his rum in a bamboo cup.

'Sit down for a moment,' the overseer said.

'Thank you.' He took a chair and Broderick sat opposite him. He swirled the rum in the wood cup and looked down into it. He tried to reassemble the night—sleeping in the mill, the hand awakening him. Was it Scipio? He didn't remember. If it was another hand, was it a joke between them, he and Scipio? Or was the other hand just afraid? The mill became a series of unanswered questions, of shadows on shadows. *Devious*, Annie Palmer had said. *The niggers are devious.*

'Are you all right?' Broderick's voice was low, neutral.

'Yes, all right.' There seemed little else to say. He clutched the bamboo cup as though it held his existence. 'I'm sorry I bothered you in the middle of the night, but I didn't know what to do.'

'Best you came. I shan't talk on about you falling asleep. No point to that. You're new enough here. You've done well enough so far. But I warn you, watch them. Devilish game they play these days. Finish up and have another spot of rum.' He drank, and Broderick poured him more.

'Are you sure . . . are you sure in case such as this that the rock was deliberate, sure that he . . .'

'Absolutely. You saw it? That big?' He measured space with his hands. 'If it bothers you killing him, be sure. And if he goes that far he has to be killed. It's common along the coast now and there's only one answer to it.'

'And they won't try to retaliate for this? They're that well in hand?' He stared into his cup but then looked to Broderick, comfortable and assured, slouched in his chair, the lamp glow heightening his sharp cheekbones, adding glitter to his hard blue eyes. Against him Arthur now felt as child to man, and the man had led him to kill as though training him. There seemed nothing in his life before that moment with the overseer. He felt strangely at home.

'Of course they could retaliate. One of Scipio's people could poison you, or grab you in the bush on your way back to the mill tonight. Or burn this house while I sleep in it. We run that risk every day. Are you afraid?' His face was quizzical, mocking.

'No I don't think so.' He was, of course, and so was Broderick, but in that moment they seemed to buttress one another, the pair of them engulfed, probably doomed, both somehow pointless.

'Fine. Don't be afraid. If you are, which I'm sure you are, don't show it . . . at least to them. You see how they give up. Like children. You didn't expect Scipio to grovel and cry like that did you?'

'Not at all.'

'I did, but then I know them. He had no idea what he was about. A rock was used at Harmony Hall a while back. The fools had no parts so the mill had to shut for a month. And that word has spread around. That's as far as Scipio was thinking, I'd wager. He never expected to die for it. He didn't hate you, or me, or her on the hill. He just wanted a week's sleep.' Broderick laughed, the sound small and dry. He took a swig from his cup and slouched back further, triumphant.

'We killed him for that? That was all? I thought there was more behind it.'

'Not enough for you, eh? I thought so. You'd need all kinds of reasons . . . Tell me Arthur, were you ever hungry in England? Did you ever go without food for a day or two, or three?'

'No.' He looked at him, not daring to question him. In Broderick's eyes was a private memory, locked and sealed like a treasure, and beyond that a hatred so distilled and abstracted that it had evolved into a calm creed, perpetual sustenance for him, its equation un-translatable except in terms of what he did. Such as having Scipio murdered without pause or question. Arthur was less afraid of than awed by Broderick, who, by the solidity of his existence, made him feel formless.

'Never really went without food? Even when the factories and all were closing, when everything went to ruin and they couldn't bring it back, for all their reasons, for all that?'

'No. My . . . my father was a tradesman. A tailor. We had bad times in Manchester but we . . . we never did without, in truth.' He looked at Broderick with pity now, knowing part of his pain. It was bad enough to be an Irishman in England, but there had been terrible hunger during the bad times. He remembered that. The overseer had known hunger pure and simple while Arthur had been shielded. And for that he felt guilt, and beyond it an aware-ness of his innocence and probable irresponsibility.

'Lucky chap,' Broderick said, his voice coldly level. 'Well, drink up and get back to work. You have about another half hour at the mill. You'll watch them now I take it?' He stood, withdrawn, sar-donic, deep in his impermeable self, that self burned and scarred but still of value, like some artifact that had withstood a fire.

'Yes. Yes. But the rest of them? I don't know who awakened me. But it wasn't Scipio and I don't know what they're up to or who to trust. Is there anything . . .'

'Nothing I can tell you. The country is in trouble. Some of it gets to us. Who is where at any moment is not known by any one man . . . and not even by her, on the hill . . . at any time, much as she thinks she knows.'

Broderick put his hands on his hips again. He put his head back, his chin jutting at the air. 'And so . . . just watch. And push them. No rest. Give them no rest. Brutes kill you if you do that.' He yawned, a wide yawn full of fatigue, put a hand on Arthur's shoulder and moved him towards the door.

'Good night.'

'Good night, Broderick. Thank you.' The door closed on him and he walked towards the mill, wondering what he had thanked the overseer for. He was numbed and drained, now an inextric-able part of Rose Hall, a pupil of Broderick by virtue of his own frailty. He may have held the gun on Scipio but it was Broderick's will, more than his own, that fired it. And he had fired the second time only against the black man's scream, only to silence him like a hurt dog, to alleviate the unbearable burden of just the sound of him. He could be, he thought, no further from home than he was that night, England and Manchester as far as the planets. If he went back he could explain nothing to anyone because, as Broderick said, there were no reasons that meant anything.

He saw the mill through the last of its work, fighting to keep his voice strong as he gave small orders, scanning their faces for hostility and finding none, their only answer to him a quiet *yassuh*, their faces bland to the point where he knew that he alone remembered or thought about Scipio, that they, in their numberless, disunified and exhausted black swarm merely went on, congealing like the mindless ocean interrupted by the fall of a rock.

He walked them to quarters, the lead man carrying a torch, he in darkness to the rear, where he could watch them, alert to trouble.

At home, Mary Lou had left some new bread and a dish of Calalu soup, but she was not there. He had some of the soup, then went to bed. He stared at the dark, the night neither accusing nor aiding him as pictures of Scipio dying, and Broderick laughing, formed and reformed in his head and he remembered, and felt, Broderick holding his wrist, gently twisting the pistol out of his hand. His mind went to his mother and father, in their other world, asleep in faraway England, innocent and benign, the simple cosiness of the morning tea together there before them, he now forever a stranger to that, to them. If he wrote to them, as he would have to, he could write only lies, fabricating a world for them because his was too unreal.

Then Annie Palmer edged into his thoughts, less thought than picture. Her delicate hands and wide eyes, her long switch of hair, the good comfort of the great house. He wondered did she lie up there alone that night, her hair on the pillow. He saw her as fragile in sleep, the house huge and silent around her. He wondered what it would be like to touch her, such a woman, after the reek and violence and fatigue of his days. Wondering and imagining, he lay awake until early dawn, slept as light broke, but awakened immediately as the angle iron clanged to rouse the whole plantation.

11

THE GUNFIRE awakened her. She prowled the house after sending Venus for the news. Venus encountered, the wagon, then Mary Lou, who had heard and seen it all from the shadows, beginning with Arthur's rush to Broderick's house. She traded the story for bread, soup and rum, half of which she left for Arthur.

Venus told it to Annie Palmer in one uninterrupted stream of words, and was dismissed. She went back to dreamless rest. No single event ever tormented her. The worst had been to go out in the dark alone, but she wore and clutched a dog's tooth against the night's terrors.

She knew that Miz Palmer would stay up, that night and maybe for days. Anything could be expected of her but at least she, Venus, was safe unless she was caught in some gross error.

There had been times when she had to hold and rock the mistress on her lap until dawn, often putting her breasts out for sucking, the white woman's face unnaturally hot at first but cooling in time, between the sucking and the rocking the slim tormented white woman subsiding, her private devils leaving her.

That was after Palmer's death. Then it was over and the mistress found other ways to fight her devils alone. All the blacks thought her a sorceress on intimate terms with the night spirits. Venus was not positive but neither did she disbelieve, knowing how Miz Palmer rode out at night alone.

Annie looked out over the land from her balcony, heard the mill going, and withdrew from the cool night air. She roamed the rooms, upstairs and down, touching a picture here, a vase there, in constant easy motion, part of her mind frightened by the two shots, another merely content with the house, taking comfort from it as though it was a sumptuous cloak around her.

In the centre of it, in the night's silence, she often stood still to listen, to wait, half-expecting a voice, a presence, an unpredictable manifestation. A white crack of lightning drawn down on the house. An eruption of the ground, an earthquake centred at Rose Hall.

In these minutes she was at the centre of a universe she almost commanded, in which she might call down fire or summon the earth to move. Jamaica often had tremors, the ground quivering for miles. When they started she waited, exultant, for them to come into their own.

That night she stood at the base of the sweeping main staircase, waiting, then passing on through the rooms, touching mahogany, Cloisonné, velvet, crystal, as though conversing with her friends in her passage. She loved Rose Hall, and she in it, and her inviolate aloneness. The shots from the mill were minor, if unnerving. She paid Broderick to keep order. If he ordered Scipio's death, that was his affair. And if the new man was learning, that was good for him, and for Rose Hall.

The new man panicked, or had, but she trusted Broderick. He was common but she liked his nerveless viciousness and the sure way he ran the plantation for her. The new man could learn from him, if he had a will to. And he might do better than Broderick in time, although he seemed unsure of himself. Possibly he was now surer, she mused.

One never knows about them, never knows. She passed through the downstairs drawing-room, pausing to look at the last of the embers in the fireplace.

Never knows except in time. She poured herself a glass of sherry and went back up the wide staircase, talking softly to herself, something she had started after Palmer's death. It frightened her then, but she came to find it soothing. A week after Palmer's burial, she sat looking at the moonlit land from the upper story, rocking in a chair and saying *Annie Annie they are not coming for you, not anyone. You killed him and buried him but no one is coming to hang you or even talk to you, to accuse you or bother you not ever because Jamaica is that way they leave you alone they left you alone they are alone you are alone and you can kill your-self if you must but there are none to kill you for killing him and you killed him because of that out there because he was not equal to that did not love that was not man enough for that. . . .* She put herself to sleep with talk that night, her eyes bright, unfelt tears welling out of them and streaming, vanishing down along her face. Thereafter she had even come to climax, Broderick surging in and out of an unknown unreached high-up place, delib-erate but unknowing, unaware of her to the point where her excitement became fright at the loss of him, or that part of him, and then fright and excitement comingling into frenzy (which he noted, detached, bemused, remembering Palmer's offhand drunken indictments of her) that urged her at and to him, resenting him but at once wondering what was about to happen, afraid it would, then afraid that the last did not exist. When it did she pushed her mouth into his rock-hard shoulder, throttling her own scream.

She was bland and noncommittal with him and kept him in his place, her fascination with what he had wrought not laid out for his inspection. He made a remark or two that verged on crudity, then went back to his work. She waited weeks before trying him again.

When she was ready he went back up to her bed but had no ambitions there. He knew she was trouble and knew of his own self-set limitations, the great house no substitute for his compact, defined existence. He wondered if he had done something Palmer hadn't, the wonder academic, a biological puzzle he discarded as soon as it occurred to him. Her food and wine were good, she was eager enough in bed if not as limber as a coloured girl, and so in sum he traded himself for food and some of the comforts of the great house. *A long, long way from that London jail*, he thought now and again, with a thin-lipped smile.

She was cautious not to indicate his peculiar value to her, which she took and considered in utter silence, detaching it from the common face and mien of Broderick, his class, and what she knew of him.

What is it then, what is it? That was all she said to herself, aloud, about it. Then she spoke the answer to herself one night while swinging into her saddle to go riding with Broderick, know-ing she would have him up later: *He was short. Broderick is . . . longer . . . there . . . further up inside me.*

The simple mechanics of it diminished Broderick in her esteem, or at least made of him a mere instrument, thus confirming his commonness, re-establishing his place, protecting her from the absurdity of any affection for him. They made love with heat and energy, driving and driving at one another, testing one another's ferocity in white-white combat in the mahogany-panelled bedroom but with a glaze of indifference over each of them and the act itself, tenderness distilled out as though by mutual agreement, their only purpose the scalding spasmodic terminus that was always there.

She retained Broderick but edged beyond him within six months, the quiet isolation of her days in the house quietly pervaded by desire and curiosity, the bright day-world baffled and diffused by the shutters, trips to that outer world impossible in any case for a known murderess, Falmouth and Montego Bay seeming an eternity away.

She took her first black man one afternoon—Flavius, the gardener. She decided that since she owned everything on the property, everything was possible for her. She ordered him upstairs, told him to undress, and hung his rags on a Hepplewhite chair. He was mystified by her close and eager inspection of him, by her lengthy fondling. After some coaxing, he finally took what was offered him with surprising gentleness, as though he were afraid she would break in two.

She went on, selecting a hand here and there if he was working near the house, acting circumspectly, as though to keep her experimentation a secret, then realizing that like everything else in Jamaica this too was known. Immersed in her newfound pleasure she had not considered Venus. But the fat servant had become a silent accomplice, providing a steady flow of new faces on some pretext or other. Annie considered punishing her for unwanted complicity but instead withdrew that time, for weeks, to consider how a well-bred governess, an educated woman who had come out nearly twenty years before as a bride, virginal, hopeful, had thus veered, first to kill, then to become an eager bedmate for black men.

Rose Hall and the island around her offered neither clue nor solution during those weeks. She looked out of upper story windows at Flavius, bent to his work in the garden, wondering what had led her to him and then wondering what he thought, what he remembered, and whether he ever desired her. She would watch for a long time, often an hour or so, but he never looked up. She had given him new pants and a shirt, but he had gone back to the old rags he had worn to her bedroom. He seemed thus to deny her existence, he a tangible memory for her, she nothing to him.

Withdrawn those weeks, she remembered, memory a river and she poised over it on a bridge, the passage of memory incessant, swift, but also interminably slow, eternal. Part of her was incredulous, detached, another part of her engulfed, swimming in the current of time past while she watched herself from the bridge, a pathetic unknown creature, for whom she had neither pity nor hope.

It was a decent enough plantation. That she knew. At first it was a wonder, vast and incomprehensible, and she new to the Caribbean, the daughter of a London doctor, who had met Palmer in London by chance, and been courted by him off and on for two years as he came and went. To her he seemed an incredible fabulist she seldom saw and who wrote her thick letters in a strong, thoughtful hand and wanted to bring her out as his bride. Born in Jamaica, he loved it and told that love, she listening as though to a mesmerist, vision on vision of hill, mountain and coast penetrating her being, an Eden unthinkable in London becoming a reality in her mind. She left, her cautious parents kind but sorrowful, her father not trusting Palmer but he tender with his prize, holding her hand as the coach rushed through the night to Liverpool, solicitous during the sea voyage, beside her on deck as they sailed into Kingston, the mountains great green majesties over the neat sunlit town.

Slavery unnerved her at first but she accepted it, it being part of his life, natural to him, serving both of them, negation of it impossible the instant it was accepted, one service leading to another, all leading to the odd knowledge that the slave's life was his pleasure, rejection his fear, freedom not even his dream.

She began to lose Palmer within months. He drank and brawled and spent more and more time with Broderick. At first she was protected by her innocence from stories of their debaucheries together. But a combination of veranda gossip, old Carruthers' intimations and the obviousness of Palmer's disappearances and his condition when he came home gradually informed her. She fought to change him, the fight centred in the quicksand of the society that had raised him, protected and nurtured by innumerable slaves, supported by the land and the unstoppable sugar, his role assured, his responsibilities virtually none, the black women always out there waiting. She fought in that quicksand, sorrow, mockery, rage, cajolery and indignation mixed with love and the hope that he might change and revert to what she thought she had married, an upstanding young Jamaica planter.

There were others like him, she heard, but few as bad as he. She withdrew gradually from the verandas and dining-rooms, from town and teas. She had liked gardening in England and tried that until it seemed pointless to her, its pointlessness heightened by Palmer's mockery. One drunken night he threw ten vases of flowers out of windows, from all parts of the house, saving the last to plummet it from the top of the stairs down on to the hall. He roared with drunken laughter, that turning to vomit which streamed out of him and down over the flowers and shards of vase.

She took up sewing and discarded that too, in the absence of a child to sew for, and caring little for her own appearance. The thought of a child entered and re-entered her mind, not as a full-blown dream but as wistful speculation. Palmer, who would have to be the source of it, made the thought unreal. Their infrequent couplings—she frightened by and withdrawn from unknown obscenities he seemed to want but she could not provide, not even knowing what they were—made a child unlikely.

But she was impregnated in the third and seventh years of their marriage, losing the first embryo in four months, the second in two. Palmer seemed unhappy at both pregnancies as though they might give her a hold on him. In his worst rages he had screamed at her to go back to England, keep a garden, lock herself in a cottage in the country and become 'another one of those dreary damned spinsters'. But she was past facing the humiliation of return and, after the loss of the two unborn children, past love or anguish but only a patient witness to and nurse for Palmer.

I love you, Annie, I love you I'm sorry, Annie, I'm sorry. At times he said that in drunken contrition, meaningless but not unaffecting, and she saw to his nursing and let him make love to her until that docile phase was done and he went back to his other world.

Then she took up riding, disliking it but enjoying attention from the stable hands who were eager for her presence, and then from one or two blacks who rode well and calmly taught her this and that without pressure or tension but with their timeless mindless quality of perpetual servitude.

Then she wanted to give that up too and just go back to the house and be alone with no challenge aside from Palmer. But between his absences and his drunkenness, and with the flowers and the sewing and the two tiny bodies she had aborted behind her, she went on, learning gradually to enjoy the solid but mobile feel of the horse under her, the elevation from the ground and lastly the liberty as she rode out through the property, slave and white alike noting her passing and admiring her.

Palmer disapproved, but not vehemently, holding it to mockery and warning her to stay out of the way of the work and out of the slave quarters. She learned to trot, canter and then gallop, finally leaving one or another attendant behind and going off alone among the hills or through Music Valley, racing and rushing when she wanted to or pausing in a far glade to rest, the horse her sole companion, witness and guardian.

Good. Good. A beautiful day. She spoke to the horse now and then and even hugged his broad chest. She wanted to ride him naked and once in this phase mounted him in the glade, undoing his saddle, pulling up her skirts, straddling his broad back, feeling the twitching of his muscles under her, sensing his eagerness to move but then getting down, fearful of being seen, fearful even for her own sanity, going back to the house, shunning both that euphoria and the glade itself for many weeks.

Riding, she encountered the deaf-mute, almost killing him by accident, in fact knocking him down and learning about him quickly from his frightened black mother. She went back and back to see him, bringing him small delicacies to eat, and then began to sew again, making the naked creature little pants and a shirt.

She brought him to the house fearfully, knowing Palmer's reaction to her projects. She fed, bathed and played with him, discovering that he enjoyed play although in his fear it confused him at first. She made a ball for him out of yarn and leather she sewed herself, and had a swing made and hung up beside the house. She noted his temper, rage and frustration surging out of him even during happy moments when, filled with wanting to cry out or say something, he could not. She soothed him with one trick or another, more and more trying to anticipate his rages. She taught him to dance although he could hear no tune but just follow a rhythm. She rocked him and hugged him and when she was sure Palmer would be away for a while kept him in her bed, loving his warm company in the night.

Palmer found out soon enough. His mockery only fuelled the child's rages. Palmer baited it as though it were a dog. Annie came to its defence, the issues between her and Palmer transferred to the dumb child, who in turn flew at Palmer in hatred and terror and even bit him one night, Palmer then dragging the child up the staircase to fling it down as he had the vase of flowers. But he was drunk and Annie, grappling on the stairs with him, managed to trip him and fling him down the steps, he reaching to save himself at the last second, she grasping the boy who was unable to sob but only cry, great tears wetting his silent face as he hugged her on the stairs, high over hall and living-room. Palmer merely fell into a drunken sleep that night, apparently not recalling why he was bruised the next day.

Those months were the worst, and during one of them she killed him. Which one, she would never recall, except to remember that he dragged her into his room one night, shoved the boy aside, pawed at her, tore away her gown, spat on her, called her a cold bitch, spewed out of his mouth words that not even he had used before with her. He held her to the bed. He told her exactly what he was then going to do to her body, how violate it, how cause her pain and for where and how long she, cold and white, would learn to love it, love him, become a nigger, act as a nigger.

She listened in passive silent last-perception of him, white cold immobile disbelief her only guardian until—as he proceeded to twist at her and turn her body over, the hairy heat of him obscene, all of him not then pitiful, weak or merely drunk but totally obscene and verging on a violation she could not even conceive of—the child mounted the bed and struck him, grunting in an extremity of fright, his little hands flying at invisible speed. Palmer flung him off the bed but in the instant he was diverted Annie had the brass candlestick on the night table. She smashed him on the ear and then across the temple. She hit the back of his head as he fell away, the lower half of him still atop her. She beat at him, striking aimlessly at vertebrae and flesh down along his back as she writhed out from under him. Uncertain that he was at last still she rummaged among his things, finding an old letter opener. She jabbed it first into his legs because he lay diagonally across the bed and then, extending herself, crawling up on the bed, whimpering, naked, jabbed and jabbed at him, kidney and lung then the back of his neck, tumbling off the other side of the bed, recovering herself, getting up to stab and stab at the back of his neck.

Her next awareness was of the boy standing against her, his woolly head against her naked groin, his arms around her thighs. She might have stood there for an hour in the soundless Jamaican night. She would never know that either. The blood on Palmer's streaked and punctured body was neither streaming nor clotted. She gazed at it, surprised that it did not exist in time, her mind searching for time, searching for guilt, fear, horror.

He's gone. He's gone now. It's all right. She spoke to the boy, who could not hear her. Then she went for Venus. She told the servant he was dead and to have him buried quickly, that night, her decision automatic, dreamlike. She ordered the burning of the bedclothes and mattress and then went up to rock in the vast living-room, sitting and swaying on a rocker through the night, the boy on her lap asleep. She drank slowly and steadily from a bottle of good sherry, wondering which was dream, those hours or the years before.

Broderick knew the next morning, as she guessed he would, but did not go even out of curiosity to see her. Venus reported only that Horace, the then-gardener, had done as he was told. She had the sense not to say where Palmer was buried, and was not asked.

That ended it, except to wait for retribution. Surely the militia would come, several of them, crude but polite, an odd mixture headed by Major Edwards or another of the planters, trotting up the drive, dismounting, leading up to a question, not an accusation. She would answer directly, gladly, ready for expiation, even for death, but not for searches, interrogations, any of that.

She waited, immobile against absolute silence, like a Roman statue awaiting and expecting its desecration and destruction, the house her peaceful and splendid museum, the barbarians coming, coming, she unafraid because only a statue, integral, alone, out of time, meaning, motion. Waiting.

12

No ONE came.

Jamaica leaves its whites alone. She remembered Palmer saying that. *We're together in another world the idiots back home don't understand. We're together in a beautiful hell.*

Two weeks later the boy, sleeping beside her, gave evidence of oncoming manhood. She got up, lit the lamp and studied him in his sleep, that odd part of his stunted body not just an anomaly but an abomination, a thing with a will of its own. She took him to Venus with orders to have him emasculated and brought back immediately. She cared for him while he healed, and he was soon as lively as ever. *He will be all right now, all right and always here with me. He's a wonderful little man, a wonderful little man.* She talked to him, stroking him, he studying her mouth, touching her lips, moving his own in mockery of speech.

Her life seemed composed until her beginning with Broderick, and what followed with Flavius and the rest, how many she could not recall. Venus's complicity frightened her, not just baring the privacy of whatever sensual phantasmagoria into which she seemed to have entered, willingly, but worse than that heightening it by institutionalizing it, the gardeners and housemen and God knew who provided for her like so many pounds of beef or bottles of wine by the cunning, silent Venus, who could not even be reproached and whom it would be useless even to kill because her replacement would in all likelihood do the same thing, *Jamaica leaves its whites alone. We are in a beautiful hell.*

She thought for two or three or four weeks, virtually immobile except to eat and a few times to ride out at night through Music Valley and up to a hill to contemplate land and sea, Jamaica like dark velvet beneath her.

She saw lights twinkling in far great houses from which she had long since withdrawn, shamed by Palmer's flagrant debauchery, known to all of them out there before she had awakened to it. And now she was further—and finally—excluded by virtue of murder (she said it aloud to herself under the stars *murder I am a murderess*) and of the self-sought desecration of her white body by black men, her own debauchery no secret. She sat alone under the sky, over the land, more and more at peace with it. Jamaica made no judgments. It was, like herself, a thing apart from the artifices of veranda and town, of reason, judgment, whispered gossip. She sat for hours at home or in the countryside, gradually more and more unshaken in her aloneness, inviolate with Palmer gone, the little boy her companion, field, mill and servant sustaining her. *They will leave you alone. They will.*

She thought of Palmer and how she had loved him with quiet pride and tranquillity at first. But it had not been enough for him. Jamaica claimed him, not she. His Jamaica, lavishing too much on him, he the impotent heir to land and the house, the dazed scion of a history not his own and he impotent to further it, he thrusting his life into the blunt dark dead end of a hundred or more negresses all at his command, looking to ignite a spark, re-create the bright white flare that had been the going out and the settling, the carving and the building of his ancestors, that light smothered by the black man's hands, the original white flame protected by those hands to the point where it consumed itself. She had loved him in London, tanned, handsome, full of talk of the land but even then a fraud or at least eroded more than she in her adoration could have guessed.

She heard from the white world only when she summoned Carruthers, less than a year after Palmer's death, for an accounting of Rose Hall's status. Broderick sent on figures about planting and tonnages to the old man. But Carruthers was the only one who knew everything—the value of the land, the percentage of profit on the crop, Rose Hall's relative position on the island.

He was correct with her, figures meticulous, his heavy ledgers in order, a boy with him to carry them, all of them written in a neat cursive script with a fine steel pen. The plantation was cash-poor, as they all were, but she and Broderick had done well with production that year. Rose Hall would hold together if they added no more hands and kept the machinery in order.

There has been less spending this year, Mrs. Palmer, consequently the accounts reflect this good state of affairs

Carruthers not having mentioned Palmer, that meant that the old man knew of his death, of the murder, but his long columns of intricate figurings—the basis of his life—accepted it.

Would you care for a sherry, Mr. Carruthers, or a rum perhaps? I still have some Haitian rum in the cellars

If you please, madam. A most excellent rum

Yes, splendid. She rang the bell for Venus.

They sipped it, the massive ledgers between them, their marbled paper covers and flaking leather binders weary with time.

You will pardon me, madam but . . . will you stay in Jamaica? Ancient and bald, thin with age, his arthritic knuckles ludicrous on the arms of the Hepplewhite chair.

I have no other home, Mr. Carruthers. Why do you ask? Abomination. He, they, all of them would know every scrap of it, and each bit magnified. The women chattering over tea. The men, white men, eager to reserve lust for themselves, calling her anything. Cold white bitch trollop.

A bad time . . . the island is changing . . . danger . . . a woman alone is rather . . . unusual. It is better sometimes to leave a place when the time comes . . . step down so to speak . . . not . . . abdicate . . . but give way to the realities . . . the society is

I do not think of myself as part of that society of which perhaps you speak, Mr. Carruthers this . . . Rose Hall . . . is my life and responsibility, as of course you understand. Gently, with the old man. And he with her, he seemingly past the age where lust or even love of the overarching concepts of morality disturbed him. Just happy to feel his pulse beat once more and once again, his swollen knuckles and knees not hurt for an hour or two. The marbled volumes of accounts his companions.

Society . . . seems necessary, my dear Mrs. Palmer. At least I have thought thus but perhaps I am of an older generation. We may be past our time in Jamaica, at least I may be. But the lone path is

Is what, Mr. Carruthers? A little smile for him, and her eyes soft with bemused affection.

Society does not always understand. Talk and speculation of course are

Society understands nothing and never did, Mr. Carruthers. Perhaps only the lone

Beyond that the dangers . . . and immorality is replacing what we once had here

Jamaica was born and built in danger, or so I thought. Soldiers, planters, builders. We drove out the foolish Spaniards as I recall, and settled this place . . . as usual they were torturing Indians, in search of gold, and as usual we came and built . . . ignoring danger . . . ignoring morality, I thought, too, for we cannot call slavery moral . . . however morality would have been a severe impediment to ours or any empire. History and morality always seemed to me to be two different things. There was another world the Greeks used. Virtue. I believe it was

The dangers are growing . . . society aside . . . subversion and violence. The old order passeth, so to speak. A sale, perhaps, could be arranged for Rose Hall and free you . . . and you would be safe

I shall maintain the old order. Perhaps in a new way. Perhaps no woman in memory ever managed a Jamaica plantation alone but I intend to . . .

It was not, then, just the veranda talk. The lean dry old man was himself beyond imagining or caring about her bedroom. He seemed to care about her life, some antique code of chivalry, oblique and deferential but still pure, speaking through him.

That was it, like the living-room, like the house around her, cloak woven on time's looms, the world Man's all time past, thick beams of Jamaican mahogany, broad planks of the floor, subjugated earth outside feeding his, Man's, creation. She the legatee, a woman alone, anomaly to old Carruthers, who excused her being a murderess, who disinterestedly overlooked the fact of her holding black men between her thighs, his own manhood distilled and gentled by three-quarters of a century, no violence, passion or hatred in him, seemingly nothing left now but that quiet old chivalric eternal sense of protection.

For your own good, Mrs. Palmer

*Rose Hall's good is my own, Mr. Carruthers. I have no heirs
as you know*

Rose Hall may . . . still endure the fate of the others

Then I shall suffer the same fate

Not necessary

*Yes of course necessary. This is my home, sir. You stay in
Jamaica*

I am an old man in

*In Jamaica, where you stay. A woman has the same choice.
You would no more leave and be an assistant solicitor elsewhere
than I*

I am old, Mrs. Palmer. You can begin

This is my beginning

They conversed delicately, patient with one another. She asked
him to lunch but he declined. After a second rum he took his
ledgers and departed, his black amanuensis absurdly laden with
the great books, Rose Hall's history in numbers between their
covers.

I hope you will consider the sale, Mrs. Palmer. He stood in a
rectangle of brightness, sun and sugar behind him, the sea blind-
ingly white in midday, heat entering the foyer as though an oven
door had been opened.

*It has always been a beautiful plantation, Mr. Carruthers, and
I shall keep it that way, and it is my only home*

Yes, beautiful, Mrs. Palmer, and I hope that we can all keep

*And I. And we know that beauty takes many forms. And so I
know you wish me well, and good day, sir.* She closed the door
against the harsh sunlight.

The Reverend Gordon came too. She knew him to be an
acquaintance of Wilson but suffered his presence on the property
because he made no effort to lure field hands to his services. Broderick had long since communicated Rose Hall's godlessness by chop-
ping off the right hand of a woman he had found on her knees, in
an attitude of Christian prayer, trying to instruct others in that
rite. Gordon knew it, preached against it, even wrote a pamphlet
that mentioned, in the ministers' usual capital letters, GODLESS-
NESS, and was published in England. When it got back to Jamaica
the idea spread among planters and one-handed slaves became more
common.

Gordon came, and she let him in, his dough-white face, red
lips and soft little hands all somehow quaint to her.

Would you care for a sherry, Reverend

I think not at midday, Mrs. Palmer, I

Day is day and even night is day. I do wish you'd join me

Well yes then all right

How nice of you to come by. Was there something special

No no, not really, not special really She saw him remember the dead black hands, the spurting wrists. He took his sherry gratefully from Venus. *Just that I have not been here in so long I must apologize for my tardiness. It is not easy for a woman alone. But a spiritual bond links us all and as . . . as God's minister I thought I should*

Should what

Well . . . well . . . hope that the Holy Spirit is . . . with you He gazed in fright, as though she might strike out at him.

I presume that he is. At least I seem to have no evidence to the contrary. My fields are productive and my health sound. Did you have word that something was wrong

Ah no no of course not. But life is a difficult path and it is so easy for us, for any of us, to go astray or to be led astray by our senses

I imagine it is. I have often imagined that as a matter of fact. Strange imaginings, I have sometimes. I suppose that part of us is much like the . . . the . . . beasts in the fields, so to speak, isn't it, Reverend? The animals around us

I think them rather fortunate, don't you, Reverend?

Oh no. No. Oh, yes, yes, God's creatures they are, as we all are, yes, God knows and loves them as he does us but only WE *can love* HIM, *while the poor beasts*

The poor beasts enjoy themselves? A bull I saw this week seemed to be enjoying himself. He was servicing a cow and with her . . . I remember distinctly . . . he was a black bull and she was tan and white

Of course of course, God's creatures were meant to multiply, to fructify the earth, to enjoy the fullness of

Everything I suppose. And we were not? She watched him knead his slim little woman's hands together. He had finished his sherry. She rang for Venus.

Ah no, no, Mrs. Palmer. Surely we should enjoy everything but without being led astray He smiled almost continuously, a weak little smile as though to prevent his being struck if he gave offence.

How astray

By . . . by excess of course, that is the most . . . most common of course

And determined by

Well we know, we know ourselves because it makes us ill, God tells us by making us sick. The evil of our ways is made manifest to us in pain and suffering

Ah yes, yes, as in eating too many apples of course. On the other hand if we enjoy something and take genuine pleasure in it—as, for example, in the manner of that bull and that cow I saw, well then

Ah no, there we differ from the beasts for we do not live for pleasure, as they do, poor dumb creatures, no no, Mrs. Palmer we live for

We live for pain?

No no for God, Mrs. Palmer, God, not ourselves just on this transitory sinful

Do the niggers you preach to live for pleasure or for God, Reverend?

I beg your pardon? He drank half of the new sherry, his eyes up at the rim of the glass, frightened little eyes. She wanted to say something quite vile to him. They had fantastic temerity, these young ministers, and were quietly destroying Jamaica, rabble-rousing Pied Pipers promising a detour to Paradise to a people eager for that detour, eager for anything but work, the niggers outsmarting them, the ministers, without the fools even realizing it.

I said do your niggers live for pleasure or for God?

Oh for God of course for God they

My niggers live just for Rose Hall, Reverend. If they do not, they have the choice of death or starvation outside these gates. Aside from that, they live just for pleasure. I have come across them in the fields here, just like that bull and that cow . . . It never quite occurred to me that they live for God. Or Paradise. Or could imagine a saint, there being no black ones, I believe. I think they are rather more aware of . . . of their living flesh, we might say.

Well, yes, unfortunately these poor people . . . but we Christians know . . . St. Paul said

And the living flesh seems to be where they had best stay. And they do seem to delight in it. Tell me, Reverend, do you like Jamaica?

*Oh yes, yes, and my work is here, so much to do and in a way
such a glorious example of Our Lord's handiwork.*

*Yes of course perhaps he created it—and then abandoned it—
and now man works at what was abandoned. This house this plantation. Have a bit more sherry, Reverend, before you go*

I do not think we can say he abandoned

Do you really like Jamaica? Do you enjoy it?

Oh yes, quite, yes. It

Pardon me but your wife did not I gather

Our life was not an easy one. She

*Yes of course. Your dedication. The difficult conditions. Tell me,
Reverend, do you keep a woman now?*

Ma'am? Venus came and went, filling the sherry glasses again
from a decanter.

*A woman. Do you keep a woman? All the white men seem to.
I hope you do. I understand they are . . . quite enjoyable. The
black women*

Ah, no, ma'am, I find it best to live alone One of his pale hands
took the sherry and he sipped at it.

*Regrettable. This could be such a pleasurable island for you. At
least it seems to be for so many men. A great . . . excitement
here. Lovely young women and men, with such . . . sumptuous
bodies. We might say . . . voluptuous. Examples of Our Lord's
handiwork, as perhaps you would say. Almost unbearably exciting. I should think a naked Jamaican girl bathing in a stream
would torment your dreams, Reverend, rather like that saint, the
one who*

*Oh No, no. No. I see only the wondrous hand of God, and pass
on*

*Very sad. I should think you might pause to enjoy, a sort of
Adam for example. Jamaica seems that sort of place. But then*

Of course

*Of course. The fall. It condemned you to an eternity without
pleasure. Cast out of Eden* She laughed. *I'm sorry, but I do find
that amusing. I suddenly saw you walking up to that girl in the
street and telling her she'd been cast out. They do have some
funny sayings in the dialect, you know. Rather crude ones too.
Got them from our ancestors and mixed up English and Welsh
and their own little words for parts of the . . . body . . . and
things they do with them . . . well, enough of that. I'm sure you
shan't try and convert little naked Jamaican girls while they're*

*washing their bottoms in a stream, will you now? Tell me, how is
your friend Wilson? I see him seldom but he appears to do his work
well enough*

She enjoyed the baffled stare in his eyes, the hard line of his
mouth, the grip of one of his hands on the other, the fingers inter-
laced.

She was genuinely glad he had come, if only to provide her with
a bit of amusement and to make her feel that age was worthwhile.
He was the spirit of all absurd seriousness. She could not,
she realized, really hate him even though he, together with
the other frocked ones, could do irreparable damage to
Jamaica.

But then Jamaica would in her eminent good sense turn on and
renounce them too, the nigger no fool but with his wayward
jungle-born cunning able to triumph over them, survival and
growth and plenitude in him as it was in the land, earth rubbed
into his flesh, scent of sugar in his skin like a perfume, moss and
flower his bed, his heavy-breasted women swinging to market,
heads up proud under laden basketfuls of yams, corn, peas all
sprung up out of the earth made fecund by rain, sun, and yes, by
the blood of both black and white because the land seemed to demand it. And drank it. And returned it, crop for blood.

And the Reverend Gordon was bloodless, thus not of Jamaica,
thus he and his heirs would vanish in time. She knew it. As well
as she knew the blackness, the women and the men, flesh their
inviolate joy, safe for all time. Knew it now. Knew a mystery
profound beyond the reverend's imagining. The mystery Jamaica's
salvation, the nigger to don but then burst out of the cloth
that Gordon and all reverends ever to come would cut for him,
interminably and surely seeking his level, that level his flesh, the
land, the simple dawn, the fire of evening, his woman, their cooking
pot, no God-insanity ever to tumble them off the sweet palm of
earth.

*Wilson is all right, Mrs. Palmer. A good fellow. A sensitive
and intelligent man. You would do well to watch him. If you
ever decide to replace Mr. Broderick as overseer*

*Intelligence has its limits and sensitivity is always charming,
Reverend, but I think your friend Wilson has . . . limitations.
Not really . . . dangerous . . . to Rose Hall, although I often
wonder. Perhaps he is. Anything that . . . undermines us . . . is
probably dangerous. As you know. And you know that we have*

· 133 ·

always dealt with . . . in any event I am delighted to have seen
you, Reverend. Do be careful. Watch yourself

Thank you. And God be with you, Mrs. Palmer. May he

Good day. Venus will take you to the door

She sensed the fright in his voice and saw it in his eyes. To him she was self-damned, a voluntary, unthinkable renegade from Christian society, even from the white world. For a second she pitied him his invincible ignorance and his own isolation but lamented the times, before Palmer, before Jamaica, when she herself was a good Anglican communicant in London, the world somehow one, innocence pervading it, benign God the creator and protector of it all. Had she been a child, then a maiden, been once a bride? And now in her forty-third year what was she?

Mrs. Palmer pray with me pray with me I beg of you before I go in God's name God will take us all He could have sensed her moment's reflection, and for that she despised herself. The fool was on his knees in the foyer, Venus holding the door open, gently scratching one of her ears and yawning.

Goodness, I thought I said he'd abandoned us. Good day now She stared at him until he got up and went, minding his manners, his fervour spent against the rock of her conviction like a wave spattered into an absurdity of spray against an age-old coral shore, she in that moment as old as earth's experience, he up off his knees to take his dream of God and Paradise out into daylight.

And that ended it, he and Carruthers the last emissaries. She settled into her own self-sustaining existence, Broderick providing her with enough news of Jamaica and Venus too, through Mary Lou and the others, the whole black stream of information that spread through the island getting to her eventually, Broderick free with it over the dinner table, Venus merely summoned upstairs for periodic recountings:

Well, ma'am, dem have trouble in Falmouth yes'day, dem runway come close to town an stop a lady carriage take him fancy hat an baggages an dem soljer come a chase cotch none but one him come to town after mek big talk an drink dem a gwine hang him fum a tree but dem built a fire cook him lak a sucklin' pig.

A-beat many neger in de Munte-go Bay square las' week, dem old han, an auction de res', fum Hartley Hall, an dem militia go mek war on dem runway up by Bogue in dem fores' kill lot of dem militia dem han at Ardmore Hall burn de crop dis week Massa Crown dey say shoot hisself all de crop gawn tree o fo rev-

rend push out of Port Maria las week an one of dem kill by Massa
Radcliffe to teach his hans to pray

She droned on, bearer of all the absurdities, a talking news-paper, Jamaica's desperation and anguish flowing through her, uncorrelated and untainted by judgment or fear or pity. She lived in a pool of knowledge unmarred by waves of crisis, the data gone once it had flowed through her. Annie saw the crises, saw the form of the seemingly shapeless sea in Venus's vanishing words.

13

'So you joined them. You know how to kill now.' Wilson spoke softly as they watched Broderick, like a general, call off the roll of slaves and give the day's assignments. The soft greens of Jamaica's morning were not unlike England's. But the sky's brightness was always a shock. Arthur, sleepless, winced at the oncoming sun.

Wilson stood unavoidably before him, his face ravaged, tired and unshaven, his eyes nursing an accusatory look.

'Joined whom?'

'Them. The killers. I understand they took you into the fold last night. Or at least he did. You're advancing quickly.'

'He told me what to do is all. He said to do it. They threw a rock in the mill. He said . . .'

'To kill of course. Follow them right up the ladder. You found yourself a good teacher, my friend. You shall be an overseer one day. I trust that killing does not . . . unnerve you?'

'I didn't want to, Wilson. He told me to. By God, I don't know about this place, I don't.' He could not bear Wilson's eyes on him, an educated man pitying and judging him.

'Ha. Don't renege now. One step deserves another. Up you go, and the cost is not your concern. Scipio may be dead but there's another to replace him. And he didn't matter. All that matters is you, getting on. There are more where Scipio came from.

Doubtless he left . . . four or five children, or more, who will of course avenge him one day. But you mustn't think of it as killing a man.'

'I beg you, Wilson, stop it.'

'Of course, and gladly. Because now you know where you are. Part of the empire. Now you belong to it. I suppose in a way I envy you. At least you shall be out there someday, where he is now, or back up there on the hill with her, or some hill, somewhere. And I shall still be back here, or gone, because I cannot commit . . .'

'Damnation, Wilson.' He knew the other man was mocking him. His vaunted education. Commenting on everything. Knowing everything. Making himself out just a sad, gentle fellow who once ran a school. Arthur looked out towards Broderick . . . *you shall be out there* . . . but he didn't want that. A vicious man, cold and abrupt. *Scipio . . . with his back to us . . . shot him now*. But a strong man. Stopping him at the gate after the Palmer woman had shamed him. Sharing his peculiar contained strength in that moment. Strange. Arthur was exhausted after his sleepless night, drained by the killing, sapped further by his imaginings about the strange mistress of the place.

'Damnation but I wish you well. Go with them. Better to be there than here, if you can, if you can bear it all. They decide things for all of us. And they eat well. No sense coming out here to hang back.' Wilson went on quietly, as though talking to himself.

'Why did you come out here then?'

'To be alone.'

'Alone?' He was too tired for Wilson to make sense. The sky was lighter. He looked at the other's face, pallid, passive, with reflective eyes that seemed turned inward on himself.

'Alone. Away from England, which will not leave you alone. And to this insanity, in which it is easy to be alone. You see?'

'No. I'm not an educated person like you, Wilson. I just came out to work.' He knew the answer fell short.

They were called forward by Broderick for their day's assignments, and strode together through the uneven dirt of the field.

'Our daily summons. How he must enjoy it, the little Irish monster. And especially ordering Englishmen about. Thinks himself one of their mad heroes. Finn Mac Cool. The same insanity, all of them. 'I ARISE TODAY THROUGH THE STRENGTH OF THE CHERUBIM, IN OBEDIENCE OF ANGELS, IN THE SERVICE OF ARCHANGELS . . .'

Wilson's voice rose, and he finished as they confronted Broderick.

'Praying this morning, Wilson? Or are you drunk?'

'Not praying. A hymn they say St. Patrick wrote, sung to deceive those who would assassinate him. You should know it. Sixth or seventh century perhaps. At least you know the saint. We are at your service, Arthur and I.'

'I am delighted to hear that, dear professor. Kind of you to join us. Take the southeast sector today and cut me no less than six acres and after supper go back and load it. That should keep you busy and keep your mind off St. Patrick.'

'He is not to be dismissed, my dear Broderick. He did after all remove the vipers from Ireland and send them elsewhere. Perhaps even to Jamaica.' Wilson tugged at an earlobe and raised his eyebrows at Broderick, who looked at him with quiet hatred.

'Make it eight acres today, professor, all cut and loaded. If it's not done by nightfall, just continue until it is. And you work tomorrow as usual. You know where southeast is.'

'Past the gate, Three kilometres out that way. Past the line of palms.'

'Good. From there to the property line and up the side of Morley's Hill. All the way up. Take ten acres in fact. Do you good.'

Arthur listened, pitying Wilson, but admiring his blind nerve. He had asked for trouble, making remarks to the overseer. Broderick could kill Wilson. A man could only work so many acres a day.

'How many men are you giving me?' Wilson said.

'Your usual twenty, less three sick today, makes seventeen.'

'That can't be done. You know that can't be done, Broderick. You know it's impossible . . .' He was almost pleading.

'Of course it is. If the going gets rough, you can cut with them, professor. Then you can all get some rest. Now go.'

'For the love of God, Broderick, there'll be two or three deaths from sunstroke or exhaustion and some will go mad. You know that. We had it last year . . . what's the point. . . .'

'I said go. But say me something nice before you go. Something you taught the little boys, besides what else you taught them, eh? What say you for us this morning?' The sun was higher in the sky. Broderick cast a long shadow on the earth. The daylight made Wilson look even more haggard.

' 'Tis sad to see the sons of learning in everlasting hellfire burning . . .'

'Rhyme, eh?'

'While he that never read a line doth in eternal glory shine.'

'Finished?'

'Yes.'

'Then go.'

'You are killing . . . you are wasting them, forget me. Them, they're dear you know, two hundred pounds if that gets to you. That woman on the hill knows it too, you'll ruin her cursed plantation faster than you'll ruin *me*, I tell you . . .' Wilson shouted his head craned out like a bird, one arm flung out behind him, pointing at the silent assembly of field hands.

'I said go.'

'Do what you will to me, man, but where's your *sense* gone, even your *sense* . . .' His voice was high and thin with hysteria. Arthur listened in fear and turned to see if the slaves were aware of the moment. A few were watching, dully aware of movement, perhaps just seeing Wilson's finger pointed at them, possibly fearing denunciation, hence violence to follow. Broderick's hands went to his belt. Arthur tensed to grab him if he drew his gun, surprised at his own daring.

'I said go.'

'And come back with the remains of my crew. The skeleton for you. Sacrifice. You insist on it. Why not give me some sponges soaked in vinegar?'

Broderick waited, immobile, quiet blue eyes on Wilson, who turned and left. The overseer scratched himself under his left armpit. He spat forcefully, not in Wilson's direction but to one side, over his shoulder, and turned to Arthur.

'You take the west field, from the road down to the sea. Take three acres this morning, leave the rest to the driver, and watch the mill this afternoon. Then go for the cattle and get them penned. I'll send someone when it's time. Take three of the mill hands with you.'

'Yes. Which three?'

'Any three, except the women.'

'All right.' He turned to go and take his usual crew.

'Wait.'

'Yes.' Broderick waited on him in his sleepless fatigue. Dawn was no longer there, just daylight, in meaningless perpetuity;

horizon, tree, earth, surgarcane, the overseer's face, swooping curve of blue sky over them, Broderick's eyes blue too, saying as much as the sky, which was nothing.

'He's not changing you, is he?'

'Who do you mean?'

'I don't mean Napoleon Bonaparte, bucko. I mean that school-teacher fool. Is he a friend of yours now?'

'No. No, we just work together is all.'

'And what was he talking to you about back there?'

'Nothing really. He . . . Wilson . . . talks a lot, about a lot of things I don't understand. He talks is all. Goes on, he does, like as he was dreaming. Like now, what he said now, poems and things.'

'And what does he say about me?' Broderick's gaze was level. Broderick wanted the truth and would use it to crucify Wilson. And yet Wilson had courage. He had displayed it. Foolish, but courage. He would pay, cutting those ten acres, and give Broderick no satisfaction, except that of nearly killing him.

'Nothing, Broderick, nothing about you. Just his talk, like you hear. He's . . . he's a comic fellow really, all those rhymes. . . .' He became eager to save Wilson, suddenly seeing the way to spare him from being crushed.

'Nothing much. I can't close your ears, lad, but I warn you, let him be your schoolteacher and you're done for here. And keep your trousers on when you're with him or he'll give you more than rhymes, understand me?'

'Yes.' He wanted to ask Broderick to call Wilson back and change the ten acres back to six.

'You're doing all right, Arthur, and he never will, here. Her ladyship knows him. She hired him for his fancy talk, and then got sick of him, so now I have to work him until he drops. He's just fool enough to keep at it. I'll have those ten acres out of him today because he wants to show me what a man he is. You give me three and go on to the cattle and that's all right.'

'Yes.' Arthur turned to go.

'One more thing.' Broderick looked at the ground, and then up at him, waiting.

'Yes.'

'You're all right. You go along here and I'll move you along, You ride?'

'Ride?'

'A horse.'

'I never did.'

'Well, in time you can. Get around some, out to Falmouth and MoBay so you can try those niggers too, and the creoles. Some really fancy ones there, and full of hell. Break it right off you. Go to town with a few pounds and you're king. Get you out of this place. Not now, but when the time comes. Harvest is the worst of it, then she eases off. That's all.'

'Yes. Thank you.' Arthur went for his crew. The ground seemed to be drawing him down. He felt as light as a shadow, hardly aware of his feet bearing weight on the earth. The thought of a horse seemed more dream than reality and he sensed it for what it was; a gift in exchange for Scipio's death and a purchase of his respect for Wilson's courage. *I am Broderick's man.* He remembered the big iron gate. *I can go through the gate. When he is ready. How long have I been here?* How strange it would be to see a town. And frightening. His rude clothes. The ingrained dirt of the plantation, dirt and molasses scent hovering around. And he imprisoned in toil, the nights short, darkness falling early, tiny cabin his home, Mary Lou there at erratic intervals, strange and haunted, clinging to him. Town seemed as distant and vast as London ever had. He called his crew and followed them to the southeast along a trail in an uncut field.

'Boss.' A black named Othello fell back a pace to talk, his head bent down.

'What is it.'

'Yu a good boss, *buckra*. Big work today, suh?'

'Three acres in the west is all.'

'Good, suh. Good, suh. Not so much. Mistah Brod'rick lak you, suh. No kill us wukkin, suh. Wuk *good*, suh, mek a *good* crew, suh.'

'Good.' By now he knew the deviousness of their praise. He waited.

'Suh?'

'Yes.'

'No trouble wid *dis* crew, suh. No trouble *heah*, suh.'

'Yes.' Scipio. They were already afraid of him. Pitiful they were, Broderick and Annie Palmer quite correct. Keep them beaten down. Give them no rest. The peculiar strength to kill was not theirs, a trick such as Scipio's natural to them. With an indefinable revulsion he saw Broderick's logic and even how he owed his life and livelihood to it.

'No trouble, suh, Pahdon, suh. You got a bit of tobacco, suh, fo him neger. Long time . . .'

'Get back with the others.'

'Suh? Yassuh. Hope, suh, dat yu mought . . .'

'Now. Back in line or you get your lashes tonight.'

'Yassuh.' He slouched back to the group, a surprisingly large man with thick arms and strong muscles across his wide back. *Kill me in an instant. Strong they are. They don't get tired, she said.* He looked down to Othello's narrow, strong waist, the muscles thick from bending all day to cut cane. Flat hard buttocks under his rags. The whole back of him a powerful V printed on the morning. *I wager he's been up there too. On the hill.* The thought enraged him.

'Get a move on.' He tried to shout but his voice sounded weak. He repeated himself, louder, and the crew, dawdling and singing softly in the dialect, moved ahead almost imperceptibly faster. The slave driver grumbled at them too, but set them no example of speed.

At the field they went to work at the silent cane wall, the *chuk* of machetes rhythmic, the driver watching and urging them on quietly.

Remembering Scipio, Arthur looked around him, half-expecting retribution, his own slayers perhaps waiting. But the borders of the isolated field were silent. He felt the sun's increasing heat, and retired to the field's edge, under an avocado tree, heavy with the ripening fruit. *Town and a horse.* He had an urge to flee, coupled with a fright that made hands and feet numb. And the day was not bearable; unending routine slashing of knives into cane, as though nothing had happened, the night's events a nightmare. And now all day, in the silence. *Broderick at the gate, waiting.* His bowels writhed and he went away from the tree towards a stand of cane. A rat rushed past him, huge, frightened and frightening, determined in his surging forward motion. He dropped his trousers and was voided by harsh wrenchings of his innards. *Sick, I'm sick.* He saw the driver fifty yards away turn and note him, squatting at the side of the field, and look away. He wiped himself with leaves, making a mess of it, and went back under the tree. A kling-kling bird lighted in the tree and made his odd, happy sounds. He heard doves cooing and then a small flight of them arose near him and flew north towards the sea, over the line of cutters. His mind's eye saw Scipio's face as it was blasted open, blood spurting from his eye socket. *Excellent people. Would you care for a pipe?* His stomach hurt and then it thrust a bitter bile up into his throat. *Sick.* The thought doubled and trebled itself. He could not leave and go to his house, or ask the driver for help. His stomach surged again. He vomited a white broth of his own fluids, bitter in his mouth and nose. And then more of it, and more while his mind raced. *You came five thousand kilometres . . .* He held the tree until his stomach had done with him. He feared lying down on the grass. Annie Palmer might come, or the slaves take advantage of him again. Some had turned to look, that he saw. He left the tree's shade and went out in the field, headed for the driver without knowing why, going to talk to him, about what he knew not. The sunshine pushed at him. He saw a flurry of white spots, like motes in the air before him. He was unconscious before he fell to the ground.

14

'HIM A-WAKIN'.'

He opened his eyes and shut them against light, aware of Mary Lou's voice, speaking to whom he knew not, nor was he curious. He felt small and light in the bed, and comforted.

'Duppy got him but go now. Obeah man kill a senseh fowl las night, a-pour him blood over rice, call de duppy a-way.'

'Sh-h, Mary Lou. He may need more sleep. Let him be now.' Arthur recognized Wilson's voice, modulated, kindly. He lingered in delight between wakefulness and sleep, not quizzical about his situation. They were there, protection and balm. He heard a cow low, and the chatter of a chicken, and felt a tiny breeze on his cheek. He thought the word Home, and it made him thirsty for tea.

He opened his eyes to Wilson, at the foot of the bed, the other's gaze mild and thoughtful.

'Good day, Arthur.'

'See him a-wakin', fevah not so bad. Duppy let him go, let him go . . .' He heard Mary Lou's excited whisper from the left. Her hand squirmed quickly from forehead to cheek and burrowed under the covers to his chest.

His eyes closed again, shutting them out. He saw the plantation gate and he with his back to it. Like a grill. *A saint they burned once. St. Sebastian, I think. Turn me over my brothers, for I am done on this side.* He opened his eyes and sat up in fright.

'Wilson, what is it, where . . .'

'In your house. All's well, man. You've been asleep a good while. Stay calm and don't move about now.'

'What not move? What not—what's happened, do I . . .'

'De duppy come again. Need anuddah fowl to-night. Hol dis, Ah-thuh, a-hol it now. . . .' She took his hand and curled it around a tiny sack hanging from his neck.

'Yes, Arthur, hold that. A bit of magic'll never hurt you. The sack contains fine medicines—a bit of chalk, a dog's tooth, and perhaps a pinch of cow dung. They've saved stronger men than you. And they had a ceremony for you, but they wouldn't let me go.'

Arthur held the sack, hung by a thong from his neck and patted Mary Lou's hair. 'Thank you, girl. . . . Wilson, how did I get here? It's been a few hours I'd hazard . . .'

'Three days, but you're all right. Have no fear. It was to be expected.'

'Three days? Three days? You mean I've been . . .'

'Asleep or unconscious or whatever. Don't let it disturb you. Food is what you need now I'd guess.'

'Mek a good calalu an some boil meat . . .'

'Wilson, you went off . . . you went off to cut ten acres, he sent you . . .'

'Quite all right, really. I talked to the driver and the cutters, poor wretches. I'll tell you about it one day. You should have a bit of food now.'

'No tell me now. How did you do it, man, how did you come out of it. I remember . . . I remember you going, you mad fool. I remember you said those crazy things to him, poems, crazy things, asked him where . . . where was . . .'

'His sense.'

'Yes but you went.'

'Sh-h-h. Mek a hot calalu an cook him a chicken. . . .' Mary Lou pressed at him as though to lay him back down in the bed.

'I talked to the poor wretches,' Wilson said. 'Like . . . like a class I suppose. And told them what we had to do, what was expected, and to cut and continue cutting as long as they could. I told them Massa Broderick wanted that and then I lied to them . . . I told them she wanted that too because the . . . plantation needed it, because the sugar might die and the mill close. . . .' Wilson spoke slowly as though wondering at his own words.

'They believed that . . . they believed . . .'

'Believed it all and I told them the field was important, that there were other fields on other plantations and they . . . they had to be strong enough to do this, were they strong enough . . . and I cut with them for a good while until they made me stop. *They* made me stop, of all insanity. And finished it that day and we loaded it that night. That is all.'

'And Broderick? He . . .'

'Is indifferent. Will find another way to kill me. And then. We only lost two men. One just dropped. One destroyed another's head in a single stroke—he and one more man went mad but I bound them to a tree for some hours and when they calmed they went back to work. But that was days ago. Lie down and rest now, my lad. It's the lunch hour and I must go.'

'Yes. All right. I'm . . . I'm sorry to be a bother, to leave you with the work, I . . .' He wept at his own feebleness, and out of concern for Wilson.

'No bother.'

The knock came but before Mary Lou or Wilson could go to the door, Annie Palmer was in the room.

'And what have we, a party?' Her hair was drawn back in a bun at the nape of her neck. She wore a long-sleeved black shirt and dark riding pants.

'He's ill,' Wilson said. Mary Lou fled to a corner and stood watching.

'Yes. Three days now. Broderick just told me. He has the fever?' She went towards the bed.

'I think now. Perhaps just exhaustion, Mrs. Palmer.'

'Oh of course. Weaklings they breed and send me . . .'

'Perhaps not weak, madam, but afflicted . . .'

'Oh yes, this terrible place. The awful work. That a white man should have to work with his body. The thought must sicken you too . . .', she turned to him, 'mustn't it, Wilson?'

'I stand before you on my feet, madam.'

'A barbary ape could do as well, I imagine.' She turned to Arthur.

'A senseh fowl take de duppy, Miz Palmer, an I med a Calalu soon come.' Mary Lou whispered from the corner. Arthur rose on one elbow. Annie sat on the edge of the bed.

· 146 ·

'And what's wrong with you now?'

'Nothing, ma'am. I took sick in the field is all. I'll be up . . .'

'You look horrible.' She pushed his hair back from his forehead and felt his face with the back of her hand. He was pale and lean, dark circles under his glazed eyes. She had seen enough of her father's patients to remember the look.

'Lie down.' She took the thick, flat bones of his left wrist in one delicate hand and found his pulse. 'Splendid. Three days of bleeding chickens and schoolmaster talk and I am not told. If you'll go now, the two of you.'

'He shouted quite often in his sleep,' Wilson said.

'I said get out. And you . . . and take this with you.' She took Mary Lou's talisman off his neck and threw it in the corner.

'About death. He shouted about it and he shouted *don't kill him don't kill him* as though he were trying to stop something. And he shouted about the mill . . .'

'I said get out, Wilson. Time you were back at work. I didn't solicit information from you.'

'And home too. And of course then he wept. I think he wept for more than half an hour and kept on about his father, his poor father, and what some lady did to him. Delirium can be strangely beautiful at times, can it not, Mrs. Palmer. The other day one of my men sang in what I swear was Portuguese and then spoke in French . . .'

'Wilson, I said get out. And take her with you. Get on, get on, Mary Lou, or I get you, girl, get you this time.' She stood up. 'You like it in there, eh? *Sizzle* inside of you, *Burn.* You scream, you *feel* it girl. I twis' it, you *feel* it. Show dem man AP on yo laig, I put it inside and yu show *nobody* heah, nobody to see and no sensay fowl save you . . .' She stood, screeching, lapsing into coloured-talk, Mary Lou paralysed, then ducking low, keening, rushing for the door.

'In French of all things. We have no slaves from the French colonies of course. I suppose he could have picked it up from a seaman . . .'

'I SAID OUT CURSE YOU . . . or you shall go too, Wilson, you shall go screaming, Wilson, I have the room waiting it's there under the house you never saw it but it's there.'

'I know. We all know,' he said calmly. 'The entire island knows, milady. Even about the collars with the spikes, and the high good time you and Broderick had there the night, is it three years

· 147 ·

now, with the runaway you found. And of course Mary Lou. Strange, how exciting men must find it, her scar . . .'

'All right, you have two seconds. One . . .'

'I hasten, despising dungeons.' He smiled at her.

'For God's sake, Wilson, get out.' Arthur spoke from the bed.

'Ah, your strength is coming back . . . good fortune with it.' His voice lingered as he walked out.

'Hateful fool,' she said softly, looking after him, 'diseased, hateful fool. It will give him pleasure to die.'

'He's a good fellow, ma'am, and works hard . . .' He was afraid to say it after her fury but Wilson needed defending. A strange man, taunting them. *More courage than I have. Lock him in her room and kill him, and Broderick there to help her.*

'Let him be. We have to survive, I suppose, with people who are running away from something. He is probably a scandal at home. But at least not a ruffian. . . . Here, let me look at you.' She turned from staring at the door.

'I'm all right, ma'am. A little weak is all. I can get to work this afternoon.'

'Lie down. Do you have a mirror here? I'll show you how awful you look.'

'It broke, I think. It's not there.'

'Broke, or that miserable Mary Lou stole it. Steal your teeth if they weren't rooted. You're pale as a spectre and you've lost a stone or so. But no fever. We shan't lose you immediately.'

'I don't think she stole the mirror, ma'am.'

'Don't be a fool. You still don't know your niggers. They have to steal to live. You know it, and they know you know it, so it becomes a matter of degree. Now be quiet while I go for a wagon. We'll bring you up to the house for a time and see that you're fed and looked after. And stop calling me ma'am. I find it tedious.'

The house. He lay still as a child in the bed, folding his fingers over his stomach. *The beautiful caw-stle,* he said aloud mocking it. *And what's going to happen to me there?*

With an effort that made him dizzy, he got up, splashed his face with water and got into his clothes just as the old driver creaked up with the wagon and came to the door.

'Sah, Miz Palmer sey yu to please come in de waggin to de house, sah.'

'I can walk thanks. Tell her . . .'

'Sah, pleas, sah, Miz Palmer say yu sho come wif me. Else him whup me.'

'All right, all right.' He smiled. They all said *him* for her.

He did feel weak, whatever it was. Overwork or an island sickness. *I've not been eating enough.* Mary Lou often brought supper but she was irregular, and it was often tripe or pig's tails and rice. When he remembered he drew from stores which were charged against his wages, but he was often too tired to build a fire and fix a meal. He drank and went to sleep very early if Mary Lou did not come. He squinted against the sunlight as the wagon creaked up the hill. *How long? How long have I been here?*

'What month is this?' He turned to the scrawny, white-headed old wagon driver.

'Sah?'

'What month is it now?'

'Don't know sah, rightly. Harves' time, sah. Close on to finishin', close on to summah, sah.'

The old man would not know, of course. They had no schooling. Even Mary Lou spoke of the moon as though it were real as a clock or a calendar, and she had unnerved him talking about the Dead Time until he discovered that meant summer, after the harvest and before the plantings. *What month is it?* As the wagon moved up the driveway he struggled to remember. *I came . . . I came . . . in January. It was late January . . . about . . . about . . .*

'Sah?'

'What?'

'Begging yo pahdon yu said sah. . . ?'

'I said nothing.' He must have spoken aloud. *I am very sick.* He felt frightened and feeble and sweat drenched his face and body. The jouncing wagon rolled past Rose Hall.

'Where are we going—where are we going?' He was conscious of almost moaning, his voice like a thin scared whine.

'De back door, sah, by de kit-chen, fo Venus tek yu in, sah. Him tell me dat, sah.'

'All right, all right.'

He watched the horse, old and slow in its cracked leather traces, as they passed around the house. The old man stopped the wagon. Venus took him into the house and to a downstairs bedroom.

'De mis-tress say you to get into de bed please, sah, after dem

· 149 ·

bath de boy soon come.' She drifted out. There was a pair of man's pyjamas on the bed.

Damnation, what am I a schoolboy or is this a hospital or what. The door opened again and a houseboy came in dragging an empty zinc tub. He went out and returned again and again, filling the tub with pitchers of warm water. Arthur sat and watched him, quietly amused.

'Lad, it will take you a long time to fill that tub.'

'Sah?' His eyes were huge and showed fright.

'A long time. A long time. Much water, eh?'

'No, sah.' He grinned, lowered his head, chuckled and ran to refill the pitcher. When he was done he stood still beside the tub.

'All right lad, out with you now.'

'No, sah. Mis-tress say him to give you baf, suh.'

'Out, boy, out.'

'No, sah, please, sah, mis-tress him whup me.'

Arthur felt absurd but sat in the tub. *Mad they're all mad they are, me sitting in a bath with a little niggerboy washing me. Good thing mum or dad can't see. Raise hell the old man would, and mum have a turn she would.*

'What's your name, lad?'

'Sah?'

'Your name, lad, what's your name?' He patted the boy's head.

'Hannibal, sah.'

'A good name. And how old are you?'

'Sah?'

'How old, how many years, lad?'

'Don't know dat, sah.' He went on with his washing, calm, serious and attentive as though there were nothing else to do at the moment in the entire world. Arthur contemplated him, skinny but seemingly healthy, his back bent to his work, content to serve, service his highest possible goal, an odd kind of selflessness his destiny until the day of his death. Arthur imagined having children—one or two perhaps—and offering them up to this kind of living death. *Service. Mawster.* He remembered the term as he had heard it in Montego Bay that first day, and despised it now. *No son of mine will ever bathe anyone, or call a man mawster.*

Contemplating the child, he thought for the first time of what it would be like to have a son, and in what society he would want to bring him up, but then his half-formed thoughts and vague visions transcended his capacity to think. His mind subsided back into the comfortable reality of being washed in the great house he thought he would never re-enter.

'You go to school, lad?'

'Suh?'

'School. Where you learn . . . you learn to read, and write.'

'No, suh. Don know dat, suh. Washin' and cleanin', suh, is Hannibal wuk. Wut school, suh?' His voice had a dying fall as though he feared his own temerity at asking a question. His eyes remained averted.

'Ah. Nothing. Forget it, Hannibal. You do a good job.'

'K'you, suh.'

When the boy was done, Arthur put on the pyjamas and got into the comfortable bed. Venus appeared with a tray and on it a full lunch—a pepper pot soup, a good cut of meat, yam and greens and a cup of tea. He was partway through eating when Annie Palmer came.

'Better now?' She wore a simple blue dress and her hair was down loose.

'Yes . . . thank you.'

'No thanks to me. You people live like idiots and someone has to look after you now and then. I suppose it's partly my fault. We are short-handed this year and Broderick has to work everyone hard.'

'The work isn't too bad it's . . .'

'It is quite bad for a white man just out of England. Did you expect what you found? Be honest with me.' She looked at him levelly, and tossed her hair with one hand.

'No. It's a bit rugged. But I . . .'

'But but. Yes I know you're a big strong fellow and can't admit weakness or be ill and just lying in that bed probably disturbs you, but we aren't *really* trying to kill you. You have a value here, and seem willing to work. Mary Lou could kill you inadvertently. Does she feed you regularly?'

'She's all right.' Mary Lou would suffer if he said the wrong thing.

'Hardly. She's erratic and a thief and a liar. Get yourself a steady, simple woman, and if not I shall find one for you. I saw no point in our losing Wilson, so I sent Mary over there. At least she feeds him and manages to keep him in one piece. She even waters his rum.'

'You did that?' He dug into the buttered yam and talked through a mouthful of food.

'Of course. My interest is Rose Hall. I can't have men coming and going every week, or dying before they've worked off their passage. I suppose you'd like to leave, being thoroughly sick of Jamaica, but of course you can't since you're under contract and I have to insist that it be honoured. But if you stay, you might find it better in time.' She looked away from him, at her fingers, at the leaded window looking out on the garden, vividly alive with red roses. She plucked the bedclothes and threw her hair, elevating her chin.

'I suppose so. It's a bit rugged but I'm not complaining. A man signs up for his work . . .'

'Yes and doesn't know what to expect . . . Surely you expected a better life, and you'll have it, if you make it for yourself. This is still a young country. It will have its troubles, but there's no need for you to run home to England. Well, I talk too much. Enjoy your lunch and get some rest. If you are well later perhaps you can dine with me.' She got up to leave.

'Thank you, Mrs. Palmer.'

'You're quite welcome.'

She closed the door quietly. He stared as though a mirage had passed through it. *I wonder what Broderick would think, me in bed with a good lunch and her ladyship here too and telling me to have a bit of a rest before dinner in her grand house. Break my back he will when he gets me again.* But then, he thought, he was for the moment protected, and wondered at the strangeness of her coming to look after him. He finished lunch, put the tray aside, looked through the leaded window at the garden, well-kept and not like the scraggly growth around his place. *Fancy. When you've got an army of niggers you can do it I suppose.*

The food made him somnolent. He went back to bed and was asleep when Venus came for the tray. She studied his pale face under the dishevelled shock of brown hair, the arms clutching the pillow, the pyjamas, which had been Palmer's, hanging loosely around his body, jackknifed in the bed, his knees drawn up under him. She took the tray to the kitchen, scraped the leavings off the plates for her children and said softly to no one *meager sho meager.* White men seemed insubstantial to her, wraiths cloaked in the power of their violence, to be feared, yes, but never as much as the deep night.

She would, she knew, and so would all her kind, rather the whip than the nights, and remembered when Arthur had come to her with Broderick, at least bringing light into the underground room at least that and the lash, once, but the worst had been after that, in the night alone.

And so the white man, white spectre, brought something even though he was meagre and doomed, no duppy to take him, no fiery-eyed roarin' calf to frighten him to death along a road; for they did not see such spirits and yet some spirit had them, something lodged in their hearts.

So she thought. Or felt. Because thinking to her was just that: Tides easing across her brain, wordless and without colour or form, except the occasional clear and definite pictures of white fingers on the whip.

She scraped away Arthur's leavings, and put them aside in a rusty tin drum, making mental note to remember to take the drum with her to the quarters that evening. Then she turned to supper work, disassembling a large head of lettuce, washing each green leaf with slow attentive care, going on to core and slice big fresh apples and then peel and carefully cut a dozen red tomatoes. The mistress had a fondness for good red tomatoes. Venus kept a small but fruitful patch of them in a corner of the garden, tending them herself.

As she worked, she hummed to herself, hummed a no-song, a mixture of African chants, Jamaica rhythms, what little she had picked up of religious music and, unknown to her, snatches of British martial airs that were also part of her extensive if wordless heritage. Part of her was quite content that Arthur slept calmly nearby in the little room off the kitchen. He seemed to keep her silent company in her work, and she enjoyed the sight of a man at peace.

15

A SINGLE CANDLE burned beside his bed when he awakened. Evening had come. The peculiar red of the Jamaican sunset spilled across the leaded window-panes and lit the garden, etching the outlines of gladioli plants and stunted palmettos against the tranquil sky.

He squirmed in the deep softness of the feather-filled mattress. He had been bone-weary for weeks and his back (although he did not admit it even to himself) had ached persistently from so much standing, beginning with the dawn invasion of the sugar fields, ending in the early hours of the morning as he watched the mill. Part of him hated to relax, but now most of him appreciated the depth of the bed where Annie Palmer had put him to rest.

Very nice arrangement, a meal and a good bed for once. Snug it is. And the fever gone now. Does a man's soul good, it does, to have warm meat and a decent place to sleep.

He stretched, luxuriating. It reminded him of home. He half-expected his mother to enter, in her quilted wrapper, to feel his cheeks and feed him barley soup. His venturing off to Jamaica had led him to a world harsher than he had imagined. Had he actually shot a man, just on orders from Broderick?

Lord luv a duck. I'm simple. And simpler now. Why's she brought me here? Kill me, like her husband. Fatten me up on food and rum and Madeira and dispatch me some dark night.

Strange one, she is, strange as they come. Best watch myself.

Ease and mistrust mingled in his mind, until the door opened and Venus entered deferentially, her face a dark moon in the candle glow, the whites of her eyes reflecting the flame.

'Suh?'

'Yes, Venus.'

'Suh, de mis-tress say if you wishes to dine with her or eat here, suh.'

'Mrs. Palmer?'

'Yassuh.'

'She wants me up for dinner?'

'If you wishes to she said, suh.'

'Great Heavens. Tell her ladyship I shall be there in a trice.'

'Suh?'

'Tell her yes.'

Venus padded out. He watched her go. *Lord, I must be feeling better. Up he is and ready for a bit of meat like that. Wonder how old she is. Be a real comforter, that would. Not like that wild Mary Lou.* There was a sense of urgency about Mary Lou's lovemaking that made it seem more like a battle. The cowlike Venus might be more comforting. He lay for long minutes letting wordless sensations overcome him, his mind turning to Venus's warm body, then the gentle aspirations of her voice, her hands and the slow, deliberate way they had served him lunch. Then (and he cringed inwardly) her uncomplaining humiliated body, exposed to Broderick's lamp, Broderick's leer. *Brute, mean brute he is. And her ladyship, the two of them the same kind. Wish I could just get away from all of it. Back with the common lot in the Smoke, or Liverpool. But better be up now or there'll be hell to pay. No dreaming, if you're to talk with her mad majesty. And why did you come among us, Mr. Arthur, and what are your fine high ambitions? At least the meal should be good, with all her land and her cook and all.*

He dressed and found Venus, who led him up the back stairs to the drawing-room.

'I'm glad you're better. Terrible, the fever. Your mind races against it. You realize how your brain is trapped in your body. I once asked to be shot when I had it. I whimpered and begged to be killed. I often wonder now if I thought that my body would die and my mind live, and go free. Did you feel so?'

She had his drink waiting in Palmer's silver mug. The two easy chairs were side by side before the upstairs fireplace. She wore a blue velvet dress, a single gold bracelet on one arm, and her hair was down long.

'Something like that, I suppose. As though all the good in you is having a war with all the bad. And you are just watching it. But I didn't want to be shot, really. Whom did you want to shoot you, may I ask?' He found it hard to imagine her poised self wanting to die.

'My husband. I asked him, or rather begged him. On my knees before him, in this room. I was younger then. And unhappy, and overwhelmed by Jamaica. It was harder than I expected, and the fever unimaginable. And it runs riot in your mind, too, if you are sensitive. Chasms of fear, and then visions of sweet release, to let your mind lose of your tormenting body.'

'Lord, I'm glad he didn't kill you.'

'He did worse. But that was long ago.' She looked straight into his eyes, as though challenging him.

'Did what?' He felt himself flush, daring to ask, but met her eyes.

'Need I tell you?' She looked away, watching the fire through the glass.

'Only if you wish.' He had heard enough bad stories from London whores to wait her out. There was a mystery here, in this fine house, for him to discover in his own way, aside from Broderick and Wilson, and she wanted to talk.

'He took me, I believe the polite word is. Here on the floor. He said I wasn't ill, but needed that. I screamed, but he held me down. He was a powerful man, you see. Physically powerful. He said . . . he said he would take the fever out of me. He was of course drunk at the time.' She sipped at her drink and stared at him again, and then turned her head back to the fire.

'I'm sorry.' He felt the inadequacy of saying that, but then he felt she had laid a burden on him.

'Don't be absurd. He went beyond it. You are no child. I can tell you. I screamed here. Venus came. He made her stand and watch my humiliation. Told her I was mad and this would cure me.'

'God. She didn't help you?'

'It's death for a slave to turn on its master. And she wouldn't have turned in any event. The coloured women defer to their men, lazy and vicious, beastly as they may choose to be. They inhabit another world. Then at his bidding she helped him with the next step.'

'The next step?'

'Ah. We started with the fever, and I got off on a tangent. Sorry. I shall finish it for you. I suppose he envied Venus's loyalty to me, and saw a chance to humiliate me. He said I was truly mad, and perhaps I was at that minute. So he made her help him tie me to my bed. Tied my hands to the bedstead, covered me, and told her to tend and feed me. That lasted a week. I think it was a week. It could have been a year the way it felt. And that was *my* fever. A shade different from yours, eh?' She smiled and looked at him as though she stood a long way off down an eerie dark corridor of memory.

'And Venus never helped you?'

'She fed and washed me where I lay, but I never asked for release, knowing the conventions of her life. The man was master in the house, so long as he lived.'

'Yes. I understand that Mr. Palmer is . . .'

'Is dead, yes, and you well know I killed him, now, don't you?' One corner of her mouth turned up in a half grin.

Hearing of Palmer's cruelty, he had wanted to touch her hand, embrace her, do something to comfort her. But she looked past sadness and past ordinary comforting, her eyes uncannily bright with secret knowledge of suffering in her times, her very words a burden on him, he helpless to assuage grief past, but still present in the room. And then the mischievous grin, as though nothing could assail her. He retreated from the thought of comforting her. There was an odd solitary strength there that dampened his natural urge to do that. But then there was the confusing softness that had brought her down the hill to care for him. *What is it she wants from me?*

'Yes I do know.' He looked away as he said it.

'And who told you?'

'I don't remember.' His eyes studied the intricate design on the Persian carpet

'Of course you do. But no mind. Broderick, no doubt. Loves to tell the new men what a monster I am. Oh, I can just imagine it. Beware of the devil on the hill. I shall protect you from her. Am I right?' Her smile was disconcerting, almost girlish.

'I don't remember, really.' He was about to grin himself.

'Good. After all you do work for Broderick, and most of the time I must leave you to his mercies, which are far from tender.'

'Well, if you killed Mr. Palmer, you had good reason, I'd say. I . . . I should have been glad to kill him myself, from what you tell me.'

'Are you serious about that?'

'Of course.'

'Well, thank you. There are . . . others who wouldn't have done the same, I'm afraid. He had more friends, or, shall we say, companions, than I. Well, tell me, how do you get on with Broderick, and what do you think of him?' Her face looked sad now, and she seemed eager to drop the subject of the murder.

'We seem to get along. Seems a strong chap. Told me right off the first day to mind my P's and Q's and get the work out with no nonsense.'

'You like him?' She drank, looking at him over her glass. *Lord what eyes*, he thought, *and pretty hands*. He felt himself flush in the warm, comfortable room, something in her eyes, something teasingly bland but still coquettish, reaching out to him now.

'I suppose so.'

'A silly question. You don't have to, really. He's Irish. And as dumb and vicious as most of them. But I need him. I should say *we* need him. Your future depends on him as well. This is no time to be choosy about culture and manners, since this is a plantation, not a *salon*. He had you kill Scipio?'

'Yes.' He paused before answering, ashamed that his act started with another's will.

'Your first killing?' She was cool, bland again, idly curious, as though discussing biscuits or bolts of cloth.

'Yes.'

'And you feel badly about it?' She rang the little bronze bell beside her, for Venus.

'A bit strange, is all. I didn't expect . . .'

'Of course. They tell you so little back home. Natives dancing happily in the sun. Colourful plantations. Conversions to Christianity, depending on what you read. Come now, admit you feel badly.'

'Yes, all right. It's not—'

'Not the usual thing. But remember there may be worse to

come. Kill more if we have to. *Expect* the unusual here. Will you do that for me?'

'All right.'

'We have unique ways of defending ourselves here that aren't everyday occurrences on London's streets. No constable came to get you yet, did he?' She grinned again.

'No.'

'Nor will he. A good thing if you didn't weaken, and I gather you didn't. One of them means nothing, and the mill is central to our work. Your cutters can laze a bit, but you'll find they correct one another. A cutter who malingers in the field has a hard time with the rest of the gang. They may even kill him themselves. More or less let them set their own pace there, but push the driver. None of *them* want to go back swinging a cutlass, believe me. Well, so much for business, always dull at best. Are you happy?'

Venus padded in, took their glasses with stubby black fingers, sighed and eased away, padded slippers shuffling along the polished floors.

'I imagine so.'

The fire popped and she rose to drag away the screen and jab it with the poker, then reached in to hook a log in the back and drag it forward over the flaming coals.

'Good. A nice lie. You're miserable with this work, of course. But it must have its compensations. I imagine that Mary Lou is pleasure for you, eh?'

Venus reappeared, setting the drinks down. She too probed at the fire for a bit, and drifted away again.

'Yes.' The subject of Mary Lou embarrassed him. Oddly enough he could listen to anything in London whorehouses, but the living-room of a mansion seemed another place.

'Needn't be shy with me. She is all right, eh? The native girls are always good when a man's fresh out. I know *that* much. Eh?'

'Yes, good.' He wondered at her curiosity. *All curious about one another. For all her glory up here she's curious about a girl works for her and even went down to brand her. Poor black girl. Think she'd be happy here on the hill with everything. Possibly not. I should ask.* He saw a witty gleam in her eye as she savoured his shyness. He wondered at her age, and guessed perhaps thirty-eight to forty-one. The eyes deep, knowing. Something in him warmed to her again. *Cussed impertinent sending me for Jason. Take her on myself, and soon, somehow. They're all the same down there, and me as much a man as the rest. Woman has two mouths, my Dad once said, and one of them's a pleasure because it don't talk.*

'Well, have a time with all of them and don't be timid. A white man is a prize for them. You can put your seed about freely, and leave Jamaica with lots of pickneys to your credit, and no need to play house with their mothers. Nothing like the deadly life in Manchester where the boys are sneaking out for their ten shilling whore. Well, at least there's that, and you'll get to MoBay now and then. Things ease up after the crop's in and ground. Then we have the dead season while the cane grows itself for us, so your life will be a shade easier later on. Tell me, you're feeling better?'

'Much, thank you. But I wish you'd take away that lad who bathed me, if I'm to be here for a time. That's . . .'

'That's Jamaica. I know servants seem odd at first, but you'll come to enjoy it. Isn't it rather a comfort to be served?'

'A bit of an embarrassment. I take care of . . .'

'Yourself. Silly man. They're here to help, and there are so very many of them. I know it's awful at first, absolutely awful. But you'll get used to us. We seem to produce only two extremes in England . . . the boors fresh out on their first plantation who surround themselves with servants to bolster up their foolish egos, and the poor meek ones who will never get over doing things for themselves, and even feel guilty about being served, and fear for their privacy. Well, I can see you'll never be very demanding but don't be meek. And forget your privacy. This is a new world and a very open one, and can be really pleasant. Even on your small wages you can live, relatively speaking, like a rich man, even though the work is a bore. Do you see that?'

'Yes, I can see that. Don't see a future really, but it's not all that bad now. As you said, Mary Lou, all that. Must say the bath felt good and the lunch too. Must say, I never had so good a lunch in London.' He looked away towards the fire, remembering his poor days as a clerk, a bit of bread and sausage and sometimes a warm pint in a corner of the shipping room his lunch then, perhaps a bit of beef and a pint or two his dinner; always a little hungry, resenting the hunger but oddly resenting, now, the blandishments of good rum and dinner to come and a woman providing his comfort in her great house for a purpose unknown to him. He felt kept.

'Future? You will find that. Don't fret about it now. Learn the workings of the plantation, and in time you'll be more useful, either here or elsewhere. You're free to go when your contract ends—become an overseer yourself one day, or buy your own land, or open a shop in the town. The vistas will open gradually, and you are young.'

'I suppose so.'

'Oh, believe so. Broderick started at the bottom here. And from prison at that. Now he has more amenities than he could have dreamed of in Ireland, and may go further someday, although he has his limits.'

'Limits?'

'Well, a good barbarian of limited education and aims. You could probably go further and lead a fuller life.'

'Really? Why do you think so?' Her charm was reaching out to him. Any ambitions seemed impossible in the face of the superiority and strength of Broderick.

'Because you think and feel. He just thinks and acts. Thank God he does, but he has no second thoughts and virtually no feelings about what he does. Simple action without reflection has its limits.'

'I'm sorry I don't understand what you mean by limits.'

'Limits, like the property limits. As far as one is able to go. Broderick's . . . soul, if we must use that word, includes just so much, feels just so much. Well, for example, there's some hope for you if you regret killing Scipio.' Her look was calm and challenging. He disliked her for being forced to ask the next question.

'I'm sorry, I thought you said killing Scipio was a good thing, that I shouldn't regret it.'

'You shouldn't, in terms of the current situation. We do really live on a razor's edge, in rather delicate balance, and have to hold our power over the black man. You did your special duty, and did it well at that instant. You fired quickly and without thought or feeling. Which is good. But the feeling, later, is important. Your regret, I mean. That's your human quality, isn't it? Perfectly natural. Hopeful. Positive might be the word. Man doesn't really want to kill.'

'But you said it was good. You said . . .'

'For that second in time. But we can't go around just butchering one another, can we? You killing me, or I you?'

'I hope not.'

'Exactly. But to Broderick it's something else. He . . . he does it in cold blood. Lives without memory or reflection. Lives without any love at all. Or even compassion. He's pure act—like a butcher. Surely you see that?'

'Yes of course. But you . . .' He cut himself short, afraid to press the point.

'I what? Be frank. We're quite alone and it's good to talk. I have no sympathy with people who are afraid to talk. And nothing you can say will affect your contract—and of course you can't fall lower than book-keeper. You can only go up from here.'

'Well, you agree with Broderick. I can't understand why a lady like you employs a butcher, really. I think of you . . .'

'Ah, how do you think of me?' She smiled a tiny smile and cocked her head to one side, her long hair dark, burnished in the fire glow. He felt himself flush and looked away, up to a painting of an old, stern-faced Palmer on the wall.

'Well, as a lovely woman . . . a gentle woman, surely, but . . .'

'Ah, but. Good. But a harridan who rushes into your field swinging a whip. Not the lady in velvet you see before you tonight, her nails polished and no boots on her ankles?'

'Quite.' He had to laugh, and without realizing it got up and paced before the fire, head down, at once amused and embarrassed.

'And of course you've heard all the other stories. How I slew John. I hit him with a brass candlestick, for your information. And you know about my chamber downstairs, and of *course* you've seen my initials up on Mary Lou's little black thigh, or is she more modest these days?'

'Ah yes, I saw that.' He squatted and then sat, tailor fashion, on the stones beside the fireplace, swinging his rum cup in slow circles, watching the rum swirling in it.

'What are you doing on the floor? Don't you like my expensive chair? That came all the way from . . .'

'I like it here. You said I could talk freely, so I can sit the same way. My father worked this way. It's really very comfortable.'

'You look like a pre-historic man. Well, to go on. I need a butcher to protect me, to protect us. Somebody decisive. You'd try, I suppose, reasoning with a nigger like Scipio, and come out on the short end of it. Everything would be peaceful for a time, and they'd smile at you, and next thing you know there'd be another rock dropped in the mill and the whole thing would go to pieces in stages. It's all right to be gentle, but we really need the butchers to protect us. You're honest enough to admit that, now aren't you? Doesn't Broderick give you food for thought? Really? It *wouldn't* make you less of a man to admit it, I can assure you.'

'I admit it. But I don't understand it.'

'You haven't seen enough of it yet. This is a new world for you. Come and cook us in our beds some night if we're not damned stern with them. And as for me, I'll have a man when I want him, and not be raped by any smelly hand has a mind to burst into my house. Oh, I want the old days too. We had a nice town house and I was brought up with all the little amenities, but we all trusted one another and didn't have a third of a million niggers around. So I really need a butcher to keep them under control. Odd, you new men often have a bad reaction. I did too at first, but it was almost too far back to remember.'

He watched her stare into the fire, memory of better times crossing her face, a softness there, a good life she had known, perhaps missed.

'But we didn't talk about you,' he said, and held his gaze until she looked directly at him.

'Me?'

'You. With the whip in my field.'

'Oh. Me. Yes, well. It depends, doesn't it, on what you think a woman should be. You've only seen women ride side-saddle, so I look queer to you right off, don't I?'

'I'll admit that.'

'Well of course you're mad. It's all convention, foolish convention. I shouldn't think it foolish if you wore a kilt, and a sporran should I?'

'I suppose not.'

'So, convention is one thing. And there's the other convention —what you should think woman's role is.'

'I suppose you're right.'

'Well, what do you think it is?'

'I don't rightly know. The home, the family. My mum . . .'

'Your mum. Surely. The stove, the needle. Iron your shirts, get you off to school and chatter over the teacups. That peculiar wasteland, woman's lot for centuries. The miasma of the daily doings, the daily gossip. No chance for real education. That privilege reserved for man, who is allegedly superior. By virtue of what, God knows. That implement you have between your legs, I presume.

Well, not for me. Without even realizing it, I left England to escape that. My father had his profession, my mother the usual tedium. I suppose I was fortunate to find . . . to find my profession here. You'd be surprised at how content I am to be Rose Hall's mistress. Is that a mystery to you?'

'Well, yes. But as you say it's not what I've been trained to except. You're rather a novelty to me you know.'

'Well, thank you for admitting that.'

'And I think you're rather a splendid bit of a woman.'

'Well, thank you. You're quite gallant.' She smiled and her eyes softened.

'But I really don't understand you.'

'Oh. I don't really expect you to. And you don't have to. Only I have to understand me. But what is it you don't grasp?'

'Well, as you say, you're a bit rough. Rather a shock to see you rush into my field on a horse, and then . . .'

'And then?'

'Lashing that man like that. Making him run and attacking him from a horse.'

'You find that unnecessarily vicious?'

'It's not something I would want to do. Perhaps not fair. Not a man's thing, I'd say.'

'Well, it's not a case of *wanting*, really, but of *having* to. Perhaps you're too gentle, still, to grasp that.'

'I don't think anybody could really explain that to me. I'm sorry, but that's the way I see it.'

'I can explain it. I have a purpose. Most of what I do is purposeful.'

'And what's the purpose?'

'Rose Hall, and with it and beyond it the land. I inherited both, and will preserve them, while I live.'

'Yes but how preserve them with . . . violence?'

'Oh, I've had time to consider that. If you are capable of love, then you are equally capable of hate. Thus you can kill for love, depending on how great your love is. Now I'm a woman alone, but my love is very great, and not for any individual but the land as a whole and this plantation in particular. Perhaps an odd form of communion for you, but something I understand. You, on the other hand, couldn't love Jamaica that much, so soon, and may never do so at all. But it is not demanded of you to love her. If you should find it in yourself someday, you'll understand what I mean. Otherwise, you never will. Now, Broderick is another thing. He kills neither for love nor for being ordered to do so, but in simple cold blood, because if he loves anything it is power alone. You see that?'

She arose as she talked and paced in front of him, under the family portraits. He enjoyed smelling the good cologne on her, hearing the soft rustle of her clothing, and getting glimpses of her slim ankles. Unaccountably, she aroused him, and he wondered how he could ever approach her. He thought again of his trip for Jason and smarted at the scorching memory of it. At least she was more pleasant this night.

'That doesn't really explain you.' He looked up at her as she passed before him.

'A rage for order, and a love of this land. I love in the abstract. I can love a meadow, a thousand acres of cane rustling in the wind, the rain that helps feed the land, love the good handhewn beams in this house, and would have it stand forever, if possible. Can you grasp that?'

'Not very easily. Why can't you just tell people—the niggers —tell them that instead of beating them in your underground room?'

'Ah, my young man, I could talk until the pyramids crumbled and they would say they saw it and go right on trying to erode it, like so many termites gnawing at it. So my defence is action. I really do it almost unthinkingly at times. If I have to lay fear upon them to get their respect, if I have to act it out to let them know this house is a power and not a myth, then that is my way. After that, someday, they might find their own love, their own self-respect, find their own version of a rage for order. And when they do, Jamaica will be the better for it. That is really as much as I can tell you.'

'What about Mary Lou?' He said it very softly, feeling that he risked her anger, ready for any answer at all. Her eyes widened and she glared at him and through him, holding off her answer or perhaps seeking it, he couldn't determine. Then she grinned, and paced back and forth again.

'Well, I'm a woman. And a passionate one. I can't deny that. She was the child of one of his nigger wenches, and then he took her, too, when she reached her teens. I thought that too much, really. I wanted her . . . to remember me, shall we say. I think she does, eh?' She turned from under one of the old portraits and grinned at him. He had to smile back and their glances joined as though sharing the happy secret that Mary Lou got what she deserved. He started to get up from the floor, and she extended a hand and pulled him up. He held on to the hand. She made no move to withdraw it.

'I see. Well, I think I know you better now. And I think you . . . I think you a wonderful woman. I wouldn't have . . . I mean . . .'

'Ah, caught yourself up. Thought me a trollop and quite mad, eh? You've heard the stories. Well, I am a good bit of both. But I do think now and again. I hope you do too. You have a life to live and might try to find some purpose in it.' She squeezed his hand lightly, then tried to withdraw hers. He held it.

'I do now. At least more than before. I suppose we are part of something . . . of something larger. Dad used to say something about that, about service. When, when I left for London he asked me to please visit Westminster Abbey. He'd been there once as a lad. And so I did. Makes you feel strange, it does. Those names you read in books. William and Harry and Nelson and so on. Men you'd like to have been with. Out there for us, and some of them dead a long time, but still there, all together in one place. I thought a funny thing there. Thought of my dad and wished he was coming to Jamaica with me instead of on his knees putting pins into ladies dresses. Thought how glad I was to be away from that to find something better here.'

'Of course. Better for you and for the world, which is eternally ready to be opened up and opened again. And in that sense you are with all those famous men—Harry and William and Nelson and so on. Going forth, instead of sitting in Manchester repeating your father's life. That is the best of us, the going forth. *Living*. That is how we come to advance, and as I said, dominate. Let the rest whine, and try to teach them not to even if it leads to violence. We have that rage for order, order on your own terms, and we need such as you, James Arthur. And now for dinner, eh?'

'May I ask you something first?' He kept hold of her hand, cradling it gently, respectful but warm, and knowing that he wanted to go further with her lean, nervous body.

'And what is that?' Her eyes remained tranquil, ready for any question, ready for more answers than he could imagine questions for.

'If you believe in going out to the world, as you say, why do you stay here—so alone, instead of getting into what is going on out there? Why keep so to yourself?'

'Ah, a natural question. A proper challenge from a bright young man. Strangely enough I have thought that out too. I am, you see, infamous. The mad Mrs. Palmer, murderous and a trollop, to use the proper term. A bit much for them. For the ladies, the embodiment of their hidden dreams. They say they prefer tea parties and flowered dresses and the domination of their boyish husbands to . . . to reality. To flesh. To genuine hatred, genuine love. Prefer well-oiled furniture to the sunrise, choose the testy little security of their well-ordered drawing-rooms over and above what to me is the joy of controlling a good-spirited horse on a ride through Music Valley or up through the hills or keeping a nigger at his proper work for the land. And so I am a strange sort of threat to them, thus hardly their friend . . . And the men. For them I am always a gossip. They demean me as a cold trollop, but wonder what I am like in bed. They rush about trying to be men, but acting like hysterical ninnies, earnestly proving their strength, which is not strength, toting their weapons, which are more like weapons against themselves, thus a form of suicide, which will not solve Jamaica, in our time. But this you shall see for yourself and perhaps see why I don't need them. I should like you to travel for me, soon, on business, to Montego Bay. Would you be willing to do that?'

'Delighted. But Broderick, he'd resent that. I want no trouble with him.' He held back a smile. *Ah, one up on the brute. Me she wants for a change, and a chance to get off this place for a bit. See it out there, and get away from the every day muck of it.* He envisioned the road, the good coastline, the towns along the way, the sight of ships on the sea, the salt-scent of the harbour at Montego Bay and a few drinks in one of the town pubs with his fellow-emigrés, to hear news of the other plantations.

'I shall handle Broderick. And now if you will let go my hand, we can go to dinner.'

He felt himself blush. He had been holding her hand tightly without realizing it. She squeezed his before letting go, then drew her fingers slowly across the palm and his wrist.

'You have a good strong man's hand, very solid in the bone but with good fingers, not stubby ones, and a nice square wrist. Let me see the palm.' She took his hand with all her delicate fingers and turned it over. 'My mother taught me. She always said

Dad was a fool with his medicines, that man's fate and his will, joined with his disposition, made him ill or well, up or down, content or forever in anguish. That a bad heart brought about the gout, an ill temper gave birth to bad eyesight and a stiff back came from too much ambition. We shall see about you.'

'Good. See shall I be governor of Jamaica one day, or inhabit a fine great house, or give it all up and be a humble tailor in London.'

'Ah, none of those, probably. A long life, a good long and a lovely one because you have a heart, a very full one. You want to love, and shall do so. You want to go forth and forth and will go on, even far from here, not for gain but for love of the world and of going on, discovering, shaping, losing fear as you go. Losing fear and finding and in turn making world within world. A very good hand, honest and brave and death has no dominion in it. You shall be an old codger, full of tales, weaving tales like a tailor, and I shall be just one of your tales when you are old and I am gone, and the century turns and you are in New Zealand or Australia or perhaps America.'

She kneaded his palm gently, felt the length of his fingers, gripped his thumb, and looked at him with excitement in her eyes, as though she wanted the future she said he might have. The fire crackled and a shower of sparks rose with a soft whoosh and a red glare.

'A grand oracle you are. Meanwhile I shall be lucky to get as far as MoBay without taking more fever or being eaten by runaways.'

'You shall have no problems. By the way, do you ride?'

'Lord no. I was a city child. The only horse I knew was under King George in a statue in the park.'

'Fine, I shall teach you this week and you can go to town a proper gentleman and representative of our fief. And now, sir, to dinner.' She led him to the downstairs dining-room, a massive oak-panelled rectangle with good silver on the sideboards and stacks of fragile china in polished cabinets, handsome oil portraits on the walls, Two candles in crystal windscreens lit the table.

'The head for you, of course, and I shall sit beside you sir.' She curtsied with a slight gay toss of her head.

'Ah no, please, this is your home. Sit here.'

'And you, tonight, the man of the house. Now take your proper place.'

He did as he was told.

16

VENUS HAD done a rich turtle soup and there was a bottle of sherry for it. Then there was a sole, broiled with herbs, and a salad, and a salisbury steak, served with greens and yams and tiny onions. There was a wine for the partridge and he opened it with a horn-handled corkscrew, his first try at opening a wine bottle. He split the cork the first time but went after it again and it came out with a soft pop. She taught him to spill a little off the top 'for the gods, or the earth, I forget which. They do it in Italy I am told,' and they had a good supper, ending with fresh blueberries and tea.

At dinner she talked of her early days in England and Jamaica —of her father and his patients, of her affable, mystic mother who preferred palms to the stethoscope for listening to people, of her trip over to Jamaica, of her first experience with a staff of blacks. *Gracious, the first time the maid came in, came in to dress me of all things. I tell you I was really abashed. But there is no privacy here. It all flows back and forth as though life in the private sense we know it were nothing. They are witnesses to everything to the point where you can't tell yourself from them. They're like . . . like your shadows in a way, and just as speechless as shadows but you know they know your every move. You either go mad to begin with or you learn to live with it. And then the casual surprises. The day I had my first party after our marriage and they came with four goats for currying. The warm, quartered, bloodied bodies of four baby goats laid out proudly for my inspection on the kitchen floor! And they pinching the meat about the ribs and telling me how good the animals were. I merely fainted, then vomited for an hour.* . . . She laughed, recalling those early days, and told him more, a genial raconteur with a history he enjoyed. Then she questioned him about his home, his parents, his work in England, his hopes for the future. She never mentioned his replacing Broderick, but suggested other alternatives in Jamaica : a civil post, a small plantation of his own, work with a Montego Bay or Kingston merchant, when his contract with her was done.

'You make me feel a fool for just coming out, not a thought in my head about tomorrow . . . a fool I am, I imagine,' he said to her over the tea. He stared at one of the candle flames, lower in the crystal windscreen, blackening it with smoke.

'Ah no. Coming out was enough for now. A true man finds his life as he goes out to it. It surprises him. He meets part of his destiny at each turn in the road, and knows it for truth or falsehood, because it strikes a chord in him, and an answer comes out of his throat, out of his heart. People who can predict their tomorrows are relatively useless, Arthur, and dull. Be content with yourself and with your searching, and you shall live well.'

'Easy to say. But I'm only a tradesman's son and at that only half my dad. And left him alone—and Mum—with no one to pass on the craft to except some stranger apprentice. Not sure I did right. Strange it is to be standing by a man with a whip behind a line of black wretches in a field out here. Feel less a man, I do, for not carrying on with Dad. He has . . . he has something steady, you could say, a place in the town. Solid work. Mum, and the little house, and me they raised. Not right of me to run, and with nothing my own. Just out to see the world. Nobody's prize.'

'Ah, you dear fool. Everybody's prize. Forget Dad and the town and the trade. At Westminster you wished he were with you, didn't you?' She leaned eagerly across the table and reached out to grasp his wrist.

'Yes, but a moment of . . . of emotion. That is for the holy one and warriors and poets and I am none of those. Just a runaway tailor's son out of Manchester with no better idea than to sail away. My dad . . .'

'Pray for your dad, and pity him. Pray that he gets as far as Westminster again before he dies. He sent you there for a reason. There is something there that he could never even try to achieve, and in his heart he hopes you will try, in your way. And in that way you will serve him better than buying buttons and carrying pins for him. And above all keep sailing away, when the time comes. And it will come and come again and each time you say no you will die a little. Tell me do you remember your history? Of the sailors. The very early ones, and what they thought of the earth's shape.'

'Yes. They thought it flat. Thought they'd sail right off the very edge of it they did. Scared they must have been, thinking it'd happen some night.'

'Right. And then one went forth and found it round. Never ending. Around and around, the horizon always there, the sun always there, rising, each day over an endless circle.'

'Yes.' He looked at her as she waved her hands, one hand three times in the air in a circle, like a bandmaster calling for volume from the trumpets.

'And you too. You saw that. The vanishing and ever-reappearing horizon, appearing even as it vanished, appearance and disappearance all one thing at one time and you not even aware of the curve of the sea but thinking it flat beneath you . . . thinking in one world but actually living in another.'

'Yes.' He had lost the words and was following her mouth and her eyes, wide, dreaming, out on the wide waters and not really on his face.

'You follow me?'

'No. I lost your words. You are a schooled woman and I am a simple . . .'

'Simple man, and this is simple. Round. Flat. You see flat. On the sea? Say yes.'

'Yes.'

'But live in the round—because you know it all to be round.'

'Yes.'

'And that is it. Flat. Round. One and the other. Two worlds. Two worlds that are really one world. Because the world is, as you already know, round. Whole. Complete.'

'Yes.' He saw it, looking into her eyes, which were focused straight on his now but not really looking at him, rather seeming to look deep within herself. He saw it as a picture—a circle, bisected by a line, as though he were looking through a telescope with a hairline across it.

'And so you need never fear again, or dwell in regret looking back towards your father—your father is not back there, but out ahead of you. If the world is round so is everything in it—everything returning always to its place of starting. And so you shall meet your father by going forward, which is the easiest path to him. Quickly now, do you see that? Do you feel it?' Her voice was urgent, but she spoke in a near whisper.

'Yes I do. I really do . . .' He had stopped thinking and his mind saw oceans and continents and the slow dawns, slow sunsets, at opposite ends of the ocean.

'You . . . you think a lot, Mrs. Palmer. I . . .'

'Call me Annie if you will. And no, I do not think. I only try to feel what the world has to teach and wants me to know, and have spent much time doing it these long years. The kingdom of heaven, they say, is within you. A most interesting line, for example. Because in heaven fear is unimaginable. And so is sustained hate. And so is finitude, hence pettiness and selfishness, because heaven is infinite—at least so we suppose. And if that is within us, there is more within us than we can know. That thought, simple as it may sound, tends to keep me alive.'

Whatever she meant, he thought, it saved her from her private demons. In the candlelight she had the air of a wraith—a vital intelligent woman full of life, full of fury but withal a wraith, death there. A tremulous balance she seemed, like the flame.

She lifted the crystal windscreen, blew out the candle, took his hand and led him back upstairs through the quiet, semi-dark mansion.

Venus brought the deaf-mute to the drawing-room. He was dressed in dark blue sailor trousers and a neat white shirt. His woolly head was big and round and his eyes too. He ran to Annie and scrambled into her lap. His fingers played with her face, then her hair, and then squeezed her smallish breasts, while she laughed and cooed at him, stroked his head and cheeks, and gave him little pinches.

'Demon, demon. All energy tonight. A fine day you must've had. Venus, what did he do today?'

'Him play wid dem fowl a lot today, Miz Palmer, a chase an' chase dem, and den ah lets him hep me cotch one for mah suppah, ma'am, and carry him to de kitchen. But him don go to de kitchen fas. Walk roun and roun wid dat red chicken get to lak him in time, an' no fight him. But den I haf to kill de chicken . . .'

'He didn't see, did he, you didn't let him . . .' Her eyes were stern.

'No, ma'am, lak you tol me nevah let him a-see no killin'. I even sen' him out behin' de garden wall so he don't heah nothin' also, ma'am. Sho him to pluck me some flowahs. Den latuh him jumpin 'an' jumpin' beside de donkey out back til I give him a ride an' he lak dat too, and den he play by hisself fo de afternoon wid de gardener's lil girl, runnin' an jumpin' and and a-hidin' in de bushes lak dey was runaways. Sech a time him have today. . . .' Venus grinned and kneaded her hands happily over her expansive belly.

'Good, Venus. I shall bring him to you shortly.'

'Yassum.'

She played with the boy for a few minutes as Arthur sat silently, sensing that she wanted that. She was totally absorbed. Her eyes glowed, she smiled and laughed and cooed at the youngster. Arthur wondered about the boy's silence, but waited. Then Annie made a sign at him, as though describing a round object in mid-air with her hands. He scrambled off her lap and dashed across the drawing-room to a cabinet, opened it and produced a red ball, threw it, pursued it, threw it again and did the same, as she watched.

'Arthur.' She spoke while looking at the child.

'Yes, Annie.'

'Arthur he is deaf and dumb. He was terrified at first but is much better now. He realizes you're here but may not show it for a bit. Just let him come to you if he wants to. If not don't be concerned about it. He . . . he has had some bad times.

'Certainly.'

He watched them play, she bouncing the ball for the lad, high up over his head, so he could catch it when it re-entered the range of his grasp. Or she rolled it, or spun it across the floor in crazy circles, he skipping after it like a dancer, then pouncing on it in silent glee. Finally she rolled it towards Arthur, and it stuck under his chair. The child advanced, then paused and watched him, his eyes still and serious, an oblong black-lacquered table between them. Arthur forced a smile, hoping it seemed real. He picked up the ball and held it. The boy brought up his right hand to his

· 173 ·

forehead, rubbing it with his fingertips, as though remembering something, or looking as though he were saluting. Arthur bounced the ball gently on a diagonal, and the boy came out and around the table to fetch it. After a second's hesitation and another glance from his eloquent eyes, he threw it back. And so they played for some minutes, until Annie said it was time for him to be off to bed. She fondled him again, then put him on his feet.

'See now if he will do something. I have taught him to shake hands. I shall bring him to you. Just put out your hand and see.'

He came across the room. Arthur stood and slowly extended his hand. The boy observed it gravely, then looked up to his face, and back to the hand, and put his in it. Arthur closed his around it gently and bowed a bit, and the boy did the same, and they let go of one another at the same instant. He went gravely and man-fully off with Annie to seek out Venus.

Arthur walked by the fireplace. Whatever stirred in him as he looked down into the fire made him want to weep. He didn't know why, except that the deaf-mute had accepted him into a world of Annie Palmer, and beyond that he himself had been taken up out of the fields and saw another world, one that frightened and confused him but one that he wanted to mend for her, for Annie Palmer, and not himself. She felt too much. She knew too much. She had been hurt too much.

She re-entered the room, carrying brandy and two glasses. 'A nightcap, eh, to celebrate your triumph with him, and then we can retire?' She poured, and they touched glasses and drank. 'A good fellow you must be. You are the only man he has taken to since John . . . died.'

'He's not yours is he?' He smiled, risking the jest.

'Ha. Impertinence. You probably think I have a horde of picka-ninnies about, because that black tramp whose brand you have fingered so often is a Palmer. No, no such bad luck, bad as I am, or have been.' She laughed and poured them more brandy.

'Just a lad you adopted then? Appealing, he is. A live one.'

'Yes and a joy to me in little ways. Neither speaks nor hears evil. He sees and feels, and now takes joy in everything. A wild flower, a horse, the sun, a sudden companion like the red chicken today, that Venus told us about. It must go strangely deep with him be-cause he cannot babble it away, or hear about something in ad-vance of trying or seeing it. So everything is immediate and new and now that his rages are almost done he is a storehouse of beauty. Do I sound foolish?'

'No you sound beautiful . . . as beautiful as you are . . . looking after that tot, and everything else you are.'

'Ah, enough of that now. To bed with you, and your first riding lesson very early in the morning. Your fever is quite gone?' She felt his face, then his neck, with the back of her hand, then thrust her hand into his shirt.

'Quite sound now, Annie.' He was ready to reach out, to touch her, to kiss her, but sensed the price.

'Good. Then get off with you. You know your way back?'

'I do. Good night and thank you.' He walked off quietly as the last of the fire crackled and sputtered. Venus had left small lamps lit all along his way, and in his room.

She came after he was in bed less than half an hour, his brain alive with her, with the estate, with odd snatches of all she had said, sleep impossible, something new stirring in him. There were four taps on the door, it opened immediately, and she entered. She wore a white nightgown, and carried a single candle which she blew out as she set it down. She slipped into the deep bed. They kissed wordlessly. She seemed to delight in him, and had more imagination than he had yet known in a woman. She soon had him warm, as though the fever had come again, and he moaned a little, wanting to get at her, as though to vanquish her, as though his body could bring peace to her fevered mind.

She spoke only once, to hold back his urgency. She introduced him into the deep subtle mazes of her experience, and he was glad she did it slowly.

She lit and carried the candle as she left the bed later and kissing him said, '*Don't* forget, riding tomorrow . . . early, my Manchester *bull*,' and in leaving left the strong traces of her scent on the pillow, for him to nuzzle, sleep delayed a while while he remembered and missed the smooth curve of loin, the shock of her small pointed breasts against his lean ribs, the fullness and softness of her hair which she had swept over the full length of him. He wondered why she had left, and then appreciated it, anticipating the next day, and fell away dreaming of that.

Annie plaited her hair for the next day's riding, watching herself in the mirror before the dressing table. Then she stroked herself with a preparation Venus provided that came, Venus said, from the nests of honeybees, and was important for love, and preserved one for almost forever. Usually Venus laid it on her, rubbing it in well, casual and impersonal about vigorously stroking every inch of her. This night she did it alone, like a sorceress taking secret enjoyment in the process. Then she went to the drawing-room for a glass of sherry and tucked herself in bed with it, arranging her mosquito net around her. She smiled and whispered to herself: *A good young one. Fresh out and innocent and perhaps a man. Or so it seems. If I could teach him enough.*

17

'YOU HEAR it now?' She was just ahead of him and turned in her saddle to face him.

'Yes. What a beautiful sound. As though the earth were whispering, I suppose you could say.' The waterfall was ahead of them, unseen, in the forest. It kept up a steady sound, like uninterrupted rain, no variance in its rhythm or tone, not a keening but a high-pitched *sheesh*, almost unnerving because of the continuity of it. Around them the forest was still, slim pines and mahogany trees intermingling, long vines carrying on motionless, relentless warfare against the larger trees, eating their way up and through their unsuspecting hosts.

'Are you tired? We've come a long way, and have some miles to go. Shall we return now, or go on?'

'No. No. Let's go on.'

'But not yet to the waterfall,' she said.

It was his sixth day of riding lessons and he had learned quickly, not wanting to be outdone by a woman, regardless of the pain involved. He had learned to sit a horse only at the price of fear. The height of it was a fright to begin with. Then it had a will of its own, bobbing its potent neck, changing its gait suddenly before he learned to control it, or learned to accept the idea that the monstrous mass of muscle-lined flesh wanted his lean, impalpable self to give it direction and purpose.

She had explained that, patiently but forcefully. *For all its size, it is just a dumb animal, nothing without you. Be firm with the reins, but not too firm. Hold the body with your knees. They are quite crucial. Use your spurs. Judiciously, but use them. And ride with it. Give it its head, when it wants it. Once it becomes well aware of you it can be trusted, to a degree, knowing you will respond. Think of a horse as part of yourself, and you will not go too far wrong. And lastly, watch your head. There is always a branch waiting, if you are inattentive.* He quenched his fear gradually and always denied his aches and pains at day's end although she recognized them, sending the little kitchen boy with pitchers of hot water to bathe him every evening, and Venus to follow him with a vigorous rubdown that seemed to search out every muscle and bone he owned, bringing his body a peace he had never known.

That week he dined with Annie only once again, and she explained his mission to Carruthers—to raise funds to buy new machinery, but more importantly to buy cod, rice and gingham to feed and clothe the slaves until the crop was sold, and perhaps later, because the crop had been smaller than usual and sugar prices were depressed. *I rely on you,* she said, *to convince him that we should go on, and not be sold out to absentee fools from abroad, who know nothing of Jamaica. I rely on whatever feeling you may have for this place, against his pounds, shillings and pence mind. Best, really, he were eliminated. But the bankers and the London money markets rely on the advice of these walking corpses.*

He heard her out, eager to get off the plantation but fearful of going to Carruthers as her emissary, unable to imagine himself facing the flinty old man. But he held back his fear of that, and of Broderick too, merely waiting for the time when the overseer would have a go at him for living in the great house, and then for becoming her messenger. He left it to her to make the arrangements with Broderick.

When they were not riding over the hills and valleys she left him alone. She said the lower part of the house was his to enjoy. He had a drawing-room and a library and a fire of his own and Venus to make his dinner and bring him drinks. He dined early each evening, and retired early. He was tempted to go down and visit Wilson (he did not dare invite him up) but feared meeting Broderick. On his second night in the house, he slept alone. On the third night he dined with Annie Palmer again, and that night and every succeeding night she came to him, shortly after he had retired, and silently and with a quiet studied fierceness made love to him. She seemed eager for his flesh and eager for him to want hers with equal ferocity but always worked and worked to contain him, slow him down, hold him interminably on the brink of his accomplishment, lead him on and on until it seemed his entire body was poised to give itself to her, becoming at the last one quivering, trembling thing, not just one part of him going to her but all of him drained, sucked out, wrenched in a beautiful way that dazed him so that he felt given over as though to the ocean or the winds, drawn away and out of himself.

When they were done she disappeared from the room as quietly as she had come, relighting the candle to take with her, slim and lovely in her white gown, her loose hair like a dark veil down her back. He always wanted her to stay, but never said so, sensing her need to go off alone and perhaps just consider him, her privacy a cocoon.

Some nights he rose alone after she left, to sit before the embers of the drawing-room fire or examine his part of the house, scanning her books, largely unread and in which he himself had little interest, or just enjoying the vastness of the panelled, comfortable high-ceilinged room, which was at least forty feet long and almost as wide. Out beyond it, on the terrace at the top of the steps, he could enjoy the depth and breadth of the deep Jamaican night, look down over half a mile of moonlit sugar to the shining sea, hear the frolicsome chattering of palm fronds in the night breeze, enjoy the strange patterings of the speechless tars.

From the steps he could look down the wide gravel path up which he had come the first day, and see the configurations of the massive gate where Broderick had confronted him. He could see a lamp in Broderick's house and sometimes the shadow of the overseer crossing a window or looming on a wall. From Wilson's house came soft fire glow. He seemed to want to be reminded of England. The sight of it roused memories in Arthur too. The fire was like a beacon in the otherwise stark blackness of the Jamaican night, alleviated only by the generalized glow from the area of the slaves' wattle huts and the subtle etching of the moonlight playing on sugar and sea outlining the far dark hills visible to the east.

One night on the terrace he had heard the low whinny of her

horse from the back of the house. Stepping into the shadow of the doorway, he saw her gallop down the gravel drive, seemingly heading for Broderick's house but then veering west and rushing into the night, the horse crashing through brush and appearing just once on a rise that had been stripped of cane that week, silhouetting itself and her against the moonlight sky as she sat for long minutes looking down over the slopes to the sea, then back to Rose Hall.

Within half an hour he heard a man screaming, short and pleading, then whimpering, in the night, and half an hour after that a woman sobbing and screaming from the east quarter, near the slave huts. The voice was unmistakably Mary Lou's. Arthur stood paralysed, bracing himself against the door, aware of the folly of interference, torn by Mary Lou's screams, confounded by whatever drove Annie to wreak vengeance on the girl. He moved back within the house, to wait, looking out of a slit between the draped front windows. She galloped up the drive, sitting erect on the horse, and then reined it to sit and contemplate the house, staring at the door where he had been minutes before. Her hair pinned up. She wore a brown shirt and black trousers. She stared at the door as though waiting for someone to come through it . . . as though sensing his presence and waiting for him.

Over her, the palm branches rustled, behind her the sea shone, around her the land lay like a dark green cloak. In one hand was a coiled whip. She stared at the door for long minutes then rode on around the house. He heard her come in the back door and go up to her room and drop her boots and then there was silence.

He sat before the last of the fire nestled between the highly polished andirons, and after his third rum smiled. *Mad bitch. Jealous of me and so went for Mary Lou. Branded her again or let her have it with the whip.* His mind's eye saw the little negress, her naked bottom squirming under Annie's lash, her eyes wild, her voice making too much of it, her Negro soul loving the drama of it. *For me. Annie did it for me and wanted me to hear it and knows, most likely, that I did. Might even know I was standing behind the door watching her. Damnation if she isn't a firebrand. A ceremony with her whip so I can hear it. Like to go up there now and take her in her fancy room and all.*

They approached the waterfall through quiet green avenues of tall, lacy bamboo, clusters of blood-red hibiscus and occasional long-leaved banana plants, heavy with their green fruit growing in improbably huge bunches.

The sound of the water grew louder and louder, an escalated surging sound, mysterious, continuous. It seemed as though they were approaching a place where the earth sighed. They came upon it through a last magnificent cluster of bamboo.

'And so this it it,' she said, reigning in her horse at the cataract's edge. 'Perhaps Jamaica's most wondrous natural thing. It flows a long way down. We are about half-way up. I come here because the native women do their wash and their bathing down below. Do you like it, eh?'

'God.' He contemplated it, the water rushing around them in a thousand thousand rivulets that were like the earth's gleaming veins.

'It *is* remarkable to see and hear,' she said. 'I find it hypnotizing and full of the wild power of the earth. I think it was Heraclitus who wrote that the universe is not still, but that everything in it flows, is in a state of perpetual flux. And this is like that. This is part of earth's story. The rain nourishes the earth, flows down the streams, gathers here in this torrent which returns it to the sea. And as you said, God. There is probably a god here for the blacks. They see a god everywhere, not one, but many and this one among many. They find gods in and on the earth, and not like those insane ministers who preach the unearthly unseen god. Let's walk into it, shall we. It's such a warm day and it is so nice in there, with it swirling about you.'

'Yes, yes. It must be good.' He gazed at the rushing, shining water, throwing up a delicate haze of spray through which the sunlight shot to make evanescent rainbows that came and vanished with the movement of the bamboo fonds overhead.

'It is good. Come now, shall you undress me or must I do for myself?' She unpinned her hair, letting it spill down her back, and sat on a rock, extending one booted leg and smiling at him. He took off her boots and then she stood and he undid her riding pants.

'Why do you wear these? I never saw a woman ride in anything but a skirt, from the Queen and ladies on down. It still seems an odd thing, you'll permit me saying so.'

'Odd it may seem, my man, but comfortable for me. It is much easier to wrap your legs around a horse than perch like a ninny riding sidesaddle. You men have more freedom than you realize, and must share it with us eventually. I am the only woman in Jamaica who rides in trousers. And I shall be for a long time. So come come, undress me, silly man, and forget conventions.' She kissed him quickly but warmly, then withdrew.

He unbuttoned her trousers and dropped to one knee to remove them. She put one hand on his head as he did so. She was naked beneath them, her legs ivory white. He rose and unbuttoned her shirt, then took her in his arms and kissed her, dizzy with excitement at the unexpected sight of her flesh in the daylit forest. His mind stayed lividly aware of everything around them—the patient horses stolidly standing by, muscles rippling, heads bobbing down to nibble at the soft green grass; her hair, a black cascade down her back; the sun, a scalding fire in the Caribbean sky, and that blue beyond imagining; the delicate pink jasmine, flaming red hibiscus petals, gentle green moss underfoot, chirping of the kling-kling birds at their weird song, startling suddenness of a butterfly seeking sunlight, to dance in it, and then ease into the shade to fold and unfold its wings with delicate grace.

She let him kiss her for a long time and then hold her, wordless but wanting to say he loved her, afraid of that but feeling her cling to him, feeling open tenderness emerge from her as she lowered her head to his chest, aware of that but unable to find words for it in his mind, more aware of the tangibility of her slender nakedness in his arms, her boots and clothes cast off and with them Rose Hall.

'All right, let me go now, and hurry, get undressed and come into the falls. We shan't have too long if we're to ride back today.' She slipped away from him with a little grin and a last glance from her strong dark eyes, tiptoed over the moss, immersed herself in the closest pool and then climbed up a step or two, the water splashing around her neck and over her breasts.

They dallied for a long time, sitting under tiny fall within waterfall to let the surge pummel them, rising up the naturally created limestone steps higher and higher into the forest towards the source of the falls, pausing to look back down the turbulent stream, a rush of quicksilver in a deep green tunnel, sourceless and endless, so it seemed, although far down below he could see the dark native girls with the sea behind them, bending to their washing, then standing to wave bright-coloured garments in the air like gay flags, then bending again to pound them on the rocks.

'They are all quite naked, Arthur. Why don't you go down there and have a look? Almost any one of them will take you into the bushes, too, if you wish. Lovely they are. Ripe and young. And you are free to seed them too. No worry about responsibility here. They are delighted to have a child by a white man, a mulatto who will rise in the world and perhaps support them in their old age. Better something like that than an old woman such as me. Take him down there and see what you can do.' She put a hand between his legs and squeezed him, whispering in a teasing voice, barely audible over the sound of the falls.

'Ah, stop now. I am very happy with you.' He put an arm around her, her naked wet body seeming tiny in his arms. She kissed him back, and drew away.

'Thank you. But you need more. A man needs much more, needs the whole world, if he is a true man, as you are. I have been watching you, on the horse this week. You put your boots in those stirrups and never faltered, although I'm quite sure that you are in pain from your back to your ankles, and as fearful as I was when I started. And you've held the line in the fields, and done well there. Better than you know. You are much of a man and have a long good way ahead of you.'

'My way is with you now. Let my way be with you. I know how fine you are, how strong you are. I'll not need washerwomen or servant girls. Come . . .' He pulled her close and kissed her. She gave herself over to him, limbs loose and arms around his body, and he felt her sigh deeply. Then she drew away.

'A kiss is silence, but there is no silence in any of us. No silence, but as many rushing voices as there are drops in this waterfall. Listen to them. Go where they tell you to go. Never stand still. Never bow down to time and circumstance, and confine yourself, the way your father did.'

'And you? Don't you keep yourself in your great house? Confine yourself. Rush out at night to whip and torture people. Ride out . . .' He heard himself shouting, his voice trying to dominate the sound of the waterfall, but love and anguish for her surging out of him too.

'Ah, I thought you saw me the other night. And heard it all too. And worried about your black servant. You can forget that. I caught her stealing cod from the storehouse. She walked away from the lash, and I left her face intact. She has a few stripes on her back now, if they might interest you. Otherwise, serve me for a while now, then forget me. I came out here long ago. My work is to hold Rose Hall together while I can. It's not work of yours.'

He saw her teeth chatter and felt her hand quiver on his arm. The waterfall was chilly, the water spilling down from high mountain streams. He took her in his arms and carried her across the water to a mossy place on the other side, kissing her and warming her body with his.

For the first time she made love with urgency, clutching him fiercely, clamping him tightly in her arms and legs, her eyes shut and body writhing on the moss. For a time he watched her, as she took her satisfaction from him again, and then again and again, curious at her transport, at the way she flung her head from side to side or knitted her brows together or flung open her mouth or dug her fingernails into his shoulder blades, at the somehow terrible but also beautiful energy in her loins, where they met. Then he released himself.

'Annie, I . . . love you. I love you so much.' As he said it he meant it.

She smiled. 'We make love in a rare setting, and I become your heroine, and you my hero. And then we shoot on like comets in the sky. Think of it that way. Without pause. Without a backward glance.' She closed her eyes as she spoke.

'No. You. I love you. I love you . . .' He moved to kiss her but she squirmed away.

'Not me. Life. Life. Love that but not me. Love this . . .' She was on her feet and pointed to the falls, vividly bright in the afternoon sun.

'You Annie. I know your goodness. The little boy you take care of . . . how you love this land . . . all that. All that is you. I want to be everything for you. Annie, I love you. I don't want your house or your land or your wealth or all that. I want to be for you, feel your head on my chest, keep you, protect you . . .'

'And you shall. While we survive. While I survive, because you shall go on. I have my love in Rose Hall. Yes you can be my man for a little while. And then pass on. But not to love me. Not that. I'm past that, past being loved.' Finality was in her voice, and she turned away, looking across the falls to the horses.

He picked her up and carried her carefully back to where their clothes were. They dressed in silence. He helped her saddle her horse. They rode for miles through deep forest, crossing rushing streams, ascending high hills looking down over the forest canopy to the sea, to the hills beyond to carpets of sugar and the scarred places where the sugar had been cut away. The isolated great houses and their outbuildings were scattered over the land like bits of paper floating on an ocean of green. No town, no church spires, no inns alleviated the upland forests. The shore stretched on for unbroken miles where land met sea. She pointed out Falmouth to him, a tiny town at best, midway in their homeward journey. It seemed pitifully small on the edge of the silent land, the placid, far-reaching sea at its back. Once she pointed out Cuba, a mysterious shadow on the far rim of the horizon, a garland of clouds hovering over it, the glassy sea intervening between the two islands. Seeing it, he felt again the original sense of awe and joy he had known on the frigate that brought him overseas, the Caribbean islands emerging on the horizon one by one through slow dawns and hazy afternoons, the ship inching towards them over the wide waters, each isle a serene implacable mystery, isolate on the speechless sea before it became its port, pastel houses and their deep verandas climbing the hills, clutter and turmoil of people and commerce on the docks. From afar, he wondered about Cuba and realized how lost he had been, cornered in Rose Hall's sugar fields, a vast world out there beyond him.

Annie rode on relentlessly, her horse walking, cantering or trotting depending on the terrain. Arthur was in pain now, his back a stiff mass of it, his legs near numb from the effort of riding. The forest ceased to impress him and he fell into near hypnosis, lulled by the movement of the horse's neck and the ship-like rocking of its body. He longed now for change, for the sight of a town, for civilization. She seemed to be at home in the forest, as alone with her thoughts as she was in the great house.

At one point they encountered a deep canyon, a washout caused by rain, and she detoured downhill to the shore road. She rode down like some ancient conqueror entering a new land.

She had a mystifying strength he had never known in a woman, at least the common girls in Manchester and London. His mother, yes. But she was the centre of a tiny world, their small home, tending only to his father and himself. Annie was something apart and unique. *Like a queen of sorts, you could say, but hidden away, nobody to know her except as she killed a man, and lay down with a lot of black fellows and rode round with her whip. But she's more than that. She does that because . . . because something hurts inside of her and she wants to kill it, drink blood to kill it. A queen is alone. That must hurt. To want good, and to be alone. And she wants good. Wants to hold it together, like she said.*

He thought, and watched her erect figure on the horse ahead of him, surrounded by the untamed landscape under the sun's fire. *Needs me. At least to do her work. To see the old man. God willing I am up to it. Proud of that. Someone like me, just out. Never tell her how frightened I am. Be a man to her. She's lacked that. She's dead right about Wilson. God, he talks a storm of words and that's all to the good but it don't buy codfish or cut sugar. I'm not a quarter the man he is in the head, but I'll not shirk doing her will. Good, she felt her head against me there by the waterfall.*

He wanted to ride up to and beside her, but she seemed inviolately alone and had stepped up the pace along the road.

As he watched her a black man appeared around a bend in the road, on her side. She passed him, then reined in and turned back to him. She uncoiled her whip. He saw the thin line of lash rise in the air and come down on the man, once and again and again and then her arm swaying from side to side as she hit him back and front, following him as he ran, hands up trying to protect his face.

'What is it? What is it?' He rode to her and heard her cursing, the lash singing in the air and the Negro screaming to be saved.

'I'll teach you, I'll teach you to keep a civil tongue you beast. Black beast. Freedman indeed. This is your freedom.' The whip snaked back and forth, a tongue of anger in the air.

'Massa, stop her. Massa, please. Ise free, massa. Ise free two year.' He ran to Arthur's horse, kneeling, his back exposed, Annie still lashing at it, his shirt becoming bloody tatters. Arthur rode to her and snatched the whip out of her hands.

'Leave him alone if he's free, damnation. You've no right to beat him if he's got his freedom.' He shouted, his love become wrath in an instant.

'Give it back, at once. Give me that whip. How dare you . . .' For the second he stared into her eyes, he felt and feared his own death. She might not stop at killing him then and there. He heard the black man, moaning, get to his feet and run. She looked after him, her fingers tightening on her reins, her legs on her horse's body, as though to follow.

'He's gone. Let him go. If he's free, let him go.'

'He's not free to address me on the road as though he were my equal. The whip. Give it me. *Now.*'

'When he's gone. I won't have you racing down the road with the lash after a free man, black or no. You're too fine for that. Do you understand? Too fine for that.' He leaned out over his saddle towards her. She swung quickly, caught him in the face with her hand, and reached for the thick leather stock of the whip. They grappled for it. He pulled it from her. She cursed him.

'What I am or am not too fine for is not for you to decide, little fellow. You may be horsed but that doesn't make you a man. More boy than man for what you know of Jamaica or even England. Best you could do was run, and hope we could support you here. Run from England. Run to us. Nothing your own, you idiot. You snot-nosed child, thinking yourself a man because you wear trousers and can straddle a horse. I'd have your head if you knew more. If you were responsible, which you're not. Keep the whip if you want, little fellow, and follow me if you can. And stay in your hut tonight, and report at dawn tomorrow and we shall see how well you do in Montego Bay, if you can still ride then.' She turned and took off at a fast gallop. He flung the whip away and followed her, gasping, terrified to ride at such speed, sure he would fall off the horse, gripping its mane then its neck, unable to sit erect in the saddle. She turned to laugh at him but never stopped her forward rush. He followed her less out of fear of missing Rose Hall (which was on the main road) than out of concern for her safety. At night she might terrify the black men, but by day she was vulnerable, a mere woman on a horse and not a near-invisible spectre with a lash that came unseen out of nowhere to scourge negroes, free and slave alike. Like the ghosts and duppies the blacks believed in, her power diminished at sunrise. On the road, for all the bunched fury of the horse under her, she seemed insubstantial.

Even in his own fright, as the ground rushed away beneath him, pushed backwards by the horse's hooves, he remembered her fragility on the moss beside the falls, her body taut and ecstatic in her accomplishment—once, twice and that day a third time— smothering her cries and sobs up against the place where his throat met his shoulder. Remembering that, he gave himself over to the horse and an hour's ride passed without sense of time, only the unabated and near monotonous agony of his sore body and the horse, real and alive in its strength and untiring forward thrust, enjoying its head, the reins slack, the animal galloping, legs coming and going like swift scissors cutting time and distance.

He was far behind but could still see her as she turned through Rose Hall's gate with just a brief backward glance at him. He turned the horse over to a black hostler with orders to have it ready at dawn and walked back to his house through the reek of molasses in the still air and the mill's distant clatter, too dazed after the ride to be furious at her, accepting banishment from the great house, consoling himself with the thought that he would be unleashed to go to MoBay the next day.

18

'WELL, TO the hill. Not everyone comes back alive and with a mission. Manage yourself carefully and you shall yet join the squirearchy.' Wilson touched glasses with Arthur.

'Ah, you joke with me always. I'd rather your knowledge than five thousand acres. You know that.'

'You have the fool's faith in books. They're a comfort, but so is action, and life is a book—a poem, rather, if you try to see it that way. Surely you have enjoyed your time up there thus far, away from your ghastly cabin?'

'Rather much.'

'Ah, you are about to smile. Is she good in bed . . . ah, pardon, you frown. I intrude on serious matters. Good God, you're taken by her, is that it? Do tell me—am I correct?' Wilson poked the logs and his evening fire flared up, lighting his gaunt face and sad, serious eyes.

'In many ways she seems a fine woman, Wilson. A bright one. Near as bright as yourself, I dare say. Many many ideas. I don't recall much of them, but she has a mind and a strength to her.'

'Surely. The strength of killers. Of our murderous empire builders riding roughshod over the globe. So you admire it? Well fancy that. Your future is assured now that you admire and believe. They need recruits, and you probably need *them*. Better to be forged in and by your times than remain a fool outside like myself. Well, step forward manfully, whip in hand. Let your heroine teach you all she knows. She's quite infamous you know. And surely more sensitive than the warden of our prison camp, Broderick. Let's have another cup to celebrate your future.' He clapped his hands, for Mary, who shambled into the room, looking levelly at Arthur, then askance at Wilson. Arthur remembered Annie's story of the watered rum. Strange, he is being protected without knowing it. *If he knew.*

'Why do you always say murderous, Wilson? There seems more to it than that. It has a purpose of sorts if it built . . .'

'Ah, now. A week in the house has acquainted you with the sweet fruits of murder. Of chains, of the quarters full of humble blacks. You've had a chance to taste the Maderia and eat the fatted calf. Crossed the wall to the other half of the world. By all means stay there. Having known one side, you shall enjoy the other all the more. In Jamaica there are only two worlds—the white and the black, life and death. We few book-keepers are walking grey shadows between them. As your friend, your *confrère*, I merely ask you, as you pass on to life, to remember death as you have seen it. Perhaps do some small thing in your time to help alleviate it.'

'Me. Me. You challenge *me*, Wilson. And you. What have you done? What will you do? Drink yourself to death here . . .'

'Not soon. I know she waters my rum. And doubtless she told you. A simple matter of drinking more. I appreciate her solicitousness, but it is not for me . . .'

'It is for the land. And that is greater than you.'

'Well said. Oh God, well said. Stand up and toot a trumpet for me. Unfurl the colours. Oh Lord. . . .' Wilson laughed, standing as he did so, leaning on the mantel. 'The land, the land. The great mystique. So much rotten tropical greenery populated by people two paces beyond Cro-Magnon and millennium behind the Egyptians. The holy land, a sponge for man's blood. As though it breathed. Man. Whatever became of him? When did we forget him and start to counting kilos and hogsheads and codfish? Does she have an answer for that, your love on the hilltop?'

'It's not the money she wants, Wilson, not that. She wants to keep it together, what was begun here. This fine plantation and the work. I suppose you see it different from . . .'

'Differently. The word is differently. If you are to be a squire, speak well. Otherwise all shall know you for a tailor's son out of

Manchester.' Wilson's eyes were cold now, and he clapped again for Mary.

'Different-ly. From there. It is so much larger than just ourselves, and a few people seem to matter less.'

'You mean a few corpses? Their blood to water the land, and make the sugar grow better?'

'All right . . . all right yes, corpses. If you will. That has always . . .'

'Always? Has always? And ever shall be? Man's blood is the price of progress? You are a convert to that too? Then you are truly lost and shall go on, with them, lashing men's backs, driving them like cattle for the Land or the Empire or whatever insane dream? Living off a herd of poor ignorant niggers?'

'It can't be changed now, Wilson. Not immediately. We have . . . we have history on our hands. All this happened before our time. It can't be changed in a day. You can't have a banquet for the slaves at Rose Hall. There are no . . . there are no loaves and fishes any more. We . . .'

'There's cod. Your woman has laid it out on the bed for them often enough. Sometimes several of them at once. She has quite an appetite, they say . . .'

'Shut your mouth, devil take you. Shut it . . .'

Wilson stood against the mantelpiece, the fire at his feet, smirking down at him.

'Quite an appetite. At least you did away with *one* of them. Scipio was up there too. Her favourite for some weeks. That should make you feel better, eh? Jason should be the next on your list.'

'Curse you, Wilson, shut your mouth.' Arthur got up and took Wilson by the shirt. The other man's soft blue eyes watched him calmly.

'No need to, really. The island is one vast mouth. Black and white alike know that you are the current . . . stud, shall we say. Or fly in the spider's web. And of course Broderick is just waiting his turn again when she's through with you. I'd imagine he knows her better than anyone. He's been in that bed so often . . .'

Arthur turned Wilson from the fireplace, hit him in the mouth and watched him fall across the table, spilling their glasses, then land on the floor. Wilson looked up, blood wetting his lips and chin.

'So. You will fight for her. Or at least attack me. A fairly good sign. You may be man enough for her. You shall find out. You shall hear more, in time, but not so directly as from me. If you can bear it, and still think well of her, you could be an answer for her, although I still doubt you can save her. It is enough you will save something, somewhere, someday for the future of what we call our civilization. . . .' Wilson got to his feet, clapped for Mary, calmly asked for a damp towel for his face, and new glasses.

'She has used and crushed enough men. God willing, you could be the last, unless tonight she sends down to the quarters for a big black . . .'

Arthur took one step and hit Wilson again, in the stomach and, as he fell, in the face, turning him sideways so that he staggered towards the door and fell against it.

'Be quiet. Now, or you'll get it again. Kill you I will . . .' He stood over Wilson, a terrible rage in him, knowing he could kill, had already killed, knowing that she was his purpose and that he could kill, for her, with ease and no conscience. Wilson suddenly seemed, for all his knowledge, less man than disease, a spectre in his isolated cabin, the old, beautiful house on the hill for all its ugly history transcending him by far.

'Killing is not for you any more than it is for me. I apologize, even though I spoke in truth. And you know it is the truth. If you can kill, then kill that in her that needs to kill, that believes it is any solution to history. I know the value of the lash and gun. And have admitted it to Gordon, but only because his disease is the idiocy of Christian mildness. If you love her, and I gather you do, teach her to be less of a terror. Otherwise I promise you she shall be lost to you. In repayment for the lash, she will have fire. You shall bury her in the ruins of her dream. The black man's time is coming. Pillage is the first step and he doesn't flinch from it, because he has nothing to lose. Even his life. When you are at the bottom it is easier, I think, to face death. Nothing to lose and a world to win. Try to convince her of that, if you love her. May I get up now, or shall you strike me again?'

'I'm sorry, Wilson.' Arthur held out his hands, Wilson taking them and rising.

'Don't be absurd. You have a right to your anger. And attractive she is. And a strange power. Not for me, I daresay, to call myself more effective than she. I hardly am, you know. Sicklied over with the pale cast of thought, and all that. Perhaps the world will be better for you, without the fool's burden of some schooling. Come, have another cup with me before you go.' Wilson rubbed his lean jaw and sat in the chair before the fire.

'Wilson, you can do something. Something. Let me talk to . . . Annie. A little school off the property. Find you a cabin for it. Give your lessons in the evening and start . . . start another world for Jamaica. Let me ask her.'

'Never. Remember I tell you now, never. Heed me or you are lost too. Your position is precarious enough. Be useful to her while she needs and trusts you, and you can perhaps help us all. Obviously, you have replaced Broderick in her esteem. . . .'

'She knows him for a beast.'

'Excellent. Step one. Let the rest happen as the fates and your own efforts decree. Look to yourself now, not me. My time is not long. And it is too late here for intelligence. Too far gone. We fight against a landslide. Jamaica's fate, for a while, perhaps a long while, shall be decided by the torch and the knife, guided by the angry heart—the angry, perverted heart. Intelligence will play a minor role, if any, justice virtually none. At long last, the island will settle and grow sanely, but long after our time. You might help Jamaica for a time, on the other hand you might leave her and find new fields. You shall see. But never speak for me. No man can speak effectively for another, especially in a strange time such as this.' Wilson stared at the fire, his voice sorrowful.

'Why do you say your time is not long? Why say a thing like that, man?'

'I have no doubt. One thing or another, in our time. The fever. Tetanus. This rum I so enjoy. Sheer fatigue. I have no great will to live. No will to power, and I know it. Brotherhood does not equate with power. The love of man, and so forth. The world admires murderers and enshrines them. Against such, Christ appears pitiful and poets sick hermits divorced from reality—or what *they* call reality, the power mongers. The cup of power I renounce, gladly, knowing it is not for me but, I am sorry to say, hoping that enough men of good will want it to change our world. Tell me, what do you think of her?'

'What? Of whom?'

'Your . . . your lady. The goddess on the hill who has so enchanted you, and taught you to ride, and is sending you on a mission for her, as though you were a knight, even though you are only going to ask Carruthers for cod. Do you, at your tender age, really love her? Or is her strength her sole charm?'

'I don't know.'

'I think you do. Are you ashamed of the word love? We English are, you know, except for the poets.'

'No, not ashamed. I . . .' He blushed under Wilson's calm scrutiny. He cringed before educated people, and always would. Those with learning, and those with some special craft or art of their own—Carruthers, secure in the mysteries of Jamaica's economy; the frigate captain, an emperor in his floating domain; his father, adept with cloth and needle and thread. To himself, he seemed a blur, and even to admit love an act of folly. Being nothing, he had no right to love.

'Yes ashamed. And if you so told her, I imagine her reaction. Poor fellow. Hold your peace. I gather you have a decent heart. The world will gladly crush it for you. Or cut it out. Hold your heart a bit and it may mellow with age. Rein it in. Give a little of it here and there. A little to her, but not all. I warn you she is voracious. Others have loved her deeply. Now do not hit me. I mean loved her, not just pleasured her. That too, but appetite is secondary, in whatever form you enjoy it. The man Broderick probably told you about, for example. One of his favourite stories. The one she galloped after and left for dead on the road. A passionate one, he was, Irish with all their peculiar passionate ferocity. Thought of her, I guess, as a citadel he had to storm. Counter her violence with his own. Melt her down and have that fierce little body nestling in the crook of his arm. He learned. Ha. Poor beast raved, fired his militia rifle into his own walls, smashed his furniture, drank like a whale, at long last went through that gate. Broderick, the fiend, sensed he would go and left the gate open. Devilish clever he can be. She was waiting, of course, probably on the upper balcony with her whip on her lap. Off he went into the night. And she out to claim him. Not reason with him or talk about his contract or threaten to jail him. Just whip him to death, a silent terror in the night. The horse and the singing lash. Her peculiar kind of black Mass. Weirdly superb when you think of it. Think of it, carefully. You have certain natural resources that will spare you from his fate, as much as you may want to die for her, and, God save us all, lovers seem to love death as well as their mates. There is, I can assure you, a *Via Media*, as the Anglicans call it. You have no idea what it means but imagine a catfooted sailor—such as you surely saw on the way here from Liverpool—a sailor high up balanced on a yardarm, the sea below, sharks waiting, that or the oaken deck, above the pitiless sky and around him wildly flapping sails and he in his unique integrity quietly presiding over all these forces, walking the yardarm as though it were the highway into Nottingham. She could be yours, if you can live like that. I would guess that you have it in you, although you will never quite understand why. And should never try. Thought is a cross, I suppose. The sanctuary of fools who cannot abide in the world as it is, as it is re-created each dawn. Consider yourself lucky to be untrained. The poets are trained in their language, their art. But they succeed in making only artificial copies of the unity of the universe. Ulysses as a story is useless. As a man, in his very being, he was all the miracle earth demands of its sons. The story must be recounted, I imagine, to give courage to a lesser breed of men that now walk the earth—I include myself—but the telling is a fool's game, the work of cripples mouthing the glories of men who in their day moved the earth. I suppose we could say that your lady, your Annie, thinks she moves the earth or has inherited the fire of the earth-movers who first came to the dark heart of this island. And she may be right. Man can fail. He thinks too much. Or dreams. Or whatever. My failing. Woman is another being. She lives in the sticky stuff of reality. Her body first. The sure pain and blood it brings her every thirty days or so, at the pleasure of . . . who is to know . . . perhaps the moon. Her home, her children, every damned act she performs is rooted in a sanity so terrible as to confound man. Indeed, to drive him mad, because man, not woman, is the dreamer in this world . . .'

'No. No, there I disagree with you. Annie dreams, Wilson. She wants very much for Jamaica. She . . .'

'For her white culture, you mean. For the few . . .' Wilson stared at him. For once he looked completely sober.

'For all, but there is a way, a way she seems to know. Believes, I mean. How can I tell you? I can't. I don't have your words, Wilson. I don't.' Arthur reached for his rum. He was sick with desire, remembering her at the waterfall, naked against the green moss. And unable to tell Wilson of that or of her night visits in the big house, all of it part of her, to him.

'A way, yes. Of torture and violence. Of the *via crucis*, for others. That way. A way of dreaming. Call it that. To establish forever the primacy of one outnumbered race while knowing it is doomed. Or does she know it? Or what drives her to it? The failure of man for example—one man to start with, her husband. And then others. White men, none to share her dream because she is . . . well, forget that.'

'Forget what?'

'I shan't have another punch from you. I grant you your strength, and respect your love.'

'Because she is what?'

'You grant me absolution from violence? A safe conduct?'

'Yes.'

'Well, because she is more man than the run of men. Which is not to deny her womanhood. I admit she is a rare combination. And fine, if you enjoy it. And can help steel your spine in a peculiar way. Some men need strong women to make them stronger. If you accept her example and will follow it, so much the better. You are found. But in turn try to find her, with your love, or she will continue to suffer as she does now. Thus she rides out under the moon, eager to hear others scream for her. Thus perhaps a score of men and women have been tortured to death in the room beneath the throne. Ah, forget what I say. Only go your man's way with her. Well, shall you stay for supper? I believe Mary has some fowl on, and Gordon brought me a wine this week while you were on the hill.'

'Dear God, you know so much, Wilson. She could use you. Use us together. Have Broderick sent off, and change this place, together. It could take time, but we could make something of it. A sort of model, perhaps, with your ideas. And I could contribute something. Train the crews to work better, do the same work in less than a dozen hours . . . make the mill more efficient . . . teach the blacks to raise more of their own food, a garden, perhaps, a large garden for all. My father kept a good garden . . .'

Wilson smiled, but said nothing.

'I'd best go. Lord, my bones are broken from the horse.'

'Ah, and everything else. A splendid week I'd guess you've had. And well fed too. Look to yourself in Montego Bay, and come back with a bit of news of the world for me. I've not been to town for a year. Good luck, Arthur.' Wilson rose and put an arm around his shoulders while seeing him to the door. Again, he left Wilson with sorrow. Oddly haunted, the man hung back, surrendering the field to Broderick. *He helps make Jamaica what it is by giving in. Damnation she can do what she will to me but I'll not back away.* He ascended the path to his house, eyes on the great house, candlelight flickering through the upstairs windows, the shutters closed. *Dawn indeed.* He imagined the pain of riding again in the morning. *Shan't injure me too much. And what a change to go through that gate.*

Mary Lou awaited him at home, the table ready for dinner, the dull earthen plates and bent pewter flatware arranged under a single candle that threw long, deep shadows in the room. He smelled boiled cod, and had no stomach for it. He would have preferred to be alone and sleep.

He began to pull off his clothes. She was naked, and he was now accustomed to be that way with her.

'Now I mek suppah. Good fish fo yu. A-long gone yu are, an' have a long trip today.' She picked up his clothing as he removed it, shaking, then folding it. As she turned to put it in the cupboard, he saw the welts on her back from Annie's beating.

'Does it hurt? Your back?' He regretted her pain, partly his fault.

'No. Obeah man med a potion and pray, turn him yeye of pain. Only pain here now.' She touched herself between her legs and came to take him in her arms and cling to him. He held her loosely, indifferent, abstractly fingering her welts. She felt soft and pliant against him but his mind repulsed her, the memory of Annie's tiny, vital body haunting him. Mary Lou was an animal and a good one, but the core of her life seemed to be in the dark tunnel between her legs. There she took, there she gave, there the world came into focus for her half-breed soul.

'I'm very tired, girl. I need to sleep. I shan't eat either. Have your supper and go.' He spoke softly. Her air of pathos always disarmed him.

'No. Long time. Need yu, an' stay now.' She pressed against him, stroking his body, exciting him against his will. He wondered at the mystery of his exhausted body being thus aroused. Mary Lou seemed like so much crude meat in his arms. Surely she had enough men in the quarters. He resented her clinging, wanting to drain him.

'I have to sleep. Now eat, girl, and go. I will bring you something from the town, eh?'

'Mistress beat me fo yu. Mek me go down like dis, and she curse she curse me for bein' wid yu.' She bent over, as though bowing before him. Her welts shone bright in the candlelight. He saw that they reached all the way down, some of the lashes having bitten into her wide backside.

'She beat you for stealing cod from stores. Tell the truth she caught you stealing, Jamaica girl. You lie, you all lie too much.'

'Hungry so I steal. Yes. But when she beat me she say about you.' Her head still down, she fondled and kissed him, her mouth hot and eager on him. He stood still over her, at once detached and aroused and then bemused by Annie's jealousy. *Those welts for me.*

'Hunger is no excuse for stealing. You work and get your wages in food and drink. Mistress Palmer protects you all, but still you steal. You must learn not to steal. To do your honest day's work and eat with the others. Whatever there is for you. And the better you and the others work the more there shall be.' Her mouth still worked at him eagerly, her wet lips and breath hot and eager at him, her hands too tugging at his manhood. His body seemed to relax, the pain of riding melting into a pool of pleasure. She was, he thought, an artful animal. She pushed at him and he let her ease him back on the bed and then take him into herself. She came to climax three or four times, violently at first then more gently each time, as though they were a series of revolutions spreading through her body, reaching deeper and deeper levels. He thought of himself as serving her, waiting his turn, detached but enjoying the ample softness of her sweaty breasts, the swell of her full black thighs, the pungent acid smell of her and the red of her mouth, the white flash of teeth. When she had subsided he had his turn, but was not with her in the room. In his mind's eye he was witness to Annie lashing her in the moonlight, the long whip singing in the air, flailing at Mary Lou's defenceless bottom, Annie naked and without saddle on her horse, triumphant and beautiful in the moonlight.

Done, Arthur rolled away and told Mary Lou to leave. He heard her pull on her dress and then take and wrap the food she had cooked and heard the squeak of the door as she went into the night.

19

ANNIE UNDRESSED, bathed and had Venus massage her and give her a bit of news while the strong black hands reached into each muscle, joint and crevice of her body. Riding by day exhausted her, the Jamaica sun too brutal, the trails, like velvet paths at night, too harsh in the afternoon. She let Venus at her face and temples for a long while to ease her eyes and head. She heard the black woman's voice as though from a distance, and let the sight of her swaying dark pendulous breasts mesmerize her. Venus seemed the spirit of all mindless comfort.

'Dem han' say times sho no so good. Dem see not so much cane an' sugar as las' year. An' cod is less now in de sto' house an' Mistah Broderick him cut down de food, dem say. Sho no lak it. Dem a'fear Rose Hall go a bad way sho mek wuss time fo neger here.'

'But there will be no trouble?'

'Dem say sho evil time a-comin Rose Hall wuss off than a lot. Some say mebbe bettah neger have Rose Hall fo demselves. Dem say very hard here and dem neger shud be mebbe free.'

'Free indeed. Free and independent. Free to wallow in their own laziness. Free to starve until they eat one another. Ah me. And you, my Venus. You are free too. Shall you leave me? You who suckled me during my bad times? Who feeds and cares for me so well? You shall be independent? Slay me in my bed, and be the new mistress of Rose Hall, eh?'

'No'm. Venus too long in dis worl' fo trouble. Sen my chillun for schoolin' mebbe. Dem not wuk in de cane but go wuk in Falmouth market. Or go a-Kingston town an' a-wuk wid figurin', or words on de papuh. Neger in de cane mebbe too long but he can hep hisself widout a-killin'.'

'There is talk of killing, in the quarters?'

'Don rightly no, ma'am.' She saw Venus's eyes glaze over, in the silent unconquerable retreat into the soul that some of them managed. No amount of torture could get a word out of Venus. She was capable of total loyalty to the inhabitants either side of the wall that separated black from white. But Annie knew she could get her information from Mary Lou, who was vain, liked beads and cloth and would gladly trade lives for them. Failing that she could torture a few of the men. No secret evaded her when she really wanted to know it. Beating was ineffectual but dark nights in the uncertainties of the underground room, and brief, intermittent torture with a hot iron or a wooden clapper fastened on the genitals served admirably, so long as it was not done regularly but came as a sudden surprise.

In the isolated silence of Rose Hall, and confronting one or another threat of rebellion, or even problems of minor theft, she had experimented carefully over the years. She had learned not to stop immediately a man broke, but to ignore it and continue her investigation, the man thus baffled telling more and more, tiny hatreds emerging, as though the base of the mind were a basket of hissing snakes. One black telling another and another, hoping to satiate her, end his own pain, pass it on to her next victims. Her terror was effective, in time no slave trusting another, all both fearing her and knowing that she was the source of whatever small good could come to them—an extra cod in their rations, a bit more rum each week, a few more bolts of material to please their simple minds.

Aware of growing success over the years, with time to reflect and experiment, she developed other techniques to amuse her in the long nights. She drove one black man mad by merely talking to him, standing unseen in the corridor outside the underground room and making irrational conversation in dialect. Before his mind left him, he confessed all he knew about a plot to rifle the warehouse that week. But she went on, and with nothing left to tell, and uncertain of whether she was a spirit or not, and unable to bear a voice without an answer for him (or even putting direct questions to him) he gave up his mind and began chanting, in a small childish voice, old Ibo chants out of Dahomey, weeping as he sang, remembering, obviously, the base of his African heritage but in the process of finding it, in that pitch-black room (she just outside his line of vision), losing all touch with his sense. She kept him on the plantation, converting him from a cutter to a hostler. He seemed to have a way with horses, even speaking to them in wordless animal language, some said.

By accident she had discovered, too, another entry into the mind. One man, a white book-keeper, whom she suspected of plotting with some of the drivers against Broderick, was shattered by her body—or (she could never be sure) by a combination of that and his memory of someone resembling her, either in spirit or in actual physical reality. She went to him at odd hours of the day and night for many weeks. She exposed herself, and him, indulged in every obscenity that came to her mind, stopping always short of climax, attenutating his desire right up to the penultimate second, which she could sense, then leaving him, in the dark, in his bonds, sometimes (if she feared having gone too far, accidental accomplishment or a night emission possible for him) flinging a bucket of icy spring water over him or kicking him, without warning, between the legs, substituting pain for pleasure in his shocked insides, his shocked brain. In time, he tried resisting her, cursing at her, laughing, spitting sarcasm even though tied and fundamentally helpless, careless of the possibility that she might torture or slay him instead of merely toying with him. But she sought her victory relentlessly, more amused than angered by his defiant spirit, resorting to simple silence in tandem with her blandishments, silence too much for him, the fantasies locked in his brain eventually overwhelming him, his thwarted desire reducing him to simple cunning, he provoking her, she feeling it, almost giving into it but the last always aware of her purpose, her need to dominate him unconditionally.

Venus massaged and Annie remembered, sure of her power to hold off revolt. Deeply sure, the need to do so a hunger within her, the depth of the hunger the measure of the terrible height of her response, her private wisdom joyous (to her) beyond speech, her will to power in her time, power for no personal gain except the perpetual joy of maintaining it, all her terrible energy devoted to it without knowing or caring why, black or white a matter of ultimate indifference to her.

She sensed the might of the other power, the black power in the quarters, not far from the heavy walls, as well as she sensed her own. She rarely trembled before it, but on some nights when the hills and fields lay silent she could feel it turning against her feel the restive stirring of a hundred and twenty-five black souls, feel them call for her as though to reassure them of her existence, her strength, her willingness to face the haunted night. It was then she saddled up and rushed out, flailing anyone she found, or, if she found no one, transmitting the message of her presence in the night by the sound of her hoofbeats. The blacks lay in their tiny cabins, shut up tight against the night air, and whispered *Miz Palmer a-go talk wid dem spee-ret*. They believed, she had discovered, that her journeys restored her powers, that she was on good terms with the shades, a true witch, possessor of the key to all the black arts, superhuman, invulnerable to bullets or knives. Many were sure she originated in Haiti, where *voudon*—Jamaica called it *Obeah*—was virtually a science, the black African soul and mystic French mind oddly wed to produce a new kind of intelligence so powerful it was said a man could be made ill, or slain, by thought alone.

She took her reputation with a smile when, a year or two after Palmer's death, she came to realize she had it. It was comforting to know that her own wild urges served a larger purpose, her special insanity making eminent sense to the haunted African mind.

Venus rubbed, and Annie became drowsy and dismissed her, asking for the deaf-mute to fan her. She dozed in the afternoon, half in and half out of sleep. She fought for the whip with Arthur again in her mind, then rued punishing him with the long gallop home. He seemed of good heart, but had come too close to her that day. She knew love for a danger. She inspired romance but men were full of it, possibly more so than women. *Their peculiar escape from reality. Wanting a woman's unconditional surrender, taking the helm of their lives only to destroy them.* John Palmer, like a Lochinvar, so devoted, so sure of himself, and then curiously ineffectual. Broderick hard, common and unromantic, holding the plantation together for her superbly after John's death. Man could be brutal but cloaked it in romantic trappings. Justice, love, freedom: words to cover the essential self, shield the vision from the red glow of eyes that lived, not as they wanted to believe, in a decent civilization, but a forest. *I know brutality. Violation.*

A woman knows it wordlessly, in her flesh, takes a man on top of her, and into her, and knows him, takes his measure in a flash, without him even knowing it. Rather Broderick in his naked honesty than all the world's Johns. Or even Wilson's hatred of me. Sure of himself. Knows his paralysis. Another kind of brutality. Brutal to himself. Arthur dreams, as too many of them do. But if he does well with Carruthers I shall have a small prize. A strong young man if not a sensitive one. Not shrewd enough yet, but time may settle him, if we have time. If I do.

Sorrow touched her, a dark awareness of her solitude. That afternoon, under Arthur on the soft moss in the forest beside the waterfall, and later in his arms, she had lost herself for a time, gone out to him (even though she used him, delaying his climax, allaying his urgency), let go of herself to the point where she merged with him and with the ground, the sound of the falls, the sun in her eyes and he like the sun, too, warm, gently protective, a good man he seemed, young, innocent and something in her responding to that.

She lay awake for a long time, alternately receiving and rejecting Arthur's spirit. *Love. They talk of love. He does, without knowing what it is. If it is. An empire, a world to win, and he talks of love as though it were a substitute. How I envy them when they can think that way. A man seems to think himself a duke or an earl when he loves. Or knightly visions, or whatever they have. A good choice I made, sending him on his little quest to MoBay. Let him prove his love. Ride that hard saddle. And he shall hurt tomorrow. Temper his romantic notions. Knit his mind a little. He has seen a knot or two of Jamaica's tapestry, and had his day off at the cataract. And already thinks himself a bit of a St. George. So impertinent snatching my whip away. Let him try now for cod and rice against the old skinflint, and we shall see what a man he is. At long last I may have found one. Beastly succession of whining self-seekers here to milk me. Come to Jamaica to live off our land and complain about the system. More here than they ever had before. Ha'penny clerks out of England, jailbirds, thieves, idiots out of London banks and Whitehall offices all wanting adventure and a high good time. No idea what work makes their wretched empire. Suckled on it. Here they see the price, and whine, or run. I shall not flee. If he at least stands beside me, I shall have a prize of sorts. Regrettable he thinks me vicious. But sweetness is too often the chief ingredient of fools.*

His sweet father on his knees before moneyed ladies. Better be born wild and suckled by a she-wolf. Ah, I shall be his wolf. Let him thus give me a purpose. I have nothing if not spirit and like so many of our men he lacks it. So I shall teach Arthur to forget his father and move the Empire one step forward, teach him where the roots the tentacles of it are so he can enjoy and cope with our frontiers. America perhaps. They say it is different there, no classes, horizons for restless people and their revolution begun by the wealthy of Boston not the rabble he might like it there if not with me surely not with me I am not for long, they will come for me a bullet or poison they have tried to poison my morning chocolate three times and a flung cutlass one night on the Falmouth Road just this year the war within Jamaica shall come to me but I shall not desert her nor shall they hunt me down like a fox running but come when they want me and at least they shall know I was here, I remained and did not flee my own service to my times, perhaps, this mansion worth preserving they surely did not die in vain the settlers, the old man on the wall out there and those before him our emigrants something has, in my estimation, drawn us apart from money, £.s.d. is not the crest engraved on the English soul plumes and helmets ours we are no lambs for shearing by hordes haunted by bogeymen they shall pay in blood for our lives, my life, insolence and wrath no answer to us we know from time immemorial power and order back through the Romans, Hadrian, Romulus-Remus and I shall be a wolf in my time little time one man perhaps would be enough.

She turned in the antique fourposter, feeling a little feverish, soft odour of jasmine in the room, haunting the afternoon, rustling of palms in the breeze, twit of an unknown bird, swift flutter of its wings beyond the mahoe louvres. She stretched and lay on her face, afternoon breeze stroking her loins and buttocks. *It would be good now. If he were here to take me now, like this, on top of me, pressing down, he there instead of the wind. He has a good hard body and when he comes into me is strong and not gentle I don't mind the hurt the slaves have been gentle with me fear me I'd imagine, only Othello has been rough, frightened me that one night, hysteria, like a tightening steel ring around my head pain lashing in there but he was so hot in my womb the head of it huge spitting hot in there I thought he'd never stop, nor I*

She rued having sent Arthur away and let her mind rove over

the afternoon, the way he undressed her, their bodies on the moss together, the gentle way he carried her across the white cataract, and then her rage at the freedman, and his intervention. It seemed less important. *A horse, and then a whip. He would naturally want it, even though in his sotfness he would never use it. Take my sceptre. But of course.* She smiled into her pillow. *Silly man.* He reminded her a little of the other, the one she had (she flinched, remembering the night) whipped to death on the road when he ran, she having rejected his love. Sean, his name was Sean. Redheaded. All the Irish passion. Yes, Arthur was like Sean but being English better controlled, more pliable, possibly more attentive to her.

One never knows about them. She smiled to herself, not unflattered by his tenderness, even if he was callow. *I am not so bad after all. Childish of him, after all is said and done, to want to protect me. But an odd feeling.* She wanted to send Venus for him, bring him to her bed. *Ha. Not the sort of thing you do with white man. Offend his ego. Nonsense. A woman should be demure, wooed and won. Either I am far ahead of my time or I should have made a good lady of the evening. A brazen one at that. Conceivably famous. Consorting with cabinet ministers and admirals and full of the secrets of Parliament. A town house in . . . Bloomsbury. Be direct with them, brazen and direct, shock their frightened little selves, dig under the crust of their respectability. Bring the Knights of the Garter to their knees. A Jason in all of them. Man more easily mastered than he knows. Spill your seed for me, oh Knight, and leave me your Garter for a memento. Vicious I am, I suppose. What is the soul of me? What is the last place? What the answer? What the question? I need not know. Surely I saw the last, on this very bed.* Wordlessly she remembered the candlestick and then her nimble, desperate self seeking and finding the letter opener, reaching out to plunge it again and again into Palmer. Momentarily unnerved by the memory she arose, first up to her hands and knees, crouching on the bed as though re-enacting that dark night, unconsciously grunting to herself as though to make a sound to hold off the room's silence. Then she went out to the drawing-room. She peered through the shutters to the hellish brightness without. She disliked the plantation by day, the sun surly and domineering, the landscape black and white, lacking the subtlety of the night. *John's passion was for the day. Why he was brutal. Unable to bear the night. Subtle-*

ties of the night beyond him. A boor. Jet black night with a trace of moon. Lifts me. There is a flame in the night, and its moth. Why the blacks think me a sorceress. They cling to day, and unreason is the night all wild joy out there in the night and not for the weak white man or the haunted black. Unafraid the old ones, Amerigo, Drake and Columbus and long long before Egyptians, like silent little foxes on their plains and deserts knowing day's secrets lay in night's stars mariners too on the water, lost by day knowing only East West until the dark night falls and the path is there written in the heavens no voice no flags there truth eternal ever there only to be sought out by one simple method or another the Quadrant the telescope poor pygmies we struggle with tiny instruments and our infantile reason and it is all there complete just waiting if you could see it all at once. I wish I could love he says he loves me, Arthur, my young man I am far gone beyond that now at my age in my time tried that with John, adoration, once upon a time banners unfurled in my young heart that is the fool's journey, never to be done again came as a bride idiocy my crime my punishment my solitude eternal I wish that dumb innocent book-keeper here tonight for no reason, born dumb knows no dominion of star or earth, happy with the simplicity of the horse, his simple quest for cod I need someone should summon Broderick for information, for the news, use his body for comfort in this night it is for fools to believe that fornicating is comfort surely not with Broderick he is so fierce but so am I as though we revel in just that as though to kill one another is that why they call it the little death I wonder

She went from the door and shutters, to perch on the top step of the main stairwell and contemplate the old man's portrait in silence. The hard face and determined eyes, thin slit of unsmiling mouth (he had, Palmer told her once, iron teeth, was thus averse to smiling), delicate lace at the throat, the fashion of the day. The portrait hypnotized her, as though the old man were alive. She often tried to imagine his life, and that of his wife. Quiet respectability of a bygone age, much less than a century before. No thought of revolt, slavery's heyday, the island secure in its peculiar kind of morality, and profitable, lacking competition from Cuba, Barbados, Antigua. Even the house, symbol of it all. Like a palace, each planter his own king. None such to be built again, but, one by one to be destroyed. She could feel the black mindless rabble stirring, a slow beast, first tentacles out, the runaways in the forests, trapping and slaughtering organized troops, and behind the mass of that rabble the mulattoes, waiting to squeeze out the white merchants, more than eager for defections, for the white go back to England and make way for the revolution. She saw it all of a piece, the oncoming shabbiness, a century or two of it as the black man foundered, fumbling to imitate the colonists, ever unable to, never able to reverse history and import white slaves from England, ahead of them only the slow terrible climb through levels of education, levels of responsibility, one to the other, that would make them stable and relatively decent. She had to regret the passing of the old order, white dynasty fading into history, the great houses one by one to go to ruin, stand on the hillsides like the Forum, the amphitheatre at Nîmes, wreck of Alexandria's library, pyramids being pocked by the wind, rifled for centuries by petty thieves. Gone: times of kings and great ladies, of rare wanderers like Ulysses, warriors like Horatius, the handful Copernicus, Bruno, Leonardo, Drake and the rest, other monuments, man looking back in awe, forward in terror, huddling in their terror, sheep in the night, eager to huddle, ready for the slaughter or the shearing, the common will supplanting or rather subverting the lone, terrible and potentially beautiful power of just one man or one woman alone, Jamaica and perhaps all mankind to drink the lees, reverse the cup, await the effect of the hemlock.

She arose from the steps before the portrait and uncorked a fresh bottle of Madeira, a good one about two decades old and consumed it slowly before the embers in the grate of her drawing-room, her white flesh reddened by the fire glow, sensing it was lost to her now, Rose Hall, but comforted by it as though it were a cloak around her, warm and comfortable cloak, a little threadbare perhaps but to be enjoyed to the last.

20

'WELL, THEN. Agreed. I doubt you can do it but I shall give you, and her, the chance, if you are foolish enough to try. Never let it be said that I was unfair. Now let's have our tot, eh?' Carruthers took out the pewter mugs and from the depths of the creaky rolltop desk a bottle of dark Demerara.

The old man had agreed to provide funds for three months' rations, providing Annie left the plantation. Arthur found the old solicitor's limits fairly quickly. His outrage about Annie, rooted in a rockbound sense of morality; oddly enough less concerned with the slaying of Palmer than her well-known nights with the black people, the one offence he could not tolerate. He had heard the ringing of chains on the dock outside his window, seen the blacks brought in like two-legged cattle, knew thus forever their place as docile, smiling servants or surly foes to be forever held in check.

'Mrs. Palmer has chosen to enter the night, cross the border of decency as we understand it. Perhaps not you but myself, if you will grant me my age, my time. Wickedness of her stripe can not be tolerated. She remains forever behind a wall she erected between herself and decent white Jamaicans.'

The old man's face implacable, decision irrevocable on it—as though he were a high priest guarding the sanctuary of white life, and she forever damned by him for having desecrated it. Arthur contained his lover's rage, a little afraid of the old man but also aware of his limited mission for cod and gingham, provocation disastrous because of the difference in their ages. Annie had been curt and clear that morning and said *he will try to provoke your rage if he succeeds you are lost from the start.*

'Sir I think her not a bad woman. The times are difficult, and for her too.' At least that. One word for her. A pain of stress in his eyes, his fists clenched on his lap, breath short, thinking *she is alive he is dead in his cold face and among his little papers and the account books.*

'Loss of perspective. In olden days we had women. Ladies. Gentlewomen is the word I seek. Knowing their place. Bringing . . . bringing Grace, shall we call it, into our world. And now a harridan like this, blot and stain on the face of this island. Thinking herself what, a man. A creature out of hell, danger to us all. To you. Utterly conscious of her wickedness, her sin, she flaunts it, knowing there are none to punish her.'

'Sir, is she truly worse than others? The planters are the same, are they not.'

'Think of your good mother. Imagine her lying down with black beasts, like an animal in a stable. God forgive me the thought. God wash and purify the mind of Jamaica when this woman leaves, that she may ever be forgotten.'

'Sir, she needs food. Funds for cod and some cloth, to tide us over the seasons. The crop.'

'Poor I know. All over the island this year. And London negotiating with the Cuban planters also taking more of the Barbados crop. We cannot coexist with them. Now, our decline. If she would go I could arrange the sale of Rose Hall. Since she will not, and must cling to her sanctuary, her eyrie, then she shall starve in it. I know the condition of the books. Money is her Achilles' heel now. This may be the end of her. Save yourself, if you wish. A packet is due in two days. I shall ignore your departure and in fact send word that you never arrived, if she queries me.'

The old man calm, confident, seemingly sure he would desert, the offer casual. *He wants her out so he can have the land.*

'No, sir. I cannot leave. We . . . we need just enough to tide us over a while.' Amazed at his own answer, remembering the mills, the fields, his rude hut, the hour on the galloping horse, punishment for defying her. We.

'She has you mesmerized. When she flings you away, devoured or dead, you shall know the truth of her. When she has sucked out your life and you are gone there shall be no investigation, either, as in the case of Palmer. The witch will hunt you down and when you hear the last hiss of the lash feel the last stroke of her peculiar justice you shall regret not taking the packet. What I offer you now is virtually a choice between your life your death you may be too young to conceive of it your blood would please her as well as the others have white and black alike. Young you are and need not seek your death thus in her in her . . . dominion how old are you twenty-four and this virago to rush you to an unmarked ignoble grave solely because she bares her body to you and feeds you quail and Madeira out of the Palmer legacy your fascination will come to a grim end, go now.'

'I shall go and take her. With me. I shall take her. I make you a promise, Carruthers.'

'Mr. Carruthers.'

'Sir?'

'You said Carruthers. Mr. Carruthers.' The solicitor tipped the rum bottle into their cups again.

'Mr. Carruthers. Make you a promise I shall take her from Jamaica if you tide us over.'

'How long?'

'Three months.' He spoke without calculating, snatching a figure from the air, controlling his breath, wanting to gasp, taking the cup and swallowing the strong rum. The solicitor's eyes said he had won. He too needed time, for whatever purpose. Sell the plantation and turn a profit, whatever. It didn't matter. She mattered. Her fury, her heart, her peculiar wondrousness haunted the room. This far, now further. Take her with me. Out of her memories, and that place. Out of that horror to where she needn't be cruel. Another place, Australia, America.

'You are positive?' Carruthers silently calculated how long it would take the week's packet to get to England, and the time needed for an answer. He could sell to absentee owners for no less than twenty-five thousand pounds keep a quarter of that for himself and arrange to take out some of Rose Hall's choicer antiques before anyone was the wiser. He had made a small fortune selling off declining plantations, hoarding it quietly and for no purpose except the satisfaction of knowing it existed. Rose Hall would be another nice plum and he would be happy to have

Annie Palmer gone, the thought of a woman owner rankling him for years.

'Yes, sir. Positive.'

The old man straightened a paper or two on his desk and fidgeted with a quill pen. His hand quivered in nervous exultation. He was eager to write England. *Two days before the packet. Time enough.*

'You are of course too young to be sure with her, but try. And it may be that I am wrong. Take her from here and she may change. There is a core of decency in all of us, was in her surely. I knew her in her younger days, before . . . the misfortune. Surely the island helped change her. Fear, bitterness. And then power. Women deal poorly with it. They have an odd capacity for hatred and cruelty that no man will ever truly grasp. Bitter, I imagine, living in a man's world all these centuries. The combination of power and grace is a delicate one. Well, you have a job of work on your hands. Take her as quickly as you can, eh, if you can, and I hope you can. You otherwise are aware of the consequences for her.'

'The consequences?'

'*Murder of course. They will think nothing of trampling her if only a handful of them will conquer their fear of her, see her as flesh and not a spirit, not a witch. Take her living body in their hands and tear her asunder or stab her through and through. How they will enjoy it, and be mystified by her blood, and the end of her breathing, and the silence. Ah, how they must yearn to do it, but of course lack the courage. But will find it, if you are not quick, young man. So you have a reprieve. Well, come back in three or four days and I shall have five hundred pounds' worth of goods arranged for you to tide Rose Hall over—twelve weeks. A bit more than four score of days. That is, we agree, your limit?*' Carruthers had picked up his bright steel letter opener and balanced it lightly in his pale fingers. He saw the fear on Arthur's face, contemplating her death.

'Yes, sir'

'*And so good day*'

'*Good day, sir.*' Arthur passed the paper-stuffed desk and wall of old sagging shelves laden with yellowing termite-ravaged plantation records and emerged on the sunlit street, noisy with the clatter of iron wagon wheels, crowded with hurrying people. He stood in the shadow of the arch of Carruthers door gazing idly at busy stern-faced merchants, lackadaisical slaves slowly unloading carts full of barrels and bales, town women white and mulatto, in long white crinolines, delicate faces luminous under dainty parasols; big-hipped black women in short, soiled dresses, swaying barefoot, necks and backs straight under fat full baskets balanced on their heads. He saw without seeing. His mind back at Rose Hall, fear of his commitment reaching him. *I said I would get her out what will she say, leave her world. With me. I must be mad. I saw it all at once the one answer to him the one thing I want too, bring her into daylight somewhere she suffers kills and it is not really in her heart, at the waterfall she was different for part of that day, happy, little in my arms and we little against the falls God, she said it was that, and the flat, round, that too she told me she doesn't want to hate surely, sees so much so much why need she be cruel rushing out to kill, cold, hard, making them scream Mary Lou too to prove nothing how shall I overcome I said so to the old man what first say to her then hear her, anger, such anger I wonder I wonder can I take her*

'Sah? Yassuh. Tek you yo lodgin', sah. Quick boy, sah. Quickes' in MoBay, sah. Two shillin', sah.' The young bearer was eager, restless, hopping from foot to bare foot. Arthur had his small bundle of clothes with him. He gazed at the bearer as though the youth had fallen from the sky, the reality of his voice a shock.

'All right yes. One shilling. Steed and Bridle.'

'Two shillin', sah. A long walk, sah, and ise hungry, sah.'

'A short walk and its one shilling or off you go with nothing.'

'Yassuh.' Nimbly, he took the bundle, set it on his long skull and sauntered off, greeting other bearers right and left, proud to have won work.

The old Scotsman at the inn took his name, and money in advance, announced that lunch was ready immediately and that he had a caller, waiting in the sitting-room.

In the shabby room, filled with tattered overstuffed furniture, a man in black arose eagerly, smiling and putting out a soft hand to shake.

'Good day, good day. Gordon is my name. The Reverend Gordon. You don't know me but Wilson does. I have heard so much about you. Yes, delighted to meet you. Did you travel well and how is dear Wilson, not able to come along I presume? Such a pity. He is in bad need of change . . . well, you are here and I shall have word of him at least . . . well, may I lunch with you we can have a good chat I trust. So much in Jamaica you have not seen, imprisoned in that strange place. You must be delighted to be away for a time. The book-keeper's life is a such a sad lot but then we all have to face up to the battle each in his own way each soul precious in its own right each of us contributing . . .'

'The lunch is ready and will soon be cold.' The Scotsman's wife called curtly through the sitting-room door.

'Yes come and join me . . . Reverend. Happy to meet you.' Arthur let go his soft damp palm and they went to table. The Scotsman's wife served a soup and a plate of curried goat, putting the dishes on the table as though eager to get rid of both them and her guests.

'And so, tell me, how is dear Wilson—do you see much of him?'

'I see him in the fields each day at dawn.' Arthur stared at Gordon. *I wonder if he thinks we have tiffin at four on the veranda.*

'Oh, oh yes. Your terrible work. Well, I hope you are as gentle with the black men, poor souls, as Wilson is. We shall all win this island away from its evil ways in time. I am sure you find it as discouraging as he and I do but faith, and courage . . .'

'I am not always gentle, Reverend. For example I killed a man last month. You must know that.'

'Well, some sort of error of course. Excusable in that harsh work. I am sure you are not the type of man . . .'

'How sure? I shot a man in the back, where he stood, and when he fell shot him in the head. He was blocking the work.' Arthur dug at his curry, surprised to be talking thus to God's minister. *Damnation I know something he doesn't. Been here on the ground in the harsh fields where they lay the cane down with a knife, in the asylum they call a mill. In the heart of it, her place her hell her dream Broderick pushing me some sort of error he says.* In his mind's eye he saw the blood again spurt from Scipio's eye socket, and stared across the table at Gordon. The curry burned at his throat, and he called the Scotswoman for some ale.

'Ah well, of course I heard about it. But still an error of course. The error of . . . that unfortunate man, your overseer, who forced you. Thus you are of course not culpable. He, dread soul, belongs in an asylum. But you . . .'

'I might just as well have shot Broderick. As it was I shot a nigger blocking up the work. Mill works well now. Not a bad curry is it, Reverend?' The Scotswoman came with his ale. He drank the mug to the lees and ordered another. She appeared to be irked at the way he rushed her. She had a lean, dour face, pale, ill-arranged hair and her dress was slovenly.

· 213 ·

'Well, but of course you don't believe that your true Christian self did a thing such as that. The church understands what man is faced with in extremeties. Forced to . . .'

'What is my true Christian self, sir? And what's that got to do with making sugar at Rose Hall, which is why I'm here?' He drank half the second mug of ale in a few gulps and went back to the good plain curry. *Fool, what would he know about my life, about the plantation. Needs a month in the fields, let the sun scorch his back, and a while in the mill, watch a man fall into the boiling pot, come up with his bones when the molasses is drained off. And her. What would he know about her.*

'Ah, you know the way and with God's grace shall play your part in converting Jamaica, strong and beautiful in the spirit you were born and shall remain, as strong and beautiful as the lovely body God gave you.' Gordon reached out and touched his forearm. Arthur withdrew it, and for an excuse moved his curry dish.

'I know the way to the morning roll call and the southwest sector and to the mill and to my hut and up to the great house, Reverend, and I know how the mill works and guess my mum and dad use a bit of the sugar we make. I don't know that the Holy Spirit uses sugar, and I didn't see him when I fell down with the fever for three days.' Arthur was surprised at his temerity but also amused. *Annie would enjoy this. The fool could never grow cane or manage a crew and a rare ass he'd make of himself trying to love a good woman. Nothing in him but words. Stick him and air would come out. What would he know about Christian self. Let him labour in the mill on a hot afternoon or walk with the cutters at sunrise.*

Arthur wanted to smile but also trembled, thus facing a man of the cloth, thus thinking. With his right hand he raised the mug again, took in the remaining ale, motioned the owner's dour-looking wife for another.

'Well, sugar is not all of it, of course. You may be temporarily diverted by the . . . by the exigencies of the work . . . but my friend you shall come to see the hills beyond it, return to yourself, your . . .'

'What's myself, Reverend?' For once he felt free of the clergy no need for amenities. They were thousands of kilometres from home over a simple dish of curry. Gordon's white round face seemed to hold no secrets he didn't know. At least he had lived!

'Yourself. Your soul. You cannot fail to hear the cry of it. I know you hear it. No need to deny it. You sob inwardly for the in-justice an inequality you see here, as we all do. Your good mother and dear father, their voices are within you. They tell you the way and of course you see it.'

'What way?' The minister was off in airy regions. Arthur queried him just to keep him talking.

'The way of truth and love, justice and equality, all of us equal under God. The new way for Jamaica, the way of Christ, when each man shall hold up his head . . .'

'Are we all equal?' Annie would like that question, he thought. He tried to visualize a lot of people holding up their heads, *like goats looking over a fence. Wilson would not like that. He would put his head down, or turn away. Annie would sit her horse and laugh. What would I do, standing in the fields? Stare.*

'Yes, equal. In the sight of God. Brothers all, and all created in his image. You know that your cutters are your brothers, your equals, under God. You carry in you the seed of the new day for Jamaica, a day when . . .'

'When we shall all sit and dine together in the great house?' He imagined Hannibal and the other cutters, cadging tobacco and trying to steal the silverware, grunting as they plucked up their dinners with their hands and laughing as they broke Annie's crystal tumblers, none ever having seen a tumbler in their lives.

'That is not impossible. If we are to commune together as God intended us to, then all is possible. God knows none of man's hor-rid distinctions and hideous cruelties. In God's eyes we are one . . .'

'Good. I'll suggest to Mrs. Palmer that we have a banquet at Rose Hall, and credit you with the suggestion.'

'Ah, now, no need for jest. We both know what a bizarre and terrible woman she is. When freedom comes to this island she will be . . . will be swept away. Eradicated. Reap the bitter harvest she herself sowed all these years . . .' Gordon's face became cold and still. The genial smile was gone from his eyes. He held a forkful of curry up over his plate, and his hand trembled.

'Harvest? You mean be killed. Do you want to see her killed . . . Reverend?'

'Certainly killing is never justified but she has gone too far, even for this country of ours, and can provoke her own end. Only her grave will still her voice and hand. She hungers for death and it will be given unto her by those she has beaten down, those whose blood she has sucked in her demoniacal greed . . .' Gordon's hands quivered and his dark eyes stared, unseeing, hypnotic. His voice seemed not his but a hollow echo of something inside him.

'I don't find Mrs. Palmer greedy, Reverend. I know her rather well. She wants nothing for herself and she leads a quiet life, with many responsibilities. Our cutters are no worse off than others in Jamaica, I'd say.' He spoke softly and levelly, controlling his voice. Gordon had frightened him with his intensity. His hatred of Annie ran too deep, hatred the countercurrent of his own vision of love and God and all of it.

'No worse off? Driven like beasts, beaten and tortured at her bidding. All their work for her profit. Going to early graves. You may have lost your perspective in that madhouse, if you can justify it so. An asylum. It should have HATE in large iron letters over the front gate. Or, CITY OF HATE, a private city, the reverse of the City of God, *Civitas Dei*. Her house on the hill the house of hell, dwelling place of a living devil, hades, I tell you and you taken in by it because she takes you to her bed of sin into her spoiled, filthy body that too part of her greed, men to her beasts to satiate that insensate greed . . .'

'Shut your mouth, man, or I'll break your jaw where you sit. You hear? With this, break your jaw and beat your face to pudding, with this . . .' Arthur moved his heavy pewter ale mug towards Gordon. He was aware of the Scotswoman, arms folded, studying them from the bar.

'Oh God oh God save us, may God save you, you believe in it, this mad country this hell on earth, butchery of the body and spirit, butchery to come of it the whirlwind, the fire, an asylum my God my God . . .' Gordon's voice rose and became a tremulous thread before he put his face in his hands and wept. Arthur looked on in silent disbelief, then waved to the Scotswoman. She crossed the room, face impassive, arms still folded.

'Bring him . . . the Reverend . . . bring him a rum, please, neat. A double one . . .'

'He never drinks,' she said, her mouth a thin red line.

'Bring one regardless, please.'

She glanced at Gordon, face cupped in his hands on the table, still sobbing softly, and turned away.

'All right but it's sure a waste and ye'll pay for it, he drinks it or no.'

'And bring me one too.' he called after her.

'For sure. And the world. A rum for all the world to keep us sodden that we'll not have to feel the flames of hell.' She spoke without turning back, and he watched her pour the dark Demerara into Jamaican clap cups. Gordon looked up only when the cups were set before them and Arthur tapped and shook him.

'Drink up, man.'

'No no thank you. I don't. It addles the brain. I . . . I apologize. Whatever I said. Your woman. There is something there for you, in her, God save you I don't understand I don't want the butchery not for her or for you or Jamaica God save us.'

'Drink your rum, Reverend, and finish your curry.' Arthur gazed at him, wondering at Gordon's sanity. *Almost smashed him with the mug, I did. Couldn't do that. A waste. Man is mad. Guess they go silly here too. Should have a parish in Sussex, drink tea with old ladies, never be this far out.*

'No. No spirits, I . . .'

'Quick, now, drink up fast. Warm your gut and settle your head a bit. Up now . . .' He tucked the cup in Gordon's hand, touched cups with him and held him with his eyes as Gordon gulped it, grimacing then coughing, stopping that and sighing deeply.

'Well thank you. Revolting but it is always warm in there. I haven't done that for some time, for many months.' He remembered the night at Wilson's house when he had fallen because of loneliness and done that with Wilson, for which in his mind he had no words. And again, been back and done it again in fascinated horror mingled with a tenderness born out of loneliness, and that of Wilson, in the alien violent world of Jamaica.

'Good for you, a spot of rum now and again. It's hard here Reverend, no easy answers. Let's have another.' Arthur's anger had passed. He felt protective towards Gordon, who seemed like a crazed boy under his official black garb.

'All right, another, if you wish. My head . . . my head hurts a bit. Thank you for bearing with me. If you . . . are taken, shall we say, with that woman, I would not mean to be crude. It's a personal thing with you that my soul cannot grasp, how you can see what she is and what this island is and still work with her and I presume admire her. You seem decent enough. I presume it is not just the body. Surely that is the cheapest commodity here. May I ask what it is? It could help me to learn more about the soul. There must be something I fail to grasp. I knew Sean, one of your predecessors . . .'

'The one she killed. If it's him, I know about that.'

'Yes. An uneducated, passionate, irreverent man with a rich soul and high ambitions but again quite taken with her . . . her power until he tried to escape it and was struck down. What is it? What keeps men enthralled, five score slaves in her quarters in check, a good man like Wilson there so long? He is on his third contract and will not see the end of his fourth or fifth and knows it in this land of . . . of doom where they die early.'

'This is the last of the Demerara. No Packet in from down the islands this week. Ye'll drink the Haitian or the Jamaican next, if ye must have more.' The Scotswoman, sour-faced, put their cups on the dark mahoe table. 'And ye'll pay me now before yer brains is too addled to remember and there's a quarrel. We keep no quarrels here.'

'Put it on my bill,' Arthur said, 'you know I have a place here for some days.'

'Paid in advance. And pay now as ye eat and drink, all of it up to the minute and none on memory.'

'How much?'

'One pound three and sevenpence.'

He fished out the money Annie had given him and she took it with lean fingers.'

'And so,' Gordon said when she had gone, 'in your youth do you really feel for this Palmer woman? Is that why you made ready to strike me?' Gordon gazed into his rum and sipped it experimentally.

'Yes I do.' He was embarrassed to say it.

'But if you are a good soul of decent family, and a reasonable young man, how can you *bear* the things she does?'

'I don't question them, Reverend. She has her purpose, a sense of purpose. And . . . and of her class we could say.'

'Then may God forgive you.' Gordon looked at him closely. 'Please come with me this evening. I have a meeting. Almost a hundred, freedmen and some newly escaped slaves. Please come, I beg of you come and see them. You need not stay for all of it. Just see their faces, see how they come, risking persecution and even death, to commune to hear the word of Christ, of brotherly love. Come to my home on Boggs Lane at nine o'clock and I shall take you from there and you shall see.'

'All right. Until then, eh?' He was bored with Gordon but his soft, pale face had a pitiful eagerness about it. In part he was curious, unable to imagine Gordon as a teacher and counsellor, wondering at the stupidity of his followers.

He found paper and a quill pen in the room, wrote *Dear Mum and Dad*, looked at the paper a long time, then went on:

I am sorry to be so late in writing. The harvest season has been on and we have been very busy reaping the crop. The cutters go out with their long knives called cutlasses and we have to follow them and watch out that they do it properly. Then the cane which looks like long sticks is taken to the mill in wagons and the mill grinds it between big metal teeth. Then it is boiled to make molasses and the sugar you buy to make cake and put in your tea. We don't have tea here but usually coffee which is a Jamaican crop. We don't eat cake, the plantation food being usually codfish and rice and some beans and pigs feet and tripe and sometimes some chickens.

The work is hard and dirty but the black people do it and we book-keepers supervise them.

He paused over the paper. What to tell them about the lashings, the stocks, Annie's underground room, his night in the mill, Annie herself? For a second he seemed to be writing from an asylum, trying to explain it to people outside the gates. And they would show his letter around Manchester, proud of it, especially his father. *My son, my son in the colonies you know. A supervisor he is, in Jamaica now.* He wrote on:

I have a house of my own here on the property. And a servant who cooks and looks after me. Our overseer is Irish but a most efficient man good at getting the work out of the Africans. They seem happy people and sometimes sing when they work, strange songs with a good rhythm, and sometimes play the drums at night. They are very strong and carry things on their heads. The owner of our plantation is a lady, Mrs. Palmer, from London. She is very handsome and intelligent. She lives in the big house, called a great house, that is larger and finer than Mrs. Tellery's big white house out on the edge of Manchester. I have been to dinner there several times and now she has give me a horse and sent me on an important business mission for her to the city of Montego Bay.

He looked out the louvred doors to the shabby, noisy town and smiled. An important mission in a big city. His father would be delighted, his mother filled with pride, reading his letter aloud to the neighbours. *And what else can I tell them?* He wrote on :

One of my associates here is a fellow named Wilson, a well-educated fellow who taught school in the Midlands before coming out. He is quite a gentleman and we have many long discussions of an evening. He plans to open a school on the island and I may work with him to do that.

He stopped again. The folks would like that too, a scholarly friend. Good thing they would never see Wilson in his cups, or hear him cutting the whole society, the whole Empire, or screaming at Broderick about archangels. Mum and Dad always thought of teachers as types of saints above the common run. He wrote on :

Another friend is the Reverend Gordon, one of our ministers. He does good work among the black folk, teaching them about Christ. He is a good friend of Mr. Wilson's and comes often to visit our plantation. I am going to one of his meetings tonight. He talks very well and is a fine gentleman.

He stopped again. At home they would see a vision of Gordon the kind missionary, not the raving, sobbing man at the lunch table talking first of equality then of burning, his mind swaying from side to side. Just as well. He thought, then finished :

Well, it has been hard work but very interesting so far and this is a very beautiful country, all green with jungles and forests and many wonderful mansions. The work of cutting and making the sugar is tiresome sometimes but it is very important for England and for Jamaica. Love, James. He put down the pen, reread what he had written as though someone other than himself had done it. *Well it sounds all right. They shall think I am content and prospering. A house, a horse. A supervisor. Decent companions.* He remembered how proud other Manchester parents were about sons way out in the colonies, all the amenities they had, servants and the lot, probably liars the lot of them now that he knew. They all sounded successful but most were probably working round the clock in India and New Zealand, Ceylon and Alexandria and all the other outposts. Still better than the deadly dull life in England, he supposed. He thought of Mary Lou, hot, urgent animal. Well, a bit of an advantage. Something Dad had not known. He smiled, licked the envelope, and went out to post it, strolling through the town, shaded by the overhanging balconies. He stood in the square to watch a slave auction, tired of it and moved on through the market area, hundreds of jabbering women squatting on their haunches selling bits of food grown on their little plots in the hills, mixed trinkets from Britain and from the other colonies around the world. He stopped by the fish market along the dock to watch them unload bright white, blue and black fish, and the multicoloured snub-nosed dolphin, the dealers haggling, each fisherman shouting that his was the finest meatiest fish and the dealers all fools and thieves. *You teef me. Yuse a teef, mon, dis a feesh,* all of them chattering interminably but the last arbiter a scale made in London on which the bodies were weighed, fish selling by the kilo and not the word.

He stopped in a tavern for two pints of ale, overheard some planters exchanging talk of problems with their blacks and cursing England's new markets in Cuba and Barbados that were undercutting Jamaica's profits, heard them as though from a distance, Annie his only concern. *We shall soon be out of it. They call it the New World. What might we do. I shall find something. Learn to be a carpenter or some trade, or find some land to cultivate, have land and grow a crop, work in the sun. And she. Hate no more. That fury. That rushing, whipping and the rage and the killing if I could take that out of her, America take that out of her a new place Rose Hall gone behind us behind her whatever she wants to prove gone no backs to lash. No, no more. My bond, that is my bond, that brutish Irishman Broderick murderous she respects him my bond is take her from him from this from Rose Hall from this Jamaica New World whatever it is find peace and no Empire no hate I hate they crawl all over you like Mary Lou like Othello begging tobacco, steal, lie, whine, beg I understand her hate beat them into line, kill or they take you take everything I am not ashamed of Scipio Broderick was right they fling a rock in the machinery curse them take their chances if they want to stop us and why put up with it kill, yes, Scipio's eye gone like a bloody red grape, yes, pay for their cod, gingham and rum yo ho ho for what to throw a rock, kill. I'll kill for her not Broderick now I know he'd kill gladly for lack of else to do but fornicate, kill, good at it, taught me, take aim, shoot, but not for her she doesn't need that wishes, I suppose, she could die too gallop out looking for it, her John gone, house hers alone, too much, take her to that New World damn me what's there, what can I do, blast Broderick, not that, not him, she's too fine for that where is she now doing what Carruthers makes me wait and then out will we have peace, yes, and love, yes, and in America what*

anything I shall find it do it for her that she shall be happy with
me and forget the killing and the hate the domination a lady
needn't be that way the little dwarf she loves him we could have
a child of our own.

He mused, heard only dimly the planters at their business talk,
and was glad to be free of field and mill, sipping good ale on a
warm afternoon and planning his future. He had a third pint, then
returned to the inn and slept until evening. On the way to his inn
he passed the slave auction again, stood for some minutes, studying the calm black man on the block, neither docile nor hostile
as his body, his age and his history were told to the crowd, his
mind off dreaming of, Arthur wondered, what.

'The meetings must be secret or there are penalties for them,
and me,' Gordon said, '. . . they can denounce me as a revolu-
tionary. They are doing it now in Falmouth and Oracabessa and
elsewhere on the coast, driving ministers into the street. Poor Jor-
dan in Falmouth was shaken out of his sleep last week, tarred and
feathered and driven out of the town. But I am not afraid. So
long as they come, the dear souls, to hear God's word. Are they
not beautiful people come from their terrible masters to the loving
light of Christ . . .'

Gordon's round face was beatific as he watched the Negroes
gathering slowly in a small outbuilding near a ruined great house
two miles from the town. The only illumination was from a half-
dozen candles on a makeshift table. Their faces were solemn and
still and empty. A few looked fearfully at Arthur.

'They are a little afraid of you, of course. Any strange white
man could be a spy. Come say hello and we shall set them at
ease . . . Arthur, this is Eddie, Eddie, Mr. Arthur, a good friend.'
Eddie's eyes were intense, suspicious, gleaming in the candlelight.
He stood mute but seemingly less distrustful as Gordon patted
him on the back then took his wrists and saw that he and Arthur
joined hands. They went on through the others, all coal black,
nervous and with damp palms, all with strange-sounding English
names, Alexander and John, Robert and Donald, Vivian and Freddy
and Elizabeth and Marion and Harold and Dick, suspicious of the
stranger, but seemingly quieted by their pastor and prophet. Arthur
wondered at Gordon's transformation. He was not the hysteric of
the afternoon, or seemed not to be. He decided to stay briefly
and see if Gordon preached damnation and the fire for Jamaica,

preached the butchery and terror he said he saw coming, the black mobs, the copper and bronze people, rushing at the golden doors. He felt ill at ease in the gathering, as though consorting openly with Annie's enemies, but was curious to see why a strange white man such as Gordon should have such power and sway over the ignorant.

'Yes, Eddie, yes, Alexander,' Gordon was saying, '. . . a friend, an ambassador from another land within our land, from the white man's world, come to join his soul with ours tonight, come out of the white world's darkness to the light of Christ we all share here in this little haven, come to hear the word, share the word, with us in the name of the father of the son of the holy ghost Amen.'

'Yassuh. Amen.' Eddie bowed his head piously, and stole a brief glance at Arthur. Alexander crossed himself, eyes fixed on Gordon as though he carried some priceless message. *Lord if they knew I was from Rose Hall*, Arthur thought, and bit his lip to hold back a smile.

'And now let us begin. Come, come, my friends, let us begin . . .' Gordon got behind the crude table, the candles arrayed around him, clasped his hands together, closed his eyes and, as the Negroes squatted on the dirt floor before him, intoned:

'Our father, which art in heaven . . .' They replied, some slower than others.

'Ow fodda which a haven'
'Hallowed be thy name'
'Hallo beethi nay'
'Thy kingdom come, thy will be done on earth'
'Tie kindumkum tie weel bed on er'
'As it is in heaven'
'Ass he teesun haven'

And so on until Gordon had finished the prayer, paused for effect, his head down, hands joined, candles flickering eerily over his pale face, over their calm, empty dark faces, their minds given over to him like so many empty gourds waiting to be filled. He gazed at them then, and then up over their heads and spoke as though to himself, his voice sonorous and rhythmic. 'My brothers and sisters we gather here in the Jamaican night unafraid of danger, the danger that is without, the terror and the horror of the prison of this world for we are free of that prison as we commune here brothers and sisters in our own world the true world

· 223 ·

here together in the heart of our land, free and independent of that prison without, where in his greed man labours for gold and builds useless treasure on earth. But we know that the true treasure lies in our souls, that we are the equal of our so-called masters and free, all free in the sight of God Almighty. And we know that those who labour for and store up treasure do so in vain for it is of no import to God Almighty who weighs us all in the same balance on the day of judgment. And we know that those who hold others in chains and worship the work of the machine are blind and deluded and evil, a curse upon the land and evil in the sight of God. And we know that the world they inhabit is verily a prison, that they are locked behind the bars of their own blindness, the blindness of their own souls. They do not walk tall and free in the sight of God as you do, worshiping the treasures of the soul, the work of the soul on earth which is man's work. And so you are greater than they, greater in the sight of God than those wealthy ones who call themselves your masters. Blessed are the poor, Jesus said, and he was right. The man who labours to create treasure labours for nothing. He is a foreigner in the sight of God, the devil's ambassador come to destroy the Eden that is your Jamaica—'

Arthur was close to the rear door and stepped out quietly. there was an acrid stench in the hut from the close-packed bodies and the sight and sound of Gordon, illuminated by the flickering candles, was making him dizzy. Some of the Negroes were already restless, looking about at one another, whispering together in the rear of the room. One handsome girl in a corner near him had stared at Arthur for some minutes and even aroused him by lifting her cotton dress and stroking her thighs, then squeezing one breast, all the while staring at him. *Whatever do they listen to him for*, Arthur wondered. *No wonder they won't work, all full of the independence of their souls. He should have his backside kicked.*

He hiked the two miles back to town through pitch darkness, seeing only an occasional oil lamp in a freedman's shack, a black family in it sitting still in the silent night. He was glad to pass on, the town ahead of him, Rose Hall after that, then America, the future not here but there. He walked quickly, the night deep, the dense foliage only partly outlined by a half-moon. He could imagine why the Negroes had their imagined spectres, the rolling calf, the bloodsucking witches, the terrifying ghosts of all their

· 224 ·

dead. The road rose over a final hill before town. Tiny as it was he was grateful for the sight of it, hugging the shore beside the clean sweep of calm sea.

In town he stopped at a smoky tavern for some Demerara and met a book-keeper from another plantation, a small Welshman, drunk as a lord, out a year and swearing he was set to risk desertion of his contract to get home.

'Mad brutes on this island. Never know until you get here. It's a cursed asylum. Gave me the whippin' job on Charlotte Hill 'cause I sassed the owner about the food. He says you're a rotten book-keeper shut your mouth. I said, Mr. Morris, I'll have none of that. He says a rotten Welsh book-keeper and you'll learn about Jamaica, my man, and puts me to lashin' backs aside my other work. Have another rum with me, Ian's me name, and you?'

'Arthur. That's a bad job that whipping. I hope you get back to England all right.'

'No, but I mean I likes it, that's the twist. And he don't *know* it. Take it out on them apes with a grin I do. I *hope* he don't know it. He thought he gave me the worst job of all. Well I sez to myself if you're in an asylum you might as well have their kind of fun, so I gleans me daily bit of amusement with the cat-o'-nine-tails, or the tamarind switch for a change. Swish, smack. I gets better at it every day. Like to hear 'em screech, I do. They don't give old Ian none of their tricks, I tell you, or their backs feel it. Caught my maid stealin' from me redhanded last week. Oh did I lay it on her. Gave her twenty-five. She come crawlin' that night crawlin' to my bed, believe it or not. Had to give it to her standin' up, I did. She says you're a white devil. I says don't play about with a Welshman lassie or I'll brand you with me initials. Oh, she did laugh. Where are you from?'

'From Manchester, but I work at Rose Hall.'

'Rose Hall? Now there's one. Give you a dozen there just for lookin' sideways at the overseer, I hear. Lord I'd love to work there. I hear she's a screamin' terror, the first lady ever to run a plantation. What's her name again, jack?'

'Palmer. Annie Palmer.'

'That's it. Knew I heard it. Lord if I could skip my contract and go with her. Pack my trunk any day and cart it over there. No secrets about her in Jamaica. Let's you swing the ol' cat-o'-nine-tails does she, or save it all for herself and that underground chamber?'

'I . . . I whipped a few of them in my day.' He almost went on to tell about Scipio as a matter of bravado, because the Welshman would have enjoyed it, but it seemed too much to tell.

'Bravo. Lay it on to them, I say. The whippin' post is their schooling. Dirty brutes play about I say teach 'em white man's language. Lord, this place is gettin' hotter every day. You know they cooked one near Falmouth last week? You hear about it?'

'No.'

'I missed it meself, but I would have gone. Wish they'd announce it and give us time off. Caught a thievin' runaway, they did, chained him to a steel pole, right up his back, and put him over the coals, toasted him for three or four hours, real show, turnin' him over to cook him nice and even, the whole town watchin'. Went right on until you know what . . .?'

'No, what.' Arthur was grateful for the next drink. The bartender, a dour Irishman in his forties, plucked up the payment from a bundle Ian had on the bar.

'His head exploded, that's what. Poof. Eyeballs popped out and everything, all of a sudden. Not a sound out of him except for his screamin' before that. Say you could hear him a long way, even up in the hills beyond town, his fellows up there thinkin' twice about any more raids on that town. Well, anyway, drink up and here's to you, friend. Lucky one you are up at Rose Hall. Hope you gets a little piece of her ladyship—I ain't askin', mind you, 'cause that's a private matter where a man sticks it but any woman with her spirit must be good and hot in the lap. You plays your cards right too and you'll have a nice plot of land and your own great house someday, if you likes this place . . .'

'I'm leaving.'

'You too? Good. Like I said it's a cursed asylum, all right for a while but one day we'll get our throats slit or get done in by the fever. I saved a few pounds and if I gets away without bein' caught I'll buy a piece of my brother's haberdasher shop in Wales. Where are you goin'?'

'America.'

'God, that's worse. Savages all around you in the woods. Everybody carries a gun there and bang bang you're dead if you even *think* wrong. No sir, not for me.'

'It's a new country. They say it's not like England. No classes. A man's his own man, so to speak.'

'You better think twice. You know what started that place.

Crazy preachers, the lot of 'em, burn a man at the stake if they catch him hoistin' a skirt or takin' a drink. And the rest a lot of jailbirds they didn't want in England. I'd stay away from that yard, man, and go back East to jolly old England. There's high talk of gold in America but you might get shot tryin' to find it. You're better off in Manchester where it's a sure thing. Slow and steady, but a sure thing and no savages rushin' around to get your head. I've had enough asylum in my time here to tell my grandchildren about and keep everybody popeyed in the White Horse inn for the next five years. Old Ian from Jamaica, they'll think I fell out of another world. You have to see this to believe it, and I've seen enough . . .'

'There's more to see, Ian. Well I'm off to rest, my friend. Nice to have met you.'

'And you. Take my advice now and get back to Manchester. And give the lady on the hill my compliments. They say she's a whore but she's in the right class for me. Tell her old Ian would be glad to swing a cat for her any day. See you in England one day, Maxwell's the last name, Ian Maxwell.'

'Jim Arthur. Cheers.'

He was awakened before dawn by shouts and saw eerie shadows thrown by flames. He thought the inn afire and scrambled to look through the curtains. A group of armed men on horses were in the street, a few of them clutching torches.

In seconds there was a rap on his door. He opened it to a tired-looking man holding a rifle.

'Militia. I'm Quarles from Merrymount Hall. Broderick orders you to come with us. There's a fight with a few hundred runaways we've found in the hills.'

'Broderick?' He was frightened. Did the Irishman want him killed in battle?

'Yes. We brought a horse for you, and a rifle. You shoot?'

'God no. I was never taught . . .'

'Teach you when the sun comes up. We'll have a little time. It's a slow ride into the hills and we'll stop now and then. Hurry, man, we're waiting for you.'

The third day was the worst because they began making contact with some of the runaways in full force. Before that it had just been waiting or cutting their way through deep thickets of forest or scrabbling over the rocky hills of the cockpit country in what seemed like a fool's quest, interrupted only by isolated attacks by tiny bands, easily overcome but always taking their toll. Four men had died by the end of the second day, wounded by arrows, spears and rifles, and one ambushed and hacked to pieces with what must have been a cutlass.

On the third day they were in the woods in force. The firing was continuous. Some of the militia deserted after the first attacks, and more left at the commencement of the third day, their nerves weakened by the heat, the perpetual assault on the clinging undergrowth, the incessant presence of mosquitoes and even the frightful screaming of the runaway slaves as they attacked, their yells almost as effective as their weapons. The militia was loosely organized, no oath binding them together, so every man was free to go as he pleased, with no excuses made to the rest. Quarles, who called himself a sergeant, asked him if he wanted to leave on the second night but he stayed on, learning to use a rifle, pushing in the powder and ball, aiming it with some accuracy.

On the afternoon of the third day they knew a force of some size was before them, with a cul-de-sac to their left and a winding river to their right and apparently nothing remaining for either side but a retreat or a confrontation.

'Now, let's get them now,' Quarles said. 'Get them and then burn out these woods so we need not come back here again. Kill every man jack of them and burn up their corpses in the forest. Let's teach them one lesson and put an end to their damnable raids if we can.'

'No. Oh no. If we attack now we could be decimated. Let's take it little by little. Take about a dozen men and go a hundred yards or so forward, under cover. Feel them out and see can you take a prisoner or two so we get more information about them. Otherwise we shall remain defensive for a bit. I've been in the cockpit country before. Oddest part of Jamaica, geographically, and they know it like the palms of their hands. Bear with me a bit, and we shall see. Remember I've seen a lot of this fighting.' Foster, the militia captain, was a soft-spoken, pipe-smoking man with a plantation of his own but with a curious patience about the fight in the forest. The day before, Arthur had heard him softly cursing the runaways, his pipe firmly clenched in his teeth, his left hand hitting the stock of his rifle.

Arthur went forward with Quarles and a dozen others, fanning out in the woods and advancing slowly, an occasional sniper's bullet singing through the leaves, an occasional yell from the other side coming towards them from the invisible enemy, until they got to a small river in the forest and stopped at its edge, because of the clear danger of crossing it. From its opposite shore came only silence interrupted by the twitting of birds, underscored by the soft rushing sound of the stream.

'And what do we do now?' Arthur said.

'Wait them out a bit. This is a bad situation. Go along and tell the others to spread out, take cover, and keep a sharp lookout. When whatever is in their black heads comes to the surface they'll either come screaming or start firing. God, I am tired. I hope this is the last of it. What is it now, the third day?' Quarles's face was blotched and swollen from numberless mosquito bites and his hands trembled steadily. He lit a cigar as Arthur left, puffing it slowly, making small clouds of smoke to ward off mosquitoes.

Half-way down the line of questioning men—wondering what Quarles's plan was, and obviously glad to take cover, as told—he met John Williams, the planter with the scarred face who had come to meet Mary on the dock, the day Arthur arrived in Jamaica.

'I know you,' Arthur said.

'Possibly, but I don't think so. What is it? You've come from Quarles? Sergeant Quarles, as he calls himself. Well, he has a master plan to cross this river, or what?'

'Take cover and wait, is his word. Ah, now I know where I met you.'

'Take cover, take cover. About all we do on these damnable expeditions. Should have had them by now. Dirty brutes afraid to fight for their plantations and their jobs. Or suck them into a trap, cut all their useless throats. What a mess.' His eyes were full of anger. He looked more gaunt than Arthur had remembered him.

'Quarles doesn't want this either,' he said softly, surprised at saying it. He put the stock of his rifle down on the green moss of the woods.

'All right. I didn't mean to include Quarles. It's Foster fights so cautiously. Thinks himself back in his London club, on a soft seat. Patience and fortitude and the waiting game. God. All right, all right. I . . . well, one serves, one must accept it.' He rubbed his hands over his eyes, then clutched his rifle, with both hands.

'I know where I met you now,' Arthur said.

'Oh? Where?' Williams kept his head down, as though totally uninterested.

'On the dock, in MoBay. Months ago, when I arrived. I came out with your wife. Mary?'

'Yes. You're the one from Rose Hall, then?'

'That's right. Arthur. I work for . . .'

'The mad Mrs. Palmer.'

'If you want to call her that. How is your wife?'

'Dead, as a matter of fact. If you must know. She died . . . she died at Eastertime.'

'I'm sorry, Williams.'

'Thank you. And now I shall take cover, as instructed, and await the next decision from . . . from out there.' He waved his hand in an arc.

Arthur went on down the line until he spoke to the last man, and turned back. As he passed Williams' position, the man spoke.

'Arthur.'

'Yes.' Williams had his back to a mahoe tree, his knees drawn up, his rifle beside him, erect against the tree.

'Good luck to you. Good luck to you, always.'

'Thank you. And to you . . .'

'Not easy to come out as a book-keeper, and now you see more. And you'll solve it your own way. Care for a drink? I've a flask of Demerara.' He reached in his bush jacket and produced the flat bottle.

'Thank you.' Arthur pulled at it, and gave it back.

'Good cure for all sicknesses, including war. Best be gone, now, and back to Quarles. Something's bound to break by night-fall, unless they want to keep us waiting for days. Can't ever guess what's on their minds, because they have none. Good-bye.' Williams stared at him, and brushed the hair off his forehead with one hand.

'Good-bye. I'm . . . I'm sorry about your wife.'

'Good-bye.' He disliked leaving, John Williams' face illuminated by a ray of sun in the forest's dense, deep gloom, but a face that told him to go, a face wanting no further converse about Mary, or anything. Arthur wondered how she had died.

For lunch they had hardtack and salt pork and waited steadily for sounds from the other side, dense with mahoe trees growing behind a thick wall of bamboo along the river's shore. Towards sunset there was audible thrashing in the brush on the other side. Quarles sent Arthur down the line again to order all to hold fire. The air was heavy with mosquitoes now, but with the sun angling away to the west the forest was cooler, the place dappled with shades of green shot through with the sun's last rays, enlivened by wild orchids clinging to moss-covered trees and wild bougain-villea growing close to the forest's floor. Arthur passed the word on to a grumbling group, two of whom walked away, working their way back through the undergrowth to where they had tethered their horses, leaving one man to guard them, two days before.

The sky was deep purple with a few cloud puffs mushrooming in it before there was word from the other part of the forest.

'White man.' It was a strong deep voice. Hearing it, they started in the silence.

'White man.' It came again, more stridently now.

'Yes.' Quarles answered the voice loudly, holding his rifle at the ready.

'You no gwine home alive from dis fores'. Finish you white man. No mo mawster fo him neger. No mo chain an' whip. No mo white man in Ja-maica. Give us food an' guns an' yu go dis one mo time, no come back.'

Quarles spoke. 'Good. We've got them. They're probably short of ammunition and they're badly off for food too. NO . . . YOU WON'T HAVE US. SURRENDER OR COME OUT AND FIGHT.'

Silence answered him. He fingered his rifle nervously, peering through the underbrush at the other side, above him skies of deeper purple obscuring the view, the long night setting in, mosquitoes gathering and fireflies visible in the twilight. Long minutes passed, perhaps a quarter of an hour, the silent forest seeming strange counterpart to the thudding of Arthur's heart, the nervous move-ments of Quarles's fingers around the trigger of his rifle, his restless feeling about for his cutlass, his powder and flint bags. Then it came.

'WHITE MAN.' The voice was softer now, but clearly audible.
'YES.'

'WANT TO TALK WID YOU.'

'TALK.' Quarles strained forward eagerly. Night was falling, and he and none of them wanted to face it again. Arthur heard some rustling along the line of men on their side of the river. They were all in a bad state after three days. The unseen black man had, it seemed, more advantage than he perhaps realized.

'TALK IN DE RIVER. ONE A-COME TALK WID YOU. COME A-WHITE FLAG, A-TALK ABOUT-IT. OLE MAN A-COME TALK. JASPER, YU KNOW HIM. COME WID US FROM HARMONY HILL. HIM BEAT A LONG TIME AN WUK A LONG TIME AN MEK NOW DE DRUM IN HARMONY HILL FO CALL DEM HAN' TO WUK OF MAWNINS.'

'YES, I KNOW HIM.' It was Williams' voice from down the line. 'YES I KNOW HIM. I KNOW HIM FOR A GOOD MAN. YES, I SHALL TALK WITH HIM. SEND HIM. TELL HIM WHAT YOU WANT TO SAY, AND I SHALL SPEAK TO HIM. I SHALL COME NOW, SEND HIM WITH THE FLAG, I SHALL CARRY A WHITE THING TOO. If you hear me, Quarles, leave this to me.'

At Quarles command, Arthur ran down the line to him. Williams reached out and took him by the forearm. 'Something white, quickly. Anything. A handkerchief, a . . .'

'I have nothing. I have nothing white. I can run to Foster. He's the leader he must have . . .'

'Your shirt, man, give me that. It's white enough. Hurry take it off, take it off. This may be our chance.'

Arthur peeled off the shirt, John snatched it and, as the lean old man from the other side emerged from the bamboo he stood up and went forward, his hands still trembling, but a hopeful look on his face.

He was almost half-way across the shallow stream before five shots rang out in quick succession from different directions and he tumbled sideways into the water. The old man ducked quickly back into the bamboo as firing started from the militia, their fire all wasted. None got up to attempt a rush across the river, then acting almost as one man they began retreating down the tiny trail they had left in the forest. There was scattered firing from across the river but the runaways obviously did not plan to follow. At the forest's edge the horses were gone and the guard's slashed body lay in the brush. It was past midnight when Arthur got back to MoBay. In the morning he left for Rose Hall.

On the long march back to MoBay, he asked Quarles what had become of Williams' wife.

'Oh, died.'

'He told me. But how?'

'Suicide. Cut her throat.'

'Good God. Why? That unhappy in Jamaica?'

'Not that. The story is she was raped, but none know for sure. He was down in May Pen for some days selecting cattle and *something* happened. After it, she took to drink. Some say kneeled and prayed every night, right in their living-room, and would never again sleep with him. That's the story, but who's to be sure. One day, she makes a gash in her throat, and that's the end of it. The word came out through the servants. That's all we know. Small wonder he walked out in the river. He'd been a strange creature since then.'

Arthur let the conversation die; there seemed no need to press it further. He began to think once more of Annie Palmer.

21

MARY LOU sensed his rage after telling him that Broderick had been in the great house since his departure.

'Him dere all da time wid her, and dem in de cellah too, an whip and a torcha dem han. Oscar dem hol one a him hans ovah flame a mek him scream a tell de truff dem yes o no gonna mek uprisin'. A hear dem scream of nights and den laffin', upstaihs, from Miz Palmer's room. . . .' Mary Lou's face was calm and her eyes deceptively gentle but she could sense, he knew, his mounting outrage.

'And so. There will be an uprising? Tell me the truth or so help me if I learn otherwise I'll kill you, you understand? A cutlass, right there, you hear me?' He jabbed a finger at her belly.

'Dem talk in de quarters. Talk an' talk. Neger all-ways a talk.' Her eyes failed to meet his. She was Palmer's bastard daughter but true to her black blood line, and lived in the quarters although, he knew, lived apart in a shack of her own.

'Curse you, woman, tell me. Is there talk of rushing the house or anything else? Are they together or just some of them talking?'

'Don know. Don *know* . . .' Tears came to her eyes. 'Some talk a blood, a killin', but dem black han all-ways talk, and afraid Miz Palmer.'

'But they say they want to murder her, is that it?'

'I ain't swearin' to it. But she torcha dem han now wid Mistah

Brod'rick, even some women han, Linda an' Birdie an' Jorie dis week fo tell if dem knows of up-risin'. An' dem in de quahtahs is talkin', I sweah is all I know, I sweah.'

If she knew more, he knew it useless to try and wrench it out of her. Useless for Annie and for Broderick too, their quest absurd, all trails leading into the maze of the quarters where there was no truth, no organization, no one man at helm even if an uprising were about to start. *And she believing she can stop it, torture it out of them, terrify them, shock them into accepting her kind of order.* A sudden wave of fright overcame him as something deep within him knew that she was going too far in her orgy of hatred with the overseer, knew it was close, the trouble, read it in Mary Lou's eyes, she sensing it but perhaps knowing it had no centre, the plantation's Negroes so well held down and divided and punished with such vigour by Broderick that any overt plot to rise would be suicidal folly.

'Well, I'll go up. Tell them down there they'll pay with their lives for any rising, every man jack of them. Tell them remember what happened to Scipio in the mill. Tell them that for me.'

'Don't go. Mistah Broderick say if you come back . . .'

'Never mind what he said.'

He went up the path towards the house, remembering what Carruthers had said when he went for the documents for three months' provisions. *She thinks herself beyond the jurisdiction of ordinary mortal life, the jurisdiction of fate itself. If need be you must tell her the penalty. Be frank with her. Remind her of what happened to Mount Pleasant and to Wilkinson of Harmony Hill and to so many of the others this past year or two. A bit of fright won't harm your cause, and may get her out of there faster. You could bring it off in two weeks or so and save us all headaches.*

I think her fearless, sir. That shouldn't work, I'd think. I love the woman and just want to see her come with me, is all.

Well, that's up to you, lad. A strange love indeed. Your business how you get her off the premises. I frankly see no signs of love in her. Haughtiness and hate, with her dungeons below, lashing niggers to tatters like a mad medieval duchess, or a Medici. Perhaps that is closer. Violence, the curse of empire. And hatred, the viper we try to conceal. I suppose to avoid either you would have to be a man in a boat alone in mid-ocean or by some magic be able to survive alone on a mountain top.

· 235 ·

He mounted the steps and rapped on the oaken door once, and once again. Broderick opened it.

'Well, if it isn't the lad from Manchester. Been off on a little trip, eh laddie?' He was drunk, clutched a goblet of rum.

'You know where I've been, Broderick. And I'm here to see Annie, if you'll step out of the way.'

'Sorry, lad, the madame is engaged. Oh, forgive me, the madame is resting, sir, I should say. Now get yourself gone, see. They're cleaning up in the southeast quarter. Just march yourself down there and supervise it. Not much of a job, won't hurt your delicate constitution, and you can tell the niggers about your trip to MoBay. Hope you got some nice black wenches there. Or did you go off to a prayer meeting?'

'I'll come in, Broderick, and you'll tell her I'm here.' He trembled but held his voice level. Broderick stood, caustic, dominant but low-voiced, in the centre of the wide-open doorway.

'You'll come in over my corpse, lad, but more likely we'll have yours to ship back to Mum and Dad in Manchester, with a Jamaica dog's tooth in it for good luck, or pig's dung or whatever the obeah man says is good luck these days.' He weaved back and forth but his face was stern, blue eyes bright, cold.

'I'll try, Broderick. I warn you I'll try. She sent me on a mission to MoBay and I'm here to report.'

'Report to me, lad. You've not risen far enough not to report to me, my man. Not forgotten the night I caught you at the gate, half out of your mind for being sent to fetch her black man from the quarters. Black man in her she wanted that night and not the likes of you, boy . . .'

Broderick saw the punch coming, almost evaded it, flung his glass in Arthur's face as it came, took the punch full in the mouth, did not waver, stood for the next one in the stomach, countered in a rush, his right fist coming up, one arm out and around Arthur's head to hold him, crack his neck perhaps, Arthur, in momentary terror recalling in a flash that the overseer was a vicious Irish street fighter, flung one foot out to trip him, Broderick, weaving, turning, punching at his body with insane fury, Arthur hitting again and again at him, realizing they had turned full circle, Broderick out of the house across the threshold, he in it, his back to the gloom of the drawing-room.

He broke and ran, Broderick catching him half-way towards the staircase, turning him by the shoulder, the two grappling, tumbling, smashing an end table, scattering china from it, struggling to their feet like two panting animals to grapple again, swinging blows from Broderick's fists smashing into his nose, crumpling bone, his mouth now ragged, taste of warm blood in it, the incredible reality of two of his broken-off teeth lying on his tongue like so much candy, shock on shock in his solar plexus as Broderick hit low and he came back high, long looping swings, the overseer reeling, falling back finally and smashing a vase of flowers, screaming as pieces of it penetrated his back screaming *I'm cut I'm stabbed Jesus God,* scurrying across the floor screaming pulling the shards out of his back with his right hand, Arthur in that split second seeing the fireplace, the screen, the rack of pokers, taking the bronze handle of one, whipping it out, the rack flying, poker and tongs clattering to the floor, going for Broderick, terrified he might rise again, merciless, obsessed, beating at his skull, the blood dripping from his smashed lips mingling with that of the overseer's, Broderick silent, trying to rise, not protect his head but rise, pushing himself up with his hands, choked breath still coming and coming until, face down, he lay still on the floor. Arthur stood over him, poker in hand, straightening slowly, panting deeply, only the sting of his wounds keeping him aware of himself, keeping him conscious.

'Well done, and now get out.'

'What?' He thought the voice a ghost right out of the body of Broderick.

'I said well done, and now go.' She was at the bottom of the steps, in her riding pants and with a pistol in each hand, the stern-faced portrait of the old man looming incredibly behind her, that calm stern white face an anachronism peering in eternal quiet determination at the woman with the trousers, the dark shirt, the two short-barrelled pistols, overseeing Arthur, Manchester tailor's son come a long way out to this strangest of all Jamaica's great houses, bloody poker in hand, a look of amazement on his blood-spattered face, contemplating the woman on the steps, ignoring Broderick's silent corpse, last of his blood oozing out of him.

'I'm not going. I came for you. I have the papers, from Carruthers. Three months' rations. But we leave before that. For America. You come with me.' He wanted to say *I pledged it to him* but stopped in time. She would not care about that. He was hypnotized by the wide-gauge pistol barrels and her solid stance on the steps, the day, the minute, not within any realm of comprehension but only to be borne out to its end, that end its purpose, that end she, now possibly about to slay him, that neither conceivable nor, if conceivable, significant, only the next confrontation the next split second meaningful, thought impossible, the poker an absurd weapon he instinctively dropped, its fall soundless because it landed across Broderick's dead back.

'I said go. Leave this house. Leave Rose Hall if you wish. No, better not. Better you work off your contract. Now that you have a taste for blood I'll make you overseer. Now that Wilson's gone you're the last. You can help me hire more, and train them. Why did you kill him?' She waved a gun barrel in Broderick's direction.

'I said I came for you, and you'll come with me. You're in more danger than you know. Where is Wilson?' He felt his mind scatter, awed by the impossibility of the day. *Overseer. Power. How she loves it. Loves even my killing Broderick. She's proud of me.*

'Your friend Wilson is gone off to Rodney's—with distinction, mind you. The first white man ever to be sent there, and I told them to be sure and keep him alive awhile, no matter what they do to him, and they do some interesting things. I imagine he screams twelve or fifteen hours a day, at least. And I hope they do to him what he did to my . . . to my little boy, the silent one who shook your hand. I should rather like to do it myself, but they work slowly, in relays, and enjoy their work. And I want the worst for him, the maximum, shall we say. Because of his education, let us say, he will enjoy it especially, he will appreciate it the more. And now go. Take Broderick's body with you and have him buried, today.'

'Wilson did what . . . what did he do? What now, God what now?' He stepped over Broderick's body to approach her. He saw her level the guns at him, and stopped.

'Someday you'll find out. He had other penchants besides political theory and poetry and brotherly love.'

'God. I am sorry. How is the boy, is he all right?'

'I sent him away with Venus. It would be rather much, don't you think, to have to look in his eyes and know what was locked behind them. I think he has seen enough, felt enough now. The slaves will probably do away with him, suddenly and painlessly. They see him as a bad omen. Now go.' She waved one pistol towards the door. Her face was controlled but he read the sadness in her eyes. She appeared almost ready to cry, but would not. He took another step forward towards her, wanting to take her in his arms.

'I came for you. I said I came for you. To take you out of here. To America, with me. You've got to get out of here. You're in danger now, more than you know. Come away with me.'

'Ah, you've come to save me, is that it? My shirtless Lochinvar flailing about with his poker, and I am to gallop off with you into a new dawn. Is that it?' Her eyes twinkled; her mouth curved in a grin.

'Don't mock me. You're too good a woman.'

'Ah, now I'm good. Indeed. And in America, what? I shall knit and bake tarts for you, eh? And hear your triumphs each night? How you bravely sold a bolt of wool or carried a hod of bricks or triumphantly totted up a column of figures in your employer's ledgers? And I—I shall tell you with what *élan* I attacked the wash. Is that your dream, my hero? How glorious. Shall I swoon now?'

'Don't be cruel. You're too fine to be cruel but you refuse to admit it. You know what beauty is. You took me to the water-fall . . .'

'To show you grandeur, which evades you. When your con-tract's done here you should wed Mary Lou and have a notions shop in Falmouth or MoBay. Or better, save your wages and be a tradesman in Manchester. Live out your domestic dream in the Midlands, have your tea and scones and play darts in your favourite tavern. Or you could do the same in America, I dare say. I imagine they need apprentices. You could be something exciting, such as a carpenter or a mason, since you have no taste for being an overseer. Now go, and report to me in the morning.'

'Cruelty, why that always from you? Why do you hide behind it? Cruelty and power. There are other ways to live. When you came here as a young woman . . .'

'The world is crueller than you know. And is guided by power. You worked for Broderick and having killed him you might learn something, because now I'll give you the chance to do his job. If you fail, it will be your skin and mine. Let's see if you are more, or less, of a man than he.'

'You yourself said he was a beast.'

'But effective. Very common but very strong, with a will to power which oddly enough you lack, but may one day find. Now carry his body out of here and as I said, report tomorrow.'

'You. I came for you.'

'And shan't have me.'

'Yes, damnation . . .' He advanced on her. She took one step back up the stairs, shouting at him to stop, then fired, the ball tearing through the flesh of his left arm, the explosion burning him. She backed away a few more steps, standing directly under the old man's portrait now.

'Now go. The other is still loaded and the next shot goes straight into your heart.'

'You're mad. *Damnation* you're mad.' He clutched the arm to slow the bleeding.

'If so, not more so than you. I'd suggest you tie up that arm so you can carry out Broderick's body. Take one of the ties from the drapes behind you, the black ones. And then go. I am rather bored with all this.'

'They'll murder you. Mary Lou said . . .'

'I suppose they will. Whatever, whenever. I am not invincible, not made of steel.'

'But we could leave. You needn't leave with me. I'll take you to MoBay. To a ship . . .'

'Desertion is for cowards.'

'You're not a soldier, damnation, damnation can't you see . . .'

'I'm the head of this plantation. And the last, now, of a long line. Someday . . . well, you do bore me. Go.'

'For the love of God, will you . . .'

'Go.' She held the pistol firmly, close to her body, and aimed at his chest. Her face held a frightening serenity. She was ready to kill him and be totally alone. *At least I can stay here and be ready for her if it comes to the worst. Overseer. I suppose I could try it. I am getting dizzy. I am bleeding.*

He took a tie from the drapes beside the fireplace to bind his arm, bent to hoist Broderick's small, light body to his shoulders, and turned once more to look at her.

'There now. A proper hero you are, with your trophy. Had you a helmet, you could be a Greek warrior at Marathon. Have Mary Lou tend to your arm and come for instructions in the morning. We shall see if you can replace him. If not you can be just another book-keeper, in the manner of your friend Wilson, who has to learn about power quite another way.'

He left, his legs weak and vision blurred, carrying Broderick into the bright sun, down the gravel path. On the way he met the old wagon driver, put the body in the wagon's bed, with orders to have it buried that day.

Mary Lou gave him some rum and cleaned his wound, listening to him babble about the danger to Annie and what he would have to try and do to stop it. He would go to the quarters and speak to them. Reason with them. She heard about the slaying of Broderick and watched him weep as he told it and saw the dead whiteness of his face from loss of blood. She made a poultice for his wound and tore up her skirt to bind it. Then she warmed a soup and fed it to him slowly. She drugged it heavily before she did so, using a powder bought the day before from a passing obeah man. If there was to be trouble, she wanted him out of it.

22

THEY TOOK their time with him. They had time and
nothing to do at Rodney's except look forward to weekend holi-
days in MoBay. McLaughlin the commander didn't like having a
white man there, thinking it denigrated his race, but when he
read the note from Broderick explaining what Wilson had done
he took personal charge of Wilson's case.

He despised perversion above all things, having once been
approached by a pale-handed priest in his town in Sligo, and
clutched to his dark black robes for frightening minutes. He and
Broderick shared a hatred of priests, deviates, and the English,
and a love of rum and nigger wenches.

'Possibly he has also been conspiring with ministers as well . . .'
Broderick had included in his note. That gave McLaughlin a clue,
a purpose however vague. It was best, he knew from his years in
the militia and at Rodney's, to challenge a man, preferably with
plotting. They seemed to find strength in the process of denial,
and the stronger they remained the better they endured privation
and torture. That strength always interested him. He had to admit
to himself, on occasion, that even the niggers could be strong,
some of them dying, he thought almost bravely, ferocious and
defiant to the end, virtually indifferent to hot coals, branding
irons, hammers pounding slowly and rhythmically on their fingernails, wood clappers screwed tighter and tighter on already crushed

· 242 ·

genitals and other, better, refinements that occurred to him from time to time.

Wilson was not questioned but merely hung up by his thumbs in a black solitary cell. On the third day McLaughlin came to look at, but not talk to, him and Wilson committed the error of lashing out with one booted foot, kicking McLaughlin in the stomach. For this he was stripped, his head shaved bald, and was taken by two guards out into the blinding sun and up to the corrugated tin roof of an outbuilding and left there for two days. He was carefully watched and each time he passed out was drenched with water and awakened by hammering on the tin from below. Then he was put back in his black cell. Unaware of being watched constantly through a peephole, he tried to ram his head against the wall, sensing what was to come, slow doom for him, for their amusement, dimly conceiving what arrangements Annie and Broderick must have made when they sent him there, what elaborate denunciations apart from the simple one arising out of what he knew was his one weakness, his one joy.

His rush at the wall across ten feet of cell did not even render him unconscious but led to his being chained by the neck to an iron ring in mid-cell, his hands tied behind his back, his food, tripe with a brown gravy and a pan of water, put in front of him to eat like a dog. He lapped at the water to ease his parched tongue, and put his head in it too. Scorched by the two days on the roof, his head aching incessantly, rage part of it, rage because he wanted to be questioned. But McLaughlin by now knew enough not to do that for a good while. He waited ten days and entered the cell one day when Wilson lay with his head in the tin pan of water, rhythmically repeating to himself *alpha beta gamma delta epsilon alpha beta*

'Taking a bath, man?' Wilson heard the loud, clear voice and looked up far enough to see the polished tips of McLaughlin's boots.

'All right, what do you want.' In the back of his brain something begged him to keep McLaughlin there as counterpart to silence, to darkness.

'Nothing at all, man. What do *you* want? A nice bath? I could arrange it for you. A nice warm bath, eh? And a good bunk instead of this dirt floor. Not for the likes of you, this cell eh, man? England respects her educated men. Tell me first about your friends the ministers, eh, man? Help me do my job, eh? Just a bit of truth is all I need.'

'Beauty is truth, and truth beauty.'

'Ah, witty you are. Bright and witty. But that shan't get you the comforts, professor, and I know what a toff like you likes. Now give us the honest truth, eh? You and Gordon and the other fellows wanted to have Rose Hall for yourselves, isn't that it? You're alone now, you know. Talk a bit and have the comforts, eh?'

'Gordon is a fool who says one thing and lives another. A failure.' He lifted his head to try and look at McLaughlin, but the short-snubbed chain held him down.

'But he's your friend.'

'Friends can be fools.' He knew McLaughlin would like that. He clung now to the talk as though to life itself, even though he sensed that worse was in store for him. *Life is pure curiosity. I must be going insane*, he thought. He was aware of his nakedness on the floor, under the other man's gaze, and his wrists wriggled against his bonds. He suddenly wanted to cover himself, was aware of a deep sourceless shame.

'Fools. Certainly. Now you're on the right road, man. Now a bit of comfort. Jenkins, McCarthy . . .' He called out to two guards outside the cell.

'Yes, sir.' He saw their boots too, and heard the Welsh accent of one of them, grasping at that, the tiny shred of recognition, of cognizance, keeping his brain alive, his headache ceasing in that instant.

'A bit of comfort for our friend Mr. Wilson. We know what a man like him is accustomed to, eh?'

'Yes, sir.'

McLaughlin had been careful to tell them about Wilson, knowing they shared his distaste for having one of their white community in the prison, niggers something else again, separated for all time from the white man's world, in another country inhabiting the world of the shadows on their flesh. But to them Wilson was now fair game, even a rare form of amusement. They had a London constable's truncheon, souvenir of Jenkins's time on the force before he had emigrated. They had lathered it with axle grease that day at McLaughlin's orders and while McCarthy leaped on Wilson, pinning him to the ground, Jenkins plunged it deep into him, Wilson reaching downward with his manacled

· 244 ·

hands, fingers outstretched, futile, his screams cut short as McLaughlin, with one foot, pushed the uneaten dish of tripe against his face, while at the same instant he felt his insides give and a hot gush of blood in him and rushed gratefully to death.

23

VENUS SUMMONED Jason, as ordered, and shepherded him to Annie's room. She had not seen him for some time but the day's disturbance had aroused her to the point where she needed company and settled on Jason for his docility. Tall and well muscled, thick shouldered and with a small waist and the Negroes' full but muscular buttocks, he was to her a mystifying study in power and placidity. She bade him take off his clothes and hang them on the Hepplewhite chair facing her dressing table.

This night she rubbed him with Venus's special oil, stroking him slowly, enjoying the gleaming of his candlelit flesh and then the uprising of his male part, stiff, turgid and abnormally long. She stroked it carefully with the oil, entranced as ever with the mystery of it. She put her mouth to it, taking in the head of it, so large it stretched her lips taut and forced open her jawbone to its limits. She pulled away suddenly and heard his first moan, and repeated this over and over until she felt that part of him grow larger, and hotter too, and felt his legs and hips tense in anticipation of his climax. Then she stopped and diverted him, stroking his fingers and palms with the oil, his neck, then his back then the back of his legs then the place where he forked in the back, slowly and meticulously until she turned him over and started again, arousing that organ he could hardly control but she, to her perpetual happy surprise, could.

'Now, Jason.' She never spoke except to say that, nor ever allowed him to touch her. He took himself in hand and commenced rubbing slowly as she watched, still rubbing parts of him with the oil, interfering with him only to slow his motion. This night she felt him approach the end, felt the little quivers in his legs and groin and then put his hand away, replacing it with hers as he lay passive and stiff and dependent on her, eyes wide and looking at the wall ahead of him. She worked him with a slow gentle rhythm, enjoying the length and heat of him in her hand, actually feeling the swelling of the head of it and putting her head down on his groin, beside it. At close range it loomed huge but she knew that in seconds, at her will, it would break into spasms, at first with a jolt, firing nothing but a teardrop and then spasm on descending spasm sink into shrunken futility and he, groaning, to relax and instinctively reach out for her, the source of, first his discomfort, then his absurd comfort, surely absurd, the delicious idiocy of it, of that, the silly rod of flesh that spat a grey fluid always a source of amazement for her *I cannot imagine having it I would like for five minutes once to know.* When it ended and the dark man's grey seed spattered out of him he reached for her in a gesture of instinctive closeness, she moving quick as a flash to evade him, bidding him dress and go.

'Yassum.' Jason arose humbly and drew on his ragged filthy trousers. They ended in tatters just above his knees. He tied them with a bit of old sweat-stained rope, then put on his blue cotton shirt, lacking buttons, tying the tails of it across his flat belly. He did not regard himself in the mirror. They were afraid of that, she knew, of their own image. He left silently, closing the door behind him.

Jason glanced towards her empty drawing-room as he shut the door, then went along the corridor to the back stairs, made the turn in the kitchen. It was black except for the light of a half-moon printing four squares on the wood floor. Venus's bedroom light was out and her door closed. He felt for and opened the door to the cellar stairs, shut it gently behind him and stood a minute, savouring the coolness but also terrified of the trip ahead through the underground room where so many had suffered and died. But he stood, as he had been told to do, before journeying on, containing his fright, as he had been asked to do by the men in the quarters who said no harm would come to him, they would chant for him, sing to the old gods, and sacrifice a chicken for him and certainly bring him back providing he did what the men had asked of him, to be sure of Venus, of what had been arranged.

So he stood and did his peculiar work, taking five and twenty breaths, all the while visualizing his hearth fire, single flame glowing down there far away. He was facing the tunnel and heard the rats scurry below in the walled room where Annie extracted her penalties. He remembered the screams that could be heard even through the walls, even below in the quarters. He half expected to meet her along the way, his primitive mind expecting a flash of light as he passed under the arch into the room and she there to catch him, his mind never considering how she might get there, he himself standing in the only path of entry to the place. He took the five and twenty breaths, counting them painstakingly on his fingers as he had been taught to do, hearing nothing, Venus not coming to lock the door, that much secure, and ran, wanting to moan but running in silence, scrambling first down the stairs and then headlong through the underground room, hearing the rats scurry, and up the other steps through the wood door into the garden, racing through the wet grass then down the reassuringly gritty noisy moonlit gravel to the quarters.

Venus heard him come, then pause, then run, and reached one fat arm out to her night table and sipped at a glass of rum. Then she dozed, her message delivered. Octavio the gardener had come that day with word she was to leave the door to the underground open. The alternative was the death of her children, her woolly headed boy of twelve, her daughter, about eight, and one smaller son, less than three.

Venus, third generation of her line in Jamaica, although she did not know it, the slaves having no records, no traditions, no sense of family or even, in time, tribe, had lived carefully, for reasons unknown to and unthought of by her, avoiding liaisons, not holding herself apart from the quarters (to do this was death of sorts, the mass of blacks mistrusting, always, any sign of distinction, of separation from the whole), but holding herself apart from the moiling of endless mindless copulation that seemed to be the slaves' sole resource, that at least a release, its issue, the children (and the quarters teemed with them), themselves a diversion, a source of hope and, more, a source of profit—some plantations encouraging breeding, paying little bonuses, capitalizing on the slaves pleasure too, each healthy male adult worth as much as two hundred pounds, a female less but still worth something.

Venus for no reason she knew or cared about stayed out of it, lived with one buck for almost a decade until he died at the usual age of about twenty-nine, was content with him, with their two children, kept her simple memories of him private within herself, yearned for no other man, her ample flesh untormented by desire, content with memory. She came to John Palmer's attention when, stricken with fever he had some of her pepper pot soup and brought her to the house as cook, before Annie's time.

She found him sick. He believed he had a congenital weakness of the glands or the liver, she of her nature disregarding that, brewing him herb and root teas and once daring to slip an alligator tooth under his mattress, that he might be better cured while he slept.

She regarded his progress with silent approval and a word to no one, not being given to proselytizing but having simple humble faith in natural mysteries she did not feel required to understand. He liked to hug her huge dark body and in jest call her his saviour. It inspired her to work up even better foods for him, scouring the markets for the freshest fish, even making for-her-complex arrangements with tough-handed seamen, who had learned that huge turtle could actually be caught from a pirogue with a hand-line, to rush their catch to her fresh and still wet from the sea for slashing up into good steaks and deep wine-flavoured soups. The tortoise shells she sold to a handful of mulatto artisan freedmen in Falmouth and MoBay via a tenuous but reliable chain of inter-mediaries, netting herself small sums which she religiously saved, always in silver, never paper, in an earthen crock buried deep under the centre of her shack in the quarters.

This was for the education of her children, not a thought but of a dim unanalysed urge within her, sensing that the white man triumphed (no matter how absurd seemed his headlong rush, how bizarre and even pitiful his violence, to himself and others) on the basis of his knowledge—the cryptic business of words, num-bers, calculations, his intelligence obviously sadly lacking in other areas (she was proud of her herb tea, mystified at Palmer's amaze-ment at it), but those mysteries, and the compilations of them amassed in the books she dusted on the shelves, were obviously to be solved if her daughter were to be more than a washerwoman in a stream, her son more than a cutter who saw only the next stalk and not the entire field as it was held in view in the young white man's, Palmer's, head.

Thus she amassed her pitifully small store of reserves her calm black hands fingering the worn pence, and the shillings, not knowing where they could be useful when the time came, or what the time could be, but sensing she needed it against the coming time of change, sensing a gap between her race and the other that could perhaps be bridged, not out of any need to conquer or submerge that other race (there being no hatred in her, the commonly shared earth, the next drawn breath, the goodness of a bit of turtle steak enough for her, for both of them, both races, she naturally assumed), but out of a simple unspoken wish to see her progeny enter, if only a little way, into the world of the complex devils and angels of the white man, who was surely of interest if he so dominated the earth.

When Annie came she liked Venus and her food and added thoughts of her own to the menus but seemed content with her cooking and eager to learn about breadfruit and avocado, Calalu and greens, cassava root, pimiento, and the yellow, egg-like ackee. And seemed to grow closer to her day by day as whatever happened between her and Palmer came to pass gradually, nothing said of it on either side. Annie sent a bolt of good gingham when Venus married (a Christian one, rare for the quarters) for the second time to a sturdy slave driver who treated her with respect and seemed, unlike the other Negroes, to respect her children and want to attend to them, and was willing to help her in small ways to amass the pence and the shillings in the buried crock for the indefinable future. Later he was to change, after Palmer's murder—possibly because of the absence of a man at the helm of the plantation—and join in an abortive try at rifling the plantation's storehouse and ended dying of lockjaw after receiving more than a hundred lashes at Annie's order and with no explanations to Venus by the mistress, and none sought by Venus, her sense of the order of things ingrained.

So when Octavio came to her with the word about the door, about leaving the door open behind Jason, and clearly indicated the consequences she accepted that, too, without panic or pain, being neither loyal nor disloyal to Annie but only there, thinking the threat against her children merely an absurd footnote to the plan. But they had included it, the house, relative to the quarters, seeming a thousand miles away, and the mistress at best an unspeakable and terrifying mystery. Octavio had come with the word, sent on by some kin of Scipio and a handful of other malcontents who, with Broderick gone, Arthur wounded, Wilson carried off by the militia and Annie either likely to rise to further heights of bloodletting or to be, for once, vulnerable, decided to chance an attack on her, no single clear reason dictating it aside from a commonly held fear that any one of them might next be summoned and emerge mangled from the dungeon. The crops in, the mill grinding its last for the season, they were also facing the long dead time, always an occasion for restlessness.

So Venus dozed, half-dreaming that she lay back-to-back with her first husband on their rude but well-used mattress stuffed with rustling cane leaves, in peace, the wordless peace of calm cohabitation, now twice denied to her by fate, that fate accepted, it being perfectly natural, as natural as whatever Miz Palmer's fate was to be, whatever was stirring below to have, she assumed, its natural accomplishment, just as natural and unquestionable as that of a man, constrained and eager and then ready, passion blooming on him like scent on a rose. Remembering her men, she fell away into relaxed sleep.

There were six and they came silently, each making his own run, barefoot, across the underground room, dashing through still air that seemed dense with fear, memory, pain. Jason leading them, they ascended the stairs, opened the door, heard the reassuring sound of Venus snoring in her room. And then went up the back way, still led by Jason, and along the hall to the bedroom door. Jason stood off, his eyes lowered to the long brass handle, and pointed to the door. Luther motioned him on. Jason ignored him, staring hypnotically at the handle. Luther, Mary Lou's brother and a member of Arthur's gang, came forward, pushing past the others, opened the door, and the rest followed, Jason last, his eyes frightened seeking out her form on the bed. They all went forward, Luther leading, and fumbled in silent panic on the bed, seeking her out with their hands.

Annie awoke with a scream, squirmed like a terrified snake in its last throes but there were too many black hands, twelve now, Jason's excepted at first, then joining, knowing in a second of extremity the penalty for him, let alone the others, if they failed, one fear cancelling the other and he at least not alone but with his cohorts.

They all found the throat at once, Luther first, then hand on hand following groping to come together in the dark. They listened intently to the last of her breathing and ignored her fingernails, tearing at their arms for the last brief seconds.

It was Jason who reached down for the silken gown, taking it in the work-worn fingers of one hand to rip it off her as though to assure himself that she was there under it, that there was nothing left, that she was as he had last known her—that she was, as he verified with one wide flat palm against her chest, immobile.

Almost as a man and without signal they lifted her by the arms and went straight to the hall and, Jason leading now, for he alone knew the way, through the front drawing-room to the louvred doors. They fumbled with its catches, failed to open them, tore out the mahoe slats and smashed the doors with their shoulders, flung her body out and down to the gravel path and ran back the way they came, Jason last this time, pausing for a few seconds to be sure she lay still, not hating her but in fact mystified by the beauty of whiteness and remembering the peculiar pleasure she had taken with him not two hours before.

They all retreated down the stairs, moved in a body, hearing one another's panting, through the underground room, and raced back to the quarters and their respective huts, her power still hovering in the air, in their minds, tomorrow a better proof of the deed, the night as ever fraught with eternal and immediate danger, even her sudden immediate appearance as a ghost fully possible.

Mary Lou saw them go up, saw the body flung off the balcony, saw them return, smiled to herself at the way they ran, Luther and one or two of the others turning to look back as though being followed. Between her forefingers she rubbed a tiny raw pearl that Palmer had given her when they had been lovers, once she'd grown to twelve or thirteen.

When she heard the last of their racing footsteps and was sure of all the familiar night sounds, and of silence from the great house, she went to the house through a side path and came upon Annie through the rose garden, the lawn and the top of the gravel path. She lay face down, limbs splayed out, head twisted to the side, hair fanned out as though it had been blown thus by a random wind.

She thought of awakening Venus, decided against it, then she sobbed in fear, suddenly realizing that change had come and she could no longer trade information for scraps of good food. Then, remembering John Palmer, she spat on Annie's back, stepping back instinctively, half-expecting her to move. Then on an impulse she lifted her skirt and squatted, urinating on the gravel, her eyes not on the body but on the half-moon, hung low in the eastern sky. Arising, she left, skipping down the gravel path, humming to herself, thinking she would go to Luther, yes, Luther. He had no particular woman that week and, Arthur being asleep and she wanting a man and Luther having led them all through the underground room and to Annie, she wanted him, and he would surely want company because even he was afraid.

24

THE BEARER preceded Arthur up the gangplank, the trunk impossibly balanced on his head. Arthur held the rope strung along the gangplank's edge, uncertain of his balance as the ship swayed gently in the harbour's low swells, the tide edging in, loading underway, the brigantine ready to go within an hour, on the high tide. He had spent his last hour in Jamaica in the tavern drinking the Haitian rum to which Annie had introduced him, and bought three bottles of it to take along in his kit, knowing that the trip from MoBay to New York would take twelve nights.

'So, you're with us again?' He looked up from the gangplank's rough surface to see the captain, in dark green jacket and cap, talking around his smoky briar.

'Hello. You're here again too.'

'Oh yes. Been far way in seven months. Plymouth. Brest. Lisbon. The Canaries. Trinidad. St. Croix. And you? Decided to leave alive, did you?'

'Yes.'

'Good. The weather looks good and we should have a decent crossing unless there's trouble in the straits between Haiti and Cuba. Quite a show here the other night. Saw it, sailing along the coast. What was it burned, you know?'

'A place called Rose Hall.' He had seen it from a hill over MoBay, most of the town turning out to watch the distant pyre, flames from the house soaring against the star-speckled sky, showers of sparks from the remaining uncut sugar drifting on the air, an east wind carrying dark snow, the ashes of the cane, over the town itself, smudging the faces of the townspeople watching. The militia, he heard, had come and gone, then the runaways had come in to fill the vacuum left by Annie's death.

'Huh. Another one. Seems it's more frequent now. Trouble all through the islands this year. Lucky you're going, eh?'

'Yes, lucky.'

'Changing all the time out here. Too bad. Not as hardy as they were in the old days. You know . . .' He took his pipe from between yellowed teeth and pointed its stem at the mountains. 'You know, there's going to be mighty bad days here and a lot of Englishmen die before it's done. Where their courage is gone to I'll never know. I tell you, I'm glad I'm on the sea. I'm my own Lord Chamberlain on this vessel and not about to die for another man's weakness. Too bad, that burning. Was it a good plantation?'

'A very good one.'

'A big great house it must have been. Burned a long time, she did. Makes you really sad, think of all the labour and good timber and planning went into it. I saw a ship burn at sea once. Couldn't get to her she burned so fierce. Shame, too, because she wasn't two hours sail from Gibraltar. I hove to and waited for survivors. Got a few, not many, with the longboats. But by God I wept for her. Not the men, the ship. First I'd seen go like that and it's hell, all that water around and a good ship burning. I suppose a ship is like a castle to a sailor. Well . . . how far you going with us? Plymouth is journey's end this time. Is it home for you?'

'America. I get off at New York.'

'A bit of the New World, eh? Well, you're young, might as well try something new. Build good ships they do, that I'll say for them. Well, got to see to the cargo. Supper's at two bells. Look forward to your tales of this place. Got a cask of Demerara down Barbados way will help loosen your tongue. Say, what happened to that young woman come with you that voyage out, to marry here?'

'She . . . it's a long story.'

'Good. We need one for a voyage. Yours is the forward cabin, on the starboard side.' He clenched his pipe back in his teeth again and went forward, shouting at the loaders and exhorting the crew.

The bearer had been waiting patiently, standing beside the trunk. Arthur motioned him down the steps, led him through the saloon and to the cabin, the trunk just fitting between the bulkhead and the bunk. He gave the departing black man a shilling. He lay on the bunk in the tiny cabin's gloom and, remembering Annie, remembering the first night before the fire, remembering the waterfall, remembering the delicacy of her hand in his, he rolled over in the bunk, and quietly cried into his pillow, fighting off the memory of the corpse he had come to a few days before.